He stroked the tender side of her jaw. His eyes glazed over with desire. Blood rushed, then pooled, hardening his body even more. She was everything he imagined she would be. "There could be no other way with you," he finally responded.

The thin-strapped gown she'd worn had ignited a burn in him the instant he saw her in it. And the wispy shawl she had wrapped around her shoulders all evening did little to hinder his surging passion. Like unwrapping a precious gift, he gently removed the chiffon fabric, turning her around as he pulled it loose to fall to the floor.

Other books by Celeste O. Norfleet

The Fine
Art
of Love

Celeste O. Norfleet

BET Publications, LLC
http://www.bet.com
http://www.arabesquebooks.com

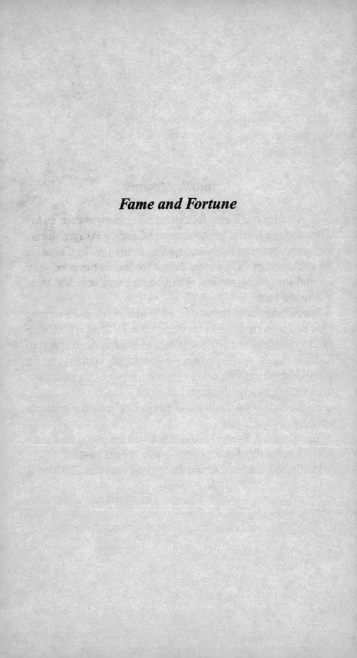

Fame and Fortune

Acknowledgments

To Amanda and Karen for always being in my corner. To my sister authors Michelle Monkou and Candice Poarch, thanks for listening to my raves and adding to my joy. To Celestine Peyton Clark of CC's Place, thanks for letting me bend your ear and for getting me out of the house every now and then. You're the best.

Special thanks to the wonderful readers who make writing a joy and who continue to encourage me. To Sharon McCalop and the Readers in Blue Bookclub, to Bobbie Austin, and to Roxie A. Jones, special thanks for your steady support and for always being there with words of encouragement. You were there from the beginning, thank you so much.

To the little ones, Damia and Aniah Norfleet. You are both blessings of the heart.

To my editor, Evette Porter, thank you for going that extra mile to make this book possible. You are the best!

Lastly, to Charles, CC and JP, my heart is yours. Hi Mom!

Prologue

The comforting solace of being surrounded by family and friends had long since found its way into Kennedy's heart. As the youngest of triplets, she had always felt the protective influence of her older brother and sister. Theirs was the path she trod with little thought. When her sister, Madison, found art history was her passion, Kennedy quickly succumbed to the relics of the past in the museums of the world and readily explored the world of art curators and historians. When her brother, J.T., delved into computers, she became consumed with the technology that helped her locate lost cities and civilizations without even picking up a shovel. Now, again, she stood at the threshold of her siblings' achievements.

Seated just beyond the circle of merriment, she observed the assembly with a steady gaze. She let the warmth of her family and the comfort of friends ease her racing thoughts. There was nothing like being back home again. Being away for so long, she'd missed so much. For the first time since she could remember, she actually considered her solitary future. Alone didn't seem as appealing as it once did.

A sadness stilled her spirit as she thought of her most recent achievement. She had finally brought the most extensive collection of ancient Nubian art to the National Museum of

African Art. It was recognized as a monumental coup in the art world, and she had done what no one else could. Yet there was no one there to cheer her on. Her family and friends, of course, applauded her. But what of that special someone? She smiled as she remembered the saying, *Success is nothing without someone to share it with*.

Kennedy glanced over just as her very pregnant sister looked in her direction. A knowing smile passed between them as Madison eased her way through the last remaining wedding guests at J.T. and Juliet's wedding, her protruding stomach clearing the way like a bulldozer plowing through snow.

"Hey there, you okay?" Madison asked as she approached.

"Yeah, fine. I'm just taking a break from all the excitement, that's all."

"Are you sure?" Madison continued. "You look a little peaked."

"I'm fine really, just a little tired and jet-lagged. You, on the other hand, look wonderful," Kennedy said proudly as her sister slowly sat down beside her. "Pregnancy truly agrees with you, Madi."

"Oh shut up, I'm a six-hundred-pound beached whale and you know it. I haven't seen my feet in a month and my hormones are in overdrive and I think I just ate a paper doily and liked it." They laughed, reaching out to each other. Madison took her sister's hand and squeezed playfully. "Seriously, Keni, I'm so glad you're back. I've missed you so much."

Kennedy looked at her sister oddly, surprised by the remark. "Madi, we've talked on the phone just about every day. And there's no telling how many e-mails we've sent each other every other hour or so. How could you possibly have time to miss me?"

"I missed having you here," she said sincerely, "with me."

Kennedy smiled. "Well I'm here now."

"But for how long? Aren't you heading back to Africa in a few days?"

"Actually, I've been reconsidering that. The emissary and the museum curator over there have everything under control, and all but two of the shipments have already arrived. I see no reason for me to be there, too. And since I'm just two months away from becoming an aunt, I might just hang around for the blessed event."

"Oh, Keni, that would be wonderful." Madison reached out and grabbed her sister, holding her close.

"Whoa, whoa, be careful," Kennedy said as she pulled away, careful not to press too hard against her sister's stomach. "Wouldn't want you going into labor here."

"Actually that wouldn't be such a bad idea. I feel like I've been pregnant for a decade already."

"A slight exaggeration I think. It's only been seven months; you're almost there." Kennedy reached over and patted her sister's belly, smiling as she felt the baby kick. "Are you sure there's only two in there?"

"That's what the doctor seems to think, but with all the kicking, elbows and knees, at times it feels more like a soccer team."

Kennedy chuckled. "Well, as I said, you're almost there, another two months and you'll be a mom," Kennedy said, smiling as a wistful expression crossed her face. A sudden stillness passed between them as the closeness of their relationship was more than obvious. Madison, being the oldest by only a few minutes, recognized the look instantly.

"It's time, isn't it?"

Kennedy looked at her sister quizzically, but then realized what she meant. "I don't know, maybe." She looked toward their brother with his new wife, Juliet, surrounded by family and friends. "Is this how you felt—alone, like something was missing in your life?" Kennedy asked.

Madison glanced at her husband. As if by telepathy, he turned to her and waved from across the room. She waved back. "It seems so long ago sometimes. Then at other times it feels like it was only yesterday. But yeah, I guess it was, I did feel like something was missing, but I didn't realize it until I was already in love with Tony."

"I'm so happy for you, Madi," Kennedy whispered thickly as her eyes started to tear.

"Don't," Madison said and she reached up and wiped the single tear from her sister's cheek. "This is a happy day for us. We finally got rid of our overprotective older brother and gained a sister in the process." They laughed as childhood memories and secrets passed between them. "But seriously, he"—she nudged her sister with her shoulder—"Mr. Right, is out there just waiting for you, I know it. No more bad boys, promise?"

"I promise, no more bad boys."

"Good," Madison said.

"Since when did you become such a romantic matchmaker? You're almost as bad as Mamma Lou."

"It doesn't take a romantic, a rocket scientist or a brain surgeon to know that you're the smartest, sweetest and most loving person I know, and any man lucky enough to capture your heart would be blessed beyond his imagination."

"Your hormones really are spiking, aren't they?" Kennedy said jokingly.

"Fine, joke if you want, but mark my words, he's just around the corner."

"Madi, you know that my work is beyond consuming. Either I'm traveling to far off continents, or stuck in the museum studying ancient relics, none of which is particularly conducive to finding my Mr. Right anytime soon."

"You never know."

"And besides," she chuckled, "it's not like he's going to just appear and I just fall into his arms as he says something corny like, 'it's you, you're the one.'"

"As many times as you've fallen in love, it's highly possible. Besides, stranger things have happened," Madison said, then looked around the room seeing Louise Gates walking toward them.

Seeing her sister's broad smile, Kennedy followed her line of vision. "Oh no, now you've done it," Kennedy whispered through a plastered-on smiled. "Here comes Mamma Lou and you know that can only mean one thing."

"Yep, that's right," Madison smile delighted at the prospect, "It's finally your turn." She stood up slowly.

Kennedy's mouth opened wide and gasped as Madison chuckled and walked away. A small helpless sound escaped her throat as Mamma Lou approached smiling innocently. "Oh, oh," she muttered beneath her breath.

"Hello, dear, let's chat a while."

Chapter One

When a telephone rings at four o'clock in the morning it's never good news and it usually means only one thing: somewhere, somehow, someone's in trouble. This was no exception. Kennedy Evans awoke startled, then scrabbled for the bedside phone, but knocked over the stack of books and magazines precariously towering on the bedside table instead. She grabbed the receiver on the second ring. "Hello," she said in a husky voice into the receiver.

It was her mother, Taylor Evans. She listened intently. The conversation was brief.

"I'm on my way," Kennedy said as she cradled the phone between her neck and shoulder and began refilling her briefcase with the notes and papers she'd been reviewing the night before.

"It's really not necessary, Keni," her mother said. "Your sister is fine and still has two more months before the baby's due. She's here at home resting comfortably now; it was just early contractions and false labor. I guess J.T. finally getting married was a bit too much excitement. The doctor simply wants her to take it easy and stay off her feet for the next few days. Tony's here, your father's here, and I'm here. Everything's fine, really. The only reason I even called you was that Madison asked for you and I promised I'd call you as soon as we got here."

Kennedy looked at the bedside clock; it was just a few minutes after four o'clock in the morning. If she hurried she could be out the door in the next thirty minutes. She glanced at the two unpacked suitcases and trunk still sitting in the corner of her bedroom. There was no time to unpack something to wear, so she had to grab an outfit from her closet. "Tell her I'm on my way. I'll be there within the hour."

As soon as she hung up the phone and stood, a dizzying swirl of anxiety surged, twirling inside of her like an emerging twister, category three, she estimated by the way she felt. Blindly building, growing, and rising steadily, the anxiety she felt was beginning to consume her. Apparently, the anxiety attacks she'd been experiencing in the past few months were gripping her again. She slowly sat down on the side of the bed, stilling her heartbeat with deep, even breaths, hoping to calm her nerves.

Unreasonable, yes. Inconvenient, always. Annoying, definitely. But she couldn't control them. Her once easy calmness and peaceful nature was now subject to unmitigated fits of nervousness and breathless anxiety.

She placed her hand on her chest. "Slow, steady breaths," she reminded herself, hoping that would do the trick. Her stomach rose and flopped uneasily; her breathing shortened and her palms moistened. It wasn't the mildest palpitation she'd ever had but, thank God, it wasn't the strongest either.

Seeking first a natural remedy, she closed her eyes to calm herself. She stretched her neck outward, then relaxed her shoulders, hoping to roll the tension away. But the sudden anxious, edgy, uneasy feelings she'd been experiencing persisted.

Panic attacks, her doctor told her after a thorough examination. *Keep your stress level down,* he added. *Relax, take time off, enjoy yourself. Get a hobby or some other distraction. Panic attacks are just your body's way of telling you to slow down and relax.* Was he kidding? Keeping her stress level down was like skiing uphill—damn near impossible. Stress and aggravation were all but written into her job description.

She was a curator at the largest African arts museum in the nation. Officially titled Curator of Northeastern African Artifacts and Tribal Customs, her job not only had her flying around the globe at a moment's notice but often had her staying away for months at a time. Acquisitions, restorations, lectures, and assessments, she did it all. Now with the museum's newest and most eagerly awaited exhibit, her personal project, she wasn't going to let anything delay the opening, especially not anxiety attacks. So she needed to learn to get them under control fast. But, for right now, she needed to get to her sister.

She realized, of course, that her mother was right. Madison still had two more months to go. She had the best medical care money could buy and had always been a fanatic about taking good care of herself. So there was nothing to worry about. Still, the pang of angst disquieted her.

She reached over and grabbed her purse, pulling out the vial of prescription pills her doctor had given her. She read the label carefully, then pushed and twisted the lid and poured the oddly shaped pills into the palm of her hand. She chose one, broke it in half, then scooped the others back into the bottle.

Without a second's hesitation she popped the small half of the pill into her mouth. The bitter tang of medication made her nose crinkle with distaste. She walked into the bathroom and washed it down with a cup of cool water, but the bitter aftertaste hung in the back of her throat like a wallflower at a school dance.

She looked up at her reflection in the mirror. The dark circles underneath her eyes reflected the eighteen-hour jet lag that her body was feeling. But it was worth it to see her brother get married and, of course, see her family, especially her sister. She smiled at the memory of her sudden trip back to the States.

She had been so busy with the exhibit that she nearly missed the wedding. Realizing that it was only a day away, she caught the first flight out barely having a chance to pack her things and say goodbye. Now suddenly the swirl of activity eased as the thought of being home seemed to calm her.

A few moments later she felt it and let the calming sensation wash over her like waves over a shore, lifting the tension and easing her anxiety. With a zest for life unmatched by most, she had an adventurer's spirit—vitality and vigor that allowed nothing to hold her down, not even her panic attacks. A few smooth, deep breaths and she felt like herself again.

Soon, she was back in control. She took a quick shower and dressed in less than twenty minutes; then she grabbed her helmet and headed for the front door.

She threw her leg over the side of her motorcycle, turned the key, angled the kickstand and drove off. It had taken all of two seconds for the thrill of her Harley Davidson XL Sportster beneath her to return. Like easing into a butter-soft leather chair, the motorcycle fit her like an old comfortable glove, custom designed to her exact measurements. She slid back into position, riding low and slightly erect. She grasped the pulled-back polished handlebars, feeling the sweet sensation of power. Her adventurous spirit was back. They, whoever *they* were, were right. Power was intoxicating.

Kennedy turned onto the quickest and most direct route to Tony and Madison's home in Old Town Alexandria, Virginia. Moments later, dawn began to creep above the line of neatly trimmed trees. The solitary headlight easily sliced through the awakening streets of Washington, D.C., leaving a stinging gust of wind in her wake.

The George Washington Parkway was nearly empty as Kennedy's bike roared across the smoothly paved bend to round National Airport's first entrance. She looked down at the speedometer, which exceeded the posted speed limit. It read sixty-five miles an hour in an area designated for far less.

But speeding was nothing unusual for Kennedy when she rode her bike. She drove her motorcycle as she lived her life—fast, hard and with no excuses. She'd had her share of tickets, but each was definitely worth the trouble. Of all the vices one could have, speeding on her Harley was certainly one of hers. There was nothing like feeling the wind whip against the force of a powerful Harley.

Approaching a turn, she blew past the second exit just under the Metro rail's elevated tracks. She smiled gleefully like a naughty child in a room filled with candy. She knew she should slow down, but she was too exhilarated by the power and freedom and it had been a long time since she'd really let go. She leaned into the next turn in dramatic fashion, her leather-clad knee almost touching the asphalt. Her bike, fitted with superior racing accessories, provided her with added safety and she took full advantage.

Pausing slightly between gears, she accelerated around a slow-moving vehicle. Then, noting a car in the rearview mirror, she eased back but continued at an accelerated speed. Traffic was beginning to thicken, so with only a few more miles to go, she amplified the torque and accelerated past the last airport exit ramp.

It wasn't until the last second that she spotted a black blur racing up behind her. Suddenly, to her surprise she was about to be rear-ended by a speeding, black Mercedes Benz limousine. The limo driver blew his horn wildly, demanding that she move out of her lane and allow him to pass. She refused. Two vehicles, one lane, something had to give.

Swerving across the left lane at the last second, she avoided a near-fatal collision by gripping and turning the polished handlebars to send the bike into a one-hundred-eighty-degree tailspin. Gravel and dirt scattered, peppering the street, as both motorcycle and limousine came to a complete stop, she on the grassy median and the limo, across the traffic lanes, on the road's shoulder.

Adrenaline pumped, she sliced back the kickstand, planted her foot angrily and leaned into the bike. Lifting her helmet visor, she stared at the black car, glaring into the dark-tinted windows. Like two lance-drawn knights about to joust at a tournament, they faced each other with equal disdain and contempt, interrupted only by a few passing cars.

Seconds passed as the two engines idled; she looked across the double lane of traffic and noted the prominently displayed dignitary license plate. "Figures," she said aloud. "Diplomats." She replaced the visor over her eyes, released the kickstand and waited to join the traffic again.

As the last car passed, she gave one last glance at the limousine, then pulled into the far right lane and drove off. The limousine followed suit, driving in the left lane. Side by side, nose to nose, they drove with equal speed until the limo finally fell back to follow in the right lane behind her.

A mile down the road the two vehicles stopped at a traffic light. Kennedy tightened her grip on the handlebars, clicked her turn signal and drifted into the turning lane. As the limo eased forward to her left, she turned to look at the rear side window. She could sense the passenger's stare through her tinted visor. Just as the window began to lower, the light turned green. She twisted the throttle and disappeared around the corner.

Fifteen minutes later she stood in her sister's kitchen.

"I told you it wasn't necessary for you to rush over," Taylor said as Kennedy entered the kitchen and sat down at the table. "Madison fell asleep as soon as I told her that I called you."

"I know," Kennedy said, toying with the teaspoon in front of her. "I just wanted to make sure for myself." The worried expression on her face remained firm. "What exactly did the doctor say?"

"Madison needs to restrict her movements and stay off her feet for a few days. The contractions have already stopped."

"Should she be having contractions this early in the pregnancy?"

"It's not uncommon to experience contractions a few months before the due date. It's just the body's way of getting ready for the big event." Taylor placed a cup of hot tea in front of Kennedy. The furrow of worry on her daughter's face caught her attention. "Kennedy," she said calmly and with complete confidence, "Madison will be fine."

Kennedy smiled and nodded. Taylor returned the gesture as she turned back to the stove. She smiled, recalling the closeness of her two daughters. Inseparable, inquisitive and incorrigible were the words she had always used to describe Madison and Kennedy. Although Madison had calmed down considerably since her marriage to Tony last year, it seemed Kennedy would never slow down.

She was the adventurer and, by far, the most impulsive of the three. Where J.T. was always responsible and calm, and Madison was ladylike, sweet and coy, Kennedy was all over the place. She had an inner zeal that oftentimes exploded. She'd enter a room and set it on fire just being herself. She was the youngest, the center of attention and the joy and jewel of the family. Her innate passion for life and her wanderlust nature had sent her circling the globe, never slowing down, until now.

Taylor knew that professionally Kennedy was successful as a museum curator and Taylor was more than proud of her accomplishments. But lately she began to sense loneliness and discontent growing inside her daughter. Something had definitely changed. She was still the same exuberant spirit, but now her zest for life seemed restless and lost. Although Kennedy would never admit it, Taylor saw loneliness in her eyes and it tore at her heart. She had first noticed it at J.T.'s wedding.

Kennedy had slipped in and sat between Madison and herself just as the last few wedding guests were being seated. As only a mother would, Taylor noticed for the first time her daughter's yearnings. Her eyes were riveted on the ceremony and a twinge of hopefulness shined. That was the moment Taylor knew that it was her time.

"So how's the museum and how are the preparations for the exhibit going?" she asked.

Kennedy brightened immediately. "Great, we're almost done. The exhibit looks amazing. I can't wait until opening night for you to see it."

"We're really looking forward to it. Did you acquire all the pieces you wanted?"

"Yes, most of them, some were already in shows. But for the most part, we got everything we asked for."

"Good. How were things at the Nubia Museum when you left?"

"It was one big powder keg. Everyone was walking around on eggshells suspecting everyone else. The tense feelings have spread to our museum."

"A theft like that affects all museums. And to find out that it was an inside job must have been devastating. I hope they get exactly what they deserve," Taylor said, having heard of the major theft ring captured by the local authorities in Africa.

"Ever since the FBI found out that it was an inside job, the museum has been on lockdown. Nobody trusts anybody else and the insurance companies are all over us to up security."

"Did you hear if they ever caught the one man who got away?"

"No, not yet," Kennedy said, flushing as the heat of nervousness stung her cheeks. There was no way she was going to tell her mother that not only did she know the man who got away but she had also dated him.

"I heard that there are several missing pieces including a small golden statue from the twenty-fifth dynasty."

"It was a beautiful gold-encrusted statue of King Aspalta. He was one of the best known kings of Kush and the last important Nubian ruler of Egypt."

"You've seen it?"

Kennedy nodded.

"I understand that the authorities seem to think it's headed for the black market."

"If it finds its way to the black market, it'll never resurface."

Taylor shook her head and sucked her teeth. "That's such a tragedy, private collectors sanction these crimes by buying the stolen items and we all suffer. I've heard that stolen art has even found its way to Internet auctions."

"Yes, I've heard that, too," Kennedy said.

"Well, as soon as they find and apprehend the thief, everything will go back to normal and the exhibit will be a tremendous success."

"I hope so," Kennedy said, knowing that it wasn't that simple. Before she left days ago, she'd been in meeting after meeting with the FBI and several African agencies regarding the theft. Because of her position and her extensive travel and the fact that she had dated the main perpetrator, she was a suspect along with a number of other employees. But this was the last thing she wanted to talk about. "Where are Tony and Dad?" Kennedy said, changing the subject.

Taylor poured tea in a second cup. "They went out to pick up some breakfast for Madi. Butter almond ice cream, walnuts, whipped cream and maraschino cherries."

"Some what?" Kennedy questioned, half-amused.

"Madison asked for an ice cream sundae just before she fell asleep. Tony didn't want to not have it in the house when she wakes up."

"He is such a sweetheart . . ." Kennedy affirmed, ". . . the perfect husband."

"He certainly is. I couldn't ask for a more perfect husband for Madison."

"Sometimes I wish I could find . . ." Kennedy began wistfully, then stopped abruptly and fell silent.

Taylor turned and leaned back against the counter. "You wish you could find what?" she asked, encouraging Kennedy to continue.

"Nothing."

"Kennedy . . ."

"Don't, Mom."

"Don't what?" Taylor asked innocently.

"I don't want to talk about it, so let's just don't, okay!"

The last thing Kennedy wanted to talk about was her single status, especially with her mother's new found obsession with matchmaking. After Taylor's success in finding her brother his new bride, Kennedy was positive that her mother had made it her mission to finish the job and have her wed by the next full moon.

"I just want you to be happy," Taylor said lovingly.

"I know, and I am happy. My job is extremely fulfilling."

"Of course it is, Kennedy, and we're all very proud of you. But your job is not your life. There's so much more to you than museum curator. You're a bright, vibrant woman with so much to offer."

Kennedy fell silent. The reality of her mother's words stung her eyes and an overwhelming swell of emotion surged inside of her. These were the same thoughts she'd been troubled with for the past two months, the feelings of longing and emptiness and the constant wondering if there was more out there for her and, if she slowed down long enough, *who* would be there.

She knew that she was a runner, not track or cross country or recreational. But she ran from emotional attachment. She prided herself on how she lived her life. Never staying in one place too long, never committing to any type of long term relationship, never putting her heart on the line and, especially, never falling in love.

As she'd done all her life, she learned lessons from her brother and sister. Their paths marked hers and she was an ardent student. She watched and learned. She side-stepped their pitfalls and avoided their pains. Madison had been hurt and J.T. had refused to even test the waters. So, as she'd done all her life, she took their experiences, learned their lessons and amplified them ten-fold. But suddenly things had changed.

Madison stood still and love caught up with her; Kennedy refused to slow down long enough. If love wanted to catch up to her, he had better be a hell of a runner. J.T. played mind games and love still found him. She refused to even play the game. Both her siblings had been hurt before, but she never would be. She was a runner—from life and her emotions. And, if by chance she slowed down, it was on her terms and only her terms.

Silence hung in the room as the two women pensively sipped their tea. "Ice cream for breakfast?" Kennedy, said finally of their earlier conversation. "I didn't realize Madison was still having food cravings. I thought they went away with morning sickness."

"Every pregnancy's different. Some symptoms last longer than others. Some never appear at all." Taylor paused as the oven timer chimed. "But to tell you the truth, eating an ice cream sundae at six in the morning isn't really such a bad idea from time to time."

Kennedy looked at her mother, stunned by her remark. "I can't believe you just said that, you the queen of balanced meals, the guru of good nutrition, the one who instilled in us that proper diet was the backbone of good health. You're actually advocating ice cream and chocolate syrup for breakfast? You never would have agreed to that when we were kids."

"Of course I wouldn't have. And I never said to make it a habit, just that it isn't such a bad idea *from time to time*. If I remember correctly, you, as an adolescent, wanted ice cream sundaes twenty-four hours a day, seven days a week. Honestly." She sucked her teeth.

Kennedy smiled, remembering the ice-cream-as-dairy argument she always fell back on. "Well, ice cream is dairy and chocolate is made from cocoa beans . . ."

Taylor laughed and shook her head as she pulled a tray of muffins from the oven and placed them on the counter. "Yes, yes, and maraschino cherries are fruit, I remember your argument well, and no, I'm still not buying it. Good nutrition and a balanced diet are the backbone of good health, but a sundae now and then as a treat won't hurt."

Kennedy shook her head. "That's still shocking coming from you." She watched as her mother dumped the hot muffins into a covered basket.

"Things change. I'm keeping up with the times. Come on, let's go sit out on the balcony," Taylor said as she picked up her cup of tea and headed toward the open balcony doors. Kennedy followed after grabbing a banana nut muffin.

"By the way, I spoke to Louise the other day."

Kennedy stopped in her tracks. "And . . ." she prompted.

"And nothing, so stop panicking. She's on Crescent Island with her plantings. Apparently there's a flower show she's entering in the spring and she needs to get ready for it before fall sets in. Anyway, as I was saying, she asked about you."

"By asked about me do you mean as in matchmaking?"

"Oh for goodness sakes! You're as bad as Trey. He panics every time I see him. And heaven forbid I even mention Louise's name."

"For good reason—she's a menace."

"Kennedy, watch your language," Taylor said.

"I know, sorry. It's just that my life is perfect as it is right now and I don't have the time or the inclination to add the drama of dating to it."

"Since when are men and dating considered drama?" Taylor asked, having no idea what was going on in the dating world.

"Obviously you haven't been out swimming in the dating pool in some time."

Taylor chuckled. "Is it really that bad?"

"Bad would be a huge step up." They laughed as Kennedy began telling her mother about the dates she'd had in the past year: the big game hunter in Africa who was afraid of butterflies, the millionaire art collector in Germany with the worthless collection of black-market counterfeits and the high-level political aide with a thing for pink toenail polish. She didn't mention the museum-robbing thief.

"The thing is," Kennedy continued, "it seems that they're always hiding some deep dark secret. At one time it was kind of exciting finding out what it was, but now I'm just not up for the challenge anymore. I guess I'm just tired of playing the game."

"You don't have to."

Kennedy knew what her mother was referring to, but she ignored the implication and instead told her about one of her last relationships with an island playboy who had been married five times, had nine children, was recently divorced, and had proposed to her on their second date.

Taylor laughed so hard tears came to her eyes. "Well, you don't have to worry about that anymore. I have a feeling that the next man you meet will be the one."

"What makes you say that?" Kennedy asked suspiciously, thinking that her mother and Mamma Lou might be back in the matchmaking game.

"I'll let you in on a little secret," Taylor began. "When the right man enters your life, you'll know it and not by anything he says or does or has, but by the way he makes you feel." Taylor reached over and grasped Kennedy's hand and squeezed softly to affirm her trust and love.

Easy conversation and banter flowed as the two women sat watching the morning sun rise above the trees across the Potomac River. The hum of morning traffic and the gentle breeze of early fall completed the atmosphere of the new day.

"So how's Dad's semiretirement going so far?"

"He loves it. Although it's been deferred slightly until J.T. comes back from his honeymoon."

"It was a beautiful wedding. I've never seen J.T. so handsome and so happy in my life. He was actually standing at the altar beaming."

Taylor nodded, "It was a beautiful day. And I can't believe how quickly it was put together. Madison was a tremendous help."

"I'm sorry I couldn't be here to help."

"Don't be ridiculous. Putting together the Nubian art exhibit is a major accomplishment. You have to be where you're needed most. Besides, your help with Madison's wedding was immense. I'm just happy that you're back home now."

"That's for sure."

Taylor and Kennedy turned to see Madison standing in the doorway, her seven-months-pregnant belly protruding a good six inches from her body. "Good morning," she said, smiling happily, obviously feeling better. She leaned down and hugged Kennedy warmly.

"Hey, shouldn't you still be in bed?" Kennedy asked.

"Yes, she should," Taylor answered and stood up. "Back to bed young lady," she said as she pointed Madison back inside the house.

"But I feel much better."

"Back to bed—now," Taylor repeated more firmly.

Madison turned obediently but looked over her shoulder to her sister, who stood and followed. "What are you doing here so early?"

"Good question," Kennedy said as she caught up to Madison. "Apparently a certain niece and nephew wanted to hear their favorite auntie's voice this morning . . ." she leaned down and said directly to Madison's stomach, ". . . and thought sending mommy to the ER at two in the morning was the best way to do it."

"Teaching them some manners is the first thing on my list," Madison promised.

"Right after potty training, of course," Kennedy added with a chuckle.

"Oh, don't remind me, twins no less. How in the world did you do all this with triplets?" Madison asked her mother as they entered the master bedroom. She headed for the king size bed, dropped her robe and climbed underneath the covers.

"You'd be surprised what you can do when properly motivated, and having triplets is real motivation," she said as she fluffed the pillows to make Madison more comfortable.

"Well, I'd just settle for a good night's sleep. It's seven o'clock in the morning and I'm already exhausted."

"Seven o'clock!" Kennedy looked at her watch. "Oh my goodness, I am so late for work. I have an early shipment due in this morning, three meetings and a representative of the Nubian government will be stopping by later. I gotta go." She hurriedly kissed her sister and mother and headed for the door just as her father, Jace, and her brother-in-law, Tony, arrived.

"Good morning," they said in unison.

"Hi. Bye. Gotta go. I have a shipment coming this morning, a million things to do," Kennedy said as she kissed Jace and Tony and rushed out, as Madison excitedly went through the bags of ice cream, chocolate and whipped cream. The last thing she heard before closing the front door was Madison asking about the maraschino cherries. She stepped outside, put on her helmet and, moments later, joined the bumper-to-bumper morning rush-hour traffic into Washington, D.C. She could already tell that this was going to be a trying day.

Chapter Two

World-weary and jaded, Juwan Mason had seen and heard it all. Cold-hearted and impassive from a childhood trauma, he was now an unfeeling man, particularly where his job was concerned. As an FBI agent his specialty was art and theft recovery, and as the bureau's top special agent, he'd seen his fill of the human condition. Calculating and shrewd, he'd gained a reputation for his cold cunning and ability to succeed at any assignment. But this was by far his most difficult mission.

The similarities had struck him immediately. That in itself should have stopped him from accepting the assignment, but it didn't. He had something to prove to himself and he intended to see it through.

Driven by personal demons, he couldn't let it go. There was no cut your losses and walk away for him. He hadn't started this but he was definitely going to finish it. This was something he needed to do and if, by chance, it got him closer to his ultimate goal, then all the better.

The Nubian region in North Africa, raped and pillaged of its name, culture and land, had been reborn. Located south of Egypt and north of the Sudan, it was a land of ancient time and recent change. Newly developed from the ravages of Sudan's civil war, it had been robbed again—this time by art thieves.

Colin Sheppard, his associate, a gung-ho, by-the-book, procedure-quoting, ex-military officer with more medals than common sense, had overseen the initial investigation. Unfortunately, mistakes had been made and, in the process, a key suspect had been released and now it was up to Juwan to make things right.

He'd studied the files and had fully prepared. He was ready to begin. He knew that he should have passed on the assignment, given the similarities to a previous mission. But he took it anyway. It was a simple clean-up from a job that had fallen apart toward the end. The main suspect had escaped and several pieces were still unaccounted for. His job was to finish what had been started, bring in the suspect and any associates and recover the art. Simple enough.

He looked around at the men seated in the back of the limo with him. All tremendously successful in their respective fields, all extremely knowledgeable and astute and all equally accustomed to positions of great power. He was the odd man out; he wanted nothing more than to return stolen objects to their rightful owners and bring the culprits to justice. *Fidelity, Bravery and Integrity*: it was the FBI motto. It was his creed.

Right out of college he had been recruited by the Federal Bureau of Investigation. His knowledge of art and antiquities, his extensive travel as a youth and his distinguished family name had given him the perfect résumé and the FBI was eager to get him on board.

His acceptance of their offer led to years of travel, excitement, personal fulfillment and eventual notice by the top echelon. He'd been promoted several times before reaching this stage of his career. Now he was on the verge of being promoted once again, this time to a prominent position in either the London or Washington, DC office. The choice was his. All he had to do was complete this one final assignment.

So here he was, sitting in the back of a limo coming from

the airport with Maurice Khalfani Kabul Mebeko, the region's ambassador to the United States and the founding member of the United African Government; Devlon Motako, recently appointed United Nations delegate from Nubia; Kofi Hawkins, called Hawk, who was Maurice's personal bodyguard; and Hoyt Collier, special envoy and Maurice's personal aide.

Juwan smiled, glancing at Maurice's feigned interest in the detailed outline of his itinerary. Hoyt Collier, his aide, had monopolized the conversation as usual. Since Maurice and UN delegate Devlon had gotten into the limo, it had been an unending drone of one appointment after another. Juwan glanced out the window as a speeding blur caught his attention and brought Hoyt's fifteen-minute detailed account of countless appointments to an abrupt halt.

The occupants swerved with the limo as five heads turned to see the cause of the vehicle's sudden jarring motion. A skintight, burgundy leather pant leg with matching high-heeled boot draped across the side of a very distinctive black and silver motorcycle sped by. Their second sighting of her drew different reactions. Hoyt, as usual, was the first to speak as he dropped the itinerary on the seat beside him.

"Wasn't that that same motorcycle driver from this morning, the one who tried to run us off the road earlier? That's the second time we've seen him in less than two hours. Should we be concerned?"

"No. As you can see, the driver already is well away," Hawk said, seldom heard yet always attentive, his keen eye watching the motorcycle speed through the traffic light less than a block away.

"Do you think it's possible that he's got ulterior motives, assassination possibly?" Hoyt asked.

"Assassination?" Devlon repeated, obviously unnerved by Hoyt's use of the word. He quickly leaned forward to get a better look at the fast-retreating motorcyclist, then reached over and picked up the limo's phone to summon assistance.

"I'm calling the local police. Are these windows bullet-proof?" he asked nervously.

"The police aren't necessary," Hawk said as he placed his finger on the switch to disconnect the call. Devlon looked at Hawk menacingly yet said nothing, choosing not to challenge him. "It's merely a coincidence to see this cyclist again," Hawk assured him, in an attempt to calm Devlon's concerns.

"I knew I should have arranged for a diplomatic motor-cade," Hoyt continued as if he hadn't heard Hawk's reassuring answer. "It might be some kind of road rage."

Talking over one another, Hoyt and Devlon began a two-man conversation about the ramifications of road rage, bulletproof glass, motorcades, bodyguards and semi-automatic weapons and the US Constitution's Second Amendment right to bear arms.

"This country's constitutional law that allows civilians to possess and shoot nine-millimeter weapons and AK-forty-seven rifles is absurd," Devlon said, continuing his verbal rant. "They're nothing short of barbaric. Everyone carries a gun here. It's like the Wild West. Homicide, genocide, how can anyone be safe?" His tone of desperation was noted and dismissed by almost everyone.

At first no one responded as Hoyt continued his dia-tribe. Then a single voice, low and composed, spoke. "Gun-carrying barbarians, genocide, that's an interesting point coming from you, wouldn't you agree, Devlon?" Maurice's voice was calm and even-toned but he had definitely gotten his point across. His slight British accent, evident only when he wanted to make a point, was punctuated to perfection.

The UN delegate to Nubia, Devlon, only recently ab-solved of his more than questionable actions in the Sudan genocidal conflicts, fell silent. Everyone knew of his culpa-bility in the atrocities. But bribing and threatening the right people won him his current post.

Accused but never formally charged, Devlon had skirted

responsibility for his actions during Sudan's civil war entirely. Yet most knew that his hands were bloodied and his pockets were lined with ill-gotten foreign aid. Friends in both high and low places had managed to secure him a position and he took full advantage of it.

The limo went silent as Devlon turned and glared at Maurice. Even Hoyt stopped his tirade. The comment, explosive in nature, hit the intended nerve. Devlon paled and immediately sat back in silence. The last thing he, of all people, should have mentioned was genocide.

Sitting up front with the driver, Hoyt turned and said, "Mr. Ambassador, if I may, security for this visit is completely unacceptable by diplomatic standards. A man in your position needs, requires, no, *demands* a full diplomatic motorcade and complement. We were nearly killed by that renegade motorcyclist earlier this morning."

Juwan and Hawk exchanged glances briefly.

Hoyt Collier, beady-eyed, bland and, oftentimes, overly zealous, gave the impression of a timid, addlebrained wimp, but he was far from what he appeared. Born into wealth, he had an IQ comfortably over 160 and had completed undergrad and graduate school in four years. He was a brilliant attorney and an accomplished linguist, fluent in over ten languages. He was a skilled interpreter and highly proficient in international negotiations.

In charge of managing the schedule and a personal aide to the ambassador, Hoyt managed everything from travel plans to personal purchases. If anyone needed to speak with the ambassador, they had to first go through him and he took his job very seriously and did it extremely well. Few were granted a personal audience and even fewer the ambassador's exclusive attention.

Unfortunately, he didn't handle crises very well, so unexpected events were a major catastrophe. As far as Hoyt was concerned, everything had to be planned and scheduled. Anything else was completely unacceptable.

"Hoyt," Maurice began.

"I beg your pardon, sir, but what if it had been an actual assassination attempt? We would have all been sitting ducks."

"Sitting ducks, there you have it," Devlon began again.

"Hoyt, please calm yourself, as you can see it is merely a person a bit eager to be on his way. I'm sure there was no harm intended or done," Maurice said firmly.

"Sir, with all due respect, I agree with Mr. Motako, life isn't as simple as black and white anymore. You must realize that."

"Thank you for that bit of insight, Hoyt," Maurice said.

"Sir, you have to be aware. People are unscrupulous and immoral. Your adversaries and those opposed to the United African Government would think nothing of taking advantage of a vulnerable situation. There are those who would like nothing better than to remove you from the political realm, particularly now that the mention of your appointment to prime minister has been made public."

The words of the over-privileged Hoyt brought a smile to Juwan's face. The man Hoyt spoke to had more knowledge of the world and the darkest souls of men than possibly anyone else on the globe. Yet the stark contradiction of his reply was bitterly ironic. Lost to the ravages of hate were most of Maurice's family and friends.

"*Akokodur*," Maurice replied simply, smiling the charismatic smile that made him a trusted prominent figure on world stage. "Have courage."

"I just wanted to point out that this motorcycle man could have been someone with mischievous intentions in mind."

"Hoyt," Juwan said, drawing attention from the others. He interceded patiently after seeing Maurice's face grimace. "Believe me, Maurice is very well aware of the dangers of his position and he takes his life and those around him very seriously. But allow me to assure you, had there been an actual emergency, the situation would have been properly and very efficiently dealt with."

He nodded confidently to Maurice's personal bodyguard, Hawk, knowing that he had a nine-millimeter gun loaded and ready at the least provocation. He, too, was armed. As an FBI agent he was required to carry a weapon at all times, especially given the recent terrorist climate. "And by the way," Juwan added as an afterthought, "the *he* was most definitely a *she*."

Book smart, Hoyt looked puzzled, an expression most were not accustomed to seeing. "What do you mean the he was a she, *who* was a she?" he asked.

"The man on the motorcycle was a woman," Juwan clarified.

Hoyt's expression instantly refused the possibility until he looked to Maurice and then to Hawk. They both nodded their heads, agreeing with Juwan. He looked at Devlon, who shrugged and looked out the window, appearing disinterested. "Really?" Hoyt said, stunned.

The three men nodded, prompting him to finally nod as well.

"I see," Hoyt added. "Interesting."

"Yes, very," Juwan said with a curious smile, revealing his curiosity.

"Now that that's taken care of, shall we get back to the business at hand?" Maurice said, ending the discussion.

"Of course," Hoyt said and picked up the itinerary but before continuing he turned around again. "Although, sir," he addressed Devlon directly, "the United States Constitution amendment's Article Two states and I quote, 'A well regulated militia, being necessary to the security of a free state, the right of the people to keep and bear Arms, shall not be infringed.' To that end, sir, nowhere does it actually mention nine millimeters or AK-forty-sevens, for your information."

His comments brought smiles to Maurice, Juwan and Hawk. Devlon's mouth opened in stunned shock as Hoyt immediately continued reciting the revised itinerary he had outlined, noting

assembly meetings, a press conference and several state receptions all perfectly timed and equal in importance.

Juwan, still amused, glanced out the window at the pris-
tine tree-lined streets surrounding Massachusetts Avenue. The
stately manors, both embassies and private residences, stood
back from the street, just clear of human contact. Behind ten-
foot hedges and iron gates stood the world's embassies:
Togo, Ireland, Haiti, Cameroon and Japan. The next one
would be Nubia and the current headquarters of the UAG,
the United African Government. And since Maurice had
spared him the interrogation so far, he knew as soon as they
got to the embassy, he would certainly be questioned about
his sudden presence.

Oddly enough he envied the early morning motorcycle
driver, her bravado. She was obviously a woman of passion who
savored and enjoyed life to its fullest—unlike his straight, by-
the-book life, which had been locked on course a long time ago.

When his parents were killed, leaving him and his younger
sister orphaned, they'd been legally adopted by Maurice.
Juwan's life had been planned to the last detail and he had
willingly followed the course that had been set out for him.
Positioned for greatness, he was denied the freedom he enjoyed as a child. The right tutors, the right schools, the right
friends, and the right job had been chosen for him and he had
followed it without question.

He looked up just as the limo turned into a slightly ob-
scured driveway lined with century-old oak trees and immac-
ulately manicured and sculpted landscaping. They drove
around the circular brick-paved driveway and pulled to a stop
in front of the brick and limestone chancery, the official embassy office. Four stories and thirty-five rooms, the lavish
mansion was both manor house for the ambassador's private
residence and the official embassy separated only by a short
hall and enclosed walkway.

As soon as the five men entered the large building, Maurice was instantly besieged on by attendants and the chancery staff. He answered questions as he proceeded to his office. Hoyt followed, also answering questions. Devlon went directly to the residence wing while Hawk paused at the front door to check with security.

Juwan turned to enter the library, then stopped and turned when he heard his name called. "Don't leave just yet," Maurice said as he paused before entering his office. "You and I need to talk."

Juwan nodded. He expected as much.

Chapter Three

The embassy, atop a ridge, had a breathtaking view of Rock Creek Park and the surrounding Arlington, Virginia. Juwan passed through the library, then stepped outside and looked around. It was late August and the gardens were still in full bloom, displaying a rainbow of colors. The peace and serenity reminded him of a time long ago.

He stood and looked into the distance, allowing memories to take hold of him. Then without warning the joy of remembering faded and was replaced by the anguish of heartfelt pain. In a brief moment his life had changed forever.

It had been many years since he'd been home. In the early years, growing up with his parents, he'd lived all over the world and experienced things few children could even imagine. From London, Nepal, and Mongolia to New Zealand and New Guinea, he had circled the globe a dozen times before settling in Washington, DC with his parents.

Unfortunately, their voices were silenced almost as soon as they arrived. They were killed in a botched robbery that had nearly taken the life of his younger sister. That night was as vivid as if it had just happened. The bright flames, the smell of charred wood and the sound of broken glass were indelibly etched in his mind. The sadness and helplessness of that moment had always weighed heavily on his heart. How could he possibly return? Yet here he was.

As the bitter memories faded, he heard the low roar of a motorcycle engine in the distance. His thoughts immediately went to the cyclist he'd seen twice already. He smiled, letting his thoughts trail astray. Thanks to her, the past two hours had unexpectedly been more interesting than he had experienced in the past two years.

"I'm curious, what exactly were you going to say?" Hawk asked as he walked up behind him.

Juwan turned, taken off guard by the sudden interruption of his thoughts. The question seemed to come out of nowhere. "About what? When?"

"Earlier," Hawk clarified as he came closer and looked out at the view, more for security than its innate beauty. Satisfied, he turned and leaned his back against the iron rail. "Just before the motorcyclist turned the corner, you began rolling the window down. What were you going to say?"

Juwan smiled and half chuckled as he shook his head. Only Hawk would have noticed and even thought to ask the question.

Aptly nicknamed for his quick reactions and equally precise abilities, Hawk was beyond reproach. He was a consummate strategist and family friend. At times he faded into the background, at other times he became a visible physical force. Either way, Juwan had little to worry about when it came to Maurice's safety.

Personally chosen for the position, Hawk was more of a friend to Maurice than his bodyguard title would suggest. Skilled at several forms of hand-to-hand combat, martial arts and weaponry, he was both professional and street-trained, having studied all forms of security, protection and defense. He had worked in security at the UN, then finally settled in the position as Maurice's personal bodyguard. He handled security both at home and abroad, and his skills and abilities went beyond the scope of many in the position.

"To tell you the truth," Juwan admitted, "I have no idea. I just wanted to see the woman behind the bravado."

Hawk smiled and nodded. "Yes, her driving skills were impressive." He paused, then added almost as an afterthought, "Among other things."

Juwan looked at Hawk. The two men often found themselves on the same wave length; this was one of those occasions. They each smiled knowingly. "A leather-wearing female motorcyclist sitting on a powerful bike suggests interesting possibilities."

"Indeed," Hawk agreed.

"But the fantasy is all for naught, twice in one day . . ." he began, then drifted off as he shook his head.

"Ah yes, but fate has a way of making a way."

"Cryptic. You're beginning to sound like Maurice."

"I take that as a great compliment."

"As it was intended," he nodded respectfully. "But D.C. is a large city and seeing our motorcycle friend again will be too much of a coincidence. Even I would question it."

"I agree."

A silence fell between them as both men turned to look below at Rock Creek Park. The view was magnificent. A continuing hum of morning traffic flowed along the Rock Creek and Potomac Parkway resembling a parade of brightly colored Matchbox cars. Beside them, a steady stream of water snaked its way beneath the line of trees and disappeared briefly below the Charles Glover Bridge.

"I thought there were going to be two bodyguards this trip, where's your partner?"

"Tyson had a few problems with immigration."

"Serious?"

"No, but he'll have to sit out a while and cool his heels until everything is straightened out."

"Can't Maurice do something about it?"

"You know Maurice would never step in unless it was serious. Tyson assured him that it was a matter of filing the appropriate paperwork.

"So, in the meantime, do you have someone else in mind?"

"As a matter of fact I do." The look Hawk gave him suggested the obvious.

"No can do. I'm laying low this visit, strictly hands off."

"Pondering other considerations I understand, congratulations," Hawk said.

Juwan turned to him questioningly. Then it dawned on him, his promotion. "I'd ask how you knew, but I'm sure that you'd have to kill me if you told me."

Hawk cracked a rare smile, something Juwan noticed more and more lately. "Possibly."

"You'd make an interesting FBI agent, if, of course, you weren't already otherwise engaged."

Hawk smiled again, letting out a chuckle this time. He shook his head. "Still going with that conspiracy theory, huh?"

"Tell me, who do you work for and what's the assignment? Because I know you're more than Maurice's bodyguard," Juwan began. Hawk turned with interest. "Secret Service, Interpol, CIA, FBI, NSA, MI-5, French Foreign Legion, which one is it?"

The question always on the tip of his tongue had finally been asked. Juwan, a trained expert, prided himself on recognizing a kindred professional. He knew Hawk was more than just Maurice's friend and bodyguard; he just couldn't figure out what. The two men looked at each other until the usual stalemate had been reached.

"I could ask you the same question, what's the assignment?" Hawk said as he glanced over Juwan's shoulder at the man approaching.

"There you are."

Juwan turned to see Maurice walking through the door of

the library. As he turned back around, Hawk walked away. His low chuckle followed in his wake.

"So, to what do I owe this honor?" Maurice continued as he approached. Juwan walked, meeting him halfway. They hugged warmly; then Maurice kissed both his cheeks and stepped back to look at him more closely. "None the less for wear, I see. Come, let's take a stroll in the garden, shall we?"

"Don't you have an appointment in less than half an hour?" Juwan asked, remembering Hoyt's busy schedule.

"Yes."

"Shouldn't you be leaving?"

"What will they do, start without me? Somehow I doubt it." The truth of his words was not boastful, just reality. He was one of the most powerful men in the world and any meeting that included him would surely be delayed until his arrival.

"How was your flight?" Juwan asked, knowing that Maurice had just flown in from New York.

"Short, bearable, and yours?"

"London to New York to DC, it wasn't exactly a hop, skip, and a jump."

"New York?" Maurice questioned, unaware that Juwan had been in New York.

"Yes, I flew in yesterday and stopped by the office."

"Why didn't you mention that when we spoke? We could have flown down here together this morning and had more time to talk."

That's exactly why he hadn't told Maurice. The last thing he wanted or needed was Maurice's input about his life. "I knew you were busy; I flew down late last night and stayed here at the embassy."

"I'm never too busy for you and you very well know that," he said, his voice firm and chiding. "Well, at least we'll be able to chat this time. How long will you be here?"

"Not long."

"Well, we'll just have to do the best we can with the time we have available."

Juwan frowned. He knew exactly what Maurice wanted to talk about. He'd been avoiding this little chat for the better part of two years, right after his last promotion. "How's Aunt Adarah?" Juwan asked about Maurice's wife, hoping to change the subject.

"She's well. She misses you. You haven't been to visit in more years than we can count."

"Business . . ." Juwan stated evasively.

". . . isn't as important as family," Maurice added.

Juwan looked away into the distance. Home was elusive as far as he was concerned. Washington was no longer his home, yet everywhere else seemed an unwelcoming refuge as well. At fifteen, after the death of his parents, he had chosen to finish his education abroad and after twenty years he never looked back.

"By the way, I understand congratulations are in order," Maurice said, interrupting Juwan's thoughts. His puzzled expression prompted Maurice to continue. "The new position."

"How did you find out?"

"Yasmine. I spoke with her earlier. She's very worried about you."

Yasmine Pole, Juwan's younger sister and a New York social worker specializing in child development, was always worried about something or someone. Just five years old when their parents were killed, she had been hospitalized for two months.

Afterwards she had been sheltered in private schools, but had always stayed very close to him. She was his heart and the calm in the turmoil he called his life. An overprotective brother by definition, he had been known to snap off a few heads of overly zealous suitors. When Yasmine had recently married his friend and associate, Kevin Pole, he had hoped that her happiness would diminish her concern for him, but apparently not.

"Yasmine's always worried about somebody," he said. "I'll call her later," he promised.

Maurice nodded. "You didn't answer the question, to what do I owe the honor?"

"What honor?" Juwan asked, still distracted from the conversation.

"The honor of your presence, of course. I haven't seen you in nearly fourteen months and here you suddenly stand before me, having shown up out of the blue accompanying Hoyt and Hawk to the airport to pick me up. I find that rather . . ." He paused briefly. "Curious."

"What are you talking about? You saw me last month."

"Conference calls from three thousand miles away hardly constitute live communication." He noted Juwan's weary silence. "Ah, I see, it is serious." He sat down on a cushioned lawn chair beneath a century-old oak tree, arched his fingers to his chin, then rested his elbows on the arm rest. "Sit," he commanded fatherly. "Talk."

Reluctantly Juwan yielded to his request. "There's nothing to talk about. I simply decided to take a break," he lied easily.

"I find that extremely hard to believe."

"It's true, there's nothing suspicious or sinister about it. I just need to take a little time out, away from the office, a long-overdue vacation."

"Somehow I doubt that the man most likely to take a bullet is simply taking a time out."

"Don't let the rumors fool you. I'm just on an extended vacation. All I intend to do is sit back and relax and enjoy the sights."

Laughter erupted, then regressed to chuckles. "Relax. You don't know the meaning of the word. You spend your free time going through old cases and spend your working hours figuring them out. There is no vacation for you. No, there is something else, an assignment, a woman, perhaps?" Maurice said hopefully.

"No." The stilted, almost final tone of his voice was immediate.

"You answered too quickly; that's not good." Maurice sucked his teeth and shook his head sadly. "Perhaps I will request the services of Adarah's friend since she will be attending this evening."

Juwan knew exactly to whom he referred. "That won't be necessary. When I find a woman that holds my interest, I'll let you know," he said, immediately thinking of Remy Poussant.

Two years ago when they met, he was sure that she was the woman to hold his interest even though he was technically assigned to draw her out. She was attractive, fun-loving and intelligent and he had broken his own rule and gotten too close, against his better judgment and everything he believed. He had hoped to save her from herself. But he had failed.

"I suggest you make it sooner than later. Adarah is anxiously awaiting the next generation." Maurice noted the troubled glint in Juwan's eye as he continued. "Besides, who will uphold the virile and virtuous Mebeko name if you don't?"

"I'm sure your sons will be happy to take on the duties."

"They're young still and too inexperienced."

"They're twenty-two and twenty-three and doing grad work at Oxford and Harvard, hardly what I'd consider too young and too inexperienced. How are they by the way?"

"Fine, fine, I just spoke to them this morning." He paused and grinned broadly. "Ah, you are a sly one. I see your FBI training is still strong."

"How so?"

"Avoidance, you change the subject well." Juwan didn't answer so Maurice went straight to the heart of his anguish. "Punishing yourself while pushing others away will not bring her back. There was nothing you could have done. You must let it go."

Let it go. He repeated the words in his mind. He had and that's what troubled him most of all.

His inability to save Remy stewed in his mind like a nightmare refusing to go away. He held on to the regret. She was no innocent yet a part of him had seen the possibility of her redemption. But he had failed her and failed himself.

"We all make our choices in life. Even the love and trust she had for you could not alter her course. She made her choice," Maurice said, as a buzz from his inside jacket pocket drew their attention. Maurice pulled out his phone. Hoyt's voice beamed through the speaker clearly.

"Sir, you have a meeting in town in twenty-one minutes. The car is waiting out front. We should leave in no less than three minutes."

"Go. I'll hang around until you come back," Juwan said, relieved at the interruption. "I still have a few things to take care of."

"I have a better idea; come with me." He stood, prompting Juwan to also stand. "This will be of interest to you as well. The National Museum of African Art is sponsoring a Nubian Art exhibit. If I remember correctly, the subject was one of your favorites."

"It used to be when I was young. I've seen enough museums in my day, I'll pass."

Ignoring him, Maurice continued. "I've been asked to speak at a small gathering on the topic of the neo-Nubian influence on the current African climate and, more specifically, on the United African Government."

Juwan's interest piqued slightly. Maurice, a founder of the UAG movement to unify Africa, had been building a strong following in the past few years. Any interest generated would only add to his cause. "I'm sure it will be informative."

"We've also been invited by the cultural liaison to a private tour and a brief look at the art exhibit while it's in preparation."

"I still think I'll pass," Juwan said as he followed Maurice back toward the library doors.

"Unfortunate. The lead curator, a delightful person, has gathered some extremely rare pieces from other museums and private collectors from around the world."

"Really, that might be of interest." His attention suddenly spiked. *Curator* and *ancient African art* rang a bell.

"Yes it is. Adarah has been working very closely with the museum. She tells me that this exhibit is truly quite remarkable. I have been looking forward to seeing it when it opens. There is already a lot of buzz surrounding a few of the pieces. Unique and distinctive, I have been told, some even I have never seen before."

"That's not surprising given the climate of the black market for art and antiquities." A slow smile spread wide across his face as his eyes glinted with the familiar rush of anticipation. "I'm sure that there'll be several pieces in question, maybe even listed in the FBI file of stolen art. I'd be interested to see the curator's papers on each exhibit piece."

Maurice shook his head. "Always seeing and expecting the worst in others. I see this job of yours has numbed your senses to the beauty of art."

"Numbed it? No. The reality of black-market activity, illegal export and the theft and pillage of archaeological sites has to be taken into account along with human nature."

Maurice stopped walking and turned toward Juwan. "Expect the worst. Is that what you've learned of life?"

Juwan looked into Maurice's tired eyes, dark and bright at the same time. They reflected the knowledge of time and the weariness of hope. "Yes, in a manner of speaking."

"Son, having a suspicious nature isn't always such a good idea. Sometimes things appear, upon first assessment, quite different from what they actually are." He began walking again.

"And sometimes things are just as they appear," Juwan responded flatly, remembering that Remy, no matter how hard he tried to change her and help her, died anyway.

"And when you are proven wrong in your assumptions?"

"I'll let you know when and if it ever happens." Juwan stepped up and opened the library door, respectfully allowing Maurice to enter first.

Maurice smiled at Juwan's stubbornness as he stepped inside. "You are certainly not your father's child."

"On the contrary Maurice, I am very much my father's child. His death gave me a rude awakening to human nature."

As he crossed the library, Maurice shook his head, understanding the pain still harbored deep within Juwan's heart. Trust and faith had always been an issue with him. The loss of his parents at such a young age was devastating, particularly since he had been close by and unable to save them. He knew that Juwan had always blamed himself for not doing more. Maurice just hoped and prayed that one day his heart would feel the joy of living and loving once again.

As he approached the door leading to the foyer, he paused and turned to Juwan. "And his life, Juwan, the life he led, filled with joy happiness and love. What has that given you?" Maurice asked. Juwan went silent. The case was complete. As usual Maurice had challenged him with eloquence and reasoning. A smile graced his lips.

"Be that as it may, we are attending this morning as attachés of the UAG and Nubia, in a diplomatic capacity, not federal agents in search of stolen relics and black-market thieves."

"And if we should by chance come across one or two?" Juwan asked, noting the widespread theft of relics from the northeastern African region.

"We'll deal with it as the need arises, not before."

Juwan nodded, understanding Maurice's meaning perfectly. As he opened the library door leading to the foyer, Hoyt immediately snapped his phone closed and hurried across the open space to meet Maurice.

"Right this way, sir," Hoyt said. Then, noticing Juwan accompanying Maurice, his brow knitted with concern. "Juwan, will we be dropping you off somewhere in town?" he asked. The angst of arriving late and disrupting his carefully laid out schedule clearly clouded his expression.

"No, Hoyt, as a matter of fact I'll be going to the museum with you. I hope that's not a problem."

"Not at all," he answered quickly as he followed Maurice and Juwan to the front door. "The Nubian exhibit is in its beginning stages and several key pieces still haven't been delivered. But as I understand it, the bulk of the space has already been set up."

"I'm looking forward to seeing some of the rarer pieces. I understand they are quite unique."

"Yes, they are. I was fortunate enough to assist the curator, Dr. Evans, in the procurement of several of the less attainable pieces."

Dr. Evans. Juwan smiled, musing at the coincidence of the excursion. Apparently his assignment would be starting much sooner than he anticipated. "In that case," he said, "I'm really looking forward to seeing exactly what Dr. Evans has to offer."

"Splendid, the car is waiting out front. Shall we, sir?" Hoyt motioned to the waiting limo as they exited through the front door.

Chapter Four

By nine-thirty the hectic day Kennedy had predicted was shaping up to be even more challenging than she assumed. She arrived early enough to be late for her morning meeting, missed a phone call from Africa she'd been expecting and then had the pleasure of listening to the museum's public liaison, Barry Culpepper, detail everything he noticed in the exhibit area as he walked through the night before. Added to that frustration, the shipment she'd been expecting was stuck in morning traffic, so she decided to take a few minutes and do the one thing that always gave her pleasure.

As she walked, the sound of high heeled boots clicking on marble flooring echoed through the empty museum halls. This was her world, this was her joy and this was her calling. Everywhere she looked she felt a sense of pride that life, beginning a continent away, was being renewed here and she was a part of it.

The museum's pale gray walls and enormous structural columns marked off and separated various galleries. Each gallery housed a select number of African art and artifacts ranging from early Nubian periods, post-colonial to modern-day contemporary. Select pieces hung on walls, were perched on pedestals and platforms, guiding patrons through a marvelous structured maze of cultural artistry.

Kennedy walked past the various displays with pride and reverence. African art, as diverse and spectacular as the people who created it, was growing in popularity. A trend begun by wealthy collectors, it was the new thing to acquire, borrow, lend or in some cases, steal. The art itself varied by region, tribe, culture and condition and usually had a recurrent theme, whether it was ceremonial or functional.

Although pleased that Africa was finally getting its artistic due, Kennedy was frustrated by the influx of amateurs, professionals and novices. Suddenly, right or, most often, wrong, everyone had an opinion about the art and the culture she loved so much. Armed with a teaspoon of knowledge some passed judgment while others used their power and positions for personal gain.

Within three years time, the museum had seen a remarkable increase in attendance and recognition. The museum now enjoyed its first real success in nearly two decades and the long struggle for credibility had taken a giant leap in a positive new direction.

The museum, closed to the public at the moment, had a full complement of employees mingling about preparing for the busy day ahead. Kennedy usually arrived much earlier but having been delayed by the distraction of her sister, had completed her morning routine of checking e-mail and answering her voicemail, including three messages from Barry reminding her about the lecture and the guest speaker. She read through the museum's online daily brochure outlining the day's special programs, noting again that Nubia's Ambassador Mebeko was scheduled to give a talk in the main auditorium later that morning. Knowing that he was a tremendous speaker, she was anxiously looking forward to hearing him but knew that she would most likely be preoccupied with the shipment scheduled to arrive, hopefully, sometime soon.

As she neared the closed off special exhibition galleries, she felt a sense of satisfaction and exhilaration. She slipped behind the dramatic mural covering and entered the gallery. She looked up at the two huge monolithic limestone figures standing pillar-like at the entrance. Formidable and challenging they stood as guards before the majesty of the exhibit. Reproduced and constructed with extraordinary care and detail from the originals which were now beneath the Aswan Dam in Egypt, she admired the exquisite artistry of the faux paint. Realistic, the wash of aged color gave the molded synthetic material a heavy stone-like quality.

She continued through the entrance admiring the progress. The museum's workmen had finished the preliminary construction and painting and only a few additional walls needed to be added. A series of step platforms and display pedestals had been staged at various locations according to the floor plan. She smiled and nodded. It was all coming together. In a few weeks her dream would be a reality.

The main walls had been painted a soft sepia tint with terra cotta trim and the flooring, a tongue and grove hardwood with a cherrywood finish, had been installed. The soft glow of track lighting softened the area, allowing a gentle pouring of light directing movement around and through the temporary walls.

Large descriptive panels sat on the floor ready to be hung in place behind each artifact. Kennedy and her staff wrote the exact wording, then handed it over to the museum's legal and art departments to vet. They in turn checked legalities and refined the wording. She read each as she walked through. Concise and informative, they described the pieces displayed. She nodded approvingly after reading each.

Eighty-five percent of the borrowed pieces had already arrived and been placed in position along with a collection of the museum's own acquired pieces from eight of its archived facilities and the official repository. Behind each display was a corresponding identifying number and description tag that had been checked, cross-checked and then triple-checked.

As she proceeded through the exhibit the peace of centuries past surrounded her and she felt the sweet sensation of pride well up inside. She had gathered the precious arts and artifacts from centuries ago and a world away. She was fulfilling a promise she made to herself long ago to bring to light the ancient world of Nubian art. And she had succeeded beyond even *her* wildest imagination.

The gallery was divided by centuries and split into two separate but unifying exhibits, the ancient Nubian world and contemporary Nubian world. Both would come together for the first time ever.

The open spaced floor plan had already been separated, designed and prepared. Additional security had been wired along with the audio and visual presentations she'd chosen. She walked into one of the seven small side rooms that had been set aside for the audio-visual presentations. Several rows of bench-style seating had been installed along with an enormous clear-screen audio/video monitor and projector. She was delighted with the room's dramatic staging. And although the film series had been completed months earlier, she made a mental note to review the films again.

Quiet and still, she stood in one of the small areas and observed the transparent screen. The subdued lighted accented the theatrical flavor and gave the room a movie theater-like quality. She walked the perimeter of the room, then returned to the main exhibit.

Kennedy sighed deeply as she approached the end of the exhibit. This was by far the best part of her day. The quiet echo of century-old art and the fresh newness of contemporary design spread out around her.

She quickly breezed through the contemporary gallery, seeing the extraordinary art and artists represented. Bonded by the pride of a culture, the unified exhibit would make a lasting statement. The abridged museum store was next. A marketplace-style gift shop had been allocated and set up to sell Nubian wares—both reproductions and originals, hand-crafted and unique, designed and created by dozens of arti-sans and vendors. The area had been stocked with toys, clothing, books, and knickknacks. Kennedy passed the front entrance and glanced through the secured mesh screen. Every possible souvenir could be bought from a two-dollar pen to a two-thousand-dollar mask.

She continued to the end of the exhibit. Several huge poster panels listing the names of the major sponsors and contribu-tors had been hung. One prominent name was the Evans Cor-poration. She was proud to have taken part in the experience.

The stress of the undertaking had been hard on her nerves. Things had gone wrong and major plans had been altered. The most significant being the theft at the Nubian Museum, the arrest of Petre Siegal, and his subsequent escape. But she refused to think about that now that she was feeling as good as new.

The exhibit was like therapy; by the time she walked through it she had calmed down considerably from the hectic start of her morning. As she headed back to her office, her beeper sounded. It was the head of security informing her that her shipment from Africa had arrived and was being unloaded in the receiving area on the back dock. She notified her staff to meet her there. As she headed for the receiving dock, she saw Barry hurrying in the opposite direction.

Barry Culpepper, jellyfish white, round and plump except for his Rudolph red nose, had an uncanny resemblance to the Pillsbury Dough Boy. He never missed an opportunity to give his opinion, deliver a lecture or dictate a directive as he rushed through the museum as if it were on fire. Thinking that his behavior made him appear more important or needed, he was pretty much useless.

His position as the museum public liaison consisted mainly

in securing private funding. Coming from a financial and business background, he knew as much about art as he did about nuclear physics. He had risen to his position by brownnosing his way from the golf course. Appointed by a member of the board, he delighted in his post, offering input as often as possible with as little knowledge as possible. Spineless and miserable most of the time, he spent his days catering to the special visitors and VIPs and his nights catering to the board of directors.

Kennedy watched as he ambled up the stairs in his typical rushed manner. She shook her head, thankful for whatever or whoever called him away from the arriving shipment. For some reason, having no explicit purpose, he always felt it was his responsibility to attend to incoming art shipments. So, with him out of the way, she felt certain that the day had just gotten better. She turned and went in the opposite direction.

"Gentlemen, welcome."

Four men turned to see a smiling man approach, greeting them with exaggerated warmth and cordiality. Hoyt, familiar with the museum and its directors, immediately stepped up to return the greeting. Hoyt made the introductions, referring to both Juwan and Hawk as Maurice's personal associates.

Barry Culpepper was flabbergasted as he met Maurice and went into a recitation of all his accomplishments including his nomination for the Nobel Prize for his contributions to resolving the Sudanese civil war. Flattered, Maurice calmed him as he had done others, by assuring him that he was merely there to enjoy the museum's offerings and to thank him for inviting him to speak.

Barry passed out identification badges that gave each man exclusive access to the museum with complete VIP privileges. "Sir, I can't tell you how delighted we are to have you attending our forum on Nubia. Having you as our keynote speaker is truly an honor. Since our other guests have already begun arriving, it will be a pleasure to personally escort you to the main lecture hall."

"Splendid," Maurice said.

"Will Dr. Evans be joining us? I had hoped we could visit the Nubian exhibit briefly to see its progress," Hoyt said as he secured his VIP badge to his jacket pocket.

"Unfortunately not, I believe that Dr. Evans is overseeing a shipment that arrived early this morning. And due to security and insurance stipulations, I won't be able to walk you through the Nubian exhibit set up as I initially hoped."

Juwan, silent through most of the interaction, was disappointed. He wanted to get a look at the exhibit pieces.

"I see, that is disappointing," Maurice said. "I was looking forward to seeing a few of the pieces my wife told me about. I understand they are quite extraordinary."

"Yes, some of the pieces are quite remarkable. Of course, I personally took charge of the major acquisitions. I choose pieces to accentuate the dramatic struggle of the Nubian culture."

"I wasn't aware that others chose the pieces as well. What are your main criteria, period or aesthetics?"

Barry looked at Maurice, surprised by his knowledge. "Well, period, of course," he guessed. "I find it demonstrates the unique quality of the work. As a mater of fact there is a piece that I found particularly interesting. It's a twenty-ninth-dynasty bas-relief of King Piye; he was, of course, the son of King Shabaka," he stated boastfully, impressed with his less-than-accurate knowledge.

"Really," Juwan spoke for the first time. "I wasn't aware that Piye, who was in the twenty-fifth dynasty, lived long enough to be included in the twenty-ninth dynasty in Nubia and I'd always thought that Shabaka was King Piye's brother, not his father. I believe I always heard that Kashta was their father."

Barry opened his mouth to answer, then, flabbergasted, said

nothing. A few "uhs" and "ums" were all that came out. Finally he found his voice and admitted that he basically counseled, oversaw and approved the various pieces and that his busy schedule didn't allow him to do the day-to-day work. He quickly changed the subject. "If you'd like, I can have someone from the staff available to speak with us about the pieces after the forum."

"Unfortunately, time constraints are pressing this morning," Hoyt said.

"Of course," Barry said, visibly relieved. "Another time perhaps."

"That would be wonderful. I'll look forward to it," Maurice said, nodding his gratitude. Barry, happy that he easily avoided a potentially embarrassing situation, beamed. "Gentlemen, this way," he offered quickly as he motioned toward the elevators.

While Barry, Maurice and Hoyt walked up front, Hawk and Juwan lagged behind. "That was very impressive," Hawk said, still amused by Barry's lack of knowledge.

"He obviously had no idea what he was talking about. And there was no way he could have chosen anything from the twenty-ninth dynasty—there was no twenty-ninth dynasty," Juwan said.

They arrived at the main lecture hall. As they were about to enter, Juwan hung back. "I think I'll have a look around."

Hawk nodded and looked at his watch. "One hour," he said, then followed Maurice inside.

Juwan waited just until Maurice entered and, hearing the loud applause, he nodded to the additional security stationed at the hall's entrance and headed for the stairs.

"Excuse me, Mr. Mason." Juwan turned, hearing Barry's boisterous voice behind him. Barry rushed over to him. "I assumed you were attending the lecture with the ambassador's party."

"No."

"Are you perhaps interested in anything in particular? Or is there any gallery I can point you toward?"

"No, thank you." He began walking away.

"Ah, Mr. Mason, question? You appear to be very astute with Nubian history. Tell me, are you a historian or a scholar perhaps?"

"No," he answered simply.

"So you are just a bodyguard?"

"I've done many things."

Barry smiled and motioned for Juwan to step to the side. He moved in closer and lowered his voice. "Tell me, Mr. Mason, how familiar are you with ancient Nubian art and artifacts?"

He smiled. "I've dealt with them from time to time."

"What about authenticating or procurement?"

Juwan's gut lurched as he played along. "I've handled a few."

"Splendid." He chuckled loudly then toned down. "I knew you were the man to speak with. It's been my impression that bodyguards, especially well-traveled bodyguards, are the most resourceful, and they have the least suspicious connections. We must chat again real soon," he said as he reached into his pocket and pulled out a card. "I have a feeling that we have quite a bit in common."

Juwan nodded, took the card and walked away. He played it cool but he knew he was onto something. He'd just been propositioned. He made a mental note to run a complete check on Barry Culpepper as soon as possible. But for the time being he continued looking around.

Because the museum was laid out simply enough, he had no trouble navigating the three stories and the one underground level. Having quickly seen the galleries on the main and top two levels, he wanted a quick glance at the sublevel. He knew that security would be tightest there since Barry mentioned that a shipment had been delivered earlier.

The entrance was blocked off to the public; Juwan was openly offered entrance because of the badge Barry had given him. Although it didn't give him complete access, it did give him a behind the scenes view of the museum's inner workings.

He noted the security doors, the cameras, and the alarm system were all top of the line. He had just completed his tour of the lower level when he decided to refocus and venture into the administrative wing.

Seeing the locked doors he slid his badge through the opening. Nothing happened. He slid it again, then heard the sound of the latch release. The doors began to open so he pulled at the handle to expedite the opening. Someone from the other side pushed, causing the door to fly open full force and the person on the other side to bump right into him. They collided with full impact.

Chapter Five

Maurice Mebeko had arrived. Excitement blazed through the building like wildfire in high winds through dry brush. Congressmen, senators, movie stars even U.S. presidents had visited the museum before, but never had such news as Mebeko's arrival caused such exhilaration. From the cafeteria staff to the security guards to the administrative staff, everyone was pumped and excited.

Kennedy was excited, but for a different reason. Not since her first trip to Nubia years ago had she been as excited. Subsequent trips to other museums around the world had yielded equal enthusiasm. But then just a few months ago she spent over eight weeks in the Nubian Museum studying and researching the different artifacts for her exhibit. While choosing and selecting the perfect pieces, she was like a child in a candy store.

A few weeks into her studies she was presented to Ambassador Maurice Mebeko and his wife Adarah. They were an extraordinary couple and she immediately adored them. In her time there she had gotten very close to Adarah. Adarah's knowledge of Nubian art and artifacts was remarkable. Surprisingly, she had not been not born in Africa but was an American citizen when she first meet the ambassador. They married and soon afterwards she became known unofficially as Nubia's cultural ambassador.

Meeting and befriending Adarah had been the highlight of Kennedy's last trip to Nubia. She was a delight. They spent many hours talking about and researching the many facets of Nubia's history.

Kennedy was indeed excited that the Mebekos had arrived but her immediate concern was two massive crates sitting on the security dock in the receiving bay.

Thankfully, both crates were intact and all the art was accounted for and in excellent condition. Fourteen pieces from the Pharaonic Age, twelve pieces from the Coptic Age and six from the Islamic, all in immaculate condition. One huge statue, which had been dismantled, from the original Abu Simbel Temple had been taken directly to the exhibit gallery and one set of mummified remains from Kashmatkh encased in the excavated sarcophagus completed the shipment.

She finished the initial paperwork for the insurance and security companies. She checked the crates' manifest for any discrepancies, then entered the particulars into the computer. She assigned specific tasks to her assistants, then left her staff to begin unpacking, cataloguing and sorting the pieces while she attended to other museum and exhibit business. One more shipment and the collection would be complete.

She made a mental note to contact her counterpart at the Nubian Museum and inform him of the shipment's safe arrival as soon as possible. Then she needed to find Barry, having received his messages that Ambassador Mebeko would be touring the facility. She definitely wanted to see him again.

But first she needed to get to her office and then to the conservation lab. There was something slightly different about one of the pieces and she wanted to make sure that it hadn't gotten damaged while in transit. She knew that she had photos and reference material in her office, so a quick side trip there, then to the lab, and then finally to the lecture hall would complete her morning.

Covered with bits of excelsior and a thin layer of dust and sand, she hurried up the stairs to her office. She was stopped twice. Then as she approached the administrative wing door, she unlocked it and pushed as someone pulled.

Stumbling, she barely caught her balance. "Kennedy," the museum receptionist said, surprised to literally run into her, "Barry's looking for you and did you hear the news? Ambassador Mebeko is here."

"Yes, I heard," she said, pulling her security card out.

"Isn't it exciting?"

"Yes, very."

"Maya's looking for you, too."

"Yes I know, she beeped me. I'm on my way to my office now."

"Oh, and you got a phone call at the main switchboard this morning."

Kennedy frowned. It was odd for her to receive a phone call at the main switchboard. "That's odd, was there a message?"

"No, he said he'd try back later."

"Thanks," Kennedy said as she swiped the key card through the administration wing lock, then closed and secured the door behind her. She quickly opened the door to her office and stepped inside.

Maya Thaddeus, her assistant of only two months, on loan from the Nubian Museum, was in her office sitting at her desk with her personal laptop computer in front of her. Her eyes were glued to the screen until a look of surprise covered her face as soon as she saw Kennedy walk into the office. "Hi," she said nervously as she stood and fidgeted with a pen on the desk. "There you are, I was looking for the shipment schedule and paperwork from the last delivery. I didn't find it in the office computer and thought that maybe it would be in your personal computer."

Kennedy looked at her oddly and came around the side of the desk. "You won't find it there; everything's encrypted."

"Yes, I noticed. I entered the division password you gave me, hoping that would covert the encryption, but it actually seemed to make it worse. The more I tried to fix it, the worse it got."

"The division password won't work on this computer." She leaned over and closed the laptop securely as Maya scooted around to the side, allowing Kennedy access to her desk.

"I've never seen anything like that before," she said, now standing in front of the desk. "What kind of encryption program was that? The more I typed, the worse it got. Then finally it just shut itself off and now it won't reboot at all. I'm sorry. I can pay for any damage caused."

"I'm sure it's fine, don't worry about it." Kennedy picked up the laptop and placed it on the credenza, then sat down behind her desk and looked up at Maya still fidgeting with the pen.

"Where did you get the program?" Maya asked.

"My brother is very good at what he does."

"He must be brilliant."

"He'd say he was," Kennedy said, joking on his behalf yet knowing that the statement was very true. "Why do you need the shipping schedule and paperwork from the last delivery? Was there a problem?"

"No, not that I know of, at least I don't think so. Petre's replacement asked about an item that was shipped. He wanted to make sure that it was on the list. I told him I'd check."

Kennedy's heart immediately stopped at the mention of Petre's name. Petre Siegal had been her friend. A native Sudanese, he had been a tremendous help to her during her time in Nubia. Unfortunately, he was also one of the men involved in the museum theft just days before she left. She was stunned when the news of his involvement reached her in Germany later.

"The list isn't in the system yet. Use the password and check the office computer in the lab. It has the most up-to-date files. The original paperwork has already gone to the insurance company for verification."

"Right, okay, thanks," Maya said as she hurried out and closed the door behind her.

"Petre," she said aloud. The thought of him had her nerves jumping; as her breathing quickened, her heart began to pound faster and a sudden flush of warmth surrounded her, then nothing. The sudden rush of anxiety that teetered inside her was just as suddenly stilled and a feeling of uneasiness settled around her.

She'd never had any reason to not trust any member of her staff, but there was something about Maya that suddenly seemed odd. She had come highly recommended by Petre. With an extensive background in both ancient and contemporary art, she was the perfect match Kennedy was looking for in a new assistant.

She had had trouble in her homeland and was desperate to start a new life. So when Petre suggested her for the position, Kennedy was happy to give her a chance.

Maya's overall work ethic was exemplary, her ideas and suggestions were visionary and on target with what the museum and she herself had in mind. She had a true passion for the art and a genuine love of the culture. But, unfortunately, it was her overall demeanor, the steady aloofness that now troubled Kennedy.

Of course, given the political strife of her country and the history of the region, Maya did as expected and stayed primarily to herself, keeping everyone at an arm's length. Apparently trust in her fellow coworkers was not in her makeup and at a moment's notice it seemed that she would pull out a pen and like a grade-school hall monitor, take everyone's name for the principal.

"What's with her now?"

Kennedy looked up and smiled. "Hey, welcome back," she said brightly. Her friend and colleague, Yolanda Chambers, the contemporary African arts curator, came into the office, passing Maya on the way out. "How was your trip?"

"Decent."

"Did you get everything you wanted?"

"Mostly, with a few exceptions," she said as she walked over to Kennedy's desk and leaned on the corner. "I heard you got a shipment this morning, anything interesting?"

"Yeah, it was like Christmas, opening the crates and seeing everything I requested." She leaned back in her chair. "I can't wait for this opening. It's gonna be a major show for us, my ancient work and your contemporary work."

"I know what you mean. 'Nubian Art, Its Past and Its Future Together as One,'" she said, holding her hands up as if to transform the exhibit's title into a newspaper headline. "It screams 'come experience me.'"

"So how was everything in Nubia when you left?"

"Okay, tense," she said matter-of-factly, with a shrug. "It's been weeks and everybody is still stunned. Then of course, there's Petre and his involvement. And after everything he got away. But the others were caught. I know he was a close friend, but the man must have gone nuts."

"You knew him before. Did you know that he was involved in the black market?" Kennedy asked.

"Nah, but I'm not surprised. He had a serious dark side. I can definitely see him doing something stupid. When I knew him years ago, he was into all kinds of craziness. I couldn't handle all that drama. I have enough of my own. But the question is—did you know?"

"No, I had no idea."

"That's a surprise. I was sure that he must have told you. I thought you two were tight and headed to the altar."

"Looks can be deceiving. Our relationship was nowhere near serious," Kennedy said. "Bad boys are not for marrying."

"Uh huh, I heard that," Yolanda said. "Still, I'm surprised you didn't know anything," she said tightly. "You were the one that he instantly fell in love with."

"What's with who? What were you saying when you first came in?" Kennedy asked, choosing to ignore Yolanda's statement.

Yolanda looked at her puzzled, then nodded, remembering. "Oh," she said of the original question she asked as she walked into the office. "Maya, she seemed more than her usual stressed-out self. She nearly knocked me out of the way coming out of here. What happened, did you finally fire her stuck-up self?"

Kennedy turned on her monitor, dropped in a CD and prompted the computer to scan several files. She highlighted one, quickly read it, then pressed the print button. "No, nothing like that. She was just looking for something in the wrong place. You know how she is about wasting time."

"Little Miss Perfect," Yolanda said, her tone biting and catty. "Listen, just a quickie, girl, I saw Ambassador Mebeko and his associates just before they went into the lecture hall. Umm-um, talk about impressive. For an older man he is very distinguished. I've seen him on television and in newspapers and magazines but never in person. He is very handsome. Plus, he's got these two security men with him and they are too tasty. Girl, I swear if I were ten years younger, I would sop'um both up with a biscuit 'n gravy. I was actually salivating when I first saw them."

Kennedy gathered the printed file and several books, then looked at her friend and shook her head. Yolanda had a way with words that made the simplest exchange of ideas a major sexual interlude.

"I thought you were still seeing that mystery man who no one has ever met or seen."

"I am, but he travels so much so I could always use a little something on the side."

"You're terrible," Kennedy said as she stood at her bookcase and continued gathering her books.

"Listen, girl, I know you're crazy busy but I just stopped by to brighten your day. I'll see you later."

"Are you still going tonight?" Kennedy asked.

"Yeah, but I might be late, my friend's back in town. We might meet up before the reception. You know how it is."

"Really, so will we finally get to meet the mystery man tonight?"

"I don't know, we'll see. He's an important man with a very visible political profile. So, for now, I'm not comfortable with everybody knowing who he is. He has a bit of a past, but we all do. He's changed. I'd like to think that I had something to do with that."

"I'm sure you did," Kennedy said of Yolanda's cryptic remark. "And I can appreciate that." Everybody knew that Yolanda had had a fling with one of the board members in the past and that she'd moved up the ladder since. But with no real proof, no one had a clue as to the identity of her latest companion.

The art world, covering everything from prehistoric cave drawings to young up-and-coming Soho artists, was a small community, and in most cases word traveled at the speed of fiber optics. Any major buy, sale, theft, anomaly or indiscretion was telegraphed immediately. The museum was like a mini-conductor; it amped up every piece of gossip.

Kennedy knew Yolanda well enough. Although their artistic specialties were different by about four thousand years, they often found themselves in the same circles and even traveled together.

So when it came to the identity of Yolanda's mystery man, Kennedy had her suspicions as who he was. And Yolanda was right. Everyone had pasts, ghosts and skeletons to deal with. Petre was hers.

Kennedy gathered the papers she'd printed, picked up a

stack of books and headed to the door; Yolanda followed. They said their good-byes, then turned in opposite directions.

She reordered the awkward books in her arms, then headed to the administrative wing's main exit to the museum. The glossy photos began to slide against each other, and then one of the books began to slip from her arms; she quickly readjusted it. Then, not paying attention, she turned, pushing the security door with her hip. Suddenly there was no door and she was off balance and pushing against thin air. Seconds later she was on her way, falling head first to the floor.

Chapter Six

Although the unexpected bump knocked him back slightly, instinctively, Juwan held his balance, reached out and in a split second grabbed Kennedy before she fell. He pulled her toward his body and held tight. The jarring impact of her body slamming off balance against his sent them both smashing against the door frame and the books she carried scattering all over the floor.

A second of shock passed. Then, sandwiched between the solidness of the door and the hardness of the man holding her and intimately pressed against her, Kennedy began chuckling at the absurdity of the sight and the awkwardness of the situation.

Safely cradled in the arms of a complete stranger, Kennedy looked up into his hazel sexy, sultry eyes. "Wow," she said breathlessly, not sure if she was referring to the situation, the almost fall or the man. A chill of excitement went through her as he continued to hold her and she continued to let him.

His smile broadened and her legs went numb. He flashed an almost dimple in his right cheek. "Yeah, wow, right back," he said. Their eyes locked as they stayed in that position a few moments longer than necessary. Then realizing that their bodies were still intimately pressed together, she spoke. "You can let me go now."

"Are you sure?" he asked. His meaning was obvious.

She smiled, knowing her weakness; she knew a bad boy when she saw one. She thought about her answer and smiled more broadly. "No, but I guess we'd better do it anyway."

The sexy smile struck him immediately. "As you like." He released her and took a single step back. She was even better-looking in person. The moment passed as they just stood there staring at each other in a comfortable silence. Then he looked down at the scattered books. "Why don't I get those for you?" She smiled and nodded as he bent down and began gathering the books, papers and photos.

Not bad, Kennedy thought as the man in front of her bent down at her feet to pick up the books. She got a nice picture of his broad shoulders, his nice tight rear end, and most importantly, there was no missing wedding band imprint. *Not bad at all,* she repeated as she raked her teeth over her lower lip.

Casually dressed in black, he had *Danger, bad boy* written all over him and she knew in an instant he was exactly the distraction she needed to take her mind off her panic attacks, although she was sure that he wasn't exactly what the doctor had in mind. But she had promised Madison no more bad boys. After Petre she should have had her fill of living on the dangerous side. But she couldn't resist. She smiled to herself. *Maybe just one more.*

Then with little provocation, naughty thoughts began to creep into her mind. And a sudden rush of heat seeped into her arms and legs as her stomach began to flutter. Kennedy took a deep calming breath. The last thing she needed was to have a full-out panic attack in front of a perfect stranger. Her palms began to moisten and her heart beat wildly. *Here it comes,* she warned and prepared herself.

As Juwan picked up the last book, which was right next to Kennedy's foot, he noticed her boots, then recognized the burgundy leather pants as the pair he'd seen earlier. He stopped, stared directly ahead at her thighs, and recalled the motorcycle driver from that morning.

"It's you," he said softly, then looked up into her eyes. "You're the one."

The panic she'd been feeling suddenly vanished as the angst of revelation hit her. "What did you just say?" she questioned, her eyes wide with surprise as she looked down at him. The tense shock of recognition clouded her expression to fearful déjà vú. She'd heard those same words before; she'd said the same words before. She immediately went still as his too familiar words reverberated in her mind: "It's you. You're the one."

Having a photographic memory for words and conversations, a strange talent she'd had since childhood, she instantly played the words back in her mind. A flash of memory appeared. It was the conversation she had with her sister at their brother's wedding reception. She heard the exact words as clearly as if they had just been uttered, and they were.

Eidetic imagery is the medical and technical term for her particular talent. She had the unique ability to remember conversations verbatim and actually see words that were in essence imprinted on her memory. Although the memories eventually faded, any recent conversation could be recalled and literally played from her memory as if by a recorder.

"Are you okay?" Juwan asked as he stood holding the books in his hands and seeing the still, disturbed expression on her face. Suddenly, the sexy siren's seductive smile seemed to fade to deep concern.

"No," she muttered breathlessly, then changed her mind, quickly shaking her head as if to clear the remembered image from her thoughts. "Yes, yes, I'm fine, thank you." She reached for the books, but he held on to them. "Sorry I didn't see you standing on the other side of the door. You'd be surprised how often that happens." She finally looked up into his face again. Her heart sank and her stomach fluttered and she knew that it had nothing to do with an anxiety attack. She smiled, then looked away. The only thing she could think of was biscuits 'n gravy. "Uh, so you said that I was the one. Any particular reason? Were you looking for me?"

Juwan paused. There had to be a mistake. This goddess-like vision could no way be the Hell's Angel on wheels from earlier that morning or the subject of his investigation, but that's also what he had thought before about Remy. Looks can, indeed, be extremely deceiving. "Yes, in a manner of speaking," he said, quickly regrouping. "I'm visiting the museum for the lecture with Ambassador Mebeko."

"Oh, right, of course." Her smile brightened again. "I hope I haven't missed seeing the ambassador and his wife."

"Mrs. Mebeko has remained in Africa this trip."

"Oh." Kennedy was obviously disappointed. "Pity."

Curiosity piqued. "You seem to know Maurice and Adarah well," he said.

"First-name basis; apparently you do, too," she said, surprised by his familiarity and use of the couple's first names. "As I understand it, few people call them by their given names." Then she glanced at his badge. It read *VIP Security* and it all made sense. He was a member of the security team Yolanda had spoken about earlier.

"Juwan Mason," he said, holding his hand out to shake. He spared a quick glance at her lanyard and badge. It read *Dr. K. Evans.*

"Dr. Evans," she responded.

"Dr. Evans," he repeated. "I don't suppose there's another Dr. Evans here?"

"No."

He smiled brighter while looking her up and down, sizing her up. "So you're Dr. Evans, curator?"

"Yes, I am. Do I know you or should I know you?" She lowered her head to regain his full attention.

It was his turn to look away embarrassed. "No, sorry about that. You took me by surprise; that seldom happens."

"Really? How so, by bumping into you?"

"No. Actually, I was expecting Dr. Evans to be a man," he lied easily.

He smiled and her stomach twisted. "Don't worry about it, most people do." She tilted her head curiously. "Are you disappointed?" she asked, flirting shamelessly.

"Not at all," he said, letting the deep timbre of his voice drop even deeper. Then he quickly dropped his eyes to her hips and thighs, then rested on her narrow waist. Her appearance was not what he expected, having dealt with many museum curators in the past. The curious contradiction of her appearance and her position appealed to him instantly. She apparently wasn't the type of woman who always played by the rules. "Quite the opposite, I'm very pleasantly surprised."

Kennedy raked her teeth over her lower lip shyly, a nervous habit she intended to break one of these days. She boldly gave him the see-anything-you-like look, which caused him to smile even more broadly. "I'll take those and I'll take that as a compliment," she said, motioning to the books he still held in his arms.

He nodded formally. "As it was intended. So why don't I carry these and walk you to wherever you need to go?"

"I'm sure you're a very busy man. And, uh, your wife or girlfriend must be looking for you." She glanced around casually, knowing that he saw right though her farce; she couldn't help but smile.

He chuckled. Her blatant curiosity about his current status intrigued him. "Since I have neither, I'd be honored to escort you."

"Handsome and gallant, a lethal combination," she said.

He blushed boyishly. She was honest and straightforward. "You speak your mind, I see. Few women do these days; I like that."

"Do you?" She nodded, then shrugged. "I've found that it saves time in the long run."

"I completely agree. Shall we?" He pivoted, waiting a split second for her to take the lead.

"By all means," she said, walking beside him.

They began walking toward the elevators. "So, you mentioned that you were here for the lecture. If you're lost, the main lecture hall is on the next level up."

"I'm not lost."

"I see. So you're here with the security team for the lecture but not necessarily to attend it." He nodded. She nodded. "And," she continued, "you're a bodyguard, I assume."

The odd question confused him until he realized what she was talking about. Since she had assumed that he was a bodyguard because of his museum ID badge, he decided to let the assumption continue. "At the moment," he said, suddenly glad Tyson had to step down.

"Are you attached to the Nubian Embassy, Ambassador Mebeko or freelance?"

"Freelance," he said, deciding quickly that it would be the least likely to be questioned.

"I see, so you move around a lot, place to place, client to client that kind of thing."

"I used to, but lately not as much."

"I'm usually very good with accents, but yours is unique, British, French, northern African, I can't quite place it. What is it exactly?"

"Worldwide."

"That's awfully vague. Care to narrow that down a bit?"

"Northern African, North American, Eastern European . . ."

"Okay, okay, I get the idea, worldwide." They arrived at the elevator doors. She pushed the button to go down to the lower level. "Well, as pleasurable as it's been bumping into you, literally, I really have to get back to work."

"Pleasurable, I like that." He nodded, agreeing, seeming

to mull over the word as the elevator arrived and the doors opened. He watched as she entered, then turned to take the books. He followed her inside, stepping in just as the doors began to close. "Maybe we can bump into each other again sometime." His exact meaning was open to interpretation.

"Maybe," she said, pushing the button to her floor and reaching out for the books.

"That's not a very convincing answer." He handed her a single book.

"Oh, wait a minute. You mentioned earlier that I was 'the one.' What did you mean?"

"The Nubian exhibit."

"Are you an art lover?"

He licked his lips seductively. "I am most definitely a lover of art, among other things."

"Other things, such as?" she questioned, her eyes focused on the fullness of his mouth.

"How about we discuss it over dinner this evening?"

"I have to work late this evening."

"Perhaps another time?" he asked.

"Perhaps," she said, smiling coyly. A silent pause drifted between them as the awareness of their mutual attraction ebbed the flow of conversation. Cautious but curious, she continued. "So," she began, changing the subject quickly, "you mentioned something about the exhibit?"

"Yes, I've heard impressive things about the exhibit and I hoped that I might get a glimpse of it before it opens to the public. I've been told that you have several unique pieces from private collectors. I'd be very interested in seeing them. I understand, of course, that it's a work in progress but I hoped for a small preview."

If anyone were to offer Kennedy a billion dollars to repeat what this gorgeous man just said, then she'd be a billion dollars poorer because, quite simply, she just wasn't listening. The only thing she saw were his perfectly formed lips and the bright white of his teeth. Then, when he licked his lips again, this time slowly and sensually, a quiver of anticipation shot through her like lightning through ice. Suddenly the thought of his mouth on hers sent the slow-burning spark into overdrive.

It wasn't until he tilted his head questioningly that she realized that he had stopped talking and was awaiting a response from her. He got it. She burst into laughter. He looked stunned.

"I'm sorry," she offered, "it's been a crazy morning and I have a million things on my mind. You were saying that you wanted to . . ." she said, hoping he'd repeat his request.

"Get a peek at the Nubian exhibit."

"Ordinarily, since you obviously have clearance, I'd be delighted to show you, but with the new shipment arriving this morning, it's just not a good time."

"I understand," he said as he took a step back. "Maybe if I stopped by another day . . ."

"Sure, that would be great. But you might want to call before you come."

"Do I just call the main number?"

"Yes, or, since you're currently attached to Ambassador Mebeko, you, of course, know Hoyt; he can give you my private number."

"Hoyt Collier?"

"Yes."

The implication of a relationship seemed vague but still highly possible. "I see," Juwan said. The elevator doors opened at her floor.

"Well, again, it was a pleasure meeting you, Mr. Mason." She stepped out of the elevator as he held the doors open.

"And you, Dr. Evans."

Neither moved. Then he let his eyes slip down and slowly roam over her body. His perusal paused at her thighs, then rose to her waist, then drifted farther up.

The surprise of his intimate appraisal of her body put a smirk of attitude in her expression. Hiding his blatant admiration was obviously not his intention. "Is there anything else I can do for you?" she asked, bringing his eyes back to her face.

He smiled his response, not at all embarrassed by his very deliberate action. So, in an explicit act of her own, she returned the favor. Dropping her eyes purposefully, she glanced at his broad shoulders, flat abdomen, narrow waist and strong legs. When their eyes met again, she nodded appreciatively. Undeniably, the attraction between them was mutual and very obvious.

"I'll get back to you on that." He handed her the remainder of the books and papers, then used his hand to keep the elevator doors from closing.

She turned to walk away, then paused and turned back to him. "Mr. Mason," she began. He hadn't moved and his eyes were still trained on her. "If the Nubian government hired you to secure the safety of its ambassador, I guess you're very good at what you do."

"I am very good at what I do," he said seductively.

"And if by chance I wanted a bodyguard in the future . . . ?" She added to his inducement.

"Do you want a bodyguard?" He answered the question with a question.

She ignored his question and asked one of her own. "How would I find you?"

"I'll find you," he said, assuring her of his intent.

Kennedy smiled and chuckled silently. The tête-à-tête, tit-for-tat had been enjoyable, provocative and very amusing. She turned and began walking away again. Juwan continued to watch her go. "You sure you don't want to reconsider dinner tonight?" he asked before she went too far.

She turned, an obvious blush having whispered across her cheeks. "Another time," she said seductively.

"I'll look forward to it."

"As will I," she said before opening the door to the employees-only entrance of the labs and ending their conversation.

Flirting for the sake of flirting had always come easily to Kennedy. She enjoyed the teasing banter and the easy, playful joking. And the perfect flirting partner was, of course, essential. But time constraints had always trimmed her extracurricular activities to a bare minimum. She'd always been too busy with her career to seriously care one way or the other. And the men who flirted with her were too obvious, too studious, or just plain too senseless. Juwan Mason was none of those. And he was attractive and very, very charming.

Although his throat had suddenly gone dry, Juwan smiled with the self-assurance and self-confidence of a man after a victory. A chuckle of amusement escaped. Oddly enough, he had thoroughly enjoyed himself. He couldn't remember the last time he took the opportunity to flirt with an attractive and intelligent woman about something other than money, jewelry and drama.

After watching her go, he removed his hand and stepped back into the elevator. Then as soon as the doors closed, he leaned against the back panel and shook his head. "So that was Dr. Kennedy Evans," he said aloud to the empty elevator. Another broad smile pulled at his full mouth as he licked his lips. She was an intriguing woman and he liked the way she handled herself and the way she handled him.

The appeal of his assignment washed over him, tantalizing his imagination and piquing his fascination. He enjoyed their conversation and definitely liked what he saw. And to say that he was very interested would be an understatement. She also seemed to enjoy herself and also be very interested. So why not take it one step further? His initial plan had been to make detached contact and keep steady surveillance, leaving a wide berth for Petre or anyone else to make a move. But after meeting her he considered a more hands-on approach.

The thought had definite merit. He then pushed the button to go to the next level. But to his chagrin there were several things working against it and he needed to handle his concerns as he would anything else—methodically and systematically—Hoyt being the first and foremost. The issue of her availability was a question he needed answered. She flirted with him with ease, that was unmistakable, but then most women did in his experience. He needed to confirm Hoyt's relationship with her before he made a move.

Then, there was the obvious—suspects were to be observed and monitored, not invited to dinner. Never had he done something so unprofessional. What was he thinking? He shook his head to rephrase the question—what was he thinking with?

The distraction of a woman was completely out of character. His mind and thoughts were definitely not on what he was doing.

When the elevator reached the second floor, he made his way to the entrance of the Nubian exhibit. The area was cordoned off and draped with a mural on canvas, and several security guards were standing in front. Two museum employees were exiting the site, giving Juwan the opportunity to glance inside. Unfortunately, the only thing he saw were huge pillars resembling the entrance to the Nubian Museum in Cairo, Egypt.

Disappointed but not daunted or discouraged, he headed back to the lecture hall. He could see that the program had just ended. Several men, some dressed in business suits and some in traditional native attire, stood outside the lecture hall talking. Juwan looked around for a familiar face. He spotted Hawk, who had just exited the hall.

"How'd it go?" Hawk asked, seeing the expression on Juwan's face. "See anything interesting?"

"No, is the panel discussion over?"

"Yeah, it ended a few minutes ago."

"Where's Hoyt?"

"He stepped out early to speak with a friend. He'll meet us at the front entrance."

Maurice appeared a few seconds later. He looked into Juwan's face and paused. There was something different about Juwan, but he couldn't put his finger on it. "Are you okay?" he asked Juwan.

"Yes, of course. How'd it go?"

"Quite well. Shall we take the stairs?" He led the way, leaving Hawk to follow. Several of the panel guests hurried to walk with Maurice as Juwan again lagged back with Hawk, giving Maurice time to talk with the other men.

"How did you enjoy the museum?"

"Very educational," Juwan said with the hint of a knowing smile. They followed Maurice into the open foyer that led to the main hall of the museum. As they headed to the front door, Juwan noticed Hoyt standing to the side talking to Kennedy. They were laughing at what seemed to be a private joke. Then she reached out and hugged him warmly. An unexplained sliver of unease shot through Juwan as a muscle in his jaw tightened and twisted and his eyes slanted with suspicion.

Their conversation and the closeness of their bodies seemed to suggest that they shared more than just a passing acquaintance.

"I didn't realize you knew Dr. Evans," Hawk said, seeing Juwan's tense reaction at seeing Hoyt and Kennedy talking.

Juwan quickly tore his eyes away from Hoyt and Kennedy. "I don't."

"Your reaction at seeing her would suggest otherwise."

"Really?" he said, sounding almost nonchalant. "What makes you say that?"

"You seem disturbed," Hawk said, smiling briefly.

"Not at all," he said too quickly.

Hawk nodded, not at all convinced by Juwan's rushed response. The reaction he witnessed was pure territorial jealousy, to which Juwan was apparently either reluctant or hesitant to admit.

"We met in the hall a short while ago," he offered in the hope of defusing Hawk's keen perception. "I noticed the burgundy leather pants, so I made a point to find out who she was."

Hawk nodded. "And did you?"

"Did I what?" Juwan asked, distracted and now overly defensive.

"Find out who she was."

"No, not quite," Juwan said, seeing Hoyt motion Kennedy to the side to speak more privately. "She's . . ." He paused to choose a non-emotional word. "Interesting."

"Really? 'Interesting,'" Hawk repeated. "That's an unusual description for a woman with her assets."

The two men watched as Hoyt and Kennedy walked over to where Maurice stood. Maurice immediately stopped talking, turned, and greeted Kennedy warmly. They spoke as if they were old friends. Juwan's curiosity deepened. The three continued talking and laughing for a while until Barry approached with several more gentlemen in tow. Introductions were made as Hoyt and Kennedy drifted off to the side, again locked in their discussion.

"I always thought that Dr. Evans was a remarkable woman," Hawk said. "Maybe you should get to know her better. You just might reconsider your initial assessment."

Juwan watched intently as Hoyt leaned in and Kennedy turned her back and nodded agreeably. Their discussion seemed to deepen in seriousness. His hazel eyes pinched to a glare. There was definitely something going on between the two of them, and whatever it was was piquing his professional curiosity. "How well do you know her?" he asked Hawk.

"Well enough."

"Meaning?" he prompted.

"Meaning, I'm not at liberty to say," Hawk said enigmatically, slightly amused. His knowing smile added to his vague response.

"Are they together?" Juwan asked of Hoyt and Kennedy.

"You might want to ask them," Hawk suggested as he spotted the limo pulling up in front of the museum. He walked over to Maurice and gently encouraged his departure. Juwan followed, noticing Hoyt was still conferring with Kennedy.

Juwan stood at the door waiting as Hawk escorted Maurice to the waiting limo. After a few more nods Kennedy looked over, seeing Juwan standing at the door waiting. She smiled encouragingly; then her expression faded, seeing Juwan's seriously impassive look. She said something to Hoyt, causing him to look to the door.

Seeing that Maurice had already left, Hoyt quickly said something to Kennedy, kissed her briefly, then turned to the door, mentioning that they would continue their discussion later. Kennedy nodded and then looked to Juwan again. She smiled. His expression was still unreadable. She nodded her goodbye, he returned the nod, and then turned and left.

An uneasy feeling drifted through her as she walked away puzzled and returned to her lab. Hoyt, not usually an alarmist, had informed her that the FBI had a strong interest in the Nubian exhibit and that a possible FBI investigation might be in progress and that it would be to her benefit to have her documentation properly ordered.

A chill went through her. Why would the FBI be interested in her exhibit? She certainly had nothing to do with the theft in Nubia. As a matter of fact, it was because of her knowledge that the theft was going to take place that the plan had been foiled.

Bewildered and feeling as though she'd been on a high-speed looping roller coaster all morning, Kennedy went back to her lab and sat down heavily at her workbench. She looked at her watch. It was a little after twelve but it seemed so much later. She turned her stool around to face the desktop, then switched on the light table and picked up the stack of art slides she'd been reviewing when Hoyt stopped by.

She chose one, secured it, then peered at it through a magnifying glass but her thoughts began to drift. The nerve-racking morning made it almost impossible to focus and concentrate. She felt a wave of anxiety threaten to overtake her. She suppressed it by clearing her mind and refusing to think about anything not related to art. It worked.

Five hours, two meetings, time spent in the lab, the vault, and the warehouse, and a very rushed lunch later, Kennedy hadn't noticed that time had slipped by more quickly than she realized. The museum had closed and most of the employees had begun leaving.

Books piled high, she sat beneath a tumble of research—review papers, photos, books, slides, catalogues, and computers. She'd been doing a detailed search for each piece in the show. She reviewed all her exhibit documentation and finalized the last few appraisals. Although a few of the paper trails had ended abruptly, she felt secure that everything was accurately documented and in order, although one piece still troubled her.

She pressed the button on her mini-projector, bringing the slide up again. The piece in question had the proper papers and documentation, but there was something about it that wasn't quite right.

"Are you still here?" Yolanda asked.

Kennedy looked up to see Yolanda standing at the door of her office with her coat in her arms. "Not for much longer," she said, then went back to work.

"I thought you'd be long gone by now," Yolanda said as she came farther into the office.

"What are you still doing here?" Kennedy asked.

"I had a late delivery for the exhibit. I hope you're leaving soon?"

"I have a few more things to take care of before I leave."

"What about the reception tonight? Barry will have a fit

if you're not there. Plus half of the board will be there. You know you can't miss it."

"Oh, man." She stopped sorting the slides and looked up. "I completely forgot."

"Well, come on; let's get out of here, I'll walk you out."

"No, you go on ahead. I have to clear my desk and make a phone call. I'll see you later."

"All right, see you tonight," Yolanda said as she walked out of the office and closed the door behind her.

Kennedy began closing the numerous books piled high on her desk. Flustered, the last thing Kennedy wanted was to attend an embassy reception. But she knew that Yolanda was right. She was expected. The receptions were usually boring and dull with lengthy overblown political speeches and blustering remarks. She had attended more than her fill in the past.

A few minutes later Kennedy looked up again as Barry knocked and entered her office. "Kennedy, I didn't get a chance to tell you that I spoke to several board members this afternoon regarding Ambassador Mebeko's lecture. They were very impressed that we were able to have him here to speak."

He continued to congratulate himself as her thoughts stalled. *We?* Kennedy mused. Was he kidding? "We" did nothing. *She* had done all the legwork. *She* had called Hoyt and Adarah asking a personal favor. *She* made all the arrangements and set up the program as a preamble to the exhibit opening. The only thing Barry did was take all of the credit, as usual. "Kennedy, we've all been working very hard with this exhibit and the board is very pleased with our results."

"Thanks, Barry." Her tone was borderline sarcastic. He had a way of making the slightest compliment sound like a pat on his own back. "It's been a pleasure."

Barry nodded proudly and turned to leave. "Oh, also I, uh, just found out that I'll be late arriving this evening. I have a situation that must be handled. But I do hope you'll still be attending."

"Yes, I'll be there."

"Good, good." He nodded, then turned to leave. "Oh, one more thing, I just got word that the Nubian authorities have officially closed the investigation regarding the museum theft. Apparently they feel confident that they've captured all the men involved."

"What about Petre and the missing statue?"

"It seems that they're satisfied with the results and decided not to go any further with the investigation."

"And the FBI, weren't they investigating, too?"

"To my knowledge, not anymore."

"That's wonderful news. I'm sure everyone will be delighted to have the weight lifted. The blanket of suspicion was making us all tense."

He nodded. "Yes, of course, I completely understand." He continued to nod like a bobble-head doll. "I'll be making a general announcement tomorrow. In the meantime it's getting late; you'd better get going." She nodded. "Oh, one more thing—I understand that you're familiar with some of the personnel at the Nubian embassy here in D.C.?" he asked.

"Some of them, yes."

"There's a new security man, bodyguard, at the embassy. He came with the ambassador this morning. Have you met or spoken with him?"

"Yes, briefly."

"He seemed quite knowledgeable about art."

"I hadn't noticed."

"Is he there at the embassy permanently?"

"No, he's freelance. I think he does a lot of traveling for his clients. Is there a problem?"

"No, of course not, I just wanted to know if he was legitimate."

"What makes you ask that?"

"Oh, no reason, I was just curious as to his background. See you this evening."

"Good night," Kennedy called as Barry left and closed the door behind him.

Kennedy frowned and then sighed heavily with wonder. But the strangeness of the last conversation didn't overshadow her relief that the museum investigation had been closed. Maybe now things could get back to normal. It was just what she needed to lift her spirits and get her through the evening. That and, of course, the interesting prospect of seeing Juwan Mason again.

Kennedy picked up the phone, dialed and continued clearing her desk while gathering her purse, jacket and helmet. The phone was answered on the second ring.

"Hi," she said. "Are you still going to the Nubian embassy reception this evening?"

"Yeah, why?"

"Good, I need a date; feel like some company?"

Chapter Seven

The phone call lasted just minutes. Juwan had requested a workup on the National African Arts Museum and all of its major employees. He told himself that it was merely a professional interest. But that didn't explain his request for a complete background check on Kennedy Evans. She was supposed to be his objective, but his gut instinct told him that she wasn't the one he should be looking at. But, just in case, he decided to continue.

Of course, this wasn't the first time he had requested personal information on a woman that he had been curious about. As a special agent, he investigated anyone he came in contact with both on the job and off, whether suspicious or not; it was standard operating procedure. But the justification should have ended when he saw Kennedy and Hoyt together, yet he requested the detailed information anyway and that troubled him.

He couldn't stop thinking about her and that troubled him, too. The memory of their short time together and their brief conversation still intrigued him. There was no way he could have misread the signals; he surely hadn't been out of the game that long. There was definite interest on both parts. The question now was what he was going to do about it.

Stepping between a man and a woman, no matter how enticing the woman was, wasn't his thing and he had no intention of pursuing her further if Hoyt was indeed the man in her life. He'd just have to reconsider his other options. But, if by chance he had misread the signals, then it wouldn't hurt to know as much as possible about Dr. Evans before he went any further. Any woman able to gain and hold his attention any longer than a passing moment was definitely worth a second look, and a background report would come in handy.

It would include every minute aspect of her life, both personal and professional, past and present. Everything she had ever done, thought of doing, and attempted to do would be listed in explicit detail. Every purchase she made, every movie she rented, even the type of toothpaste she used would be listed.

It was scary sometimes when he considered the power of certain government agencies, his in particular. Within minutes he could order a person's entire life, unvarnished, placed before him to be scrutinized and examined. A more zealous or unscrupulous person with the power could do any number of things with complete political justification.

Satisfied that he would soon know everything there was to know about Kennedy Evans and other principals at the museum, Juwan decided to join the reception. He left his suite in the embassy's residence wing and wandered down to the main hall. It was still early, but most of the guests had already arrived; a few stragglers still entered. He estimated that nearly three hundred guests were already in attendance. He recognized several high-ranking federal officials and a number of Hollywood celebrities. Not impressed, he continued his stroll through the crowd.

Delegates, guests and dignitaries lingered and lounged as they laughed, talked and amused themselves while enjoying the entertainment and the bevy of edible delights being circulated on silver trays. The strategically placed open bars were well used as were the buffet tables stationed around the perimeter of the hall. Waiters carried large trays, traversing in and out among the throng of guests.

Dressed in his stylish black tuxedo, Juwan drew admiring glances from a number of women standing around. But he barely noticed as his eyes constantly roamed the room. He was looking for only one guest and as yet he hadn't found her. Disappointment bit at him as it seemed that she had indeed chosen to work late and not attend. Eventually he moved to the side and lingered.

As with all embassy receptions, security was tight. The D.C. police secured the local area and streets around the embassy, a private agency took care of the immediate outside and embassy grounds, and the Secret Service and embassy's internal security mingled with the many invited guests.

Juwan stood by the interior door. The private security agency Hawk had hired was thorough as invitations were checked and confirmed before attendees gained entrance.

"I see you finally decided to join us," Hawk said as he came up beside Juwan at the front door. His right ear held a tiny earpiece connected to the main security office.

"I was working," Juwan said simply.

"I thought you were on extended vacation," he said as he continued scanning and observing the arriving guests, searching for any anomalies.

"I am."

Hawk shook his head, knowing the feeling. Standing down and at ease had never been easy for him either. "Enjoying yourself?" he asked.

"I'll let you know."

"Relax, get a drink, take the night off. We have everything under control," he assured Juwan.

"Of that I have no doubt," Juwan said confidently enough, knowing that security was the least of his concerns. "But old habits are hard to break. Letting my guard down even when I'm not on duty is impossible."

"I know what you mean," Hawk commiserated.

"Have you seen Hoyt this evening?" Juwan asked.

"I saw him earlier. He's around someplace. Find Maurice and you'll find him." Hawk glanced back into the foyer and the surrounding area.

"Do me a favor, if you see him, tell him I'd like a brief word with him in the library," Juwan said as he turned to return to the reception.

Hawk didn't reply but nodded in the direction of an attractive couple walking up the driveway arm in arm, talking and laughing as they approached. "I see that the good doctor has decided to join us after all."

Juwan, who was just about to walk away when Hawk spoke, stopped and turned around. Delight then annoyance momentarily cemented him in place as he just stared. Kennedy had arrived but she wasn't alone.

Napoleon's retreat, McCarthy's retreat and his retreat would all go down in history as the greatest battles never fought. Juwan turned and left. Moments later he found himself alone in the library, staring at an old model toy prominently displayed on the fireplace mantel. It was a reproduction of the 1839 schooner *La Amistad*, carefully modeled inside a glass bottle. The model belonged to him. He had asked Maurice to care for it in his absence. It was the last thing he and his father had made together. He had been twelve.

Indecisive and conflicted were unlike him. What was it about this woman that tore at the very core of his soul? In the brief moments they shared, she had somehow drilled a hole into his logic, skewing his judgment. His thinking was awry and his hesitation was intolerable. She was attractive, that was true. But he had been with women just as attractive. Why her? Why now? She was intelligent, funny and intuitive, important qualities in his mind. But how could one brief encounter, albeit enticing and alluring, disrupt a lifetime of focused dedication?

"Hawk said that you wanted to see me? We have to make it quick, the ambassador will be making a short speech momentarily," Hoyt said as he walked into the library, seeing Juwan standing at the fireplace. His back was turned away from the door. Receiving no answer, he called Juwan's name a second time before getting a response.

Juwan turned around, surprised to see Hoyt standing just a few feet from him. "Juwan, you wanted to see me?" Hoyt repeated.

"Yes," Juwan said as he turned. "Question, are you seeing Dr. Evans?"

"You mean romantically?" Hoyt clarified.

"Yes."

"No," he answered simply as he looked at his watch. "Is that it?" Juwan nodded. "I'll see you outside. The ambassador will be delivering his speech shortly. You might want to attend."

A moment later he was out the door and Juwan turned back to the schooner with a slow, easy smile.

Chapter Eight

The bright lights of the Nubian embassy lit the way even before the car turned into the driveway.

"Remind me again why I'm here?" Trey Evans said as he opened the car door for his cousin while adjusting his already perfectly tied tie.

"You're here because we were both invited. I needed an escort, you needed a cover and one of your best friends, whom you haven't seen in months, will be here. And you had nothing else planned for this evening," Kennedy said, "so stop complaining. I do it for you all the time."

"Correction, you did it for J.T., not me."

"Oh please," Kennedy said. "Don't let's bring up the Investor's Ball at Union Station last spring or the Clayton-Hall-Keller Gala at the State Building on Pennsylvania."

"That was different. Those were two unique occurrences. In both cases my date backed out at the last minute."

"Backed out?" she remarked as they approached the embassy's security at the open door. She handed Trey the invitation. "If I remember correctly, in both cases your dates found out that you had another date right afterwards and dumped you, leaving me to fill in at the last minute."

"Neither one dumped me," he protested formally. "One had a previous engagement and the other came down with the flu."

"They dumped you like a hot potato," Kennedy teased.

"I have never been dumped in my life," Trey protested indignantly. Being a financier and investor, the owner of Evans International Finance, and a very eligible bachelor in Washington, D.C., he was indeed coveted by half the women in the city. And now, since his cousin, J.T., had recently married, he felt as if it was open season and he was fair game, particularly when it came to marriage-minded, husband-hunting females and, most particularly, a matchmaker named Louise Gates.

"Whatever, the point is I stepped in and bailed you out a number of times, so shut up and walk me inside. It's not like you weren't already coming here tonight."

"You realize, of course, that this is all Mamma Lou's fault. She's got everyone in the family scared to death to walk out of their houses alone for fear that we'll be seen and, therefore, next on her matchmaking radar." He handed the invitation to the security attendant at the door, took Kennedy's arm and walked inside. "My theory is . . ."

"Ugh," Kennedy moaned and rolled her eyes to the twenty-foot ceiling as they entered the embassy foyer. "Give it a rest, Midas," she said teasingly, using her childhood nickname for him, one he always hated and one she took great pleasure reminding him of. He got the nickname because of his penchant for picking stocks that oftentimes doubled or even tripled in value. "The last thing I need to hear tonight is one of your brain-lame, off-the-wall theories."

"I beg your pardon," he whispered in her ear. "My theories are neither off-the-wall nor brain-lame, which isn't even a word, I might add. My theories are *insightful*."

"Fine, whatever. Are we gonna stand out here and argue all night or are you gonna act like my escort and walk me into the reception?"

Trey didn't answer, as usual, knowing that it would drive his cousin crazy. With her just two months younger than Kennedy, they were as close as brother and sister and their constant battles and bickering proved it. Although Madison and J.T. had chosen to attend different universities, Kennedy and Trey wound up going to the same college, she for art history and he for finance. Fiercely protective they would do anything for each other including bailing each other out when needed. So when Kennedy called, he came to the rescue. Of course he couldn't let her off the hook too easily; he had to needle her for old time's sake.

"Well?" she questioned.

"I'm still considering my options," he quipped, smiling his usual Cheshire cat grin.

She elbowed him in the ribs, causing a strange unexpected sound to escape. Several guests nearby turned in their direction and smiled politely. Barely able to contain her laughter, Kennedy turned and walked away. Trey followed, rubbing the part of his chest her elbow had poked.

The pair was worse than brother and sister. Kennedy had played tricks on Trey all through school and he had evened the score all through college. As relentless as their pranks were, they were also fiercely loyal and completely protective of each other. Now that it was just the two of them left single, they closed ranks even more.

"That was totally uncalled for," Trey muttered as he caught up with her. She lifted her elbow to hit him again and he ducked away. "Okay, okay, I surrender. Come on, I'll get you a drink."

They chuckled on the way to the bar. As they approached, Kennedy paused, seeing a woman she recognized. "Oh my goodness, isn't that Tony's friend, what was her name . . . ?"

Trey instantly panicked. "Mamma Lou?" he said louder than he intended, then began searching the immediate area for the nearest escape route.

"No, would you just chill and relax? Mamma Lou's not

here. Last I heard she was back on Crescent Island with her flowers."

"Relax? Easy for you to say, you're not topping the hit list."

Kennedy squinted across the room, "That is her, Laine . . ." But before she could finish the last name, a woman came up to her and blocked her path.

"I know you, don't I?" she said, her voice rich with an overly pronounced southern drawl. "You're Tony Gates' sister-in-law, aren't you?"

"Yes, I am, nice to see you again." The dread in her tone was ignored. But Trey, standing at her side, looked at her oddly, confused by her questionably bad manners.

"You, too, dear," the woman said briskly, barely seeing Kennedy anymore. Her attention and newly purchased breasts turned in Trey's direction. She licked her front teeth and leaned in. "And who do we have here?" she asked, openly admiring Trey like a full course Thanksgiving dinner. She puffed her chest and held her hand out delicately while boldly introducing herself before Trey could answer. "Mimi Brown. And you are?"

"Yes, I remember, Mrs. Brown. We met briefly at my cousin's wedding."

Mimi looked surprised. "Your cousin?"

"Madison and Tony Gates."

"Oh yes, of course. You're the stockbroker, aren't you?"

"Something like that."

"Well, isn't this a small world? If I remember correctly, you own that investment company by the White House."

"Actually it's between the World Bank and the International Monetary Fund headquarters."

"Yes, of course," she brushed off quickly. "Tell me, have you met my daughter, Laine?" She began searching the immediate area.

"Yes," Trey said quickly. "Actually I met your daughter at Tony and Madison's wedding . . . but . . ." Mimi continued looking around as Trey made a face, pleading for Kennedy's assistance.

"Actually, Ms. Brown," Kennedy began, interrupting, "Trey and I were just going to the bar to get a refreshment, then step outside into the garden for some air. So, if you'll excuse us . . ."

"Excellent idea," Mimi replied before Kennedy could finish her statement. "We'd be delighted to join you." She took Trey's arm and tucked her arm beneath his and walked away, leaving Kennedy standing there. "Laine," she called out as they approached her daughter, "look who I just ran into."

Trey turned and gave Kennedy an accusing glare, causing her to shrug her shoulders and openly laugh. His expression was priceless. Being trapped by Mimi was unpleasant, being sandwiched and trapped by Mimi and her daughter was downright distressing. This was by far the best prank she'd ever pulled on him. Kennedy smiled and shook her head sympathetically. The uncomfortable animated look on his face brought a twinge of guilt to hers but not for long. She knew Trey could handle himself and would slip away in no time.

That was his unique talent. He could assess a situation, analyze his options, then either use it to his advantage or walk away with ease, yet always leaving in the best light. That was, of course, how he dealt with his many short-term relationships. Women were attracted to him like pins to a magnet and he, as her brother once did, took full advantage of it.

Together Trey and J.T. had trolled the streets of New York and D.C., leaving a trail of sad and broken hearts behind. But they were never hurtful or cruel. They always stated up front that their work was their main focus. Most women felt, wrongly, of course, that they could change them, but when the inevitable happened and J.T. or Trey felt that it was time to move on, hopes and expectations fell like bricks in a shallow pond.

Oddly enough that's how Kennedy lived her life as well. Her work had always come first and relationships, few that there had been, came afterwards. Seriously tempted only once, she'd since decided never to let her heart overrule her judgment. Committed relationships were fine for others, but she was too headstrong and far too assertive to contemplate one. Most men were either intimidated by her indomitable spirit or just had no idea what to do with her. Then her thoughts slipped to another temptation, Juwan Mason. He posed a serious question; what was she going to do about him?

Kennedy took a step toward the bar to follow Trey, then stopped. She spotted Juwan coming in her direction. As if she'd summoned him, he appeared. His smile was sexy and open, completely different from the last time she saw him. Just fifteen minutes earlier she had spotted him at the front door for a brief second; then he disappeared.

He was temptation personified, bold and audacious; he was the kind of man to whom she was attracted. He had an air about himself that exuded power, strength, and confidence. He was a formidable and apparently skilled opponent; his bodyguard position seemed to afford him the right amount of charm and danger. Just being around him made her feel adventurous.

His stunning good looks were pure African American yet spiced with cultures from around the world. Clean-cut with abundant masculinity, he was charming and gallant and his bold awareness caused a twinge of anticipated excitement. Sitting behind a desk was definitely not for him. She sensed that he was a man of action and it excited her.

Unfortunately, it also gave her pause. The thought of another Petre in her life was definitely out of the question. Petre's extreme nature, although enjoyable at first, had later unnerved her and when he admitted that he had had dealings in the black market and stolen art, she was horrified. In the next breath he told her that he was planning another robbery in the next few days. So she did what she had to do. And now here she was—throwing caution to the wind again.

But her immediate reaction to Juwan was too overpowering. The instant he looked at her she felt a stirring sensation in her stomach that had yet to dissipate. And when he had handed her the book and their hands touched, a spark hit her like a bolt of lightning. She shuddered. He felt it, too. She could see it in his eyes. The question now was what she was going to do about it.

The answer came almost immediately. Enjoy him, every delectable part of him. And since she had no intention of staying around for more than a few months, he'd be the perfect distraction. So, for the time being, she'd take pleasure in him.

"Good evening, Dr. Evans," he said when he stopped in front of her.

"Good evening, Mr. Mason."

"You look . . ." He hesitated a second, letting his eyes drift slowly down the curves of her body, obviously admiring what he saw, then roguishly grinning, continued, "Stunning."

She did.

As soon as he had come back into the room, he spotted her instantly. She was impossible to miss. Of all the women in attendance, she was by far the most dazzling, dressed in elegant couture of dusty rose silk taffeta. Her flawlessly tailored gown fit her body like a second skin, molded to perfection on every curve. She was lusciously provocative as her bountiful cleavage tipped forward. At the thighs the dress flowed slightly outward like a shimmering graceful waterfall, fluid and ultra-feminine. Accessorized with diamond teardrop earrings and a diamond choker that sparkled as brightly as her eyes, the gown overwhelmed him as soon as he saw her.

"Thank you." She looked up at him, the deep rich chocolate coffee of his complexion contrasting beautifully with the stark white banded-collar shirt. "But that's not what you were going to say, was it?"

"No," he admitted freely.

"Well, what were you going to say?"

He glanced around, then quickly leaned in, whispering for her ears only, "I was going to say that you look . . ." He paused a split second. "Delicious."

His warm, minty breath traveled along her ear and down her neck, sending a ticklish tingle through her that danced all the way to her fluttering stomach. She smiled and laughed. "Good word, you look delicious yourself."

He nodded his thanks, then paused a brief moment to examine her face as if to memorize every inch. "Can I get you a drink, or perhaps something to eat?"

"No, thank you."

He looked around again. "Are you here alone?" he asked, already knowing the answer.

"No." She nodded toward Trey still standing at the bar. "I brought a friend with me."

Juwan nodded, then looked toward the bar, seeing Trey uncomfortably sandwiched between a buxom older woman and a rail-thin younger woman. "And he left you alone?" Juwan said as he turned back to her.

She grinned, seeing Trey's glare at her. "He actually didn't have much of a choice."

"Well, it appears that his loss is my gain. Since it looks as if your friend is otherwise engaged, would you like to join me on the dance floor?" He offered his hand.

"Actually I was just about to . . ."

"Please?" he asked, taking her hand in his.

His eyes were soft; how could she resist? "Yes, I'd like that." She spared one last look in Trey's direction, then followed Juwan to the center of the dance floor. He stopped, turned, then slowly wrapped his arm around her waist and pulled her gently toward him. She fit into the curve of his body with ease. The music flowed and they danced.

Their conversation was comfortable and easy as if they had been together forever. Art, music, travel—they had a lot in common. He asked about the exhibit and she answered. He queried further, she answered in greater detail, which he seemed to follow with little trouble. "Are you sure you're not in some way connected to the art world?"

He remained casual where others would have stiffened. "What makes you ask that?"

"You seem to know a tremendous amount about the art world—for a bodyguard, that is. Why is that?"

"I know a tremendous amount about a lot of things," he said with his usually evasive response. He looked down into her eyes with purpose.

She smiled sweetly. "You didn't answer the question."

"Do you want to talk about art all night?" he asked, still avoiding the issue.

"No," she said. "Not really."

"Good, let's talk about you."

He asked more questions; she answered, and then, for some reason, she began telling him about the time she slipped and fell into an open tomb in South America, sending her to the hospital with a sprained ankle and injuries. His interest was genuine but soon waned as his thoughts wandered.

The sweet scent of her expensive perfume made his nose tingle and softened his edge. Having this woman in his arms was probably not a good idea. But he had started this game and she played it better than he expected. He knew that he needed to be extremely cautious. She was smart, quick and intuitive and was the kind of woman that men fell for whether they wanted to or not. He could see any man begging this woman to be his.

So his reasoning outweighed passion as desire was held at bay. He wanted her, that was a given, and from the moment he looked down into her soft brown eyes, he knew that he would have her.

Then he felt her relax and melt deeper into his arms. He held her closer. It felt right, too right. When the music stopped, he stepped back and joined in the applause. He looked into her eyes and his heart stopped. He noticed the man she came with watching them from across the room. "It appears that your friend is looking for you. So, Doctor, if you'll excuse me," he said, not waiting for her response, then turned and blended into the crowd.

Doctor, if you'll excuse me? What was that?

Trey came up beside her and handed her a glass of champagne. He watched as Juwan moved through the crowd. "Was he a friend of yours?" he asked.

Kennedy shook her head to clear the cockles of her stupor. "Maybe, I don't know yet." She took a small sip and followed Trey to the buffet table.

Had their bodies *not* moved so seductively that she was ready to smoke a cigarette even though she didn't smoke? Had their body language *not* promised possibilities of more in a dance that could only be classified as borderline seduction? And had his hands *not* pressed along the curve of her back, tempting her to move closer? Then she definitely could understand his abrupt departure. Hell, she would have done an about-face herself. In actuality, it had, they had, and it was nice. *So*, she questioned herself again, *what was that?*

Okay, she'd run men away before with her single-minded ambition and her sharp tongue, but that was intentional. Never had she scared one away without opening her mouth. She chuckled and shook her head again. This was definitely a first for her.

Moments later she was back on the dance floor with Trey, yet she was still wondering what had happened with Juwan. Then it hit her as her focus drifted to where Juwan now stood on the other side of the room. His head was lowered and he was in deep conversation with Hoyt and the ambassador. They talked for a few minutes; then Hoyt walked away and Juwan remained to confer with Maurice Mebeko.

She began smiling, understanding. He wasn't running away from her, he was going to work. As the ambassador's bodyguard, he didn't dance with a guest; it wasn't in his usual job description. She made a mental note to be more aware of his position and never to jeopardize his job.

"You look good out there. I'm glad to see you finally out dancing and enjoying yourself. It's high time you start acting like you're on vacation. Dr. Evans is a delightful woman. Adarah and she got along wonderfully when she was in Nubia a few months ago," Maurice whispered happily when Hoyt walked away and Juwan stayed at his side.

"It's not what it looks like."

"What it looks like is that you've found the one."

"The what?"

"The one." Juwan looked across the room, seeing Kennedy on the dance floor. "She is the one who now holds your interest and possibly your heart," Maurice added.

"No," Juwan denied immediately. "We were just dancing, that was all. There was absolutely nothing more so please don't read anything into it."

"Ah, but you're very wrong, there is much, much more. You didn't look at her as a dance partner. You looked at her as a life partner."

"Maurice . . ." Juwan began but was cut off when he saw who Kennedy was dancing with. It was the same man who escorted her here. A fierce protective expression crossed his face and his eyes narrowed.

Maurice nodded and smiled. "I see even now, you don't look at her with your eyes but with your heart. It's the same expression your father had when he looked at your mother." Maurice smiled and nodded to himself, remembering the couple fondly. "He called her his one. He'd say that she was the one woman that held his heart and he knew the instant he saw her that she would be his."

"Well, it seems that you're mistaken; as you can see, Dr.

Evans is otherwise engaged." Maurice turned and saw Kennedy on the dance floor again laughing and dancing with the other man. "They arrived together," Juwan added.

"Looks can be deceiving. Perhaps they're just friends or business associates."

"Perhaps," Juwan said, then turned away. "At any rate, you're mistaken."

"I think not," Maurice said as he glanced across the room at Kennedy still on the dance floor. "She is your one. It's up to you to be the one for her."

The music stopped and after the polite applause, Hoyt stepped up to the small podium. He cleared his throat, gaining everyone's attention. His remarks were pointed and brief, directed mainly on Nubia and its politics. Then he focused on the ambassador, his numerous accolades, his current position and his founding of the UAG.

Afterwards he introduced delegate Devlon Motako, who stepped up and proceeded to bellow on about his recent accomplishments. The evening took a serious dip into boredom.

Chapter Nine

A credible cover was crucial and bodyguard was his. Thanks to Barry Culpepper and his museum tag, she already assumed that fact so he decided to go with it. She seemed attracted to him; he needed to use that attraction and vulnerability to get to her. If he could penetrate her emotionally, he would have exactly what he needed. But he had to be careful. She was no fool. She was intelligent and quick and would instantly spot an opportunist. No, everything had to appear genuine, even his feelings for her. He had to make her believe that he was attracted to her, which wouldn't be difficult in this case.

Juwan had been undercover many times in the past. He'd played a janitor, a gigolo, an art buyer, an appraiser, a thief and even a smuggler. So experience wasn't the issue. But as with any undercover assignment, getting lost in the role was always a danger. He knew that playing the part fully was always the key. This part included seducing a curator into revealing secrets. Secrets she might or might not know. But he needed to find out one way or the other. And if she knew nothing and was innocent, fine, she would still make an excellent cover for him to get into the museum.

All he had to do now was find her and continue his little charade. He smiled in the dimness. Charm had always gotten him what he wanted when it came to the fairer sex; he knew he would have no trouble this time. Then, uncharacteristically, a twinge of regret and remorse shot through his heart. No, this had to be done and he was the man to do it, even if it meant putting his heart on the line. The end justifies the means. He hardened his heart and prepared to go inside and begin.

The focus on his assignment was still his primary concern even as his attraction to her surged. Yes, he wanted her but it could never happen. The ethical conflict of fraternizing with a potential suspect was clear. He had to get close, he had to gain her trust, but he also had to keep her at arm's length. And she, desirable and tempting as sin itself, would not make it easy.

He looked off into the night as the battle inside raged. His heart and his mind fought as Maurice's words echoed over and over again, "She is your one. It's up to you to be the one for her."

"You're missing the ambassador's speech."

Juwan turned quickly, seeing Kennedy standing in the garden path right behind him.

"So are you," he said; his smile was genuine.

"Must have been something important," she continued as she approached.

"What?"

"Whatever it was that drove you out here, whatever it was that you were just thinking about. Pensive, brooding, deep in thought, you looked troubled, so I assume it must be something important."

"I was thinking about a woman I met earlier."

"Really?" she said, coming closer. "Tell me about her."

"Not much to tell. We just met, so you see I don't know her that well."

"That's a shame."

"I think so too."

"So what are you gonna do about it?"

"I don't know. I haven't decided yet."

"You haven't decided? Okay, I'm a little confused about something," she began as she leaned back against the iron rail beside him. "Maybe you could help me out. We, you and I, seemed to get along well, very well, I thought. But now I'm a little puzzled. The whole flirting-teasing thing, is that just your charm or are you actually interested?" Juwan smiled at her directness. "Or," she added, "do you just like to play games?"

He took a deep breath. "You are direct."

"I believe we've already covered that ground."

"Yes, I guess we have."

"Are you married?" she asked.

"Would it matter?"

"Yes."

He smiled. "No, I'm not married, are you?"

"Would it matter?" she asked.

"Yes."

"No, I'm not married."

The moment stilled. "I apologize if my charm, as you put it, implied anything other than what it was."

She chuckled quietly. "Spoken like a true diplomat." She pushed up from the rail and took a step to walk away. If he wasn't interested, there was no reason to stay.

"I'm a little confused, maybe you can help me out," he said, quickly grabbing her hand before she could retreat. "It appears that you are already spoken for."

"Really?" she questioned. "That's news to me."

He looked momentarily puzzled. "Actually." He leaned up away from the rail and began to walk, releasing her hand and leading the way through the embassy garden. "I was under the impression that you were with Hoyt. But I spoke with him earlier and he dismissed my concerns. Now here you are tonight with another man. So again, naturally, I assumed you were otherwise engaged."

"You might have asked."

"True."

A moment of silence drifted between them as they walked through the well-lit path. She looked beyond the trees; a mist hung heavily in the darkness. In the distance a blur of red and white vehicle lights danced in line across the bridge. The thick smell of a passing shower was in the air. She looked up at the sky as a burst of lightning streaked through the darkened clouds in the distance. "Looks like the storm will pass us by."

"Looks like," he responded, his eyes riveted on her.

"I think it just might be a lovely evening."

"Possibly," he assessed, still gazing at her.

"Well," she began, "are you going to ask or not?"

It was his turn to chuckle. "Are you otherwise engaged?"

"No, I am not otherwise engaged. My cousin and I often attend these types of functions together."

"Your cousin?" He stopped and completely turned to her.

She stopped, too. "Yes, my cousin. So what's it gonna be, Juwan, friend or lover?" She had barely gotten the words out when his mouth captured hers, soft, gentle and firm. Their hands at their sides, neither attempted to embrace the other. They just leaned in, forming a bond between them, allowing the firmness of the kiss to hold them in place.

When the kiss ended, they just stood there looking into each other's eyes. Then a slow easy smile spread across both of their faces. Without words he had made his choice. "That was nice," she whispered quietly.

"Yes, it was," he replied, then noticed her vague expression. "Although it looks like you've changed your mind."

"No, I haven't, I was just wondering . . ."

"Wondering what?" he asked.

"Whether or not you're a good idea," she said.

"Am I supposed to admit otherwise?"

"No."

"Okay, then I'll guess I am a good idea."

"And, can I take that to mean you're interested?"

Juwan chuckled. "Yes, that would be a safe bet," he said as he leaned down to kiss her again. But before he could capture her mouth, another couple walked by, followed by a few other stragglers from the party inside. They greeted them as they passed by. "Come on, let's go this way," Juwan said. Kennedy followed as they walked in silence around to the side of the building toward a secured gate.

He opened the small black box on the post and keyed in several numbers. A quiet buzz hummed for a few seconds and he unlatched the gate's door. The private garden was small but well lit. She followed him inside, then along a path to an enclosed gazebo situated a short distance away from the main structure of the embassy.

"In here," Juwan said as he opened the door for her. As soon as she entered, he closed the door behind them and pulled her to his arms, joining their lips instantly in a kiss a thousand times more passionate than their first. Stirring and powerful, the kiss pierced her with the power of its intensity. The kiss deepened even more; giving and taking, they surrendered everything.

He took her breath away, and her heart pounded in her chest louder than the thunder's rumble outside.

This time he held her tight, molding her soft body to the firmness of his. She yielded, letting the passion and desire they both felt take them in only one direction.

He beckoned that she enter and she willingly obliged. She opened up to him. He plunged his tongue deep into her mouth, exploring while giving in to her hunger. His hands grasped her, pulling her body closer and closer to his. As the kiss deepened he felt her body shudder with desire, the same desire he felt.

The driving need of their passion pushed them further. Boldly she reached beneath his jacket and pulled at his shirt. Spreading her hands wide, she felt the unyielding firmness of his chest. Then she wrapped her arms around his body, pressing his torso against her with all her might. It had been a while since she felt the strong power of a man holding her. Her mind muddled as she drifted on a cloud of desire.

His hands awakened her body and she reveled in his touch. The promise of their pleasure sent a blazing fire. Now wrapping her arms around his neck, she held on as he lifted her up and held her in his arms, cradling her to his chest.

He buried his face in her neck, ravaging her with a trail of burning kisses. Kennedy closed her eyes and reveled in the blissful sensation. *Oh God.* The spicy scent of his cologne mingled enticingly with the aromatic fragrance of her perfume, arousing senses she'd forgotten she even had. Madison was right, a new love, a hot romance, a lustful layover were exactly what she needed.

As the kiss deepened, breathing became less important. The only thing they felt at that moment was the need and desire to be in each other's arms. A rash of passionate kisses was planted, then slowly subsided to end with a sweet peck and nuzzle at her neck. With his heart beating like a kettledrum on hyperdrive, he released her, then stepped back to regain some measure of control.

Moments later he reached down and took her hand and kissed her fingers lovingly. His eyes burned with desire, but the caution in hers gave him pause. She pulled at the shawl haphazardly draped on her arms. "Are you chilly?" She shook her head no. "Do you want to go back inside?" She shook her head no. "Dance?" She shook her head no again. "What would you like to do?"

She looked through the gazebo's openness, down the path farther. "Where does this lead?" she asked.

"To the ambassador's private residence."

"Do you live there?"

"Yes, at the moment."

"Show me."

"Are you sure?" he asked. She nodded.

Without words he wrapped the shawl across her shoulders and placed her hand in the crook of his arm and escorted her out into the night. The short walk inside the gated garden led them to the mansion's back door. He entered a code, releasing the security latch. The door clicked open to a small buzzing sound. Inside he entered another code and the buzzing stopped.

"This way." He took her hand and led her through a maze of doors, then up a flight of stairs and down a long hall. When they finally reached the closed door of his suite, he turned to her. "The reception is down that hall to the left and down the stairs. If you'd like to return . . ."

She grinned. With the reception long forgotten, she boldly opened the door and walked inside. After a slow turn around the dimly lit suite, she stood across from him, smiled sweetly, then raked her teeth over her lower lip. This was what she wanted. He was what she wanted. And now was when she wanted him.

"Nice suite," she said.

"Thanks," he responded.

"I heard that there'll be a special guest later this evening, someone very high up in politics."

Juwan watched her every move. She was a vision to behold. He had walked away from this woman before, but he had no intention of letting her go again. He didn't speak right away but just began walking toward her slowly. "Really?"

She nodded and hummed. "Uh-hum."

"Does that impress you?" he asked.

"No, not really." She slowly circled across the room away from him.

"What does a man have to do to impress you?"

"Orchids are always nice."

He chuckled. "I'll have to remember that."

She continued to walk around the room, looking around,

peering into his closet and fingering his row of neatly pressed shirts and suits.

"So this is my suite," he finally said. "Shall we continue with the tour or did you want something else in particular?"

"In a manner of speaking, yes. I would like something else."

"And what would that be?"

"I want a bodyguard," she said seductively, letting her shawl slowly drop down her arms.

"What a coincidence, I seem to be available at the moment."

She continued walking slowly around the room. He followed. She knew he would. "Well, how much do you charge? I don't know if I can afford you yet. A museum curator is just a federal employee. We don't make a lot of money."

"I'm sure we can work something out."

"Really?"

"Um-hum."

She turned, catching his eye. "Do you know what you're doing?" Her brow rose as she tilted her head questioningly. "I mean, ah, are you any good at it?"

He chuckled and shook his head. Double entendres drifted between them like endless foreplay. He liked this game they played so well. "Yeah, I'm very good. But I guess the only way to know for sure is to try me." He licked his lips, sending a hot flash of excitement through her body.

"Well." She cleared her throat, turned and began walking away again. "I guess I could give you a try, just to see if we'd work well together."

"Sounds like a good idea," he agreed.

"But"—she turned again and waited until he got closer so that there'd be no mistaking her meaning—"I wouldn't want you to think that this was a permanent arrangement, bodyguard-wise, of course." The implication in her words and tone was completely understood. He, like her, had no intention of making the arrangement anything other than what it was. But unbeknownst to her, his motives and intentions were far more focused on his mission to gain her trust and get her to talk.

"Not at all. We'll take it one day at a time." He stopped walking and stood still in the center of the room.

"And what about the nights?" she asked as she slowly walked toward him, closing the short distance between them. As she neared, she reached up to the crisp lapels of his tuxedo jacket and felt the satiny softness of the material. Her hands fanned out over his broad shoulders, down his chest, then slid beneath his jacket and circled around behind him.

"Definitely nights." He leaned down, brushing his lips against the gentle curve of her neck. Her body swayed in response, so he instantly gathered her in his arms and held her close, pressing her lower body firmly to his.

The unmistakable throbbing power of his manhood, eager to please, sent a tingle of anticipation through her. She closed her eyes, knowing his need and feeling the swelling passion of her own. This was what she wanted and being held by the power and strength of Juwan was what she needed. Her skin tingled, sensitive to his touch, burned each time his lips kissed and his tongue teased. The madness of the moment drove her to want more. There was no beginning or ending. All there was was Juwan and the way he made her feel.

"Good, when can you start?" she finally asked as she maneuvered her hands to his shoulders from beneath and removed the jacket, allowing it to slowly fall to the floor.

"How about now?" His voice was low and husky, barely audible as his mouth rested on her bare shoulder. Then tiny gentle kisses traced a path up her neck to just below her chin. When he reached the corner of her mouth, he stopped and looked down into her impassioned eyes. He waited for her answer.

"Perfect, you're hired," she muttered.

In an instant their lips met in an explosive kiss that rocked the universe. She reached her arms up to his neck. He gathered her waist even closer to his body. Their mouths joined as one, as if they had never been parted. A moment of stillness surrounded them, and the only sound heard was the faint echo of music from the party downstairs and the rhythmic pounding of their hearts.

When they finally parted, they held each other smiling at nothing and everything. The oneness of their thoughts and the mutual understanding they'd come to were crystalized in that moment. An unspoken agreement had been forged and neither seemed to expect anything more from the other than a simple fleeting romance.

"I'm glad you came this evening," he said as he fingered the wispy shawl still entwined in her arms.

"I'm glad I came, too."

"You are so beautiful."

"Juwan," she said, then paused slightly. "It's been a while for me. So can we go slowly?"

He nodded his understanding. He had no intention of rushing through this moment. He wanted to savor every tender touch and every sensuous stroke of her body. He had nothing but time. His desire for her had been building since the moment he'd read her profile months ago. The many pictures he'd seen didn't do her justice. And now looking at her wrapped in his arms, she was beyond breathtaking.

He stroked the tender side of her jaw. His eyes glazed over with desire. Blood rushed, then pooled, hardening his body even more. She was everything he imagined she would be. "There could be no other way with you," he finally responded.

The thin-strapped gown she'd worn had ignited a burn in him the instant he saw her in it. And the wispy shawl she had wrapped around her shoulders all evening did little to hinder his surging passion. Like unwrapping a precious gift, he gently removed the chiffon fabric, turning her around as he pulled it loose to fall to the floor.

As she turned away from him, he rested her back against

his chest, planting his hands on her scented shoulders. A slow, gentle, sensuous massage followed. Softly yet firmly he kneaded her neck and shoulders and rubbed the erogenous areas behind her ears and at her temples. Her hair, once pinned up with tiny diamond-studded bobby pins, now hung in tendrils along the nape of her neck.

Floating on a cloud of erotic stimulation, her head dropped to the side. He leaned down and muttered something near her ear, but she had no idea what he asked or said or wanted. All she knew was that his mouth, his tongue and his hands were wreaking havoc on her senses and slow or not, if he continued much longer she was going to turn around, rip his shirt and pants off, and take him right there in the middle of the floor.

Then one of his hands delved lower down her arm to her hand. He raised her arm, bringing her hand to his lips. He caressed her hand lovingly, kissed each finger in turn, then laid her hand on his shoulder behind him.

He repeated the same action with the other hand to have both her arms above her head holding his neck tenderly. Then in one smooth motion he dipped his mouth to the crook of her neck, drawing a moan of pleasure from her that was loud enough to be heard in the next state. Her eyes fluttered closed as a hot burn sizzled through her body. She continued to hold on and he continued to ravage her neck, her ears and her arms. Never had such a simple act been so exciting and so damn erotic.

Relentless to the point of frenzy, her breathing quickened and her mind and thoughts soared. His touch, like smoldering lava, caressed her in every way possible. His hands melted onto her skin like sweet dark milk chocolate. The madness he brought to her with just his hands promised an evening of true delight. Her mind wandered and her thoughts faded to barely conscious passion. *If this was foreplay then making love with this man would probably kill me. Oh but what a way to go.*

Her arms, weak with surrender, collapsed down and her head fell forward, her chin resting on her upper chest. *This is too much.* He immediately brought his mouth to the back of her neck, then lowered his assault through the taffeta gown down her back to her waist. He fell to his knees behind her, then slowly turned her around. *Have mercy.* She heard the words echo in her mind.

She looked down at him and with trembling, anxious hands pulled at and released the knot of his bow tie, then miraculously with anxious fingers unbuttoned his shirt and pulled it from his pants. He gathered her body close and buried his face in her stomach, kissing the rose-colored material softly. A hiss escaped from her mouth and a low guttural groan escaped from his throat.

He held and gently massaged the backs of her thighs through the soft material, caressing them as he held her balanced and in place. He felt so good, his mouth, his tongue, his hands. Her brain sizzled and her heart pounded through her chest as she held his head and stroked the lobes of his ears. Thoughts mingled incoherently; her body was awash with sensations and desires as fireworks exploded before her eyes. Falling forward was all she could think to do. Just as she was about to let go, she stopped herself. *Oh God, now I'm hearing melodies. Wait.* "That's my phone," she muttered breathlessly as she held the side of his face, then his shoulders.

Under protest Juwan released her. He stood, stepped back, and turned away to compose himself. Several long drags of heavy breathing added to the thunderous pounding of his heart. Clearing his head was more difficult than he expected. Fifteen minutes alone with this woman had his senses turning to mush. He rebuttoned his shirt but left the bow tie hanging loosely around his neck.

Kennedy found her phone in her purse. It was a 911 alert from Trey. She answered. "Hello," she said, trying to compose herself to at least sound aware. "No, I'm . . ." She paused and looked around the suite. "Upstairs. Why? Who? Yeah, okay, I'll be right there." She looked over to Juwan. He had turned away from her. She closed the phone and walked to him, placing her hand on his back. He turned slowly, gathering her into his arms in one motion.

"I have to go back," she said.

"Yes, I heard." Juwan took a deep ragged breath. "Your cousin?" She nodded. He released her and walked to the center of the room and picked up her shawl and his jacket.

"Apparently there's someone else looking for me."

"Another bodyguard, should I be jealous?"

She grinned. "No, not at all."

He nodded and walked back over to her. He wrapped the shawl around her shoulders, then leaned in and gently kissed her forehead. "I'll walk you back." One last kiss parted them. He opened and held the door for her. Together they walked down the hall, this time in reflective silence. When they approached the stairs, Juwan held back, then stopped.

"I enjoyed our tour," she said with a knowing smile.

"I did, too," he said, returning her smile. "Maybe we can get together again?"

"I'd like that."

"May I call you, or should I still go through Hoyt?" He leaned down and kissed her gently. She reached into her small evening bag, pulled out her museum business card and handed it to him. He read the raised script.

She tiptoed up for one last lingering embrace. "I've gotta go," she whispered after their sweet embrace.

He nodded as his grip released her. She moved toward the staircase, then stood waiting. After a few seconds she turned back to him. He was still standing there gazing at her. "I don't usually make a habit of what we just . . ." she began awkwardly. "I mean I don't just . . ."

"I know," he said, not allowing her to finish.

"I just wanted you to know that. I'm not the kind . . ."

He nodded and smiled. "I know," he said sincerely, knowing more about her than she could possibly imagine.

She took a step down, then turned again. "Are you coming back to the party?"

"Later."

She nodded her understanding. "See you downstairs." She took another step but stopped when he called her name.

"Dr. Evans, wait," he said, turned to a beautifully adorned floral display on the side table, and plucked an orchid from the long stem. He walked it over to her. "For you." He handed her the solitary bloom. "Impressed?"

She nodded. "Very."

"And for the record, just in case there was any doubt, I am *very* interested."

"After what just almost happened I think we can drop the Dr. Evans thing. You can call me Keni." She turned and continued down the stairs, letting his words rest on her heart. A slow, easy smile as wide as the Grand Canyon spread across her face.

The feel of his hands on her body still pulsated against her skin. And the sensation of his mouth on hers sent a shudder of exhilaration through her. Deep and searching, his kisses were meant to seal a promise, and had they not been interrupted by her phone, she would have loved to see just what that promise was.

A diversion like Juwan Mason was just what she needed. He was absolutely perfect, a man with whom to enjoy a brief non-committal relationship. They could keep it light and casual but still enjoy the intensity of the obvious attraction she knew they both felt.

After a quick stop in the ladies' room to refresh her makeup and lipstick, she found Trey standing at the buffet table talking with a gorgeous woman dressed like Li'l Kim and every bit as endowed. As soon as she walked up, she threaded her arm around him possessively, causing a surprised expression on the woman's face. "Hi honey, I'm back. It was the babysitter; the kids are fine," she announced. The woman, stunned, soon excused herself and quickly moved to the opposite side of the room.

"That was totally uncalled for," Trey said.

"But it was fun," Kennedy said, giggling like a schoolgirl.

"Well, I'm glad you're in a jovial mood because you'll never guess who's here."

"Who?" she asked.

"Hello, lovely lady," a deep male voice whispered close to her ear.

Kennedy turned and opened her mouth, surprised. "Shawn." She wrapped her arms around him and embraced him warmly. "How are you? You look wonderful."

"And you, lovely lady"—he held her arms out and backed up to see her better—"look divine as usual."

"When did you get here? How long can you stay?"

"A few minutes ago, although I'm only here for the night. I have to fly out tomorrow and get back to the set."

"Starting or ending?" Kennedy asked. Shawn knew exactly what she meant.

"Ending, thank goodness, I'm bruised and worn. I think I'll leave the action stuff to my brother next time," Shawn said, smiling. There had always been an unspoken code among the three of them not to talk about his acting career in public, but asking a simple ambiguous statement inquiring as to the beginning or ending of shooting was fine.

The three instantly began talking about the last time they'd been together and the trouble they'd gotten into. They joked and laughed for the next ten minutes, drawing interested looks and pleasant smiles from others standing nearby.

"Trey, Kennedy, hi. I'm back." They turned to see Laine standing just to the left of Shawn. "Sorry it took so long to get back to you guys," she said, overly friendly as she fanned her face with her fingers dramatically. "I got stuck on the dance floor since forever." Then she turned to Shawn as if she had just noticed him standing there. "Hi," she said brightly.

Kennedy and Trey looked at each other and smiled. "Laine, this is Shawn Anderson. Shawn, this is an acquaintance of ours, Laine Harrington," Kennedy said, making the introductions. Laine smiled and held out her tiny hand.

Shawn shook it warmly and stepped back to include her in their discussion. The conversation continued, they were talking about sports, and although Kennedy was right in the mix, Laine was completely lost. The conversation shifted several times from cars, art and financing to the stock market, world affairs and upcoming holidays. Several times Shawn, Trey or Kennedy would make a remark to draw Laine into the conversation, but the only thing she wanted to talk about was Hollywood, actors and actresses and his movies. Shawn eventually asked Kennedy to dance with him. She did.

As soon as Juwan returned, he looked around, sensing that something was different. Then it hit him, the sudden appearance of numerous Secret Service operatives immediately drawing his attention. Apparently a very high government official was on the way. Two minutes later the official arrived.

Hoyt walked up beside Juwan. "Impressed?"

"I don't recall your mentioning that the vice president and the secretary of state would be coming when you read the guest list in the car earlier today."

"Classified."

"I see," Juwan said absently.

Both Juwan and Hoyt continuously scanned the room, but for different reasons. Hoyt looked for any situation needing damage control while Juwan looked for a woman dressed in a pale pink gown. He spotted her across the room dancing with a man different from the one he'd seen her with earlier.

She had said that he was her cousin. Maybe this guy was,

too. But his body language gave Juwan pause. He was definitely no relative. Juwan frowned, his first inclination was to go over, introduce himself, and then escort him outside. But he suppressed that urge. Then upon closer examination of the man's profile, the familiarity became clear. He'd seen him before. Then he realized who the man was. He was just about to go over when he was stopped.

"Juwan, Juwan Mason, is that you?" Juwan turned to the slightly familiar voice. "It is you. Welcome home." He looked down into sweet loving eyes that he hadn't seen in years. But they were unmistakable. They were the eyes of Adarah's good friend, Louise Gates. She smiled and opened her arms, welcoming him.

He remembered her instantly and slipped comfortably into a warm adoring hug. "Mrs. Gates, how are you?" His voice was patient and gentle.

"Wonderful, just wonderful. Adarah told me that you were back in the area, but I had no idea that you would be here tonight. What a wonderful surprise."

"It's good to see you, Mrs. Gates." This woman was remarkable, he thought to himself. Not only had she apparently learned the secret to longevity and good heath but she still had the twinkle in her eyes that he remembered so well.

"Oh, please call me Mamma Lou. Everybody does." He nodded. "So, how have you been, how's work?" she asked.

"Fine, I'm on vacation for the next few weeks."

"Well then, you must come and visit Crescent Island."

"I might just do that. Yasmine's been a few times and raves about it."

"Well, of course she does." Louise Gates took a quick glance, focusing on Juwan's eyes and face. Then she frowned and he knew he was in for trouble. "So what's this I hear about your not calling your sister?"

Juwan chuckled and shook his head. "Does she send out an SOS, smoke signals or beat drums every time I forget to return her phone calls? Everyone I've talked to so far has mentioned the same thing."

"She worries."

"Too much."

"That's what family is for. Call her; set her mind at ease. That's what brothers are for."

Juwan nodded, knowing that there was no way he was going to even come close to winning a disagreement with Louise Gates so there was no need to even bother. "Yes, ma'am," he said humbly.

"Good." She began looking around. He turned to follow her vision. "Now, where is the forgetful young lady who let you loose this evening?"

"No date this evening," he admitted, then regretted it instantly, remembering her tendency to play matchmaker.

"Well, that just won't do, will it?" She began looking around in earnest. "It's a shame I didn't know you'd be here this evening. I know a lovely woman, a museum curator, who I'm sure you'd be delighted to meet."

Juwan choked and unconsciously ran his finger between his neck and collar, feeling the noose of Mamma Lou's matchmaking beginning to tighten quickly. "Actually, Mamma Lou, I'm waiting for someone."

"Oh, good, I'd love to meet her. Make sure you introduce us as soon as she gets here." She nodded, knowing that he wouldn't dare lie to her.

"Hey there, young fellow, go find your own girl. This one's already taken."

Delighted by the interruption, Juwan turned, seeing the permanent staple by Mamma Lou's side, Colonel Otis Wheeler. He smiled with relief and delight at seeing him. Colonel Wheeler handed Louise the glass of punch he'd brought over and kept the other for himself. Then the two men grasped hands, shook then hugged briefly. "Colonel Wheeler, it's good to see you. How've you been?"

"Doing well, doing well. How goes the battle?"

"It goes," he said evasively.

"We'd heard that you were headed back this way."

"Yes, I'm on vacation for a bit."

"Needed some downtime, uh?"

"Yeah, something like that." The look in Colonel Wheeler eyes was both knowing and understanding. As a retired Marine intelligence officer, Colonel Wheeler had seen more than his share of undercover assignments.

"Juwan and I were just talking about the young lady in his life. I can't wait to meet her."

"Is that right?" Colonel Wheeler said as he noticed the panic in Juwan's eyes. "Well, he's going to have to get back to you on that one because if I'm not mistaken, they're playing our song." He took Louise's glass and handed it to Juwan along with his own. "So if you don't mind, Juwan, I'd like to take my pretty lady here for a slow spin on the dance floor."

"Not at all, enjoy." Juwan's face was calm and nonexpressive to most, and his relief was evident only to Colonel Wheeler. A knowing wink secured their little secret as he took Louise's hand and led her away. "Always faithful," Colonel Wheeler said in passing.

"Semper fidelis," Juwan responded with the Latin Marine Corps motto. As he watched them go, he breathed a long sigh of relief. In his career he had been undercover, under pressure and under fire but never had he been so completely and totally cowed by a five-foot-two dynamo named Mamma Lou. He set the two glasses on the nearest buffet table and, seeing his escape, broke for the other side of the room.

"Playing our song indeed?" Louise remarked as she fit comfortably in her escort's arms. She shook her head and sucked her teeth, making a tisking sound as if she were disappointed with a young child. "That was the worst and most blatant rescue and getaway I've ever seen, and I've seen many."

"No doubt." Colonel Wheeler chuckled joyously. He knew there was no fooling his love. They had been together too long and knew each other too well. "Just giving the man a little breathing room. I'm sure you'll find him and his young lady later this evening."

"I'm sure I will," she affirmed.

"Here we go again," Colonel Wheeler said under his breath.

"I have no idea what you're talking about."

"I just bet you don't." Colonel Wheeler chuckled again, this time louder and more joyously. He knew that Louise would never change and he'd have it no other way. "You're asking for trouble this time," Colonel Wheeler warned as he gracefully moved her around the dance floor. She smiled in his arms while keeping an eye on the situation around her.

"I beg your pardon?" she asked innocently.

"Now don't give me that innocent expression, which one is it this time, Kennedy, Randolph or Trey?"

"I'm sure I have no idea what you're talking about."

"The last time those three saw you they were as nervous as jackrabbits in a dog kennel. You had them nearly jumping out of their skins as soon as you looked in their direction." He chuckled, remembering the look of fright on their faces as soon as they saw Louise walk in their direction.

"Of course I didn't. They were just surprised to see me."

"Surprised," he snickered. "They were scared witless." He chuckled again, this time more openly. "You're asking for trouble," he repeated, shaking his head sadly at the prospect of another matchmaking mission.

"Don't be ridiculous, I have everything completely under control."

Colonel Wheeler smiled and shook his head patiently. Having been in several wars and countless battles, he knew a doomed mission when he saw one. "They're wise to you. You'll never pull it off."

"Of course I will. I always do," Louise said confidently. "And never say never, particularly to a woman with a talent for finding romance. Love is like a complex recipe, a pinch of this, a dash of that, a little time, a lot of patience and anything is possible."

"Louise, you can't create happy endings in the kitchen like your banana bread pudding. One of these days . . ." he warned.

"Vision, you see, that's all it takes. I'll let you in on a little secret."

Colonel Wheeler looked down at her, his eyes bright with admiration and love. "Okay, what's the secret?"

"Proximity."

"What about it?"

"Proximity, that's all it takes in most cases."

"All it takes for what?" he asked, completely lost.

"Matchmaking is a lost art. Very few possess that talent and those who truly see the possibilities realize that you don't always have to do something and that mere proximity works just as well."

Colonel Wheeler let out a boisterous laugh. After a few minutes he calmed down. True to his nature, joyful and pleasant, he adored his Louise. He even adored the swirl of adventure that seemed to constantly surround her. The talent she had to set things into motion was truly remarkable.

"It's only the truly defiant who actually require my hands-on assistance. The others merely need my presence to ignite the spark."

"That makes absolutely no sense," he said.

"Of course it does." The music stopped and applause surrounded them. Colonel Wheeler and Louise moved back toward the buffet area and continued their conversation.

"Okay, we're here this evening, I assume it's because you have matchmaking in the works. And since we're in Washington, I assume that it's either Senator Randolph Kingsley, Trey Evans or Kennedy Evans. Or is there some other lucky person of whom I'm not aware?"

Louise smiled innocently as she nodded across the room.

Colonel Wheeler followed her nod. "Isn't that . . ." he began, then stopped, smiled and shook his head. "Now that might just be worth the drive here. If you can pull that off, it'll indeed be a miracle." He chuckled and his whole body shook.

Louise smiled. She was right on target. Then her eyes brightened again as she spotted a couple standing just a few feet away. Surprised and delighted, she walked over.

"Kennedy, Trey?"

"Uh-oh." Kennedy froze as a splinter of recognition spiked down her back. *It can't be.*

Mamma Lou came up to Trey, kissed his cheek and hugged him warmly. Then she turned to Kennedy and repeated the action. "You look divine this evening," she said to Kennedy as Kennedy kissed Colonel Wheeler's cheek and Trey shook his hand.

"Thank you, Mamma Lou, so do you." Kennedy looked over to Trey, who was easing away from the two of them.

"Trey," Louise said just before he dashed away. "Do you mind if I borrow Kennedy for a few minutes? There's someone I'd love for her to meet."

Kennedy turned to glare at the smirking Trey. But he was enjoying this too much. "Not at all, Mamma Lou, help yourself, please. I'm sure Kennedy would love to meet someone new. As a matter of fact, she was just saying that the other day."

"As were you, Trey," Kennedy remarked, trying to get even.

"We'll talk later." Mama Lou winked at Trey as she took Kennedy's arm and led her away. "Now, dear," she said as she began scanning the crowd, "there's a young man here who needs some attention. He works for the FBI, he loves art, and he's a sweetheart. Now." She continued to look around the room. "Where did he get to?"

Colonel Wheeler and Trey watched Kennedy and Mamma Lou as they walked away. Trey shuddered. "Oh, that can't be good," he muttered, not feeling as bad as he should have. Colonel Wheeler chuckled at the relief in his tone.

"That's probably gonna make her evening," Colonel Wheeler said with a broad smile.

Smiling and nodding his head, Trey enjoyed the moment. Then he snickered, then chuckled, then laughed so hard he nearly choked. This was by far the best prank he had never played on Kennedy.

Shawn returned from the dance floor and the three men talked until Colonel Wheeler decided to hit the buffet table and Shawn was asked to dance again. Trey, pleased with his short reprieve, glanced around the room then spotted the Li'l Kim look-alike from earlier. He walked over and they resumed their previous conversation.

Laine Herrington stood alone, fuming, as she pouted and hissed in the corner. She watched as Kennedy openly, shamelessly flirted with the actor, Shawn Anderson, on the dance floor again. Earlier she had watched as Louise Gates walked away with Kennedy and then seen Shawn following to ask her to dance again. It was just too unfair. She huffed loudly and knotted her arms over her small chest. Trey and Shawn, two gorgeous men and they both ignored her, how rude could they be?

It was Crescent Island, Tony and Madison all over again. Just when she and Tony were all set to get back together, Madison arrived and stole him away from her. Now it was happening again. She had a good mind to walk right over there and slap Kennedy silly.

As soon as Kennedy came into the room, both Trey and Shawn directed their attention to her. They completely ignored everyone else but Kennedy. It wasn't fair. Even when she went over to them, they ignored her to talk about art, old broken pots and stupid pictures. So what, who cared? She pouted. It was all ancient history as far as she was concerned. Who cared about dirty old stuff from millions of years ago when you could just go out and buy something brand new? Why anyone in their right mind wanted to put together a show of mummies was beyond her.

Dressed in her usual head-to-toe pink ensemble, she crossed her arms over her toothpick-thin figure and scoured the room for her mother. She'd know what to do. Concentrating hard, she completely missed the first invitation.

"Excuse me, would you like to dance?" he repeated as he tapped her shoulder.

Startled, Laine turned around sharply. Hoping to see Shawn standing behind her, she was disappointed. It wasn't him. She eyed the man there for a second until he nodded and began to walk away. "No wait," she called out louder than she intended, "I mean, yes, I'd love to dance with you." The anxiousness in her voice was obvious.

Hoyt smiled and walked back to her. Mrs. Gates was right, he thought, she was lovely, small, petite. He liked that. "Shall we?" he requested, taking Laine's hand and leading her to the dance floor. He nodded and smiled at several guests, including the guest of honor, Ambassador Mebeko himself, as they maneuvered through the crowded dance floor.

Laine proudly followed, knowing that all eyes were drawn to her and the man she was with. This was even better than Shawn Anderson, she decided.

A sudden rush of excitement shimmered through her. She had seen him earlier as he introduced the ambassador. Tall, handsome, a little nerdy, but she liked that. She'd made up her mind instantly, he was definitely a possibility. He obviously had excellent taste in dance partners and pretty much that's all she needed to know.

* * *

Across the room Mimi glanced at Louise, smiled, and nodded her approval and gratitude. Louise returned the approving nod. Everything was going just as she'd planned—perfectly—because no matter what anyone said, proximity worked and miracles were indeed right up her alley.

Chapter Ten

By Monday morning a slow, easy smile still rested comfortably on Juwan's lips. He reached up and touched his mouth. The feel of Kennedy's lips still quickened his pulse. An unrequited hunger had been burning in the pit of his stomach since they had parted Friday night. She was a remarkable woman and he had more than enjoyed being with her. She was vivacious and exciting with an electric spark that outshone the room. He knew from the instant they met that there was something special about her. Her eyes had captivated him and her smile held him mesmerized, even now, two days later.

Existing on little sleep was part of the job, he knew that. But last night the unthinkable happened, he dreamt about her. He seldom dreamt, at least he never remembered his dreams. But this one was vivid and clear. They were together in his suite; they were making love. Then suddenly it was Remy all over again, the arrest, the phone calls, the pleas for him to help her, and finally, her lying in the morgue with a dark corded band around her neck. But it wasn't Remy in the dream; it was Kennedy and the makeshift noose around her neck was the diamond choker. She called to him but he turned away. He saw her as she prepared to jump from the chair. He ran to stop her but he was too late; she jumped; he was unable to save her. Her calls to him echoed in his mind until he awoke. Tangled in the sheets and drenched with sweat, he awakened in a panic.

It was imperative that he be on top of every situation as a special agent on assignment in the field. All he had to do was make a case, then walk away. He'd done it hundreds of times before. But now, for the first time in his career, he felt his focus slipping. He thought about her constantly. When he slept, he dreamt of her and when he was awake, he thought of her. She had gotten to him and he'd willingly let it happen.

Sitting alone at the desk in his suite, he stared out the window, seeing only her. He'd become fixated. But he knew that he needed to stay objective. He had a job to do and she, not knowing, was a necessary part of it. He needed to focus and stop the wistful fantasizing.

He looked down and pressed the key, sending a detailed briefing to his superiors. Then he checked his assignment files and initial report for any changes. Satisfied that everything was in order, he completed his morning ritual by requesting additional data from his support associate. He waited for the reply, then ended his transmission by closing the laptop.

He stood up, stretched, crossed the room and grasped the doorknob, then paused when the vibrating of his cell phone grabbed his attention. Recognizing the number instantly, he flipped the phone open and answered.

"I got your message," Kevin Pole said, starting the conversation by jumping right to the point as usual.

"Good, I need you to pull some background intel for me. I sent a list, but start with Kennedy Evans."

"Yeah, that part I already have. But since I understood that you were officially on leave of absence for the next two months before the big move, I assume this intel you requested is regarding the ingredients of a Caribbean tropical drink or possibly the bartender mixing it."

"Not quite, I'm on assignment." Juwan listed in detail the

information he required including personal dossiers and Interpol database files.

"What's the case?" Kevin asked, not at all surprised by the assignment revelation.

"The Nubian Museum theft."

"I didn't know we were still interested. I thought that case was closed when we captured the three men involved and recovered all but one of the pieces," Kevin said as he entered Kennedy's name into the central database and began a preliminary search. Several files flashed on the screen; he scanned them then continued.

"That's the word we put out. Officially it was closed, but unofficially we have intel that Petre Siegal had more help than we first thought. There's a high probability that someone in the National Museum of African Art was working with him."

"I see, so that's why you're at the embassy, a cover."

"Yes."

"Does Maurice know?" he asked as he continued scanning the files.

"No, and I'd prefer he didn't, at least not yet."

"Got it," he said, finding the file. "I just pulled a preliminary on Dr. Evans. She is a curator at the National Museum of African Art."

"I've got that part, what else?"

"Okay." He began to read through the onscreen file. "She travels extensively. As a matter of fact, her passport reads a lot like yours: parts of Africa, Europe, Asia, US, and, most recently . . ." He paused to recheck his findings. "She's now back from Nubia and Germany where she was red flagged."

"Flagged for what, by whom?"

"Now this is the interesting part." Kevin ran his finger along the computer monitor and pointed to the name listed. "She was red flagged by you."

"What?" A cold chill sliced down Juwan's back.

"You flagged anyone with an A class passport making

regular business-related visits to Northern Africa and Germany and connected with the Nubian Museum. Nine people showed up on the grid. She was one of them."

"When exactly was she in Nubia?"

Kevin read down the list of passport notations. He stopped and rechecked the list. "Five months ago for three weeks. Two months ago for two weeks and two weeks ago. She's just getting back. Looks like she was in Nubia a day before the robbery, then flew out a few hours before." He paused. "She was in Germany for three days after that. That's an awful lot of coincidences. Didn't Colin track Petre to Germany just after he was mistakenly released?"

"Yeah, that's probably why he targeted her."

"It does look like they might have been there at the same time, a possible meet?"

"No, there's no proof of that. All we have is speculation. We're gonna need a hell of a lot more intel. Other than the red flag in Germany, what's her record look like?"

"She's clean. Just speeding tickets but all paid on time. But, as you know, these prelim reports don't cover everything."

"I requested a full run," Juwan said.

"I'll expedite it," Kevin replied. "You know, it's possible that she was in it for the thrill, like Remy was."

"No, for Remy money was the key. That was her pull."

"Well, you can cross off that motive; Kennedy Evans has got money, plenty of it. She's the daughter of Jace and Taylor Evans of E-Corp Industries; they're an international computer software company. Plus in addition to a hefty inheritance, she's worth quite a bit of money in her own right—stock, investments. At this point there're no prior connections, no records, no motive, no proof. The wrong move on her could seriously damage future operations. The Evans family has a lot of political power."

"Something doesn't feel right," Juwan wondered out loud. "Why would Petre go to Germany?"

Kevin made the connection. Germany was where Remy killed herself. "Juwan, listen, I felt bad about the way things went down in Germany with Remy, too. She was a beautiful woman who had gotten herself in way over her head. You can't take this on as your own personal crusade because of guilt. You didn't do anything wrong. You did your job. There was nothing anyone could have done to save her. Remy fell in love with your undercover persona, not you. And no amount of contrition on your part will bring her back."

Juwan ignored Kevin's unsolicited input. "Anything else?"

"No," Kevin said, knowing that Juwan hadn't heard a word he had said.

"Make sure I get the full profile on those key people as soon as possible and send Petre's along as well. I want to compare."

"I'll have it to you by this evening. I'll send it by diplomatic courier since you're at the embassy."

"How's my little sister?" Juwan asked.

"Ready to strangle you if I'm not mistaken. Apparently you were supposed to call her last week and the week before that, and the week before that and didn't. Then you suspiciously disappeared, no word, no contact. She immediately assumed you had been swallowed up by the earth."

"She does worry, doesn't she?"

"Only when it comes to you."

"She knows the job."

"True, she also knows that as of two months ago you were no longer a field operative and the undercover operations thing was over, putting you behind a desk. Not to mention, you're supposed to be on vacation."

"Okay, tell her I'll catch up with her later this week."

"Better idea, you tell her," he said.

Juwan smiled. Kevin was no fool; telling his wife that would only have her asking a dozen more questions. "Fine. I'll call her myself."

"Good idea."

They hung up. An hour later Juwan stood in the lobby of the National Museum of African Art. He noted the private seminar announcement and saw that it was being taught by Dr. Evans. He smiled. There were still thirty minutes left in the program. Without a second thought he took the steps to the main auditorium.

He slipped inside, then found a seat in the back row. The room was dark but he could clearly hear Kennedy's voice as she talked about the slides of the Nubian artifacts being shown on the screen. Each time the projector clicked she explained the slide and its relationship to the exhibit and why she had chosen to display it or not.

Several questions were asked and comments made, but by and large the discussion remained on target. He sat back and listened to her present the exhibit facts and details. She talked about the folklore and gave specifics on language and details about Nubian religion. Juwan was impressed. She was even more knowledgeable than he'd thought.

A few minutes later the program ended and Juwan was one of the first to slip out the door. He hung around in front of the main auditorium until most of the participants had gone. He stood at a display near the entrance.

"Juwan?" He turned, smiled and buckled her knees. *Damn he was gorgeous.*

"Dr. Evans, Keni."

"Hi," Kennedy said as she walked up and stood beside him. She looked at the piece he'd been observing. "Do you like this piece?"

"Not particularly," he said, not taking his eyes from her profile.

A flush of heat instantly began to burn inside her. He had a way of setting her body on fire with just a glance. "I thought you told me that you loved art."

"I do, just not this particular artist or this particular piece.

I've seen some of his other work. I find it extremely predictable, nothing particularly extraordinary."

"Is that right?" she asked, surprised by his detailed analysis of the popular artist.

"Yes, he seems to favor the works of Demonte in his basic approach, but he misses the mark with his use of color and abstract line."

"Demonte," she repeated, nodding, impressed by his sharp artistic eye. "You have strong opinions and I see that you do know your African art. Did you study?"

"In a round about way."

She started smiling. "What does that mean?"

"It means not directly," he patiently informed her.

"Anyone ever tell you that you're extremely evasive when it comes to personal questions?"

"What makes you say that?"

"Because you are, you never answer direct questions about yourself, at least not fully. You are evasive and never quite answer. It's a fascinating quirk or is it a professional habit?"

"That's an interesting observation."

"My point exactly."

He laughed, with joy and amusement. "I thought I could possibly steal a moment of your time and have a peek at the exhibit."

"I thought you were supposed to call first."

"I like living dangerously."

"I bet."

"Would it help if I bribed you?" he joked.

"It might, what do you have?" He smiled. She smiled. "Come on." She led the way down to the main floor and across to the special exhibit's gallery. "It's an amazing exhibit and I'm incredibly excited about it." As they approached, he stepped up and pulled the draped mural aside, allowing her to pass easily.

The moment he stepped inside, he was drawn to the

massive power of the statues standing guard. Juwan stepped closer to have a better look. The onyx black skin of the male figures was astonishing. "Wow."

"They're Medjay militia from the New Kingdom made of black granite."

"This is incredible, I had no idea."

"It is, isn't it?" Kennedy said proudly. "And it's only the beginning." She led the way around a corner. As soon as they turned, Juwan stopped, surprised and delighted by the sight. "Isn't it wonderful?" she said, knowing the usual reaction.

Juwan walked around. Kennedy followed, giving him a brief history of each piece.

"As I'm sure you already know, the country we refer to today as Nubia, before Ambassador Mebeko was instrumental in its secession from Sudan, was called Nubia or Cush in ancient times. That was over 2,500 years ago. Kerma was the capital and black African pharaohs ruled major territories along the Nile River including Egypt."

Although the Cush Empire pre-dates Egypt, they were still the two most powerful cultures and were indelibly linked as one. They fought constantly—enemies one day, allies the next. For about a hundred years Nubia ruled Egypt. That's when art, architecture and artifacts become really interesting."

Juwan was amazed by the pieces in the exhibit. He stopped in front of a small mural-like relief. "It's from the tomb of Huy from around 1320 B.C. It depicts Nubian notables paying homage to the gods and to Huy."

As they came to the end and Kennedy explained some of the contemporary works, Juwan was speechless, realizing that she was right. The exhibit was amazing. Together they walked through the exit. He was in awe as she closely observed his reaction. It was the first time that anyone other than museum employees had seen her work. "That is phenomenal," he exclaimed as he turned to her.

"Thank you, it was a team effort, we worked really hard.

We still have some things to do, the audio and video, the background sound, things like that."

He stood shaking his head, still stunned by what he had just seen. "You did a remarkable job."

"I'm heading back to my office. Would you like to join me?"

"I'd hoped you'd ask me that. Yes, I would."

"Come on," she said and she directed him away from the open atrium toward the stairs.

He observed every inch of her as she walked. The business suit she wore was anything but strictly business: Clean-cut lines with a strong edge of femininity. She looked beautifully stylish while still presenting a businesslike image. She turned, seeing his eyes cemented to her.

"You seem different this afternoon," she said.

"Do I?"

"Yes, you seem slightly distracted. Is everything all right?"

"Fine," he responded, then realized that either she was too intuitive or he was becoming too transparent. Either way he needed to rectify the matter. "You look particularly businesslike this afternoon, a far cry from the leather pants last Friday," he remarked after giving her body another quick once-over.

"Friday was unique. I had to make an early morning run to my sister's house in Alexandria and most of my clothes were still packed."

"Packed?"

"I've been away for a few months."

"Really, where?"

"Feels like all over."

"Was it a procuring trip?"

She nodded. "Something like that."

"Now who's being evasive?"

She looked over at him and smiled. "Touché."

When they reached the door where they first bumped

into each other, she turned again. Knowing smiles broadened on their faces as they continued through.

As they entered her office, she immediately walked behind her desk and took a seat. She cleared her throat nervously, thankful for the distance. Juwan troubled her and her focus on him was more than she realized. Thinking about a man whom she'd just met was unusual for her, but nearly making love to him their first night together was disturbingly over the top. "I'm glad you enjoyed the exhibit. Maybe you can come back when it actually opens. I know that Ambassador Mebeko and several members of his staff will be coming. I hope you can come, too."

"I'd like that. I hope I can," Juwan said after standing at the door for a few moments and getting a quick overview of the layout and particulars of her office. He moved closer to the desk.

"So, did you only stop by to see the exhibit or was there something else you were interested in seeing?" she asked seductively.

He smiled, knowing that this conversation would ultimately lead them down a wanton path. He responded easily. "Actually I came by to invite you to dinner this evening. Are you free?"

"Yes, I'd like to have dinner with you."

"Wonderful, any particular restaurant or would you like me to decide?"

"I'll tell you what, why don't you come over to my house? We'll send out for something."

"Don't you cook?"

"I don't often have the time, do you? Or is that also too personal a question?"

"No it's not too personal and yes, I do cook. As a matter of fact, I'm a very good cook." Her expression was pure shock.

"You look stunned. I have many talents."

"I am stunned. You don't look like the domestic type."

"I'm full of surprises."

"Apparently. Might I inquire as to your other abilities?"

"In time."

A knowing glance passed between them that was hotter and more erotic than anything either could have said out loud. A sly smirk and an inviting smile added to the flirting.

"I'd better leave you to your work," he said, taking another quick glance around the room, sizing up as much as he could. Several piles of well-used art books, some opened, some closed, cluttered the top of her desk. Two stacks of 35mm slides sat on top of a small light box on her credenza along with a small laptop computer open to a screen listing several e-mail messages waiting to be read. A second desk computer with the monitor in save mode had a colorful ball bouncing round the screen. All in all, he decided, it was a typical office with few surprises.

"Okay." She stood and walked him to the door.

He opened it, then turned to her. "Until this evening," he said. "Seven o'clock okay with you?"

She nodded. "Sounds perfect. See you tonight."

He turned but not before leaving her with his signature smile. But this time there was something behind the smile that seemed to suggest that there was a lot more than he was able or willing to say at this point. It was the look in his eyes that was more than just awareness. The whole time he was in her office he seemed to be always observing. But she assumed that it was just the nature of his business.

She first noticed it Friday evening as she watched him interact with the embassy guests. He didn't just glance at people and things, he absorbed them, taking in everything at once, flaws, blemishes and imperfections. He seemed to be more of the situation than in the situation. She couldn't quite put her finger on it, but she knew that there was definitely more to Juwan Mason than what he led people to believe, what he led her to believe.

Kennedy watched as he strolled confidently down the hall to the exit doors. He was dressed casually in an open-necked shirt and relaxed slacks that hugged the curve of his rear as if they had been made just for him. She chided herself. She wasn't in the habit of watching men walk, but there was something about Juwan's body that begged for her attention. She smiled naughtily, then looked away.

But that would be for another time. Right now she needed to get some work done, and standing in the doorway watching him walk wasn't exactly what she was paid for. She closed the office door and went back to her desk and buried herself in work.

Juwan had noticed the names and titles on the doors when he first passed by with Kennedy. At least he was honest about hoping she'd ask him back to her office. He needed to get into the administrative wing and she was his best opportunity.

Hearing her close the office door behind him, he stopped and backtracked to the door he wanted. Barry Culpepper's name was prominently displayed on a brass plate outside. He knocked twice, then entered.

As soon as he entered, he gave the office a quick once over. As he sat down in front of Barry's desk, he picked up a magazine and opened it to a random page. The office was much like Kennedy's. It was filled with art books, mostly brand new and unused, piled high on the desk, credenza and coffee table. His office was larger with a side window and a second exit door. Juwan made a mental note to review the museum's blueprints and floor plans to see where the door led.

Barry walked into his office and stopped, stunned to see a strange man sitting in his office reading a magazine. "I beg your pardon, who are you and what are you doing in my office?"

Juwan stood and turned around.

Barry recognized him immediately. "Mr. Mason? What an

unexpected surprise, please sit, sit." They shook hands and Juwan sat back down in the offered chair. "I trust everything is well with the ambassador and at the embassy?"

"Yes, everything's just fine. Ambassador Mebeko was delighted that you invited him last Friday. He speaks very highly of you."

"Really?" Barry said, obviously impressed with himself. He openly beamed brighter than a Broadway spotlight. He must have made a better impression than he thought.

"Yes, of course," Juwan lied effectively.

"Well, that is good to hear. You know, the ambassador and I have known each other for years. As a matter of fact his oldest son and I often go fishing upstate."

"Is that right?" Juwan nodded, looking as if he believed every word, knowing, of course, that Barry was lying through his teeth.

"It's always a pleasure to see him again and you, too, of course. So, Mr. Mason, how can I assist you?"

Juwan purposely didn't get to the point. He needed to test the waters so to speak and get a better feel for Barry's character and motives. He extended their conversation by exchanging general pleasantries—weather, politics, and then, finally, travel. The opening he needed had been inadvertently supplied.

"Barry." He leaned in casually, a sign of trust and confidentiality. Barry, sitting behind his desk, also leaned in. Juwan smiled, knowing the predictability of the trusting mind. "I'm sure you heard of the horrendous theft that took place in Nubia a few weeks back."

"Yes, of course," Barry said, his eyes widened. "Terrible, terrible."

"Indeed," Juwan agreed. "I wonder whatever happened to the last stolen piece. I believe it was a small golden statue," he said, deciding that if Barry often fished with Maurice's oldest son he might as well go for it and toss out some bait.

"I couldn't imagine."

"Of course not." Juwan paused, smiled and shook his head. Barry observed every move he made. "But of course . . ." Juwan began, then stopped, waving his hands, dismissing the thought.

"What were you going to say?"

"Oh nothing, forget about it."

"No, please. I insist, go on. We're all friends here," Barry offered.

"It's just that if that piece was to somehow find its way to an auction, it would make quite a profit for whoever has it."

Barry scoffed. "Sotheby's would never touch stolen property and the Internet auctions are all being watched by the FBI."

"Right, of course," Juwan said, then smiled again. "But possibly a private auction, say the black market. Interest might be phenomenal." Barry's eyes lit up. "As a bodyguard I know a lot of interesting people. Some travel in very interesting circles. I'm sure some collectors would pay just to have the opportunity to place a bid," he joked and chuckled; Barry joined in.

"Hypothetically speaking, Juwan, how much would something like that go for, hypothetically speaking, of course?"

"Hypothetically speaking, of course, I'd say the high five figures, maybe even into the low six figures."

"That much." Barry nearly salivated.

"Hypothetically speaking, of course," Juwan added.

"Of course, hypothetically speaking."

"Well, Barry." Juwan stood, deciding that it was time to slacken the fishing line and let Barry rest a while. "I'd better let you get back to work." He turned and headed to the door.

"Ah, Juwan, wait." Barry hurried to the door. "I may have something in my possession that you might be interested in." The bait was taken and Juwan waited for the inevitable pull on the line. It happened more quickly than he expected.

He laid out his planned story and Barry absorbed every word. They talked another ten minutes. Although Barry hadn't admitted anything, he did ask very interested questions about

Juwan's contacts and he was more than interested in the names he dropped and the items he mentioned. Greed was a powerful motivator and money was ultimately the key to most crimes. Everything was going exactly as he'd predicted.

The remainder of the afternoon seemed a blur. The museum, crowded all day, was finally closed, making it easier to maneuver the larger pieces of the exhibit into place. With dozens of matters still to attend to and not a lot of time before the exhibit opening, Kennedy found herself relying more heavily on her assistants.

As queen bee to a hive of workers she focused her attention on the big picture in the center while others were delegated to deal with the particulars. This was her element, this was the part of the job she loved. When everything came together, the result was magic. She just wished that everything in life could work out just as perfectly.

Kennedy went out onto the floor and stood at the elaborate entrance of the exhibit, which was still cordoned off. She passed the massive wooden partitions and entered the main gallery. The first sight was of four black Medjay militia statues from the tomb of King Tuthmosis III, standing guard. Stoic and intimidating, the statues immediately brought Juwan to mind.

It was a powerful opening, equalled only by the remainder of the exhibition. She continued walking through. On either side of the wall were reproductions of murals from the Thebes tomb of Huy, viceroy of Nubia buried at Qurnat Murai circa 1320 B.C. Impressive, the images showed the elaborate burial ritual.

She reread the text on the attached plaques that she had approved earlier. The wording was informative and interesting. And exactly what she wanted to convey.

As she continued, an array of equally impressive art pieces

greeted her. The main pieces, after clearing the insurance and appraisals, had already been delivered and installed according to the floor plan. The initial floor plan had been altered several times to accommodate security issues.

The centerpiece of the show had yet to arrive and would be located toward the back of the exhibit. Several pedestals and temporary risers had been set up and new walls had been constructed to allow for easy flow and security. Kennedy walked the exhibit path as if seeing the space for the first time. She nodded, pleased with the revised floor plan. It worked well, she thought. She continued walking through. Reliefs, statues, urns, pottery, sculpture and masks were all reflective of the ancient Nubians and would be perfectly arranged throughout the exhibit.

Maya, wearing cotton gloves, came around the corner and saw Kennedy looking up at the lighting. She immediately hurried over. "Kennedy, we just arranged item number NBE 032."

Kennedy followed Maya around the corner to the far pedestal where an elaborate striated wig and broadcollar headpiece of gilded silver was mounted. She nodded her approval. The mask of Queen Malakaye sat perfectly mounted on a base held in place by a rod. Borrowed from the Museum of Fine Arts in Boston, it would be surely an impressive piece.

"Looks good, I like it," Kennedy began, then looked up at the overly subdued spotlight. "The lighting still needs to be adjusted. We need the piece visible but still dramatic."

"Okay," Maya agreed, making a brief notation in her notebook, "I'll work on that tomorrow. Do you need anything else before I go?"

"No, have a good night. See you tomorrow." She looked at her watch. It was getting late and she wanted to change before Juwan came over. Then it hit her like bolt of lightning out of the clear blue sky. She never gave Juwan her address. He had no idea where she lived.

* * *

The three sealed dossiers were waiting in his suite when Juwan arrived back at the embassy. He opened the first packet and pulled out the contents. Kennedy's file was on top. He picked it up. The words "Dr. Kennedy Evans" were printed in block letters on the cover. He'd seen her file already, having read it weeks before. Now it was much thicker; Kevin had apparently included some additional information.

He sat at the desk, leafed through the file and began a detailed reading just as he had done with every other undercover assignment he'd accepted. Fifteen minutes later he knew everything there was to know about Kennedy, including the fact that she didn't cook and that shrimp scampi and lobster with garlic butter linguine were her favorite foods. That she was allergic to penicillin and had just begun taking an anti-anxiety drug for stress and after the fall she had in South America when she sprained her ankle. She aiso received medical treatment for a serious internal injury not listed in the report.

The third child of triplets, she had lived a charmed life of wealth and privilege, although it seemed that she insisted on making it more difficult. Extreme adventures and activities motivated her. She drove cross-country motorbikes, surfed the waves in Hawaii, skied the mountains of Vail and jumped out of airplanes for fun. She was a high-stakes risk-taker and seemed to thrive best on an adrenaline rush.

But he knew that it was all a sham. Her profile shadowed his exactly. She was a runner. He recognized the traits because he had done it himself for so long. She chose risky adventures; he chose undercover work. Taking risks made him feel alive. After his parents were killed and he survived, he had delved deep into his psyche and come out with nothing—no emotion, no feeling, no joy and no pain.

He went undercover to feel alive. She parachuted from a plane to feel in control. They were the same, one having everything with too much feeling and one having nothing with too little feeling, two sides of the same coin, both running from the same thing—life.

He smiled at the description of Kennedy's lifestyle, then focused his attention on her personal report, more specifically, her past and current relationships. He read impassively, though his mind lacked the objectivity he usually possessed. There, listed in black and white, were the men in her life.

Having had only sporadic relationships that lasted for as long as she stayed in a particular place, she apparently only lived for her career. Commitment-phobic, a word he was very comfortable with, was usually associated with men. She was a new breed of independent woman, making her own way, enjoying life and staying single without the trouble of a long-term relationship.

He understood her.

The men in her life were listed chronologically starting with the earliest. He recognized one name instantly. Hoyt Collier's name appeared. They had had a relationship, but it seemed to have lasted for only a few weeks, then cooled to more of a friendship.

Following Hoyt were three others, two lasting slightly longer than a month. Then the third, a motorcycle racer and sky diver, a man without visible means of support, lasted nearly six months. Juwan paused to consider him. This man had kept Kennedy's attention for nearly six months. Then upon closer inspection, Juwan saw they were apart more than they were together and seemed to be kindred spirits rather than lovers.

Among those three were several other men who seemed to be more casual acquaintances, dates and buddies than romantic entanglements.

Juwan stood up and walked away from the file. A stinging sense of jealously bit at him and he knew why. He was beginning to have feelings for Kennedy and that was dangerous. He didn't pity or feel sorry for her as with Remy. Those he could handle. No, these feelings ran deeper, too deep. He was physically attracted to her, yes, but there was more. Her open personality had drawn him in and her exuberance for life had aroused the stillness in him. She was what he'd been looking for, the spark of excitement that had been missing. Unfortunately, he also had a job to do.

Next he picked up the files entitled "Petre Siegal" and "Barry Culpepper." He read the files, scanning both reports side by side. Coincidences and circumstances were rampant, same times, same places. The confluence of their lives was unmistakable. Then he saw it, the one notation that sent up a red flag. Petre met with someone from the National Museum of African Art the day he was picked up. As far as they knew, Kennedy had left the country suddenly a day earlier. So whom did he meet with?

Juwan pondered the question as he continued. The only other unexplained event was the Germany trip. Petre had been mistakenly released, then had disappeared. He was spotted on a flight to Germany. That would put him there the same time Kennedy was there. Juwan read the three files again. If he wanted to make a case against her, this was a damn good start.

A cold chill cut through him like a frozen spike. The similarities of the three files brought back haunting memories. He knew that Remy wasn't working alone. When she received stole African art, she immediately fenced it on the black market or on the Internet. He knew that there were others involved. He was just never able to catch them.

He closed the files and sat back, recalling the past as if it were yesterday. The ploy was easy. To Remy he was an art buyer from London interested in black-market African art for his employer. He was charming and gallant and she instantly fell for him, believing every lie he told her. She trusted that he would not betray her. The closer he got, the more he knew that she was in over her head. Just as their deal was about to go down, he'd cut his ties.

She panicked, calling him twenty times in an hour. Phone call after phone call went unanswered. When desperation set in, it was time. His boss had insisted that Remy be brought in, thinking that she would identify the other players when faced with extended jail time or a more lenient sentence. He agreed. They were both wrong.

They followed her to a café where she made five phone calls, three to his bogus number, one to another address lasting over ten minutes and the last to an unknown number. Then she sat and waited for nearly an hour. As she stood to leave, the police showed up and arrested her. She was stunned and ran. Her phone shattered in the clumsy struggle. Two hours later while in police custody, she killed herself. Her phone, which was destroyed, held unrecovered data. They never found out who the other two people were.

The troubling memories of her suicide still haunted him. But hindsight was 20/20. Two months ago he vowed that, given a second opportunity, the outcome would be different. He would settle things by finding out who her partners were and bringing them to justice. But for now, he had a dinner to plan and another woman to betray.

Chapter Eleven

"Are you sure you don't need any help in here?" Kennedy asked as she walked into the kitchen after changing into a silk knit sweater and jeans. She spotted a beautifully potted orchid sitting on the kitchen table with a bottle of champagne poured into two flutes, and formal table setting by candlelight.

Juwan handed her a glass of wine as soon as she entered. "No, just sit back and relax. I've got everything under control."

"Wine, candles, dinner cooking on the stove, soft music in the background, are you trying to impress me or seduce me?"

He turned to her. "Either one, I'm open." She smiled and shook her head. "Speaking of impressive, the paintings in the living and dining room are magnificent. One is unsigned, and the other is signed *Evans*. Are they your work?"

"The one hanging in the dining room is mine."

"You painted it?" he asked, surprised.

"Yes."

"It's beautiful. You're very talented. Why didn't you become a painter instead of a curator in a museum?"

"I paint as a hobby. I know first hand how consuming art can be."

"You didn't sign it."

"I never do."

"You should, your work is very impressive."

"Thank you."

"So what about the painting in the living room above the sofa? It's signed, *Evans,* you signed that one."

"Actually, that's my mother's work. She's a professional artist, a painter. We obviously have a similar style."

"Does she still paint?"

"No, lately she's focused her creative talent on building a school for the arts on the Potomac."

"That's right, of course," he said mistakenly.

"Have you heard of her or seen her work?" she asked.

"Yes, in a manner of speaking," he said, remembering the file he'd read earlier that afternoon. "I meant that I can see where you get your talent for painting. She's wonderful. You're wonderful."

"Thanks," Kennedy sighed longingly and looked away at the table setting and the romantic presentation. "The table looks lovely. You were obviously a good Cub Scout." He looked slightly confused. "Always prepared," she clarified. The comment still seemed to confuse him. "Oh, that's right, I keep forgetting you're not originally from the States. Do they have Boy Scouts wherever you were born and raised?"

"Where I was born, yes, they do. Most countries around the world have some form of scouting program," he answered, choosing again not to correct her assumption that he wasn't born in the United States when in fact he had been born in Boston.

"Well I'm glad you could get the evening off although I had heard that Ambassador Mebeko was going to the White House this evening. Did you need to be there?"

"No, he'll be fine. He's well covered."

"Oh right, of course, the Secret Service." She sipped her wine and watched him as he stood at the stove pouring salt into a pot of rapidly boiling water on the back burner. His back was to her so she leisurely enjoyed the splendid view of his body.

He'd worn a long-sleeved cotton shirt, sleeves rolled up to the elbow, tucked neatly into a pair of casual slacks. Casual loafers and an apron she recognized from the peg on her wall. Then with a keen eye, she went into greater detail. Broad masculine shoulders to a neat tapered waist to a firm, luscious butt that begged to be touched. She followed downward to his legs, strong and powerful. He was the perfect specimen of a modern man, powerful and gentle, comfortable at work, the bedroom and even the kitchen.

She nodded her head, mentally agreeing with her assessment, and reconsidered her initial impression of him. Maybe he wasn't such a bad boy after all. Bad boys certainly didn't cook dinner, set tables or wear aprons. Maybe he was just a nice guy with an interesting job.

He looked as though he belonged here, perfectly at ease and perfectly at home in a kitchen preparing a meal for a family. Her mind began to wander and questions about his life drew her brow to furrow. What did she really know about Juwan other than he was a freelance bodyguard on temporary assignment who knew almost as much about art as she did?

Her curiosity had already begun to grow. There was something very different about him and that also seemed odd. He seemed cautious and distracted. Half an hour ago when she arrived home to find him gathering grocery bags from a car with diplomatic plates, she was elated that he had found her house. His timing had been perfect. But then it seemed that everything about him had been perfect. And that bothered her as well. She obviously didn't know him well, but she knew when someone was hiding something, and he definitely was.

She looked over to where he stood at the stove. Juwan continued stirring and sautéing shallots and butter, filling the kitchen with sublime aromas. It was the first time she could actually remember anything smelling that good coming out of her kitchen. Although she loved to cook, she never seemed to have the time to do it. "Umm, that smells wonderful. What exactly are you cooking for dinner?"

"It's a favorite of mine. I hope you like it. It's shrimp scampi with lobster and linguini."

"Seriously?" she asked, more than a little surprised by his offering. "Are you kidding? That's my all-time favorite dish. You must be psychic."

"No, just a good guess," he said.

She nodded, feeling the tug of curiosity again. "Are you sure you don't need any help?" she asked again.

"No, I'm fine, sit back and relax. Dinner will be ready in a few minutes," Juwan said over his shoulder.

Kennedy moved closer to the delectable aromas. She watched as Juwan expertly prepared the seafood. "Where did you learn to cook like this, or is the question too personal?"

Juwan smiled, remembering their earlier conversation. "It's a necessity of bachelor life. Learn to cook or starve."

"Really, I would have guessed CIA."

Juwan went still until he remembered that the Culinary Institute of America was also called the CIA. "No, I'm more or less self-taught."

"Well, you did an excellent job. Dinner smells fabulous. Did I happen to mention that lobster and shrimp scampi with linguini is my all-time favorite dish?"

He smiled. "Yes, you did."

"Wow, I can't believe you just came up with it like that. And I still can't believe that you found my house so easily."

"It wasn't that difficult."

She turned away and moved back to the small kitchen dinette table by the bay window overlooking the brownstone's small backyard garden. "But it's not like I'm in the phone book or anything."

"You forget my occupation. I have found a few people from time to time." He walked up beside her and added more wine to her already full glass.

"Thank you," she whispered quietly.

"Hungry?" he asked, as he gently kissed her on the cheek. She nodded slowly. "Starved," she responded.

He took her glass and set it down on the table, then put his hands around her waist and drew her to his body. She went willingly. A smile curved easily. "Sexy, smart, loves and knows art and can cook. If I didn't know any better, Juwan, I'd say you were too good to be true. You're perfect. It's as if someone created you in some laboratory just for me."

He smiled. "Is that a bad thing?"

"It's a questionable thing."

He released his hold on her waist and went back to the stove and continued sautéing. "You have a suspicious nature."

"Tell me, Juwan, who are you really and what do you want? What is it you're hiding, a secret life of crime fighting or maybe a wife with six kids?"

"A very suspicious nature." He laid a sharp knife down on several cloves of garlic, then smashed down with the palm of his hand.

She waited patiently for him to respond to her question. This was one question she needed answered. He walked over to the sink and washed his hands, then grabbed a towel from the rack and turned back to her as he leaned against the sink. "I'm not married, never have been, and I don't have any children and if I'm not mistaken, you asked me that already and I told you."

"So what *are* you hiding?"

"What makes you think that I'm hiding something?"

"Aside from the obvious, you have yet to answer a straight question about yourself."

"I just did." She nodded her acceptance of his answer. "Where is all this coming from?"

"I have rotten luck with men."

He found that hard to believe, yet from her dossier he knew it was true. She was beautiful; even in the casual jeans and sweater she wore, she was breathtaking. A jolt of honest sincerity hit him as his heart softened and reached out for her. In that moment he felt something that he hadn't felt in a long time. "I find that hard to believe."

"It's true," she said, slightly amused. "I've dated personalities ranging from Attila the Hun to a comatose Quasimodo. Then I bump into you, literally, and you're seemingly perfect on paper and off. The universe isn't that kind to me."

"You're not very trusting, are you?"

"No, I'm not."

"Maybe it's your time and our time together," Juwan said, then shuddered inside. The words slipped from his lips before he thought. He was feeling too much for her and it was jeopardizing his objectivity. He needed to detach but he knew that it was too late; he couldn't walk away, not now, maybe not ever.

"Maybe," she said, feeling a pull from her heart toward him. "And as you said before, I'm direct. I don't believe in wasting time, yours or mine. I know what I want, Juwan, plain and simple, no ties, no strings, no commitments and no drama when it's over because I don't intend to be around." He smiled and shook his head, knowing that he had read her perfectly. "I have money and my family has money. So if you're a gigolo, it's already been done too many times."

He turned off the heat beneath the pot of boiling water and the sauté pan, removed them from the stove then turned around to face her. Her expression was somber and serious. "I don't want your money, Kennedy."

"So the question remains, Juwan, who are you really and what do you want?"

"Honestly?" he offered as he approached her.

"Preferred." Kennedy steeled herself for the inevitable.

"My name is Juwan Mason . . ." He tipped her chin upward to his mouth, then paused just inches away from her lips. ". . . and I want you." He kissed her with consuming passion. She yielded, willingly blending her desire with his. The kiss lasted an eternity as their tongues intertwined in a maddening, erotic dance of seduction. Then the kiss slowed, ending in a gentle pull. He licked her lips, then his own, sending a burst of heat straight to the pit of her stomach, then further south.

". . . I want to kiss you and hold you and make love to you all night long. Then I want to start all over again in the morning. I want to taste every inch of your body from the top of your forehead to the bottoms of your feet. I want to fall asleep with you in my arms, then wake up with you pressed to my hungry body. I want to fill you completely, satisfy every fantasy you ever imagined. I want to find that sweet small spot on your body that makes you weak. Then I want to love that spot until you beg me for mercy. I want to hear you scream out my name when you reach your pleasure. And I want to do all this right now. That's what I want."

Juwan leaned back slightly, then reached out and touched her face. He gently stroked the sweet soft edge along the side of her brow down to her chin. He looked deep into her chocolate eyes, seeing the pain where layers of mistrust had built up over the years. Being used by others was apparently a part of her reality. It was what she was used to and what she expected.

And here he was—using her again.

But she had bought his line. He recognized the subtle change. She wanted to believe him, believe *in* him. And, for the time being, he'd let her. That's how he got close. He gained trust and then secrets flowed like water. He had succeeded; he had gotten to her, but deep down inside she had gotten to him, too.

"Is that okay with you?" he finally asked.

"Yeah." She nodded her head slowly, taken aback by his honesty. "That's okay with me." The perpetual runner in her had slowed down.

"Good. So I know what you want and you know what I

want. Are we gonna eat now or am I gonna find that small sweet spot?"

She smiled at the possibilities. "The only thing better than shrimp scampi with lobster and linguini . . ." she said as she reached around his neck and removed the apron he'd borrowed from her kitchen hook, ". . . is warmed up shrimp scampi with lobster and linguini." She slipped the ties over his head and tossed the apron on the table. He reached down and pinched the lit candles, extinguishing the flames. She took his hand, kissed the singed fingers then walked him from the kitchen, through the dining and living room, then up the stairs to the second floor.

In silence they went to her bedroom. She opened the door, he followed. He watched her as she walked to the nightstand, pulled out a couple of small golden packets and tossed them on the bed. She turned, their eyes met and held. Seeing him still by the door, she walked back to the center of the room, crooked her finger and beckoned to him. "Come here," she whispered, barely loud enough for him to hear. He came obediently. She reached up and slowly slid her hands down the front of his chest and stomach, feeling the taut firmness beneath his shirt. His muscles contracted, tightening at her touch.

Smiling and venturing further, she reached up and slowly began unbuttoning his shirt, keeping her eyes focused on his. When his shirt was completely undone, she spared a glance at her handiwork. Pleased, she draped the shirt back to his shoulders by spreading her hands wide. The chocolate smoothness of his chest was exposed. She reached up, guiding his shirt from his body with her hands, stopping along the way to enjoy the brawn of his body—pectorals, triceps and biceps.

He watched intently as she worked her magic on his body, enjoying every second of her exploration. When the shirt finally slid down his forearms to the floor, he leaned in and gently kissed and nuzzled her neck. Then he reached down, grasped the hem of her sweater and pulled it up over her head, letting it drop beside his discarded shirt.

He continued by unzipping her jeans, then bent down to ease them from her hips, thighs and calves. With little effort she stepped out of her jeans and kicked them away. Now, standing before him in black bra, matching hip-cut panties, heels and a smile, she boldly reached for the band of his pants.

She undid the belt, snap and zipper of his pants, then slowly eased them down his long muscular legs, purposely letting the back of her hand breeze past his groin. He breathed in deep and quick, then hissed, tensing at her touch.

She liked what she saw. He was solid, firm and powerfully built for long nights of leisurely pleasure. He gently coaxed her to turn around. She did. He laid his hands on her shoulders, relaxed, then took the elastic straps of her bra and pulled them down her shoulders and unsnapped her bra. It instantly fell away, releasing her pert breasts, nipples already hardened and pebbled.

From behind he ran his hands up her back, over her shoulders, then down her arms to her hands. He lifted her hands to his neck. She smiled remembering this same position from a few nights before. He gently slid his hands down the sides of her body, tempting her breasts, hips and thighs with the slightest touch. Then his tongue traced moist circles along her arm, shoulder and neck.

His hands came up along her hips and encircled her stomach. He ran his fingers along the elastic edge of her panties, sending a burning sensation through her body like lava flow from a swelling volcano. She moaned in anticipation and bit at her lower lip for relief. It didn't come.

He pressed her closer, back against the hardness of his body. She closed her eyes reveling in the sweet sensation of his touch. Feeling him so hard, so wanting, so ready, took her breath away. Her arms fell down of their own volition. But his assault continued. Tenderly teasing and tempting her, he was driving a maddening burn into her with every touch as he cradled her body, keeping her in place.

He stepped back but held her firmly until she regained her balance. He took her hand and together they moved to the side of the bed. He sat down, bringing her to him. When she was standing tucked securely between his legs, he opened his mouth and let his tongue barely touch the tip of her nipple. A sensation shot through her with the speed of a bullet. Her legs weakened and she instantly grabbed his shoulders to steady herself.

With torturous twists in scintillating circles, he teased the underside of her breast until she was completely breathless with anticipation. Seeing her reaction, he looked up at her. "Is this the sweet spot?" he asked, then answered his own question before she could reply. "No." He held her waist firmly and let his mouth trace a burning path down between her breasts to her stomach, then around the side to her hips just beneath the band of her panties. He nipped, sucked, kissed then licked. "Is this the spot?" he asked again. "No," he responded to himself again.

Incoherent rambling was all Kennedy heard. She had no idea what he was asking her and didn't much care. He was the artist and she was his willing clay, molding and stroking her at will. She was his for as long as he wanted.

"Is this the spot?" He rubbed his hands down the backs of her thighs as his kisses toyed with her navel. "No," he decided and proceeded further.

Working his way upwards, he lifted her to straddle his body as he sat on the side of the bed. She sat back on his knees, holding on as he captured a breast and suckled. The urgency of her desire and the slow torturous foreplay had her completely breathless.

She trembled as her nerve endings danced on edge and her fingernails dug into his shoulders. His hands, tongue and lips continued the search for the elusive sweet spot, feeling, touching, caressing every part of her body. He leaned down and kissed her and it came from nowhere, a gasping scream of blinding, uncontrollable pleasure. Her secret was out. He found it, her erogenous zone, her sweet spot, the one place on her body where desire was born.

She collapsed into him. Juwan held her close, secure in the knowledge that this was only the beginning of their pleasure. He smiled a knowing smile of a man having succeeded. He gently lowered her to the bed, then removed the last hindrance of their joining.

He reached onto the bed, opened one of the packets, and protected them. She reached out to him and he came to her, leaned down, barely touching. Her breast was in easy reach and he captured it with purpose and determination. She grabbed his shoulders, holding him as his kisses lowered. His tongue circled her stomach, his teeth nipped her hips, then his kisses devoured her. Writhing in ecstasy, she pulled at him but he refused. He had found a new pleasure to tempt her.

Blinding lights exploded before her as she held on and closed her eyes tight. He lifted her leg away and lovingly stroked the soft underside of her thigh while working his way down to her red toenails. Then his sweet sensual kisses continued back up. When he reached her neck, he stopped. Kennedy opened her eyes.

She had sizzled and simmered just to the brink of pleasure each time he touched her. He had mastered her body and was prepared to give her the ultimate pleasure. Strong, hard and ready, he hovered above her, eager and willing to seal their bond. His breathing was ragged and edgy. He wanted her. He needed her. The pain of his readiness was beyond even his endurance. But he needed her to be sure.

She focused on his eyes, she recognized the question he didn't ask. She smiled, then arched her hips as she grabbed his waist and pulled him down. Her unexpected move caught him off guard and his body slammed into her, filling her completely, in one thrust. She gasped with blinding pleasure. By the time he leaned back up, she had begun the rhythm of their joining. She led, he followed. He led, she followed.

The ultimate pleasure awaited them as each thrust propelled them closer. The hunger of their carnal appetite was unrestrained. The fierce intensity of each thrust signified the focused power of their desire. Pumping, throbbing, stroking, pulsating in a sexual binge surging ever forward, closer to the prize that awaited them. Back and forth, in and out, in rapid rhythmic movement they reached for the stars.

A moment later they captured the stars and the momentum of their passion burst through. In an instant the source of their release came and they opened up to it. In each other's arms, in a blasting, vibrating array of rapture, they found their ultimate sweet spot.

Then, drained, they lay in each other's arms, breathing the last remnants of pleasure. The release they'd sought and the blissful contentment they found left them sated and satisfied. The thirst, the hunger, the need, had all been quenched.

Juwan leaned up, then twisted his body to lie at her side. As he did, he reached out for her. She curled her body to his and together they held tight to each other until the next time she reached for him and found him needing her.

Later they ate and still the insatiable passion pulled at them until their explosive release came. Always wanting more, they made love again.

As dawn approached, Juwan slipped silently from the house. His last look at the sleeping Kennedy aroused the now familiar need to bury himself inside her. The too vivid memories of their lovemaking and the open sensuality of her body's movements beneath the sheet sent a burning desire surging through him. Anticipation began to swell but he resisted waking her.

The note he had left, worded precisely, gave no specifics. It only stated that he'd be away for a few days and would call her when he returned. But he knew that seeing her again would be dangerous, not mortally or physically but emotionally. He had opened his heart up to her to gain her trust and she had captured it. The game he had played so skillfully for years had finally turned on him. The seducer became the seduced and the hound became the prey.

He sat in his car, staring at the neat brownstone two stories up at the bedroom window fighting the urge to return to her side. His body craved her, his mind wanted her and his heart needed her. Like no one before, she had gotten to him. But he had set an operation in motion and had to finish it. No matter where it led. His basic instincts had always proved correct. Now, for the first time in his life, he prayed that he was right.

Chapter Twelve

The week went by in a blur of activity.

Friday had been a long day that seemed to drag since the week began. But the perpetual smile on Kennedy's face had outlasted her exhaustion. Memories of Monday night kept replaying in her mind. Juwan Mason was incredible. And if their one night together was any indication of his bodyguard abilities, then she was in for the major shake up she'd been searching for.

After working all week finalizing the displays, in the storage vaults at the museum, then spending all day Friday with insurance appraisers and revising the layout of the exhibit to suit their new requirements, the last thing Kennedy wanted to do was go home to an empty house. So she called her sister. "Are you up to some company?"

"Are you kidding? Definitely," Madison said. "Tony's working late, so bring lots of food and don't forget the milkshakes and desserts."

Reminiscent of their carefree, single days when either Madison would visit her in Washington or she would go to Philadelphia and visit, Kennedy prepared the usual. She went to their favorite eatery and purchased an elaborate spread of edibles ranging from barbecue ribs to shrimp and lobster, vegetarian pasta salad to double-dipped chocolate cake, apple cinnamon turnover pastries and lemon mousse cheesecake.

Madison met her at the front door just as Kennedy set the bags of food down to retrieve her sister's front door key. She pulled it out as Madison swung the door open to greet her. "What took you so long? I'm starved."

"You're always starved. Hey, what are you doing up? Shouldn't you still be in bed resting?"

"I have officially been given a reprieve, no contractions and no labor pains. I went to the doctor this morning. She said that everything looks good and the babies are in perfect health."

"Thank God," Kennedy said as she led the way to her sister's kitchen.

"Yumm, something smells fantastic, what did you get?" Madison said while rubbing her hands together.

"What didn't I get," Kennedy said as she placed the three gourmet bags on the kitchen table and began pulling out containers of food. As she placed the containers on the table, Madison immediately opened each one, taste-testing each.

Two hours later after laughing, talking, gossiping and eating, the sisters ended up out on the front balcony drinking thick chocolate milkshakes while flipping through baby catalogues and magazines, picking out last minute accessories for the two nurseries.

The evening sun had long since dipped its early fall rays beneath the lush landscape across the Potomac and the huge harvest moon emerged to shine brightly in the night sky. A comfortable breeze blew and the night sounds of traffic in the distance and the lapping waves added to the ambiance of the tranquil evening.

"This one is so adorable, I'm getting it," Kennedy announced, holding up the catalogue and showing Madison a large stuffed bear with a bowtie and top hat.

"Aw," she said, smiling brightly. "That is so sweet. That would be perfect in the Philadelphia nursery."

"How are you and Tony going to keep all of this straight? Two houses, two nurseries, two careers and two babies."

"Well, since I'm on extended leave of absence from the university, my career is pretty much on hold at the moment."

"Are you okay with that?" Kennedy asked, knowing her sister's love of teaching and her ambitious nature.

"Oh, yes," Madison smiled brightly. "Don't get me wrong, I have every intention of going back to work in the future. It's just that right now I want to take some time off to spend with the babies." She unconsciously rubbed and stroked her stomach, soothing the perpetual kicking.

"If I were in your place, I'd do the exact same thing."

"You will be—especially if Mamma Lou has anything to do with it," Madison said, jokingly. "She'll have you married so quickly you'll have no idea what happened. But you'll love every minute of it."

"I still can't believe how she does it, you and Tony, Raymond and Hope, even Dennis and Faith. And now that she's helped Mom match J.T. with Juliet, that woman is unstoppable."

"She certainly is," Madison said as she held up a magazine photo to show Kennedy, who crinkled her nose and shook her head disapprovingly. "I still think that either you or Trey might be next."

"Me, no way, I don't think so, not anymore, hopefully. She tried, but thank God, whoever the man was was nowhere in sight and she missed the opportunity. I haven't heard anything and neither has Trey. So we're thinking that she moved on to someone else a lot easier to deal with than either of us."

"I wouldn't bet on it," Madison said. "Just because she's not physically here doesn't mean that she doesn't already have something in place or already worked out."

"What do you mean?"

"She'll get you so panicked and worried about her matchmaking that you focus on her while you unconsciously let your guard down. Just look at J.T. and Juliet. He was so sure that he was being brilliant by getting Juliet to pose as his love interest and fool Mamma Lou that he never even realized that Juliet was the one Mama Lou had picked out for him all along."

"You make her sound like such a schemer," Kennedy said.

"No, she's not, really. She just loves the art of romance and the fine art of love. And once she gets you in her sights. . . . Talk about a lost cause, you might as well just give up and buy a wedding gown."

"True, but to her credit, her matches are perfectly suited." Kennedy paused to consider the couples she just mentioned.

"Yes, they are," Madison agreed, thinking of her husband and how Louise deceptively paired them.

"Speaking of Mamma Lou," Kennedy began, "why didn't you tell me that your grandmother-in-law knew half of the people in the Northern Hemisphere?"

"That doesn't surprise me at all. When did you see her?"

"She was at the embassy party Trey and I attended last Friday night. And, as I said, she tried to match me up with some art-loving FBI agent but thankfully she couldn't find him. He must have been hiding someplace."

"That's hysterical," Madison chuckled until she saw Kennedy's stern expression; then she laughed more. "Seriously, I didn't know she was even in town," she said, now slightly suspicious of the coincidence.

"Neither did I. I thought she was still tending her plants on Crescent Island. Oh, and you'll never guess who else was there." Madison took a long sip of her milkshake while shrugging her shoulders. "Mimi and Laine."

"Get out," Madison said as she set her cup down beside her. "Talk about coincidences."

Madison shook her head steadily. She knew that when Louise Gates got it in her mind to play matchmaker, she was as single-minded and determined as a category-five hurricane, completely impossible and unstoppable. The most innocent chance encounter was actually a major gain for her matchmaking schemes. "Are you sure that everything *was* just a coincidence—her being there, I mean?"

"Of course, she had no way of knowing in advance that I was going to be there or that Trey would be accompanying me. We didn't even know that she was in town." Then Kennedy paused, put the magazine she'd been flipping through down in her lap and looked over to her sister. "Wait, she knew, didn't she?"

Madison shrugged and chuckled. "Probably not, but you know Mamma Lou, she's a real piece of work."

"Do you think she could still be after me?"

Madison shook her head, seeing and knowing the outcome as clear as day. "Honestly, I have no idea."

"Find out," Kennedy insisted.

"How am I supposed to do that?"

"Ask her."

"I am not going to ask her. You want to know, you ask her."

"No, then she might think that I want her to match me up."

"Do you?" Madison said.

"No," Kennedy said immediately.

"Wait a minute," Madison said abruptly, "Mimi and Laine were both at the party—" Kennedy nodded while sipping her shake. "And Mamma Lou was there, too." Kennedy nodded again. "What if Mamma Lou wasn't there for either you or Trey? Maybe she was there for someone else."

Realizing what Madison was suggesting, Kennedy grinned, then began chuckling. "You don't think?"

"It's possible. Mimi's been trying to get Laine down that aisle since forever. Her best bet might be with Mamma Lou."

"Actually, that's an interesting supposition."

"I wonder who the guy is," Madison mused.

"As long as Mamma Lou's attention is focused elsewhere, I don't care." A slight pause in conversation lingered and Madison shook her head and Kennedy chuckled again.

"So how was the embassy party?" Madison finally asked.

"It was great. I think Trey fell in love with a Li'l Kim look-alike."

"That sounds about right."

"Shawn Anderson was there."

"How's he doing now?"

"Great, he looks good, real good," she emphasized.

"Really? Anything I should know about—like you making a sudden move to Hollywood?"

"No, movie stars aren't exactly my thing, you know that."

"Since when? You had a crush on his brother, Lance Morgan, since forever, at least before he got married."

"Well, that was before."

"Before what?" Madison questioned, knowing that Kennedy was up to something and wanting to make sure she wasn't leaving the house until she told her everything.

"Before Juwan."

"Juwan," Madison repeated with interest.

"Juwan Mason."

"Wait a minute. There's a Juwan Mason who's making you blush just by saying his name and you weren't gonna say anything to me?"

"I'm telling you now."

"That's not the point." She looked down at her watch, then back up at Kennedy. "You've been sitting in my house for over three hours and you just now decide to mention that there was a Juwan Mason in the picture."

"The conversation didn't come up until now."

"Don't give me that. Since when does any man who can make you blush not get top billing in our conversations?"

"Madi, really, there's not much to tell."

"Details, I need details. I've been stuck in that bedroom for days. I'm about to go insane and you have juicy gossip and you wait until now to say something. Girl, if you know what's good for you, you'd better talk fast."

"Okay, okay, but as I said, there's not much to tell, I

actually just met him last Friday. He's a freelance bodyguard at the Nubian embassy and he protects Ambassador Mebeko. He's tall, dark and handsome with the most sinfully devilish smile I've ever seen, although he doesn't show it much. He does that whole bodyguards-never-smile-stern-face thing most of the time. He's traveled the world and apparently lives abroad, but is here on assignment. I don't know for how long."

"He sounds perfect for you. Tall, dark and dangerous—the typical bad boy. Just your type."

"No, not anymore. I've learned my lesson. No more bad boys for me." Madison arched her brow, looking doubtful.

"Okay," Kennedy continued. "Granted they're usually a lot more fun and exciting as long as you don't get caught up in their drama or emotionally involved with them."

"Because they break your heart," Madison said.

She nodded. "Because they completely obliterate your heart if you let them."

"But you never do."

"That's right, I never do, never will." Kennedy spoke from experience. She often found herself attracted to men with exciting careers or who lived extraordinary lives. Petre was one. He was bold and daring and had his finger on the pulse of just about everything happening in Nubia. But he was too much even for her. And although she had tried to change him, he was too far gone. The lifestyle he led had too strong a pull on him. And she wasn't at all surprised to find out that he was involved with the museum theft.

"A world-traveling bodyguard and he's not a bad boy?" Madison asked skeptically.

"Well, maybe just a little."

"Okay, tell me more, what else?" Madison asked.

"He's funny, sexy and smart. He can cook and dance and as usual, he's hiding the biggest secret in the world."

Madison, having inched forward in her seat and been

completely enthralled by Kennedy's description, was taken aback by the last remark. "What?"

"He's hiding something."

"Hiding something like what, is he married?"

"No."

"Gay?"

"Most definitely not."

"Bank robber, drug dealer, number one on the FBI's ten most wanted list?"

"No, nothing like that."

"So what makes you think that he's hiding something?"

"You know how you get that feeling that something is wrong and you dismiss it? Then you find out later that your first instinct was right. And you've been dating a jerk all along."

"Are you kidding, remember me? I was the original jerk magnet for years."

"Ditto. I've dated enough men to know when they're hiding something."

"Well, maybe that's the reason you're so suspicious. You're used to dating men who aren't up front with you. You've become jaded."

"I don't know, Madi. I tell you, if I didn't know any better, I'd say he was leading some kind of double life."

"You mean like Clark Kent and Superman? Now that would be too interesting."

"No way. I don't think I could date the cloak-and-dagger type, too many secrets and way too many lies. There's no way I could trust a word he told me."

"But he's not, so don't worry about it. This is probably all for nothing and your imagination is just on overdrive because of everything that's goin' on at the moment. What else about him?"

"He loves art and, believe it or not, actually understands it. He's got this quiet brooding passion thing going on that's just too sexy."

"Okay, now the good stuff," Madison prompted, arching her brow meaningfully with a giant sisterly smile.

"He's built like an African warrior, tall, strong, firm, but not that bodybuilding muscle type. He's got light-colored eyes, hazel green, with rich milk chocolate skin. He looks incredible in his clothes and, believe it or not, even better without them."

"No, you didn't," Madison said, her mouth wide open.

"Yes, we did."

"No. What?" Kennedy nodded her head slowly, affirming her sister's assumption. "You did?"

"We did."

"When? I thought you said that you just met last Friday night at the embassy."

"Actually we met earlier at the museum. We literally bumped into each other and I nearly fell on my face, but he caught me just in time. In the process I wound up very intimately pressed against him."

"Hell of a first meeting," Madison remarked.

"Tell me about it. Anyway, we kissed that first night at the embassy reception. Talk about curling toes, the man has serious kissing talent. We were out in the garden, then in his suite, and if Trey hadn't called on the cell and interrupted us, I actually considered dragging him down and ripping his clothes off."

"I can't believe you did that! You are so bad." They laughed like silly school girls. "Well, you've always been wonderfully spontaneous. You're bold and extraverted. And when you see something you want or something you want to do, you just go after it, full force. I've always envied that about you."

"Don't envy that, being impulsive has gotten me into major hot water over the years and will probably get me into serious trouble some day."

"Nothing you can't handle and get out of." Madison shook her head and grinned at her sister. "Sucking face in the garden and in the suite of a man you just met? Talk about not playing hard to get."

"I know, I know. It's crazy, but what can I say? I was possessed."

"Possessed nothing. You were horny."

"Yeah, well, that too." They laughed so hard that Madison had to make a quick run to the bathroom. As soon as she returned, she sat back down and insisted that Kennedy continue. She did, outlining Monday night in careful but limited detail.

"So where is he tonight?"

"Away," Kennedy said. The noncommittal answer seemed to suggest more. "He's been away all week, working."

"I guess that makes him perfect for you."

"Yeah, I guess it does." Kennedy's expression sobered.

"So what happens next since you insist on dating only men with a limited shelf life?" Madison teased.

"Casual dating has always worked for me."

"I know, transient and temporary. It's always the same. Either he was leaving or you were. I bet even this guy has an expiration date stamped on his forehead and he doesn't even know it."

"For me, falling in love is way too much responsibility, you know that. It always seemed overrated, messy and a waste of time. But I have to admit Juwan does make the idea awfully tempting."

"Now that's something new. I've never heard you say anything like that before."

"I know, I know," she smiled wistfully and continued. "He's a phenomenal lover and an interesting man and if there was any man out there who could stop my running, he'd be the one."

"Seriously?" Madison asked in all sincerity. Kennedy nodded. "He got to you, didn't he?"

Kennedy didn't answer. She didn't know what to say.

There was no way she could fall for a guy after knowing him for a single week, could she?

"I don't know, maybe all this running away from life has finally come back to haunt me. Or maybe after all these years I'm just finally falling in . . ." Hearing footsteps, she turned to see who was coming.

"What?" Madison prompted. Excited to hear the next word, she followed Kennedy's line of vision to the doorway where Tony stood smiling.

"Hi, Tony," Kennedy said sweetly.

Madison, anxious and completely impatient for more gossip, moaned, knowing that she wasn't going to hear the rest of Kennedy's last comment. "Hi, honey," she said as he approached and kissed her on the forehead and stroked her belly.

Kennedy chuckled at Madison's obvious lack of enthusiasm.

"I get the feeling that I arrived at a bad time," Tony said.

"No, not at all," Kennedy said as she stood to leave. "I just stopped by to keep Madi company until you got home. It was just girl talk, nothing special." She winked at her sister, then reached down and gave her a hug. "See ya later, sweetie. I'll call you tomorrow," she said as she headed to the balcony door.

"You'd better," Madison warned.

"Oh and Tony," Kennedy said. He turned to her. "Your grandmother was kind enough to introduce Trey and me to the vice president of the United States and the secretary of state."

"Why am I not surprised?" Madison said, shaking her head.

"I never am," Tony admitted, "not anymore."

Chapter Thirteen

Tuesday afternoon Juwan flew to the New York field office. Wednesday morning he went to London's attaché office and Friday afternoon he was back in the New York office. After slipping back into his black market supplier persona and going back out into the field, he came up with some interesting information. He'd been meeting with informants, securing intel and gathering data. In essence he was building his case and as always it was going to be rock solid. But, unfortunately, everything he'd turned up so far pointed in a different direction from what he expected.

Barry Culpepper, his suspected connection to the Nubian Museum theft and his new target, had covered his tracks extremely well. He had faded into the shadows, letting the men in Africa take the fall. Now, by the looks of the investigation, it appeared that Barry had done more than just cover his tracks. He had effectively cast suspicion completely away from himself. But Juwan's gut feeling was strong. He saw Barry's interest when he mentioned his black-market ties. The glint in his eyes was unmistakable. He'd seen it many times before. It was greed. He left Barry considering the offer, tempted by the proposal.

He was interested and Juwan knew that the money they

talked about was too tempting for Barry to pass up. Juwan had played it as one last score before retiring. There was no way Barry would pass on it.

For two months he had searched for the elusive connection between the two museums. But the only name prominently mentioned in Petre's notes was Kennedy Evans. All leads pointed to her; she was the connection. There were three meets listed, each right after a major theft had taken place. Petre was picked up with two pieces in his possession. One more was still missing and that was unacceptable. The agency, the local government and the insurance companies were after someone's head and his job was to find that someone.

He had a responsibility to report his findings. But his findings didn't satisfy him. He needed more time. He needed to find proof that Kennedy wasn't involved and that Barry was Petre's partner. He needed to be sure. Could she be playing him? Was she good enough to fool a professional? He knew Kennedy's file. She thrived on excitement and a crime like the museum robbery could be an adrenaline rush.

He pored over Kennedy's financial records with a fine-toothed comb. She was independently wealthy and didn't even need to work, yet she did. Daughter of the entrepreneurs, Jace and Taylor Evans, owners and founders of Evans Corporation, a multi-national computer company, she could buy and sell most of the art she treasured so deeply. Why then would she chance stealing and involving herself in the black market?

Everything he had on her and her family checked out clean. She was an ordinary woman paying taxes and living the American dream. Granted she was worth millions, so that was hardly motive for becoming an art theif. No, he had to be missing something. Something not as obvious, something, of course, he muttered aloud. "Love, the ultimate motive."

Love, he concluded. Shameless and without reason, the power of love could make the sanest, most completely lucid person do the most irrational, foolish and bizarre things. A man in love was useless; a woman in love was putty in the right hands.

Remy was in love and it had killed her.

Had Kennedy been in love with Petre?

"Welcome back to work. How was your vacation? What was it, all of seventy-two hours?"

Juwan looked up. His friend and associate Kevin Pole stood in the doorway with a file in his hands. "Yeah, something like that, give or take an hour."

"How long are you staying?" Kevin asked.

"Don't get your hopes up. I have a six o'clock flight to D.C." He looked at his watch to confirm the time. "I'll stop by and see Yasmine before I go."

"Good idea," Kevin said as he moseyed into the office while reaching for his hand-held computer. He scanned several screens until he came up with the one he was looking for. He made an exaggerated face and shook his head miserably.

"What?" Juwan asked, annoyed, seeing the dramatic production.

"Oh nothing, just checking to see who had seventy-two hours in the office pool. Ouch, looks like we owe Ian lunch. Damn," he said, shaking his head again. "Have you seen that man eat? There goes my pension."

"You guys either need more work or seriously need a new hobby." Juwan shook his head, not at all surprised at the office wagering on how long it would take for his return to the office or Kevin's joking.

His office staff knew him well, and Kevin in particular knew him too well. They'd been good friends since he had taken Kevin under his wing; Kevin had come up through the FBI ranks in Juwan's shadow, following his career footsteps perfectly. Over the years they had faced danger, tragedy, and death and now they were in-laws, brothers.

"Heard you were in London."

"Yeah, I needed to check a new lead."

"Did you get what you needed?"

"No, not quite."

"Anything I can help with?"

Juwan sat back in his chair. "Yeah, tell me about the National Museum of African Art," Juwan said.

"Washington, D.C. Major offerings in contemporary and ancient art. Classified as division three. Cited a few years back to section G9."

"Receiving stolen property," Juwan said.

"The piece in question was returned almost immediately."

"Nothing after that?" Juwan asked.

"I can check but if there was a more recent red flag, I would know."

"See what else you can dig up about the principals, especially Barry Culpepper, his background, previous connections to Petre and other museum robberies."

Kevin nodded. "Sure, you think he's involved?"

"Yeah, but it's just a gut instinct."

"Your gut instinct is oftentimes better than a room full of intel. You'd better get going."

"You're right. I have just enough time to make a quick stop to see Yasmine, then catch my flight." He stood up and grabbed his briefcase. "Keep in touch."

After coming home from her sister's house, Kennedy relaxed across her bed as visions of Juwan and their night together brought the smile back to her lips. She picked up his note and read it again. Something she found herself doing too often. Simply worded, it was exactly something she would have written before. She paused. *Before.*

Impulsively she picked up her cell phone and called Hoyt. He answered on the first ring. "Hi, Hoyt, it's Kennedy."

"Hey, how are you?"

"Fine, I know you're busy, but I have a quick question about one of your security men, Ambassador Mebeko's bodyguard. I was told that he'd be unavailable for a while. Do you know when he'll be back in town?"

Hoyt immediately assumed that she spoke about Tyson, Maurice's missing bodyguard. "I really can't say. I don't know exactly what the problem is, just that it has something to do with immigration."

"Immigration?" she repeated.

"Yeah, we're trying to sort it out but it doesn't look like he'll be with us long. Why, do you have someone else in mind that we could use?"

"No, I was just curious as to what happened to him."

"Listen I have a meeting in a few minutes, I'll call you back later tonight."

"No, don't bother. It was just a quick question."

"Okay, I'll call you next week. We'll do lunch."

"That sounds great, bye."

As soon as she hung up, the phone rang again. She picked up. "Hello."

"You're a hard woman to catch up with."

"Petre?"

"Yes."

"What do you want?"

"I need money." Petre was rushed and nervous. His accent was thick.

"I can't help you."

"You have money."

"Yes, I do. But I can't help you."

"We need to talk."

"We don't have anything to say to each other."

"I think we do. I can offer you information, important information. You can buy it. I'll call you back in a few days."

He hung up but Kennedy held onto the phone. She

couldn't let go. Why is it that nightmares never leave you? They just fade into the background and wait patiently for a moment of weakness. Then when that weakness comes, they pounce, rearing up from the sewer, bringing you back to reality.

Her heart sank as her thoughts spun wildly. It hit her like a ton of bricks. A cold chill shot through her as her breathing became labored and her palms moistened, cold, clammy and icy. Her mind dashed in a thousand different directions and her heartbeat thundered so fast it felt as if it would jump from her body. The weight of an anvil sat on her chest and her nerve endings spiked through her skin like millions of needles. She was frenzied, about to jump out of her skin, and she couldn't stop herself. She'd been besieged by her traitorous body again.

She stood up and paced the floor in a swift rapid tread, going nonstop to nowhere. "Stop it," she told herself to no avail. But the panic symptoms continued full force. Beleaguered and overwhelmed, she plopped down on the chair with her eyes closed and her hands still holding a murderous grip on the telephone. She took in large gulps of air through clenched teeth, hoping that the rush of oxygen would lessen the anxiety. It didn't.

So she sat in full panic mode waiting for the end. It came ten minutes later when her breath caught and finally eased. She lay back against the cushions of the bedroom chaise. Her heart still pounded and her breathing was still choppy but not as it had been moments ago.

She got up and went into the bathroom to splash cold water on her face. Then after wiping dry she looked at her reflection in the mirror. Although Petre had called, it was Hoyt's words that echoed through the muddled uncertainty of her mind.

"Immigration. Deportation," she whispered aloud to the empty room. The words often went hand in hand these days. That's what he was hiding; he was having problems with immigration. He was being deported. And here she was feel-

ing sorry for herself because he didn't call and he was strug-
gling to stay in the country.

Then the blaring sound of the phone off the hook drew her
attention. Realizing that she'd dropped the receiver by the
chair, she picked it up and placed it back in the cradle. Just
as she hung up the receiver, the phone rang.

She picked it up instantly. "Hello." Her voice was notice-
ably shaky.

"Kennedy?"

"Yes."

"Hey, it's Juwan."

"Juwan?" She questioned her hearing. Was she imagining
him? Could wanting something really make it happen?

"Are you all right?" he asked, immediately concerned by
the pause in her tone. "You sound upset."

The tremble in her voice remained. "No, I'm fine. I'm glad
you called."

"I told you I would."

"I know but . . ." she paused, not wanting to let on that she
knew about his problem. "Things happen."

"Feel like a little company?"

"Uh, sure. Where are you?"

"About to ring your doorbell."

Just then the sound of her doorbell echoed through the
house. She looked to the open bedroom door. He was already
here. She ran her fingers through her frazzled hair and went
downstairs trying to calm herself with each step. When she
reached the front door, she paused to mentally will herself
to at least seem relaxed and in control. The bell rang again.
She took a deep breath and opened the door.

Juwan stood on her doorstep impatiently waiting to be let
in. There was something going on, he could hear it in her
voice. She was tense and edgy and although she denied it,
there was definitely something wrong.

As soon as she opened the door, he saw it in her eyes. She

looked away, allowing him to step inside. He continued behind her as she walked away. "Are you going to tell me what's going on?" He looked around the immediate area for any sign that someone was there or had been there recently.

She turned, smiling brightly. "Nothing's going on. I told you before, I'm fine. It was a long day, a long week. I'm just tired and I didn't expect to see you."

"I left a note. You were sleeping so peacefully I didn't want to wake you." His smile was hesitant. Then he shrugged. "Actually," he continued, "that's not exactly true. I did want to wake you."

"I got that part in your note. I just wasn't sure if you'd be back. It is okay for you to be here, isn't it?"

He was puzzled. "Of course it is; why wouldn't it be?"

"No reason. I know you're busy with the ambassador. I don't want you to jeopardize anything just to see me." Although she didn't know him well, she did know that he was a proud man. So she'd keep his secret and Hoyt's confidence and not bring up their immigration conversation.

"You're worth it."

"I'm glad you came by."

"Do you want to tell me what's troubling you?"

"It's a long story."

"I have plenty of time."

"What do you do about nightmares that won't go away?"

"You wake up," he said simply.

"Easier said than done."

"Tell me about this nightmare."

She paused and sat down on the living room sofa. He sat next to her.

"I had a friend who messed up pretty bad; got himself in deep trouble. He did some stupid things. He stole from his job and was about to sell the stolen goods. But apparently the whole thing was a set up and the buyer was an undercover agent. Everybody got caught but now he's on the run."

A cold chill went through Juwan. She had just described his associate Colin's last assignment. "Where is he now?"

"I don't know."

"Has he contacted you?"

"Yeah, he just called a few minutes ago."

Juwan went still. Petre had contacted Kennedy. He made a mental note to get a phone tap release on Kennedy's phone lines. "What exactly did he say?"

"Nothing much, just that he needed cash and that he'd call again."

"When?"

"I don't know. He didn't say."

"Kennedy, this is important, were there others involved, other than the men you said were caught?"

She shook her head. "I don't know, maybe."

"Did your friend ever mention anyone else, a partner?"

"I don't know, maybe. Yeah, I think he did once. He said something like, 'we have it planned.'" Then she relayed the conversation word for word.

Juwan was beyond amazed. "How did you do that?"

"What?"

"Remember the exact conversation like that."

"It's called eidetic imagery. It's like having a photographic memory but I have it with words. I remember conversations."

"That's amazing. Does your friend know you have this talent?"

"No. Few people know. It unnerves them for some reason."

Juwan nodded. That definitely wasn't in her file. "Okay, getting back to your friend's partner. Have you ever met him? Do you know who he is?"

"No, I have no idea. Can we talk about something else?"

Juwan nearly broke. His patient easy interrogation was about to become a lot less gentle. But he couldn't chance it. He couldn't push her by asking too many questions and appearing overly anxious. He decided that there'd be another time and he'd get his answers then. But for right now the important thing was that Petre had resurfaced and he had contacted Kennedy just like he knew he would. "Sure."

"Thanks."

"For what?"

"For listening, for not playing the macho hero and attempting to do something about the situation when there's really nothing anyone can do."

"Your friend needs to give himself up."

"I know, but he won't."

Juwan stood up suddenly and grabbed her hand. "Come on, get up, I want to show you something."

Kennedy stood and followed. "Show me what? Where are we going?"

"You'll see. Come on. Trust me."

Chapter Fourteen

In another fit of laughter Kennedy shook her head, still in the afterglow of the night they'd just spent together. "I can't believe we just did that. That was incredible. You are incredible. I really needed that."

"I did, too," he chuckled to himself, remembering their adventurous evening. "But actually I believe it was the company that made the night incredible," he added as his eyes grazed over her in the darkness. He reached out, took her hand and gently squeezed it. Then it hit him soberly, she was the best thing to happen to him and he was going to lose her.

He turned away just as she looked over to him. There was a steadily growing part of him that hated lying to her. But it was his job to get the truth. Unfortunately, his job was getting too personal and for the first time that he could remember, he was getting too personal about his job, about her. He was losing his objectivity and the feeling stilled him. From the start he had been too attached to her, even before they'd actually met.

He remembered the time when he first read her dossier. On paper she was his ideal counterpart. They were both adventurous loners with a love of art and a sense of justice and beauty. And in every action they seemed to fit perfectly. He could easily see himself being with her for a lifetime.

Their relationship, such as it was, was confusing and complicated. And in the short time since they'd been together, he was well on his way to falling in love with her. But he knew that as soon as she found out what he was, who he was and what he was actually doing, she would despise him and he would lose her. What he needed was more time, time to think and time to circumnavigate the inevitable outcome.

The psychology of manipulating outcomes was his specialty. He'd maneuvered and controlled situations, events and people to suit his purposes for a living. He studied their faults and frailties and desires, then used subtle tactics to effect the outcome. He'd done it time after time, why couldn't he do it this time? Why couldn't he manipulate this outcome?

The answer came as soon as he formulated the question. He was betraying her friendship, her trust, and—he looked over to her profile—her love. His feelings for her were jeopardizing the mission and his job. His sense of duty was strong. But he needed to protect her as well. Barry had covered his tracks and in doing so he had maliciously paved a path directly to Kennedy. On paper she was as guilty as the rest of them. But Juwan knew better; he just needed more time to prove it.

When this went down and Petre and Barry were caught, he needed to make sure that Kennedy was completely absolved and safe. But there was no way to guarantee that outcome. He'd have to find a way to save her.

"I should have known that you were an adrenaline junkie," Kennedy said jokingly, interrupting his troubled thoughts.

"Me? No way," he said, trying to sound lighthearted. "I didn't know that you were such a daredevil. Ten roller coasters in one night? That has to be some kind of record."

"I know, I'm still dizzy," she confessed with a bright smile and a devilish chuckle.

"Some of those drops were unreal."

"And I loved every minute of it," she said, "especially that whirling, twirling and spinning-out-of-control one that did a 360-degree triple loop. It spiraled backwards, then forwards, and in a split second hits you with zero gravity as you hover in midair."

"Which one was that? You just described every roller coaster we went on tonight."

She laughed again. "I guess you're right about that. After a while they all seem to be about the same. They were all pretty heart-stopping."

"You're pretty fearless, aren't you?"

"That's one of my bigger problems, I love the adrenaline rush. That's why I only drive my motorcycle early in the morning. Usually no one's out and I can pretty much tear the road up. That is if there're no cops around, of course."

"So speed demon, what else do you do?"

"I jump out of airplanes, hang glide, and surf and pretty much anything else I can think of. I love the thrill."

"That's way too much for me."

"Really? That's surprising. I would have thought that you were exactly the same."

"What would make you think that?"

"You're a bodyguard. Isn't that why you became one, the danger and excitement of the life?" she asked, changing the subject to something more personal.

"Maybe," he said noncommittally. "I guess I never thought about it like that before."

"You put your life on the line every day for clients you hardly know. How do you do that?"

"It's a job."

"But it's more than that. It's a way of life, isn't it?"

"Yeah, I guess it is," he responded truthfully. "I love my work. It's satisfying. I get to right a lot of wrongs and in the long run that's what it's all about. I protect people and save people from themselves."

She nodded her head slowly, appreciating his candor and honesty. "That sounds incredible."

"So," he began, sparing a quick glance at her as he drove, "is that why you're attracted to me, the danger of my job?"

"I am not a danger groupie, if that's what you're asking."

"Now who's being evasive and not answering questions?" Kennedy smiled as he tossed her words back at her. "No, that's not why I'm attracted to you. I'm just a sucker for a sweet line from a handsome face."

Juwan burst into laughter, then nodded, having enjoyed the compliment. "That's good to know."

"What about you, why me?" she asked.

"I love your personality. You're sweet and funny and have a good heart. You're smart, talented, love art and that's only for starters. You respect yourself and others and I enjoy being with you too much for my own good."

She smiled, liking the simplicity of his answer.

"Oh," he added. "Did I mention that you were also sexy as hell?"

Kennedy laughed happily. "Ditto."

The moment passed as she relaxed back against the car's leather interior. The smooth ride was exactly what she needed after the excitement of the evening.

"So what are we gonna do with all these?" she asked as she brushed at the stuffed-animal fur and spiking its whiskers.

"I thought we'd drop them off," he said as he pulled off the highway several exits before leaving Virginia.

"Oh, no," she protested. "We can't trash them. You worked so hard to win them, shooting basketballs and hitting silly clown faces. I don't care how easy you made it look. All they need is a good home. I'm sure some child would love to play with them," she said, turning around to look in the backseat, which was filled with teddy bears, snakes, kittens, dogs, superheroes and other stuffed animals, dolls and toys.

"No, we won't trash them," he said as he pulled into the

hospital parking lot. He checked the sign and followed the arrows to the emergency room children's ward. "My sister has a friend in the pediatric ward here. She's always talking about how the kids love having cuddly stuffed animals with them when they're sick. It makes them feel better."

Kennedy smiled. It was the perfect solution. She looked over to Juwan. So much for menacing bodyguard and strong, silent type. He was just a sweet softy who apparently had a soft heart for sick children.

He parked. "I'm gonna run in and see if she's on duty tonight. I'll be right back." He got out and disappeared through the sliding glass doors, then returned a few minuets later with a huge empty rolling cart. As he approached the car, Kennedy rolled down the window. "She'll take them all."

"Wonderful, I'll help." Kennedy got out of the car and together they loaded the toys onto the three-tiered cart and rolled it back into the hospital.

An older woman in her early sixties dressed in a Bugs Bunny and Daffy Duck smock with white pants and sneakers greeted them as soon as the entered. With salt-and-pepper hair, deep chocolate skin, and a warm inviting smile, she began chuckling as soon as she saw the overloaded cart. "Oh, Juwan, look at them. They're so sweet. The kids are gonna love these." She grabbed one of the smaller stuffed animals and fluffed its fur. "Thank you so much. You are such a dear." She reached up and gently patted his face. Then she glanced as if noticing Kennedy for the first time. "Hello, are you a friend of Juwan's?"

"Yes," Kennedy said as she extended her hand to shake. "Hi, I'm Kennedy Evans. How are you?"

"Fine, just fine. I'm Barbara Cole."

"Where would you like them?" Juwan asked.

"Just put them in my office. I'll see that they get distributed between the ER and the children's ward tomorrow." Juwan nodded and continued rolling through the large double doors.

Kennedy and the older woman followed at a slower pace. "So you must be the young lady responsible for getting Juwan to finally slow down and stop by for a visit. He's always so busy traveling with that job of his."

"Yes, I can imagine. He's very busy."

"So how long have the two of you been seeing each other?" Kennedy's jaw dropped and she went speechless. She was surprised by the forwardness of the question. "Oh, don't mind me, Kennedy. I've known Juwan and his sister since the accident. You must be very special to him. He's never brought anyone else here. But a word of advice," she said. Kennedy nodded encouragingly. "Take care of him. He's not as tough as he lets on, but then again none of us are."

Kennedy's brow rose. The word *accident* jumped out immediately, but since the woman didn't elaborate, Kennedy didn't question it. "Actually Juwan and I have only just recently started going out."

"Really, and he brought you here?" Kennedy nodded, slightly interested. "Already?" she continued. Kennedy nodded again, even more curious. "Now that's interesting."

"Is it?" Kennedy said, completely fascinated.

"Very," she said, her smile broad and bright as she nodded her approval. She apparently knew something that Kennedy didn't. "Come on, Juwan's probably in there with the kids and forgotten all about us."

True enough, Juwan was sitting in the hall talking with a little boy holding firmly onto one of the superhero stuffed toys from the cart. They were nodding their heads, agreeing to something. Juwan stood up as the little boy handed something to him and he put it in his jacket pocket.

The woman leaned over to Kennedy. "They love meeting him and seeing his badge. It makes them feel safe somehow," she said in a hushed tone, so as not to disturb the special moment.

"Does Juwan come here often?" Kennedy asked curiously.

"Not for a while. But before, after the accident, he was here every day for two months straight."

Kennedy's brow rose again. That was the second time she mentioned *the accident*. She wanted to ask questions about the accident and about Juwan's past, but she held herself back. Whatever she needed to know, Juwan would tell her in time.

She watched with lighthearted amusement as Juwan reached down and shook hands with the young boy. Then they slapped hands street-style. And finally the young boy giggled, then burst into laughter as he tried to jump up to reach Juwan's hovering hand to give him a high five. Afterwards they nodded a secret agreement.

"Ready?" he asked her as he approached. She nodded. He leaned down and hugged Barbara, promising to visit again as soon as possible. They left as the young child, holding Barbara's hand, walked back to his hospital room.

"That was so sweet," Kennedy said as they passed through the inside door.

Juwan turned for one last look at the little boy and Barbara. "He has another operation tomorrow and he's scared. He said the Spiderman was his favorite."

Kennedy couldn't speak. She was too moved. They walked back to the car in silence, she with her thoughts and he with his.

The appeal of a strong man giving comfort to a small child brought a tear to Kennedy's eyes. She was touched.

The lingering doubts about Juwan hiding something faded away in the night as he drove her back to her house. "Do you want to come in?"

He smiled knowing that neither one of them was in the mood for a night of passion. "No, I'd better go. Can I see you tomorrow evening?"

"Yes. I'd like that."

"Good, I'll call you."

She nodded. "I had a wonderful time, Juwan, thank you."

"You're very welcome." He leaned in to kiss her. With passion and fire, it was long and lingering and the perfect ending to the perfect night.

As she walked upstairs to her bedroom alone she realized that she had fallen for Juwan. He had opened her heart and that this night was the beginning she'd been searching for all her life. Juwan was the man and the dream. He was everything she'd ever hoped to find and more. Unfortunately, it was only a matter of time before immigration caught up with him and he was out of her life.

Chapter Fifteen

The steadfast dullness of her heart's pain had eaten at her from sunup to sundown each day for the past three weeks. Her mornings and afternoons were spent at the museum with the exhibit and evenings and nights were spent with Juwan. Knowing that she had approaching deadlines on both, she felt each was frustrating and stressful in its own way, but to her surprise, she hadn't had a panic attack. The clock was ticking deafeningly louder and louder and she felt as though she was spinning her wheels on both.

Hoyt's words echoed in her mind like the chime of a vibrating bell. *Something to do with immigration.* She knew that could only mean one thing. Given the current climate of suspicion and unease in the nation, it was completely possible for Juwan to be deported at a moment's notice. It was frustrating to know that any minute she would get a call from Juwan saying that he could longer be with her because he had to leave the country.

The phone rang. Her heart jumped. She looked at it sitting on her desk as if it were a foreign object she'd never seen before. "Hello," she said tentatively.

"Hey, beautiful."

The sweet sound of Juwan's playful voice immediately

lifted her spirits. "Hey, yourself." She smiled, relieved by his upbeat mood and the reprieve.

"Are you busy tonight?"

"Well, actually I was going to work late tonight. There are a million things to do still and hanging around with you is bad for my work ethic. And also I have a late meeting with Barry."

Juwan hesitated. Barry had just called him and set up a meeting for this evening to discuss his purchase of the stolen art. "Not tonight, tonight is special."

"Why is tonight special?" she asked.

He paused a moment to quickly think of a valid reason to get her out of the museum and out of the house. "It's our anniversary."

"Our what, anniversary?"

"Sure, we bumped into each other exactly four weeks ago today."

"No, we didn't, we met on a Friday, today is Wednesday."

"Close enough," he said.

"Since when are you the frivolous sentimental type?"

"Since I met you."

She blushed. "What do you have in mind for tonight?"

"Let's dance."

She laughed happily. The man had of way of amazing her at the oddest moments with the most wonderful surprises. "That sounds like a fantastic idea."

"Great. How about dinner at seven-thirty first? If you leave there by six, I'll meet you dressed and ready at your house at seven with dinner in hand."

"I can't wait, it sounds perfect, but let me take care of dinner, you bring the wine." He agreed; then they said their goodbyes and hung up.

Afterwards Kennedy sat at her desk and stared at the blank computer screen with a silly expression on her face. Just a few moments earlier she'd been dreading the future. Now, all of a sudden, she couldn't wait until tonight. She shook her head. Juwan had an amazing effect on her. How do you stop thinking about a man who's only temporary, both in your life and in the country?

It was her fault. It was how she set it up, how she always set it up. Love 'em and leave 'em. Now the joke was on her. She wanted more. She wanted the whole thing.

She left her office and headed to the exhibit area. Just as she entered the exhibit, Barry called her name. She turned to him.

"Kennedy, about tonight," he began as he approached, "I have a personal situation that just recently came up. Can we change our meeting tonight until ten o'clock tomorrow?"

"I'll be in New York tomorrow. How about Friday? I have my final shipment coming in so I'll definitely be here."

"Actually, that would be even better for me," Barry said.

"Good, I'll see you then." Kennedy smiled happily. The exhibit was almost complete, her meeting tonight had been canceled, and she was going dancing with Juwan. "Perfect," she said aloud just before entering the exhibit.

Juwan, having finished his briefing and reading the transcripts of the wiretap on Kennedy's phone and learning of Barry's current movements, was completely stumped. He laid the data on the desk and frowned as he looked away. Kennedy had mentioned that she had a meeting with Barry this evening. So why would Barry want Kennedy in on their meeting? The thought worried him.

He had called Kennedy to get her out of the museum so that he could meet with Barry unseen and here it seemed that Barry had already included her in their arrangement. "No," Juwan said aloud to the empty room. "That can't be right. There has to be another explanation." Juwan drummed his pen on the desk in anxious frustration. If he had to testify to this meeting in his final report, it wouldn't look good for Kennedy.

He haphazardly tossed the pen across the desk. This wasn't going to work. He needed to follow his first instincts. He needed to voice his concerns, then back off. Gaining her trust and getting close to her had jeopardized everything. He had never allowed his heart to rule his head until now.

He needed a valid reason for her to be there with Barry tonight. But the facts were the facts and every plausible scenario he conceived came up empty. So, if she was to be there this evening, then it would be for just one and only one reason, Kennedy was somehow involved.

An hour earlier, Barry, extremely nervous, had called him on his private cell requesting a meet at the museum as soon as possible. Since he hadn't heard anything from Petre since the night of the embassy reception and was desperate, he needed Juwan to help him sell the stolen art to one of his buyer contacts as soon as possible. Holding onto the stolen statue was getting too dangerous.

Juwan, amused by the meeting place and the amateur clandestine tone in Barry's voice, cautiously agreed. The meet to discuss the particulars and for Juwan to see the statue was set for six o'clock, just as the museum was closing.

Juwan looked at his watch. He had nearly three and a half hours to kill before meeting Barry. The troubling thought of Kennedy's involvement kept spinning in his mind. If she was in too deep, he knew that there was very little he could do about it. A desperate sense of regret washed over him until a knock on his door drew his attention. He answered.

"Maurice!" Juwan said, surprised to see Maurice standing at the door of his suite.

"Juwan." Maurice smiled, genuinely pleased to see him.

"Aren't you supposed to be in meetings all day with Devlon?" Juwan asked as he motioned for Maurice to enter. He did and crossed the room and stood at the open terrace doors. Juwan followed.

"There was a brief window of opportunity so I took the liberty of seeking you out."

"I'm sure Hoyt is pleased to hear that."

"Hoyt had a meeting to attend this afternoon, leaving me free to have a little chat with my favorite son." Maurice patted Juwan on the back proudly.

Juwan smiled happily. "It's good to see you, Maurice," he said, realizing that they'd seen little of each other over the last four weeks.

"Duty calls," he acknowledged. Juwan nodded in agreement. "I was afraid I'd missed you again," Maurice continued. "You're a hard man to catch up with lately, even in the same house." He chuckled.

"I've been kinda busy," Juwan said.

"Yes, so I hear." Maurice turned, smiling even more broadly. "I am pleased to hear that you've found a nice young lady to keep your mind off business. Kennedy Evans is a wonderful person. I can't tell you how pleased Adarah and I were to hear the news. And you see, she is the one just as I predicted."

"You have the wrong idea. What's between Kennedy and me is business."

A scowl of disappointment and concern shadowed Maurice's face. He knew exactly what that implied. Juwan had decided to investigate Kennedy. "Business? Juwan, I hope that this is not one of your investigations or your personal quests. Does she know that she is just business?"

"No."

Maurice's scowl deepened. "Juwan . . ." he began.

"Maurice, this doesn't concern you."

"It does when you're throwing your heart away."

"My heart has nothing to do with this."

"She is your one. You can't ignore that."

"And you would have me ignore the obvious. She could possibly be involved with black market theft."

"What proof do you have that she is anything other than who she appears to be?"

"Getting proof is exactly what my job entails."

"By using someone, by trickery and by lying?"

"By any means I deem necessary."

"Juwan . . . ," Maurice began, his tone disapproving.

"Maurice, you don't pick and choose your moments to be ambassador any more than I pick and choose the times to be a federal officer. When an opportunity arises, I act. My gut feeling tells me that something is going on at that museum. Someone there is using their position to move stolen property. So yes, it is my personal quest, my duty and my responsibility." He paused briefly and took a deep breath. "I have an appointment. I'll see you later." He walked away without another word.

Once outside he breathed a heavy sigh of regret. He did choose this assignment; it was his idea. And now it was his obligation to see it through. Someone was responsible for stealing art and artifacts and it was his job to stop it. Yes, even if it involved Kennedy. He had no choice; if he didn't do it, someone else would.

He got into his car and began driving aimlessly. An expression of resolve and a tight grimace etched across his face as he steadily lowered the accelerator. In his world no one was above suspicion, not even him. His heart and his mind were at war and the battle continued.

He slammed his fist against the steering wheel. *Damn.* It wasn't how he expected to leave, but there was nothing he could do. Maurice had unrealistic expectations of his relationship with Kennedy. Juwan stopped the car and looked up. Without thinking, he had driven straight to Kennedy's house. Disgusted with himself, he drove off.

A few blocks away from the museum he spotted a familiar face. It was Barry Culpepper, hurrying to the Metro. He continued past. After a quick call, he parked, then grabbed a baseball cap and doubled back. He watched as his target hurried from the parked car and entered the Metro station. Juwan followed discreetly.

Close but not too close he shadowed the stout figure as he paid his fare and hurried down to the lower platform. Juwan picked up a discarded newspaper and stood watching a few feet away.

The Metro train arrived. Juwan angled for a better position just in case he needed to catch the train. He didn't. The last passenger to exit brought a knowing smile to his face. Chance had a way of making a way. The coincidence of his driving down the small side street at that time of day at that exact time was an unforeseen event that had proven extremely advantageous. He stood on the side, watched and waited.

The two men talked with exaggerated anger. Juwan smiled. Although he was able to read only one man's lips accurately, the gist of the heated conversation was evident. The small ring of thieves had gotten larger by one. It was an unexpected disclosure but not at all surprising.

Using his cell phone, he zoomed in and took several photos of the two men, then made a notation of the date, time and place. He continued to watch when the vibrating of his phone got his attention. He answered, nodded twice then hung up. His backup had arrived. With visual confirmation, they had orders to follow but not apprehend, leaving Juwan free to continue with his meet. Maybe this wasn't going to be as bad a day as he thought.

At twenty minutes to six Juwan strolled into the museum and stationed himself by one of the smaller exhibits. He kept a keen eye out for Kennedy as the museum announcement was sounded, ten minutes until closing. He moved to the Nubian exhibit entrance and waited. As he predicted, Kennedy came rushing out with two other woman all saying goodbye at once.

Juwan looked at his watch and smiled. Good, she'd be leaving just as he hoped. He was relieved. Apparently the meeting she had with Barry had been called off.

A few minutes later, he called Barry. They met at the entrance to the administrative wing, then went to Barry's office. The conversation was brief. Barry needed something sold fast. Juwan agreed to arrange the transaction. Everything was going exactly as planned until Barry mentioned that he didn't actually have the piece. He said that a friend had it and that he would bring it to the next meet.

"Who is this friend?" Juwan asked, already knowing, having seen the two meet in the Metro earlier.

"Don't worry, she's fine."

Stunned trepidation gripped him, but his stern and cautious expression never changed. "She?" he asked, then shook his head and stood. He hadn't considered a contingency. "Not good enough. I'm calling the whole thing off," he proclaimed with finality. "There're too many people involved." He turned and headed for the door.

"Wait," Barry said anxiously as he hurried from behind his desk. "Trust me."

"How do I know I can trust this person, whoever she is?"

"She's all right, she . . ." Barry began to stammer, "she . . . ah . . . she works right here at the museum."

"Exactly what does she have to do with it?"

"She's holding the product."

"Who is she?"

"I'd rather not say at this time."

A muscle in Juwan's jaw tightened and pulled firm. He glared at Barry angrily, then nodded his approval. "Have her at the meet, too."

"That's impossible," Barry exclaimed.

"Just do it," Juwan insisted. "I want to meet this woman."

Barry agreed reluctantly, already planning to wiggle out of it later. They finished their business, agreed on a price then set up a new date to exchange the art for the cash. Juwan checked his watch as he left. He had plenty of time to pick up wine for dinner with Kennedy.

Word from both overseas and local informants had confirmed that Petre was no longer in Africa but he was still trying to make contact with his supplier and buyer. He needed money to run and hide, but apparently, as suspected, he didn't have the stolen art. His partner did. Either way, Juwan needed to finish this. And if he could do it and protect Kennedy, he would. But if she showed up at the meet, there'd be nothing he could do.

Kennedy. How do you stop thinking about a woman who you know will despise you as soon as she finds out that you're not who you said you were? He was playing with fire and sure enough going to get burned.

Juwan arrived at Kennedy's house. She had left the door unlocked and he walked right in. As soon as he stepped inside, the wafting aroma of grilled fish greeted him. He followed the scent to the kitchen, but it was the loud singing that quickened his pace.

Kennedy was standing at the counter holding a head of lettuce, the music blaring, while singing at the top of her lungs. Juwan couldn't believe his eyes or ears. He put the bottle of wine and flowers down and leaned against the door frame and enjoyed the one-woman show.

Shimmying and sashaying, her hips moved seductively and her head shook with serious attitude. There was a "Heat Wave" in the kitchen and Martha and the Vandellas would have been extremely proud of her. Juwan nodded his head to the joyous rhythms, enjoying the performance. He was surprised; she was good, very good. Then as soon as the song went off, another one came on and she started all over again.

This time he decided to join her. He picked up a spoon from the table and came up behind her. She turned around instantly. Smiling as their voices harmonized, they sang each part with laughter and joy. By the end Marvin Gaye and Tammi Terrell's "Ain't Nothin' Like the Real Thing" never sounded so good. They ended by comically hand-dancing. Each dancing a different step, they bumped into each other, stumbled against each other and nearly knocked the table over as he dipped her and tickled her. She laughed so hard he nearly dropped her.

The music continued as she grilled salmon and vegetables on the indoor grill and he finished the salad. He poured the champagne he brought with him and they celebrated their almost-anniversary in joyous style.

The night was magical. They never made it out dancing, but they danced that night, hand in hand, slow, fast, to Motown oldies, to R&B soul, to reggae, and even to rock 'n roll.

In a moment of quiet they sat outside on the deck and watched the sun set behind the trees. The setting was relaxed and tranquil. Soft jazz played in the house and the last chirping of crickets added to the night sounds. The smell of faded summer flowers whispered in the warm September breeze.

Kennedy smiled. This was absolutely perfect. If she could capture this moment to last a lifetime, she would. She looked over at Juwan seated in the lounge chair beside her. He was the perfect man. It was as if God created him just for her. She had found her other half, the man she'd been looking for all her life.

Then the thought of his having to leave hit her and saddened her mood. She knew that it was only a matter of time. But she didn't want to think about. All she wanted was for this time with him to last forever.

"That meal was delicious. I thought you couldn't cook," Juwan said, interrupting her thoughts. He had deduced that fact by reading the extensive list of take-out orders from her most recent credit card file.

"No, I said I seldom have time to cook, not that I couldn't cook."

"And you can sing," he added.

"No, not even close, you should hear my sister, Madison. Her voice is incredible. She should have been a recording artist."

"What is she?" he asked, already knowing the answer from Kennedy's file.

"She's a teacher, art history at the University of Pennsylvania. But she's on leave right now. She's about eight months pregnant."

"Is this her first?"

"Yes."

"Boy or girl?"

"Both."

"Twins? Wow. That'll be a handful for first-time parents."

"Multiple births run in my family. I'm the last of triplets."

"So you're the youngest."

"Yeah, J.T., my brother, just got married and Madison and Tony married just last year. This is their first."

"And second," he added.

"That's right," she laughed happily.

"That's great. You're gonna be an aunt." She nodded, then went still and somber. "Do you want to have children someday?"

"I can't."

"What do you mean?" he asked. That wasn't in the file.

"I fell into an open tomb a while back, sprained my ankle and apparently shook some things up inside. The doctor said that conceiving children would be difficult."

"But not impossible."

"No, not impossible but it would be extremely difficult."

"Did the doctor run tests?"

"Dozens."

"Did he say exactly what the problem was?"

"Trauma, scar tissue, internal scarring. I guess all my motorcycle stunts finally caught up with me." Kennedy took a deep breath and shook her head. "Whoa, I can't believe I just told you that. Nobody knows that." She frowned and tears welled in her eyes and she looked away. "I never even told my parents that." A tear slipped down her face in slow motion as her breathing increased.

Juwan reached up and touched it before it fell. "I'm glad you told me. Thank you." He touched his finger to her chin and turned her face to him. She resisted firmly. "Kennedy, Kennedy, are you all right?"

She suddenly stood and walked away. He followed. Her palms moistened and her pulse sped up, keeping time with her stampeding heartbeat. She needed to get away. She hurried up the stairs and into her bedroom. She closed the door just as he was about to enter.

"Kennedy," Juwan said, blocking the door before she could close him out. He knew about her medication and the reason she was taking it. His sister had taken the same medication a few years ago. It was obvious that she was having a panic attack. "Calm down, just try to relax." He took her hand and firmly walked her to the bathroom and turned on the cold water. He tossed a towel into the sink, then wrung it almost dry and placed it on her face.

The cold icy sensation of the towel surprised her.

A few minutes later she calmed down considerably and Juwan left her alone in the bathroom. He walked into her bedroom and paced the floor. He was nervous and felt completely helpless. His heart raced at seeing the panic she experienced. Helpless, his heart went out to her. There was nothing he could do but wait. She needed to calm herself—that he couldn't help her with. But he could be there when she was ready to come out.

He needed to set a calming mood. While walking and pacing he had noticed the candles on her dresser, nightstand, bookcase and fireplace mantel. He went downstairs put a couple of cups of herbal tea into the microwave, then brought them back to the bedroom. When he returned,

Kennedy was still in the bathroom so he lit the candles, dimmed the lights and turned on the fireplace. The room was warm, calm and tranquil. He was standing at the fireplace when Kennedy came out of the bathroom.

She looked around the room surprised by what she saw. It was a dream. She looked back to him and smiled. "Thank you," she said quietly.

"You're welcome." He walked over and sat down on the side of the bed. "Come here," he said in a whisper. She came to him and sat down next to him. He wrapped his arms around her and pulled her closer. "Are you okay?"

She nodded. "Yeah, I'm fine." He kissed her forehead as she closed her eyes, feeling protected by his strength and understanding thoughtfulness.

"Panic attack?" he asked.

"Yes, I just started having them. They come now and then. No rhyme or reason, they show up whenever. Did it scare you?"

"No, my sister used to have them."

"So that's how you knew to use the cool water and towel."

"It worked for her sometimes."

"Thank you," she said a second time, filled with even more emotion. He held her closer as the silence rested comfortably in the room, covering them like an old blanket. She opened her eyes, seeing the calm and soothing ambiance of the room. "You did an incredible job," she said, smiling adoringly. "It's so beautiful."

"You're beautiful," he said, his eyes still on her face.

She ran her hand haphazardly through her tousled hair. "You're either blind or nuts."

"Neither." He leaned away to gauge her expression. "I'm in love."

Kennedy's heart leapt into her throat. Hearing him say the words was a dream come true. But she knew that a scare like witnessing her panic attack was most likely the catalyst. After all—he was a bodyguard, used to always being in control and protecting the weak. He was probably trained to save others from harm and here he was, helpless to save her. Saying that he loved her was probably just a gut reaction and the ultimate reassurance.

"Bet you didn't mean to say that," she finally said teasingly.

"You'd lose," he said very seriously. The sincerity in his eyes was unmistakable.

Kennedy panicked, then stood to walk away. He quickly reached out and grasped her hand. She turned to look at him. "In case you didn't notice, that was me giving you an out."

"In case you didn't notice, I don't want an out. I want you." He pulled her even closer and wrapped his arms around her body. The position had become comfortable to them. He opened her shirt and kissed the flat of her stomach as if it were delicate porcelain.

"Juwan Mason, you're a bad influence on me."

"Umm, that's good to hear," he muttered, still tenderly kissing her stomach.

"What am I gonna do with you?"

He stopped and looked up at her. "Love me."

"It's too late for that. I already do." They kissed and the night lasted an eternity as they loved and made love.

Chapter Sixteen

Juwan stood at the window and looked down onto Pennsylvania Avenue. The sidewalks were thick with local and federal workers and tourists and sightseers crazy enough to attempt venturing out at this time of day. It was just after five o'clock and the mad rush hour traffic had congested the streets and stalled movement in all directions. The sound of horns blowing bellowed endlessly as bumper-to-bumper traffic had come to a standstill.

The conversation he'd been having had gone in circles and he was beyond annoyed. The three of them had reached a stalemate. It was the first time that he and his associates completely disagreed on a plan of action. But a directive had been issued and he was expected to implement it to the letter, and that included bringing Kennedy in and finding out exactly what she knew.

But how could he? He'd told her that he was in love with her. There was no way he could bring her in and interrogate her after last night. She was right. He hadn't intended to say it but the moment drove him to it. But also in that moment he realized that he truly did and expressed his true feelings.

"Okay, okay, where is she now?" Kevin asked, trying to calm the room.

"New York City, the Metropolitan Museum, she had a lecture to attend," he said, his back still to the room.

"Okay, when she gets back, we can close this," Colin insisted.

Juwan shook his head. "No, it's too soon. I need more time." He turned around. "And we need more intel. There are too many unanswered questions, too many unknowns."

"Juwan, we have everything we're going to get at this point," Colin said. "Look, I understand your attachment. She's a beautiful woman. But there have been dozens of beautiful women. You've never allowed a pretty face to sway your judgment before. What's so special about her?"

"We were wrong, Colin, you and I were both wrong," he said simply.

"It's a little late for that, Juwan," Colin complained. "You could have passed on the assignment, but you didn't. This was your call. I exposed the relationship with Petre. This was your idea, your setup. You found her and outlined the plan."

"I was wrong," he admitted again. "She's an innocent. She has no idea of the whereabouts of Petre or the stolen art."

"Her innocence isn't based on any valid evidence. I suggest you follow the directive and bring her in," Kevin said.

"On what grounds? The circumstantial evidence isn't exactly overwhelming," Juwan pointed out.

"We have enough to hold her and get some answers," Colin insisted.

"No, it's too early and I don't want to blow this with her, not now."

"Here's the deal. If her level of cooperation meets or exceeds expectations, then she's off the hook. So bring her in," Colin repeated, firmer this time.

"No, not yet."

"We need to finish this, Juwan," Kevin said. "Everyone is anxious to have it over with, including the top. With your testimony we can do it. She's the only other viable wild card. She's the mule. You said it yourself that Culpepper implicated her. She has the piece. Bring her in. If she's as innocent as you say, then fine, she's off the hook. But if not, she can cut a deal like everybody else. You know the game. The first one that cooperates wins the prize."

"No. I said that she might know something, not that she has the piece. I checked the house while she was asleep the other morning. It's not there."

"Of course it's not there," Colin said. "Do you seriously think she'd leave a stolen statue worth that much money just sitting on the fireplace mantel in her house?"

The vivid image of Kennedy's candlelit bedroom instantly flashed to mind. He needed to protect her. There was no way he could testify against her. "We need to follow the plan. We should let the meet with Culpepper play out. Petre has tried to contact Kennedy before. I know he'll do it again. He's on the run and he needs money. Other than selling the piece, which we know he can't do because he doesn't have it, she's his next best bet for getting money."

"Culpepper doesn't have the piece. She has it," Colin said.

"Actually, technically," Kevin began, "we don't know to whom Culpepper referred. He only said that *she* worked at the museum. They are hundreds of women working there."

"But Evans is the only one with complete access. She procured the art, knew the shipping log and even dated one of the principals. Not to mention that she has a travel itinerary that reads like who's who in the black market," Colin said.

"She doesn't have the temperament," Juwan said.

"What the hell are you talking about? Temperament has nothing to do with it," Colin said as he looked closer at Juwan. "What's wrong with you? You've never hesitated on an assignment before. Why are you losing focus now? What happened to you?"

The standoff had gone on for nearly an hour. Colin was firm. Juwan was unmovable. The two men went back and forth, each firmly set on a course of action. Juwan looked at Colin sternly. "She's not the one." His adamant tone leveled Colin.

"Everything in your report points directly to her."

"And that's what bothers me. The case is too pat. It's like we were meant to go after her."

"You're thinking that it was a setup all along?" Kevin asked.

Juwan nodded. "And we went for it."

"Fine, if not her, who do we target now?" Colin said, finally giving up. The ringing of his cell phone sitting on the conference room table drew their attention. He let it ring a second time before answering. He didn't speak, only listened. "We have a lead on Petre. One of our informants in Africa has him arriving in D.C. a few days ago."

"That sounds about right," Juwan confirmed. "We'll wait for him to make contact again. In the meantime let's stay on Culpepper and the third party facilitator. What did field recon get?"

"Nothing useful, so he's been scrapped."

As expected Juwan's expression was fierce. "What?"

Kevin held up his hands in surrender. "There was nothing we could do—diplomatic immunity. It comes to the rescue every time."

"What about his history . . ." Juwan began.

"Invalid, it has nothing to do with this. The order came from upstairs," Kevin continued. "The meet you witnessed proved nothing. The two were followed. Culpepper went back to the museum to meet you and our new friend, to a third party, his mistress. The only thing we have is that they know each other and both are fond of standing in the Metro station. Other than that, there's no other connection."

"You gotta be kidding me, did you check everything?"

"Nobody wants to touch it—too political. It's a directive, hands off and stand down until further notice. Devlon Motako is not to be touched."

"Fine," Juwan said, exasperated by yet another directive.

"So how do you want to work this?" Kevin asked.

"We follow protocol and proceed with the current plan," Juwan said.

"Whatever you say," Colin said. "The current plan calls for your target to be brought in. I guess you have to bring her in." Juwan looked at him fiercely. The battle was about to begin anew.

"Forty-eight hours, then clean-up," Kevin said suddenly. "Something breaks in forty-eight hours or we follow original protocol and bring her in with what we have."

Both Juwan and Colin looked at him, then understood. "Fine," Colin said and began gathering his files from the conference room table. He looked over to Juwan as did Kevin.

The look on Juwan's face was classic. Although this might have been just another assignment at one point, it certainly wasn't now. He finally nodded his agreement.

Sitting on a lecture panel at the Metropolitan Museum of Art in New York City all morning discussing the recent heightened interest in ancient Nubian art and artifacts would have usually been for Kennedy like sending a child into a candy store and saying, *enjoy*. It was exactly what she loved doing, and that, coupled with the opportunity to talk about the upcoming exhibit at the National Museum of African Art, should have been beyond exciting. But not today, today she had other things that weighed heavily on her mind.

Fulfilling a promise she'd made months earlier to a friend and colleague, she sat distracted, half listening and only vaguely hearing the other panelists as they spoke. She was too preoccupied with thoughts of Juwan and what Hoyt had told her. He was the best thing to happen to her. There was no way she could let him just be deported without at least trying to do something to help.

She smiled, remembering the night before. What started as a wonderful evening had turned out to be an incredible night. Cooking dinner for Juwan, sitting out on the deck, then dancing under the stars had been the perfect ending to a strenuous day. Even the panic attack she experienced hadn't ruined the night. They made love and talked long into the early morning hours.

She couldn't imagine anything more incredible than waking up in his arms this morning and every other morning after that. And with only four hours of sleep she felt as fresh and relaxed as if she'd slept for ten straight hours. Since she needed to catch a commuter flight to New York, she left, leaving him to clean up the dishes. Actually he had volunteered to stay and clean up. He was definitely a godsend. Kennedy smiled and shook her head, still unbelieving how they met. It was as if the universe had smiled down and had finally given her the gift of love. There had to be something she could do to keep Juwan in the country.

Realizing that applause had begun, she quickly joined in. Now aware that her friend and the event's coordinator, DeWitt, was about to introduce her, she prepared to give her abbreviated talk. She looked at her watch; it was still early and since she had decided to double check with the museum's shipping department and return to D.C. instead of doing her usual visiting or shopping, she had cut her talk down to just twenty minutes.

Her name was announced; applause greeted her. She stood at the podium with her notes and looked out into the faces of the attendees. Then it hit her like a bolt of lightning out of the clear blue sky and her abbreviated talk of twenty minutes lasted just under fifteen minutes.

Hitting the high points of the ancient Nubian dynasties, their rulers, achievements and downfalls, she noted the important ramifications of the Egyptian and Nubian contributions to both the ancient and contemporary art world. Though brief, the talk was thorough with insightful facts and interesting details. Specifics were kept to a minimum.

She noted that the people of the region were exceptional strategists, brilliant inventors and accomplished warriors. Nubia, having conquered Egypt and other neighboring countries, was a formidable power.

By the time she wrapped up her talk, she was confident that the audience received a fair assessment of the Nubian people, their art and its cultural importance.

Her audience, attentive and open to her remarks, was surprised when she finished quickly and thanked both them and her friend for inviting her. As she returned to her seat, her mind whirled with numerous possibilities for solving Juwan's immigration problems. She considered several alternatives, most less desperate, but realized that the one obvious option would be the best. So she settled on it. If he agreed, he could be in this country permanently and she would never have to worry about Mamma Lou and her matchmaking again.

Not only would she have beaten her at her own game, but she could quite possibly be the first Evans or Gates to ever outsmart Mamma Lou. A smile of premature success pulled wide across Kennedy's face. Sometimes the most obvious answer was the best and this was by far the best idea she'd had in a long time. Now, she figured, strategizing her next move, all she had to do was gather additional information, then talk Juwan into going along with her plan. But she saw no real problem with his accepting her offer. After all, it would make him a permanent resident of this country and he could work here as long as he wanted.

As the last speaker gave his talk, she mulled over the best way to get the information she needed since time was of the essence. The sooner she got the information, the sooner she could implement her plan and the sooner Juwan would be safe from deportation. She decided that the government office of immigration and naturalization would certainly be her best bet. Nodding absently, she realized that she needed to make a few calls.

The panel question and answer portion of the program lasted longer than she anticipated. So when it finally came to a close and final applause ended, she was overjoyed. Then during light refreshments and coffee she found herself surrounded by curious audience members. She stayed and greeted every patron and personally invited them to learn more about ancient Nubian art by attending the museum's exhibit opening.

As usual, she was welcoming and patient with all questions, but her mind was definitely miles away. So when the flurry of additional questions dwindled to just a few, she graciously made her excuses and departed.

"You were wonderful," her friend DeWitt said as he hurried to her side and thanked her with a warm hug.

"Thank you," she said as she hugged him back, then gathered her things together to leave.

"I know you have a commuter flight to catch, so do you still want to double check with shipping?"

"Yes, definitely," she said. "After everything I've been through to get this exhibit off the ground, I can't leave anything to chance. After this I still have one more shipment from the Nubian Museum, and that arrives tomorrow afternoon."

"I heard about Petre and the Nubian Museum thefts." DeWitt shook his head as he walked with Kennedy toward the exit and headed down to the security and shipping offices. Once in the elevator they continued talking. He mentioned that several special agents had asked him questions as well.

"Really?" Kennedy asked. "When was this, right after the theft?"

"No, just a few weeks ago. I assumed that they are still investigating anything and anyone connected with the Nubian Museum. Have they contacted you?"

"No, not yet," Kennedy said. Although she suspected that

both the FBI and Interpol were still after Petre, she was surprised to hear that they were still investigating the Nubian Museum theft and also investigating those with connections to both Petre and the Nubian Museum.

She knew that she had to be on the top of their list. But not having heard anything from them since the actual theft, she was curious. Then she remembered Hoyt's warning earlier to make sure that everything was in order. She paused to consider; maybe they were investigating her and she didn't even know it.

Chapter Seventeen

There was nothing more frustrating than the nagging ache of suspicion eating its way into her every thought. The theft at the Nubian Museum and its continued ramifications, the upcoming exhibit and, of course, Juwan. All three weighed heavily and had continued to pull at her for the past few hours. In the cab ride to the airport, during the flight back to D.C., and even now as she sat waited in the INS office for her turn. Maya, Yolanda, Barry and Petre—she knew and trusted them all, yet now she questioned them. Petre could not have acted alone. He needed help on this end and the thought of someone she still trusted being involved weighed heavily on her heart.

Then Hoyt's concerns about the exhibit and DeWitt's warnings about the FBI's continued interest concerned her as well. The rush of angst flooded her mind like a runaway tsunami. She remembered Petre's call and his promise to call her again. With everything that had happened, that was the last thing she needed. If the FBI was indeed still looking at everyone connected to the Nubian Museum and looking for him, his contacting her could be misconstrued as something it wasn't.

With endless concerns and questions, her wayward musing

was only made worse by restless sitting and waiting. She looked around at the people in the small waiting room with her. Although it was crowded, she was still alone.

Being alone and anxious, with troubling thoughts, was a miserable way to be. Aggravated, Kennedy was never good at waiting. Everything she did, wanted, or needed happened immediately, either by her own hand or her family's. So the torture she now felt was magnified tenfold each time the child behind her kicked her chair, the man beside her blew his nose and the woman behind the desk clicked her nails and popped her chewing gum.

The silly ring of cellphones and the constant chatter of different languages all spoken at once were annoying. And the boredom of waiting continued as the numbers called slowly proceeded and the crowd of applicants slowly dissipated.

The waiting area around her was pleasant enough with oversized photos of purple mountains and billowing wheat fields. Pen-and-ink sepia etchings of the Grand Canyon, the Statue of Liberty, the Golden Gate Bridge, the Liberty Bell and the Washington Monument hung prominently. And a fitting tribute to New York City's Twin Towers, the Pentagon and the Pennsylvania field added symbols of remembrance of 9/11.

The mingling of cultures brought a sense of renewed pride to her. So many people wanted to be here and so many had tried. Oftentimes the strife and dissension of their native land drove them to give up everything for a glimpse of hope and the promise of peace and opportunity. She smiled, knowing that what she was doing would turn out for the best. But her selfish reasons for wanting to be with Juwan gave her pause.

She was doing the wrong thing for the right reason and the right thing for the wrong reason. She loved Juwan with all her heart and she knew that he cared for her and maybe that would be enough for now. He'd told her that he loved her, but that was during the stress of her panic attack. She saw the pain of worry and concern in his eyes. Telling her that he loved her was exactly what she needed to hear, whether he truly felt it or not.

It could work, she nodded convincingly, promising herself, they could work. Love could grow from affection, kindness, and friendship and she was sure that, in time, he could truly love her as she loved him.

Kennedy looked down at the slip of paper pressed tightly between her fingers, then looked up at the board behind the counter. According to the last number called, her turn should be soon. As she relaxed back in her chair, her thoughts centered on Juwan, and her mind continued to wander, interrupted by the vibration of her cell phone. She checked the phone number; it was the museum. She answered.

"Kennedy?"

"Yes," she said, not recognizing the voice on the other end.

"It's Maya Thaddeus, at the museum." Kennedy paused a moment, surprised to hear her voice. Few people had her cell phone number and she knew that Maya wasn't one of them. "I'm sorry to call you on your private cell phone like this, but I'm leaving early today and I wanted to let you know that the last shipment from Africa arrived a few hours ago. I know you're still in New York, but I just wanted you to know before I go."

"What? It arrived today?" she asked.

"Yes. I'm a little surprised that you changed the delivery date to have it arrive when you wouldn't be here."

"I didn't change the delivery date. It's supposed to arrive tomorrow. Yolanda's shipment arrives today."

"There must have been some kind of miscommunication. Anyway, they're here and since Yolanda's not here, Barry wants us to start unpacking the pieces. I'm leaving a copy of the shipping paperwork on your desk. Barry took the original with him."

A miscommunication was impossible, of that she was certain. Since she would be in New York all day, there was no way she'd purposely arrange and schedule the last crate to arrive when she couldn't personally be there to receive it. This was no scheduling mix-up. Someone changed the two shipping dates.

"Number 82," the woman behind the counter called out.

Kennedy looked up at the woman through the crowded waiting room, then at the paper in her hand. She was number eight-two. She stood and began walking to the counter. The oddity of the phone call and the strangeness of Barry unpacking her shipment struck her as peculiar.

"Kennedy, did you hear me; are you still there?"

"Yes," she said hurriedly. "Thanks for calling, Maya. I'll be there as soon as I can." She closed the phone and was directed to an office down the far end of a hall.

An hour and a half later she was driving back to D.C. The appointment at the Fairfax, Virginia district office had taken longer than she expected. But she had gotten all the information she needed, received the necessary forms and looked them over briefly as she drove to the museum.

Although the laws were a lot different from what she'd expected, she had no qualms about continuing her plan. If it worked, and she saw no reason for it not to, then she could save Juwan and permanently get Mamma Lou and her mother off her back.

Her plan was risky and, if anyone found out, would carry serious ramifications and could even mean possible jail time. But with steadfast commitment she decided to go ahead with it. She smiled to herself and wondered why she hadn't thought of it earlier.

Arriving at the museum just before it closed to the public, Kennedy went directly to her office. Maya's phone call had completely surprised her. She hadn't expected the shipment until the following day. She went to her desk and picked up the shipping paperwork that Maya told her about. It was a copy. She looked through the other papers on her desk for the originals, then assumed that Barry still had them.

Moments later she was headed to the shipping area to see her delivery. As soon as she unlocked the security door and walked in, four beautifully preserved bowl fragments greeted her. With shards of excelsior still on the floor and the crate still against the wall, she unlocked the bin, picked each one up in turn and examined the pieces. Centuries old, they were perfectly preserved and just as she remembered seeing them in Nubia months ago.

She looked at the paperwork again and noticed that Barry had strictly adhered to protocol and procedure. He noted that each piece had been checked and confirmed. He signed off on the consignment paperwork and the insurance papers.

Afterwards she studied the customs report and cross-checked it against her original paperwork. The crate had cleared customs a day earlier and was sent directly to the museum instead of being held until the following day. She was still puzzled.

Why would someone change the date to arrive a day earlier? She continued checking the paperwork, then saw something else that appeared odd. She cross-checked the usually inconsequential packing weight. The total weight of the crate was different from what she had previously calculated months ago. The additional poundage confused her. She knew that her original weight had been exact. She was precise, particularly when it came to correct shipping weights. Every additional pound cost money and even though her budget was far larger than normal, she used her funding wisely.

Kennedy went directly to Barry's office. He wasn't there, so she went to Yolanda's office. Poised to knock, she heard her name called.

"Kennedy, what are you doing here?"

She turned, seeing Barry walking toward her. "Barry, just

the man I was looking for, we need to talk. Do you have a few minutes?"

Barry looked at his watch. "Actually, I'm running a little late for a meeting. I'm on my way out now. Can this wait until our meeting tomorrow morning?"

"I don't think so. It's important, it's about the shipment."

He nodded and proceeded to his office. He walked in, laid his briefcase on the desk and stood, leaning back against it, not bothering to offer her a seat and impatiently waiting for her to begin. "How can I help you?"

"You unpacked my crate this afternoon."

"That's right. Everything checked out perfectly. The consignment pieces will be a wonderful addition to the exhibit."

"There's a problem with the shipping crate weight. The final weight isn't consistent with my original calculation."

"I wouldn't worry about that, I'm sure it's just a mathematical error."

"That's unlikely. The crate was heavier by almost twenty pounds. I was there when Petre weighed it."

"Petre," Barry said scornfully. "How can you still trust anything he said or did after the trouble he's in?"

"Because I was there, too. I did the calculations with him. And it appears that something had been added before the crate was sealed, then removed when it arrived from customs."

"That's impossible. I personally saw every piece as they were unpacked and there was no missing or additional piece. I would have surely noticed."

Kennedy shook her head. "Still, the crate was twenty pounds heavier when it left Nubia. So whatever was included is not there now."

Barry looked at his watch anxiously. "Well, it appears that there was a shipping miscalculation at some point. But I assure you there was nothing else was in the crate." He picked up his briefcase and began walking to the door, obviously ending the discussion. "Now that that's settled, I have to go. Good night." He stood at the door of his office and held it open for her to leave. She walked out without saying another word.

Moments later Kennedy sat at her own desk looking at the shipping paperwork. There was no mistake. There was something going on. She turned on her computer and was preparing to work when the phone rang. She looked at her watch. It was nearly seven-thirty. She hadn't expected anyone to call her this late, and only family and close friends knew that she'd still be at the museum. Hearing a friendly voice would certainly ease her frustration. She picked up the receiver.

"Kennedy."

She frowned. Her day had gone from bad to worse. "Petre?"

"We need to talk."

"Where are you?"

"I'm here in D.C. Can you meet me tonight?"

"You're in D.C.? Petre, you have to turn yourself in. You can't keep running away from this."

"Will you meet me?"

"Fine, where and when?"

Chapter Eighteen

"I missed you," he began as soon as she approached him. She remained silent as she watched him anxiously looking around. He checked behind her a second time. "You weren't followed, were you?"

"By whom?"

"Never mind," he smiled, still devilishly handsome. Like melted dark chocolate, his smooth boyish face was exactly as she remembered, glowing black eyes and bright white teeth and the same mischievous smile that had caught her attention months ago. He was sin itself. "You look good."

"Thank you."

"You look *really* good." He reached up and stroked the side of her face gently. "Maybe after all this is over we can . . ." She looked away. "All right, maybe I deserved that, but there's more to this than you know, and more than what the police and FBI know."

She looked back to him with interest, but didn't speak. He opened his mouth to speak but closed it again. An uncomfortable moment of silence sliced between them. This was not the man she remembered. The Petre she knew in Africa was joyful and adventurous. This man was fearful and desperate. Where deep affection once was, now pity filled her heart. "Turn yourself in, Petre."

"No," he said adamantly.

"Well, then what do you want from me, money?"

"I can get money. I need a favor."

"No," she answered without hesitation.

He continued anyway. "Your last crate is being delivered tomorrow. I need you to get something out of it for me."

Kennedy's heart sank. A part of her wanted to believe that all of this was a big mistake and that Petre, a man she had cared for, was really innocent. But she knew that it was just wishful thinking. He had added something to the crate before it was shipped and now, whatever it was, he needed it back. "I can't do that."

"Of course you can. It's your department. No one knows what's in it except you. When the crate arrives, unpack it alone and whatever you do don't let . . ." He paused and looked around cautiously, then continued in a whisper, "anyone else at the museum know what you're doing."

"Anyone else, like who?" she questioned, wanting to confirm her suspicions about Barry and maybe even Yolanda and Maya.

"That doesn't matter. Just make sure no one else is there."

Had he known her better he would have known that the abhorrence in her expression and cool chill of her tone had already decided his fate with her. All pity, empathy and lenience she once felt for him and his predicament had turned to disgust. He was trying to implicate her in his crime.

"I can't do what you ask," she repeated.

"Please, Kennedy, do this and I'll be out of your life for good."

A small upward pull of her mouth sealed her response. "You already are," she said quietly. He looked at her with anger and hurt, not believing that she would desert him in his hour of need.

"Kennedy . . ." he began.

"I have to go." She took a step back.

"Please, Kennedy." He reached out and grabbed her hand. "You'll do this for me, I know you will. And what you find inside hold it for me. I'll contact you in a few days." He looked around, then hurriedly ran across the street and down into the Metro system.

Kennedy watched him until he disappeared down the escalator. She saw him turn at the last second and wave to her. She shook her head and walked back to her car and sat.

Juwan lowered the camera. He had focused on Kennedy and not on Petre as he should have done. It wasn't until seconds had passed that he realized he had just allowed Petre to get away. He turned the camera over and quickly ran through the pictures stored on the small memory card. Kennedy's face was stern and emotionless compared to Petre's obvious jittery edginess. But there it was nonetheless, in full color and in still reality, Kennedy and Petre had met.

Reading lips was a necessity in his field and he had mastered the technique with ease. He knew what Petre had asked of Kennedy and he knew her response. But he also knew her heart. If she could help someone in need, she would. Petre was in need and the question was would she do as he asked?

Juwan mulled over the question, but before his mind settled on a single answer, his thoughts were interrupted by the sound of his cell phone ringing. He answered.

"Juwan."

"Keni," he said, surprised to hear her voice.

"Can you get away tonight? I need to talk to you."

"Sure," he said, his eyes focused on her still sitting in her car a half block away. "Are you at home or at the office?" he asked.

"I'm parked at the mall. I'll be home in about ten minutes or so."

"Okay, why don't I meet you there?"

"Thanks."

"Keni," he said before she hung up. "Are you okay?"

"I will be after we talk."

Juwan hung up and watched as she drove off in the direction of her house. He waited a few moments, then pulled away from the curb. The case was closed. The pictures he'd taken and the information he'd gathered were enough to get a search warrant and bring her in. All he had to do was drive to the FBI office and make his report. The police and local agents would take it from there.

He could meet with Barry and bring him in and wait for Petre to make contact with Kennedy again, meet with him and bring him in, too. He'd have his promotion and be back in London within a week. The neat package would be complete.

The words hung in the air like a heavy fog. He had said those exact words before. Then it occurred to him, the similarities to Remy's case were even more alarming. It was the exact same scenario. He had followed her to her meet. She led him to her partner. Her partner was picked up. She was picked up. Then afterwards she called and asked to see him. But he never went to her. Instead he went to the local office and filed his report. A week later he'd received word that, while in custody, Remy had hanged herself in her cell.

The idea of that happening again sickened him. But he had to do his job. He called his office and gave a preliminary status report. The response was immediate: "*Bring her in.*"

But he turned his car away from the FBI building and in another direction, toward Georgetown and Kennedy.

Kennedy rehearsed the wording all the way home. Usually extremely eloquent and fluent, she'd never searched for words to express herself. But now the confidence she had had abandoned her, and the closer she got to her home the more anxious she became. As she pulled into her driveway, she looked in the rearview mirror and saw Juwan's car pull up behind her. She took a deep breath but sat there waiting. She was sure that this was what she wanted to do. She couldn't save Petre, but she could save Juwan.

The car door opened and Juwan stood there with his hand out to her. She looked up into his eyes. She was home in more ways than one. His smile was exactly what she needed after the horrendous day she'd had. She took his offered hand and stepped out. Juwan instantly pulled her into a warm loving embrace. "I missed you," he said quietly into her ear.

The perfect moment reverberated in a sweet wind chime fashion over and over again. The sincerity of his words and the sweet hug of his arms put to rest all doubts she might have had.

Mamma Lou and her matchmaking could search the world over for the perfect man for her, but she knew at that moment he was standing right in front of her. He was the man for her and if by chance he agreed to her plan, she would do everything in her power to make him love her, too.

The embrace ended and he followed her into the house. As soon as he came into the house, she turned to him with arms open. She kissed him passionately, long and hard, giving him exactly what he needed. If time stood still, she wanted it to be at this moment so she'd have him with her forever. As the kiss ended, she felt the joy of power and nervousness about the question she'd be asking in the next few moments.

"You weren't gone that long, were you," he said jokingly as he turned and closed the front door behind them.

"Actually," she said, walking into the living room, "I was gone too long."

He followed, noting her cryptic response. "How was your lecture at the Met today?"

"Good, it went well. How was your day, dear?" she asked playfully.

He came up beside her and wrapped his arms around her just as he'd done when she got out of the car. It was a satisfying habit he'd grown accustomed to. "Too long." They stood face-to-face and he looked into her eyes questioning what was going on behind the softness of her smile. "Anything interesting happen in New York or D.C. today?"

"Plenty," she said awkwardly. "But we can talk about that later." She pulled away and moved to the sofa.

"Are you okay?" he asked.

"I'll know in a few minutes," she said hastily. "Come sit down, I have something to tell you."

They walked over to the sofa and sat. She took a deep breath and smiled. He didn't. She started. "We need to talk," she said, then paused a moment.

"Start at the beginning," he instructed.

"Good idea," she said, then took a deep breath and burst. "It was a crazy day," she began. "The commuter flight to New York was miserable, the lecture, talking to my friend DeWitt afterwards and finding out that the FBI is still after Petre and anybody connected with him. Then the last crate from Africa came a day early. I wasn't there to meet it and the shipping weight was off. Barry is into something at the museum. And then I met with an old friend, this man I knew when I was in Africa, a few minutes ago. He's in serious trouble." She freely spilled everything that had happened without taking a single breath.

"Hold it, hold it, start from that part, the end. What about your old friend from Africa. Tell me about him first."

"That's not important right now. I'll tell you about all that later, but first I need to talk to you about something that's about to happen." She paused. "Actually it's more like something I'm gonna do, or rather would like to do if you'd agree."

"What's going on, Keni? What are you about to do?" he asked, steeling himself for the worst.

"Believe it or not I've been asked this question several

times and each time I've said no, obviously. So now I know what it feels like to have the shoe on the other foot . . ."

"Kennedy," Juwan said, holding her waving hands still. "What are you about to do? Tell me."

"I am. It's just that I'm not sure how to say it."

Juwan was immediately confused. This wasn't the heartfelt confession he expected. "Kennedy, just tell me. I'll understand whatever it is, just say it," he said, hoping to draw her out.

She began again. "I guess I should have talked to you before now, but I didn't want to embarrass you so I didn't mention it. I was told in confidence and I'm not sure what you'll think about it, but I left New York earlier than I expected today. I made a stop in Virginia, Fairfax, Virginia."

"Did you meet someone in Virginia?" he asked, not having a clue as to what she was talking about.

"Yes, I did."

"Who?"

"I'll get to that. But first I know that you really don't know me very well, but if there is a way that I can help someone, I try my best to do it. Playing it safe never appealed to me. I was always attracted to the thrill of excitement. And to me you were exciting, a bodyguard, a bad boy and not the kind of man to get serious with or expect a long-term relationship with. I suppose that's why you and I began this thing we have. But somewhere along the way things changed."

"What exactly are you trying to say?"

"I'm saying that I've changed. I didn't mean for this to happen but it did." The completely puzzled and confused expression on his face made her pause. "I'm not saying this right, am I? What I'm trying to say is that I know about your problem and I have a solution."

"A solution, to my problem?" he asked.

"Yes. I've never done this before." She blushed.

"Done what?" he asked, beginning to get anxious.

"Proposed."

"Proposed what?" he asked in all seriousness.

"Proposed, as in marriage," she said calmly even as her heart raced a mile a minute.

"Proposed, as in marriage?" He repeated her words.

"Yes, Juwan Mason, will you marry me?"

Juwan was shocked speechless for the first time in his life. Of all the things he expected to hear this evening, this wasn't one of them. He stood up, walked away. The shock of the moment had him completely flabbergasted.

Kennedy watched as he stood at the window. "I know this is a shock. And it's really none of my business, but in the short time that we've been together . . . I guess what I'm saying is that I just don't want you to be deported and leave the country."

He turned around to face her. "Deported? Who said that I'm being deported and leaving the country?"

"Hoyt."

"What? When did he tell you that?"

"I talked to him a while ago. Actually it was shortly after we met at the museum. He told me that there was a problem with one of the ambassador's bodyguards. He didn't know that we'd just met. And since I knew Hawk was born and raised in Detroit, I naturally knew that he was referring to you. Of course I didn't tell him that I knew it was you. So, since you were having problems with immigration and deportation was a strong likelihood, I thought this could be a solution."

Juwan understood. The shock of the moment began to clear. Suddenly her reasoning dawned on him. She was saving him. He had come to save her and she was saving him.

"No pressure, of course, but if we marry, you could apply for citizenship and be in this country freely as long as you like."

"Why would you want to do this for me? You don't really know anything about me."

"I know that you're a good man. You work for the Nubian embassy as a bodyguard for its ambassador so you must be well trusted. And I know that you make me happy and that at times I can't wait to see you and I know that I want to have you all to myself even if it's just for a little while."

"But . . ."

"This is sudden, I know. You don't have to answer now."

"Tell me about your friend, the one you met today from Africa."

"Petre, what about him?"

"Who is he?"

"Petre Siegal, we dated months ago while I was in Africa selecting the pieces for the Nubia exhibit. He was the art specialist. But he was also into black-market dealing."

"Did you know about what he was doing?"

"I found out later. I told him that he should turn himself in, but all he talked about was one last job."

"Did you help him?"

"Yes, I tried."

Juwan's heart sank. "What do you mean, you tried?"

She paused. "There was an anonymous call"—he knew exactly what call she was talking about—"to the FBI. They were told about Petre and what was suspected. They apparently listened and checked it out. A few days later Petre and some of his friends were under arrest. But he got away. He's here in the States now."

"And you met with him; what exactly did he want, money?"

"No, he needs my help."

"With what?"

"He wants me to recover something that he put into a crate that was scheduled to be delivered tomorrow."

"Are you gonna do it?"

"Of course not. But I couldn't do it even if I wanted to. The crate was delivered early. It arrived today. Someone changed the delivery date and I wasn't there to meet it. Barry, the museum's public liaison, unpacked it. Technically, as upper management he has the authority to do so, but theoretically he has no idea what I should receive. Of course he had my staff there to assist. I think there was something else in the crate. But whatever it was, he must have it."

"Tell me what you know about Petre and Barry and their connection with the theft at the museum."

Kennedy talked and Juwan listened. His mind buzzed. This was perfect. He was getting a wealth of information about their movements and those attached to them. Some information he already knew but most he didn't. He was correct in his original assessment of Kennedy, she did have knowledge she didn't even know she had.

When she finished telling him about Petre and Barry, she paused and apologized. "Sorry about all that. It feels good to finally talk about all this to someone. I know that there's nothing you can do about it, but it's good to just talk."

"I'm glad you told me. Now I have one more question."

"What?" she asked.

"The marriage you proposed, what about you, what do you get out of this arrangement?"

She smiled. "I get to help you."

"Is that all?"

She smiled. "I have a matchmaker on my back. This will take the wind out of her sails. Plus I've always wondered what it would be like to be married. So for now, yes."

"Don't you want to marry for love?"

"There's always time."

He nodded his head, agreeing with her, then paused and looked into her eyes. "It's really none of my business, but I have one more question. Since your relationship with Petre was evidently months ago and things have obviously changed since, I'd like to know something. You don't have to answer it if you don't feel comfortable."

"Ask and I'll let you know. What's the question?" she asked.

"Your friend Petre, did you love him?"

She smiled coyly. "You were right, it's none of your business. But I'll answer anyway. Contrary to popular belief, speculation, and interoffice gossip, Petre and I were not intimate or lovers. He wanted to be but . . ." She shrugged and let the sentence end there. "We were friends, nothing more, nothing less. I loved him as a friend. Is that what you wanted to hear?"

He nodded.

"So, Juwan," she began again, more confident this time, "will you marry me?" she asked as she smiled easily at his stoic expression. "Some people would call that a deafening silence."

Juwan, realizing that he'd stopped breathing, looked at her and half smiled. She was brilliant and she was right, she did have the perfect solution, but for a different reason. Their getting and being married would solve everything. Even though he knew that the INS marrying clause no longer applied, another law would. If he married her, there was no way he could be made to testify against her, that too was the law. A husband can't be forced to testify against his wife. Impulsive and spontaneous, the decision had been made.

Juwan stood up and held out his hand to her.

"Do you have your driver's license?"

"Yes." She looked at him oddly.

"Good, let's go."

"Where to, dinner?"

"No, Las Vegas. We're getting married tonight."

Chapter Nineteen

Barry had called the phone number Juwan had given him and left a message. It was the second message he'd left in as many hours. His nerves were on edge and his temper was short. By mid-afternoon, when he still hadn't heard from Juwan, he was ready to climb the walls. Distracted, he sat in his office and replayed their meeting in his mind. It had gone well. He showed the photos and Juwan seemed very interested and confident that he could make a deal with his buyer.

Barry eased back and debated whether or not to leave another message for Juwan. Just as he leaned in to make the call, his phone rang. He picked it up. The line went dead. That was the second time that had happened this morning. He hung up only to have the phone ring as soon as he released his hand. He picked it up instantly.

Work beckoned. Yolanda's shipment had arrived and since she was out, he needed to sign off on and oversee its release and unpacking. Two hours later after giving a visiting VIP a tour of the museum, he stopped by Kennedy's office to make sure that he'd successfully calmed her concerns the night before. She wasn't in her office and it looked as if she hadn't been in at all.

When it occurred to him that he hadn't seen Kennedy all

morning, he decided to go to the Nubian exhibit. He quickly walked through expecting to see Kennedy making her last-minute arrangements, but instead he found her assistant and her staff. "Where's Kennedy? We were supposed to have a meeting. I haven't seen her all morning," Barry said to Maya as he made a mental note to inform Kennedy that the lighting over a few of her pieces seemed too harsh and needed softening.

Maya immediately jumped to her feet. "She's not here."

"I can see that. Kindly tell her that I'd like to see her this afternoon."

"She's not in at all today."

"What, where is she, when did this happen?"

"I don't know where she is exactly. All I know is that she left a message on my voice mail saying that she would be out of town and would be back on Monday morning. I guess since the last shipment arrived and is being processed she decided to take a long weekend. But if you need something, I'd be happy to . . ."

Frowning, Barry left before Maya finished talking. Apparently he hadn't successfully calmed or assuaged Kennedy's concerns. This was getting too complicated, first Petre now Kennedy. He wasn't sure who to trust. He suspected that they were together since they'd dated, but she didn't seem concerned about his being caught until he spoke with her the night before.

Kennedy taking an unscheduled day off weeks before the opening of a show was unheard of. Barry was troubled and his thoughts began to fray. What if she contacted the board? What if she had contacted Petre? What if she wasn't with Petre and had contacted the FBI? His mind whirled with possibilities. Then, settling his thoughts, he tried to resolve his suspicions. The obvious one struck him first.

She knew that one of the missing pieces had been hidden in the crate, he surmised. Why else would she be so concerned about the crate arriving early? That could be the only reason she was so anxious about the weight. He smiled at his deception. He'd arranged for Kennedy's and Yolanda's shipments to arrive on opposite days. So Kennedy's crate arrived when she was in New York yesterday and Yolanda's would arrive today when she was in Boston.

He wasn't sure which crate the statue was in, but, either way, he was sure to be the only person unpacking both crates. The night he planted it was a jumble of confusion. Petre and a number of museum employees had been arrested and nobody knew where anything was. It was the perfect opportunity for him to accidentally misplace one of the pieces.

Now, all he needed to do was make the deal and sell the statue before Petre found out. And since Juwan had the contacts to make it happen, he was going with him. Things around him had gotten out of control. It was time to get his life back on track.

As soon as Barry got to his office, he opened the door and pushed it closed behind him. Not hearing the soft click of the latch, he turned around. He noticed someone standing in the doorway. "Petre? Are you crazy? What are you doing here?"

"Nice to see you too, Barry. How are things?"

Barry closed the door and hurried over to his desk, tossing the papers he'd been carrying down and going back to face Petre, who was still standing at the door. "Are you completely out of your mind? There are people looking for you! You can't just walk around here like you own the place."

"Your security wouldn't know me from Adam, and since both Kennedy and Yolanda are out today, I figured that this was the perfect opportunity for you and me to have a little chat."

"We had our chat a month ago. Nothing's changed."

"I think they have and we need to talk."

"What about?"

"A certain missing statue that the FBI would like to talk to me about. You see, I know you placed it in one of the crates being shipped here. So I figure I'd get my cut from you now and you can sell the statue later."

"I have no idea what you're talking about."

"Don't you?" Petre challenged. "It was you. You set us up. You called the authorities and had them waiting for us."

"You're dreaming! Why would I call the authorities? I'd have just as much to lose as you."

"But this way you get it all. So I want my cut now."

"I don't have that kind of money."

"You're lying," Petre accused. "And double-crossing your partner can be extremely dangerous." The phone rang. Both men looked to the desk and then back at each other. It rang three more times with both of them just standing there looking at it. When it finally stopped, Petre continued. "All my contacts have gone to the wind, I need cash now. You know people, investors, sell the statue."

"I don't know anyone. And even if I did, I don't have the kind of money you're looking for. Maybe you should ask your girlfriend."

Petre knew exactly of whom he was speaking. "Kennedy has nothing to do with this. This is between you and me. Sell the statue and get me my cut."

"How am I supposed to sell it? You've got half the art world looking for it."

"I don't care how you do it. Just get it done. I'll be around. I'll contact you in a few days. I want to be there when the deal goes down."

The phone rang again. "You have to get out here," Barry said anxiously. "Whoever it is calling will be coming to the office next. And if it's Maya, remember, she does know who you are." Barry hurried to the desk and picked up the phone. He turned to look at Petre. The door was open and he was already gone.

* * *

Colin Sheppard stopped at the open door to Kevin's New York office. The wire to his cellphone ran from his belt loop to his ear as usual. He held an open file in one hand and had just ended a conversation with the second cellphone he held with the other hand. "What's going on in Washington? Juwan hasn't reported in this morning. Has he brought in his suspect yet?"

Kevin looked up from his computer screen. "No, not yet."

"Why not?"

"There might have been several new developments."

"Such as?" he prompted with a long exaggerated sigh, annoyed that speaking with Kevin and getting information was like pulling teeth from a cheetah. He had to be quick and steady.

"There's a possibility that the initial suspect isn't directly involved as first assumed." Kevin smiled as the words left his mouth.

Colin's jaw tightened. This was his call. He had run the dates and available information and come up with the most likely person to be involved. He read of the close relationship between Evans and Siegal and he reasoned that she knew exactly what was going on. "And his reasoning is?"

"There are mitigating circumstances."

"Which are?" he questioned.

"The relationship between Kennedy and Petre wasn't as first assessed."

"That's ridiculous, all data point directly to her. She was his girlfriend. She had to know what was going on. Therefore, it stands to reason that she's involved," Colin said decisively. He had personally connected all the dots and come up with the suspect. He waited, expecting a debate with Kevin. There was none.

Kevin didn't reply, which caused Colin's jaw to tighten and pull again. Kevin never gave more information than was necessary and he never speculated one way or the other. Everything was fact-based and evidence with him, thus, no questions asked, no response given.

"So what's Juwan's solution? His forty-eight-hour window is up."

"He's got another, more viable suspect."

"Who?"

"Barry Culpepper."

"Culpepper, the public liaison?"

"Correct."

"I ruled him out. He had no direct contact with Siegal. He's not even close to the art. How does he figure in this?"

"Apparently he has more contact with the art than we were led to believe."

"Everything went through Evans. Where is Juwan getting this?"

"He analyzed that latest data."

"Then it's all speculation, correct?"

"Negative."

The circular conversation began to irritate Colin. "Why not?"

"It's in the report. Juwan met with Culpepper and suggested that he had black market contacts. Culpepper showed extreme interest. Remember, since Petre had the contacts, Culpepper's in need of a middle man to move and sell the goods. Juwan offered his service and Culpepper bit."

"Does he have the missing statue?"

"No, not to my knowledge."

"So all this is futile. It still doesn't prove anything. We know for a fact about Evans's relationship with Siegal." Kevin remained silent and the last straw had been broken. Colin decided to assert his directorial privilege. "I don't care if she's directly involved or not. She has information and possible knowledge. We need Siegal in custody and this thing cleaned up." He paused. "Have her brought in."

"On what charges?" Kevin asked, the stern seriousness and disapproving expression on his face evident.

"For questioning," Colin responded; his expression was equal in its seriousness.

"On what charges?" he repeated.

"There is such a thing as probable cause. I want Evans brought in, and I want this thing finished, and that's a direct order." He walked away without another word.

Kevin sat at his desk and digested the conversation, searching for anything he could use to stall the request. But Colin's words were exact. He picked up his phone.

Chapter Twenty

Beckoning with the seductive arms of a new lover, Las Vegas was everything anyone could have imagined and more. Built with an appetite for life, it stimulated and quenched desires, twenty-four hours a day every day of the year. Wickedly addictive, the thrill of gambling enticed as the promise of never-ending frivolity endured. Everywhere you looked the senses were shocked, heightened by the exotic dream of the small desert resort where "what happens in Las Vegas stays in Las Vegas" is its motto. It was an over-the-top, neon dream feeding an unending hunger for excitement.

But the extraordinary glitz of the city was lost on Kennedy. She saw little, heard little and did little. The only thing she truly remembered experiencing was the man standing next to her and the words of the judge standing before them.

Unlike the traditional Vegas weddings officiated by Elvis impersonators and drive-through-window preachers, their wedding ceremony was officiated by a federal court judge. With the backdrop of a wall of law books they stood in the judge's study, with his wife as a witness.

Somewhat surreal, the blur of the night and the ceremony finally crystallized when she heard the words *I do*. Moments later she signed the certificate, Juwan signed the certificate, the judge looked at them, nodded, added his signature and bid them a good life.

They kissed with passion and the reality of Kennedy's dream began to form. She was married. A smile of satisfaction pulled wide across her face. This was the ultimate adventure. She looked up at her new husband. The assurance that life would never be the same sparkled in his eyes. Having arrived as singles, they left as man and wife with a legally binding paper that legitimized their joining.

The limo ride from the judge's home to the hotel followed a direct line down the famous strip. Kennedy thrilled at the excitement of the moment. She'd of course seen the brochures, the movies and had on occasion watched the television shows that promised, but the actual reality of Las Vegas was much more.

She looked out at the bright lights during the wee hours of the morning. The lavishness of the twenty-four-hour city was a world away from the sedate tradition of Washington, D.C. Wild and brimming with energy and excitement, Las Vegas was the epitome of pleasure and delight, but oddly, not as she imagined. "I thought it would somehow be more . . ." she said softly, then paused thinking aloud more to herself than to her new husband, ". . . outrageous."

Juwan leaned closer and followed her line of vision into the night. He smiled. "Were you expecting Sodom and Gomorrah?"

"Well, maybe not as extreme. But yeah, something along those lines," she admitted.

"Disappointed?" Juwan asked.

She looked at him and reached up to stroke the stubble on his chin. "Never."

"Good," Juwan said as he kissed her tenderly. "But you're right, this is no way to see Las Vegas." He pushed a button, opening the limo's sunroof. He pulled a center panel down from the back seat and helped Kennedy to stand.

Then all of a sudden, the magnificent grandeur of Sin City

was at her fingertips. Crowded with passersby at four o'clock in the morning, the unbelievable dream had been realized.

She looked up at the monstrous casinos designed with every conceivable theme from Roman palaces to volcanic eruptions. This was exactly what she expected. Her eyes darted from side to side as bright flashing luminous streams of light, spectacular attractions, outlandish locals and the greatest sky spectacular since the aurora borealis welcomed her.

Moments later they arrived at the hotel. They were greeted at the curb by the honeymoon concierge. He escorted them to the top floor, then made a discreet exit after giving Juwan the key and pointing them in the direction of their suite.

Juwan slid the key card, then opened the door to one of twelve honeymoon suites on that floor. But for all intents and purposes this was the only one in the world as far as he was concerned. Kennedy, about to walk inside, was immediately swooped off her feet, lifted and carried over the threshold. Stunned by the unexpected surprise, she giggled and wiggled, then wrapped her arms around her husband and kissed him hard.

He stepped inside and kicked the door closed. As he let her slowly slide down the front of his body, he smiled with delight as he dropped the three bags on the floor and cuddled her closer. Kennedy glanced down at their luggage—three plastic shopping bags, one from the local drug store and two from the boutique in the downstairs lobby.

"I can't believe we pulled it off," Kennedy said as she looked at the white gold band on her left-hand ring finger. Tilting her head from side to side, she held her hand up to admire the ring. Simple yet distinctive, it was beautifully adorned with an overlaid crosshatched pattern. "Mr. and Mrs. Mason, I love the sound if it."

The sincere happiness in her voice sent a pang of guilt to Juwan's heart. Although he knew that he had done the right thing, he knew that soon the elation would end and the reality of his actions would create a wedge between them like an axe splitting wood.

He gently lowered her to the floor while keeping her close. She was his to protect and he would never allow anyone to harm her, and that included himself. "Kennedy, I promise you," he began softly, "I will never allow anything or anyone to ever hurt you."

"So being married to a professional bodyguard is paying off already, I see. I guess that would automatically make me the safest person in the world."

"Yes, it does, but right now we need to talk about my career and about my life. There's a part of my life you don't know, and you need to," Juwan said, taking her hand and leading her to sit on the bed beside him. She sat, then leaned and kissed his neck.

"About being a bodyguard? Tell me about it," she whispered seductively, then reached under his sweater and stroked the tiny hairs on his chest, slowly going downward.

"There are things you need to know," he said anxiously, closing his eyes as she pressed tiny kisses down his neck.

"I'm listening," she said. "Tell me more." Her fingers grabbed the edge of his waistband and she was wreaking havoc on his senses. He held her hand still.

Juwan took a deep breath, every nerve in his body tingling and the thickness of desire deepened his voice. "My job is a lot more detailed than just that. I do a lot of traveling and I, uh . . ." He moaned as the kisses continued.

"Of course you do," she said, interrupting him.

"I often go undercover and as such we . . ." he tried to continue, but she interrupted again. He was losing track, getting caught up in the passion of being with her.

"Yes, let's go undercover now," she said as she reached for his waistband again, but he instantly took her hand.

"Kennedy, listen," he said firmly, "this is important. You need to know this."

The seriousness of his tone stopped her and she looked at him. "Tell me."

"At times I'm assigned to go undercover to infiltrate or . . ."

"Undercover? Really, that sounds exciting, is it?"

Juwan frowned. This wasn't going to be easy. "Sometimes, but other times it's very difficult, like now. I have to do things that I really don't want to, but that's the nature of the job."

"You said *we* and that you were *assigned*. Do you work alone or with a company or organization?"

"I work with an organization."

"Do you have a gun?" she asked with interest.

He nodded. "Several."

"Have you ever shot anyone?"

"Yes."

"Killed them?"

"Kennedy, I'm trained to shoot to kill in self-defense."

"Wow." The shock of her new husband's profession surprised her. Apparently there was much more to being a bodyguard than she imagined.

"One of the reasons I'm telling you all this is because I've been offered a promotion and asked to fill one of two positions that would dramatically curtail that life."

"Juwan, that's wonderful. But would that mean you'd have to still live abroad even though we're married and you could be a US citizen?"

"No. There are two positions available. One of the positions is in London where I live now and the other is here in the States."

"I see."

"Kennedy," he began.

"No, Juwan." She stood and moved away, knowing that this was his way of telling her that he still needed to leave. "I don't want to talk about this. Not tonight. I don't want to deal with it and I don't want to think about it."

"We have to, Kennedy. I need to make this right with you."
He stood and went to her.

"This is our honeymoon and it should be special so all that
other real life stuff doesn't matter, not now. It can wait until
tomorrow." She paused. "Is that all right with you?"

Juwan smiled; loving her was so easy. "Yes."

"Good." Kennedy looked around the room to a door leading to the bathroom, then found two. "Now I'm gonna take
a shower, then change into something more appropriate for
the occasion." She winked, making his eyes sparkle, and a
deep ripple of anticipation streaked through him.

"What exactly would that be?" he asked, peering into the
bags sitting in the middle of the floor.

"You'll see, I'll be right back." She picked up two of the
bags and headed for the bathroom.

"Kennedy," Juwan called to her. She turned but still stood
in the doorway of the bathroom. "I want you to know that
whatever happens in the next days or weeks, I do love you."

She smiled blissfully, never tiring of hearing those words
from him. "I love you, too."

Juwan nodded as she disappeared into the bathroom. He
walked back to the bed and sat down heavily. Moments later
he collapsed back, then lay there looking up at himself in the
bed's overhead mirror. His feeble attempt to come clean
was nothing less than pathetic. He shook his head; he knew
that he needed to tell her.

Standing, he grabbed his bag and walked to the door across
the room from the bathroom and found a second bathroom. He
walked inside and dumped the contents on the marble counter.
A quick shave and shower later he donned the silk drawstring
pajama bottoms and matching robe Kennedy had picked out,
then went back into the bedroom. Kennedy was still in her bathroom, so he walked over and stood at the window and looked
out at the approaching dawn.

The penthouse suite afforded him the perfect view of the

landscape spiked by the glittering light of Las Vegas. The flatness of the desert stretched for miles and he looked far into the distance, wishing that he could somehow take Kennedy away from all this.

He had mastered the art of deception and it had served him well over the years. He learned to work undercover in all circles, from the boardroom to the bowery. He hung with criminals and company CEOs, parasites and presidents, and in all that time he never wavered in his convictions. Detached and unemotional, he did whatever he set out to accomplish, no matter how difficult, no matter how troubling, until now.

Since the age of fifteen when he had witnessed the brutal killing of both his parents and his sister's ensuing trauma, he set his life on an unswerving course. At that moment he knew that he'd given up a part of himself and for the rest of his life, he would never be the same.

He had severed his feelings and distanced his emotions, going through life expecting the worst in human nature and never being disappointed. Regret was never part of his equation. Then, two years ago, at the end of a routine field assignment, he'd walked away as usual, expecting to feel nothing and, as usual, he didn't.

Unexpectedly, the death of Remy weighed heavily on his mind. Remy, who was gullible and trusting, was killed by her own hand. And he'd stood by helplessly, unable to stop her. Trusting others was her greatest weakness. She trusted him and he had betrayed her. But that was his job and he was good at it. She was a means to an end. And, ultimately, she was expendable. He'd walked away as he'd always done. But this time he felt something. Maybe doing the right thing wasn't always doing the right thing.

The uneasy emotions settled around him, alien and unfamiliar, regret and guilt. He had done many things in his career to get the job done and he had never felt regret because he always knew that the ends justified the means. But now he wasn't so sure. Remy, vulnerable and susceptible, had been manipulated by her accomplices, her boyfriend, and then again by him.

The haunting thought of fate replaying itself settled on his heart. He hadn't been in love with Remy, but he knew that she loved him and he used her love against her. Now, as fate would have it, he was in love with Kennedy. And as sure as the sun would rise tomorrow, he knew that when she found out about him, he would lose her.

Gradually, he looked down, letting his eyes drift to the streets below. The energy of the city was beginning to reawaken. A new day was coming.

Juwan looked at his reflection in the window glass. He remembered the moment he saw Kennedy months ago. Her photographs in the file had given him pause even then. Candid and playful she was with Petre in one, another had her alone walking with a backpack on her shoulder in a Nubian market.

The days and nights after that he had fantasized about her, her face, her smile, and her touch. A slow smile spread wide across his face as the fantasized image of Kennedy slowly appeared behind him. Juwan's smile broadened as the conjured image walked closer. She reached out to touch him, but instead vanished.

Juwan lowered his head in frustration. Reckless was a word that would never be used to describe him, but he hadn't been himself for some time now and feeling off-balance had become the norm, and he didn't like it. He turned and walked back to the bed and lay back as he had done before.

Kennedy opened the door and came out of the bathroom. She spotted Juwan lying on the bed. His thoughts were obviously miles away. For the first time in a long time the possibility prompted a smile. She went to him.

"I have no idea how you did all this, the flight, the judge, the room. But I'm so glad you did," she said, approaching.

He opened his eyes and sat up as soon as he heard her voice. She had appeared out of nowhere, dispelling his troubled thoughts into puffs of smoke. The moment he saw her, a rush of heat hit his groin like an arrow hitting the center of a bull's-eye and his heart skipped a beat. His eyes roamed the length of her. She was beyond just beautiful, she was dazzling and captivating and sexy.

Her gown, fitted in silk and satin, shimmered on the curves of her body as she approached like black ink. She seemed to be flowing in enraptured waves; he stared, fixated and trancelike with each step she took. His eyes glazed and glistened. She watched his response and smiled inwardly. Seeing the spark of arousal dance in his eyes, she knew that she definitely had his attention. "You like?" she asked.

Dry-mouthed, he licked his lips and nodded slowly and steadily as his mouth gaped. She smiled openly. This was exactly the reaction she wanted. He was still nodding when she came to him. She reached out to him, touching and fingering the loosely tied drawstring on his pajama pants. She touched his chest, then spread her hands, moving his robe aside. He looked down and watched her hands move over his chest. He closed, then opened his eyes and groaned, prompting her to bolder action.

She pulled her nightgown upwards then straddled his legs to maneuver her body on top of him. Then she sat back on his lap and looked down into his misty pale eyes. "Thank you," she whispered.

Juwan licked his lips a second time in as many minutes. He didn't have the slightest clue why she was thanking him. All he knew was that she was his and he was hers. "Kennedy, you are . . . breathtaking," he said, choking the words in gasps of passion.

She took his face in her hands and caressed him. Flushed and amorous, his skin was on fire. She kissed his forehead, his eyes, his cheek and the corner of his mouth. She playfully nipped at his neck, then licked and kissed the tingling spot. She tasted the lobe of his ear and ran her tongue around the curve of his jaw. She found that teasing him was a pleasure she fully enjoyed. "I think I'm gonna enjoy being married to you," she whispered into his ear. The heat of her breath made his body shudder; his hooded eyes closed and his mouth opened but he didn't answer her.

She combed her nails over his short-cropped hair and down the smooth softness of his freshly shaved chin, then leaned in and kissed the underside of his jaw. He smelled like heaven, sweet, strong and sensual. She continued raking her nails down his neck, over his shoulders, and then down the front of his chest. The tiny silk, soft hairs on his chest made her even more playful.

"Keni," he moaned tensely, using her shortened name as he grabbed at her hands to still them, but she avoided his grasp.

"Yes?" she hummed calmly. He groaned a low throaty response as she continued her decent. When she reached the drawstring of his silk pajamas, he took her hands and held them still. He leaned in and kissed the thin lace covering her breasts. She shifted on his lap as anticipation arched and stiffened her back. He moaned his satisfaction as he noticed the narrow strip of satin holding the scant lace in place over her swollen breasts. He bit at the ribbon-like tie and the paisley webbed fabric, tasting the sweetness of her nipple through the lace. The two swatches of lace loosened. She leaned away, but just as quickly he wrapped his arms around her and held her close.

It was his time to play and he knew that he would savor every minute. He reached up and pulled the lace robe down her shoulders, then ran his hands over the soft silky satin of her raised gown. Her arms were pinned to her sides by the robe, but she somehow clung to his shoulders as her limbs weakened and her head rolled back. He immediately took advantage of her position and pulled the ribbon completely away.

Her breasts, brown orbs, plump and pert, beckoned to him and he obediently obliged.

He devoured her, tasting, licking, pulling and lapping, flicking his tongue and surrounding her until she surrendered everything to his will. She moaned and groaned in ecstasy as the heat of his mouth scalded her tingling skin. He reached and gathered both breasts, then tucked his face between the deep cleavage, going from nipple to nipple, sending torturous pangs of pleasure and nerve endings riotously dancing.

The mounting need of his body instinctively moved him to gather her against his body as he continued to nuzzle his face into the swell of her cleavage. The subtle scent of her perfumed body compelled him even closer as he inhaled the sweetness of her skin. He looked up to her. "You are so beautiful," he muttered.

She released her arms from the robe and the gentle brush of her lips along with her tongue on his mouth sent a shockwave of renewed desire through him. He tightened his grip on her waist. She kissed him passionately, lazily wrapping her arms around his neck and holding him tenderly. The kiss was intended to seduce and entice, but instead it merely added gasoline to the already burning fire.

Juwan returned her kiss with equal fervor. When it ended, she let her hands drift down his neck and over his shoulders. Her nails gently dug into him, leaving a trail of fire across his skin. He shuddered as a muscle in his jaw tightened and he fought back the need to make love to her instantly.

The passion of their embrace erupted into a succession of pulsating kisses, hard, long and searing. He leaned back, allowing her body to lie on top of his. Ending the kiss, she rose up and looked down at him. The sun's first rays beamed into the room illuminating the curve of her body as she slowly, completely removed the lacy black robe.

Her negligee, satin and silk, was all that separated him from his desire. He released the thin shoulder straps, letting them fall onto her arms. She reached up and seductively pulled the gown over her head and tossed it to the floor.

He in turn wiggled free of his silk pajama bottoms and impatiently tossed them aside. They were both naked; he looked up at her. She was the most perfect sight he had ever seen. He reached up and cupped her breasts with his hands, feeling the weight of their fullness. She shifted her body upward, hovering over the stiff shaft of his passion. Hard and full, the fierceness of his hunger throbbed for satisfaction.

She stroked the length of him, causing a deep intake of air and a gasping exhale. The power in her hands so excited her. She taunted and toyed with her newfound pleasure. Strong and virile, he pulsated and she loved the unrestrained hardness.

He released her breast and reached down to her pleasure; in one smooth gesture he captured her core and she nearly fainted. His talented hands, fingers and thumbs, relentless in their pursuit, teased and toyed, sending the burning fire into her.

She centered her body over him, then dropped, sending the blade of his manhood deep into her core. She gasped and cried out. The pleasurable sting of him held her timeless as she held her breath. Long and hard, he was deep inside of her. She moved up slightly, feeling his escape, then plunged down again, repeating the motion. In purposeful, slow strokes she rose and fell, increasing her pace each time. The cadence had begun and their bodies moved in unison, quickly building a wave of sensual rapture.

Thrust after thrust they met as one in a vigorous fever. He held her waist to guide her as she leaned back, rocking her hips and sitting on the power of his thrusts. Her nails bit into his arms and her eyes rose heavenward. Then as the rapture approached, she leaned in over his body and his mouth instantly grasped her nipple and she screamed in pleasure as his tongue licked the sweet dark center of her breasts.

Frantic tension sent their need to the edge. The crescendo approached. He arched his body up, meeting her one last time, head on. They erupted and as one, cresting at the peak of rapture. She collapsed on top of him. Breathing raggedly, she lay there pillowed by his body and wrapped in his embrace.

Moments later she slid to his side and he wrapped his arm around her again and pulled her close beside him. She looked up, surprised to see herself looking down onto his body. She smiled wickedly at the surprise. "There's a mirror up there," she said huskily, still slightly breathless. He moaned his response, then kissed her forehead lovingly and gathered her even closer. Together they stared up at the reflection of a loving couple.

His warm, loving embrace was everything she needed.

She closed her eyes and allowed sleep to take her. She slept in his arms in peace and comfort. This was where she belonged and where she intended to be for the rest of her life. Sated and satisfied, she was aware that the end of her long day had been more than she could have possibly imagined. She smiled blissfully. There was no way anything could go wrong.

Chapter Twenty-One

Midday Juwan opened, then closed his hooded eyes, feeling the gentle weight of Kennedy's hands roaming across his shoulders. He rolled his neck and opened his eyes to see her hands spread wide across his chest, then slip low to his waist. They lay naked, entwined from a lovemaking marathon. He'd lost count after the third climax. She released over and over again, her body twitching and shuddering with each orgasm. He smiled, remembering her screams of passion as he brought her to ecstasy and watched with pleasure.

The dream, the vision, was now a reality. He looked up into the eyes of his reflection, then over, seeing her still asleep. He sighed deeply with satisfaction as she moaned and moved, now lying half on and half off his body. He gathered her closer, resting his chin on the top of her head, then closed his eyes. A peaceful sleep took him again as the sights and sounds of the city below surrounded and engulfed them, but they were a world away in their own dream.

Toward evening, Juwan awoke in their bed alone. He looked at the clock; it was much later than he expected. Kennedy came out of the bathroom with a scanty white towel wrapped around her. His mind instantly followed the pull of his body.

She smiled when she saw that he was finally awake. "I called room service again. They should be here any minute."

"You look wonderful," he said, sitting up against the pillows as he relaxed back, taking in the full view of her as she stood in the bathroom doorway. "Come here."

"I hope you're hungry. I ordered half the menu."

His brow arched knowingly and a cocky smile sparked in her eyes. It was a look with which she had recently become very familiar. "I'm hungry, but not necessary for anything room service has on the menu."

"Oh really," she said as she sashayed over to the bed, then kneeled close to him. He immediately grabbed her waist and drew her beneath him. The towel slipped away. A shower of kisses followed as she giggled and wiggled and he kissed and ticked relentlessly.

Then suddenly he stopped and looked into her eyes. "I love you," he whispered. He kissed her passionately, expressing all the emotion he had saved up his entire life. Lips soft and tender pressed together as mouths opened and tongues playfully intertwined, hands fondling and stroking, teasing and tempting. The heat of their passion readily surged once again.

The gentle knock on the door was ignored the first and second time. Then finally Kennedy drew herself away, realizing that room service had arrived. "That'll be room service with our breakfast, lunch and dinner," she said, pulling away from him to get the door.

"Let 'em wait," he protested, being too comfortable with his wife wrapped in his arms. "Or they can leave it outside."

"They need a signature, Mr. Mason." She escaped and darted away quickly as his hands reached for her one last time.

"Come back," he begged as she hurried from the bed to the bathroom and grabbed one of the big white fluffy robes supplied by the hotel. She disappeared into the living room of the suite. Juwan sat up, hearing her talking with the

server. He looked over to the clock again, then to his phone.
The red light was blinking. He reached over, picked it up and
opened it. The urgency of the text message made him smile.
It was exactly what he had been waiting for. He responded
with his own message, agreeing to the specifically noted time
and place. He flipped to voice messages and listened to the
same urgent message repeated twice. His smiled broadened.
This was getting better and better.

An hour later Kennedy and Juwan laughed and talked,
eating out on the terrace overlooking the city. Dusk was approaching and the distant mountains lit up with a red purple
haze as sunset approached. Kennedy stood at the chest-high
rail and looked out over the wondrous view. The sun's last
rays lit her profile and Juwan sat staring at the beauty of the
moment. She was the vision he had dreamed. "We have to
come back here again," she said.

Juwan stood behind her. A warm gentle breeze blew through
her wayward hair as he tucked his face into the crook of her
neck and kissed her. His hands drifted down, opening the
thick tie of her terry cloth robe. He slipped his hand into the
opening and felt her soft bare skin. Her stomach flat, her
breasts round and plump, he traveled lower touching the tiny
hairs, causing her to moan and reach for up for him.

She draped her arms around his neck and he plunged
deeper, causing her moan to echo louder. She wiggled away,
but he kept his taut body pressed to her back. She turned to him,
opening his robe and seeing his readiness for her. She lifted
her leg, he caught it and pulled her up to wrap completely
around him. Holding her tight against the high-backed rail, he
pressed deep into her and rocked until a blinding surge of passion released. There in the muted sunlight, standing on the terrace surrounded by ornamental trees, bushes, decorative
sweet-scented flowers and the city alive with passion and excitement, he loved her once more and the rest of that night.

The next morning Kennedy awoke in bed beside Juwan.

She quietly crawled out, turned to see him roll to the side. She went into the bathroom and took a cool shower; her body relaxed as the tepid water ran over her. She washed her hair, sprayed on her favorite body mist, slipped on her new jeans and sweater, then went out into the living room.

She sat comfortably on one of the two big overstuffed sofas and picked up the phone. She dialed the number and waited, figuring out the best way to tell her family. Before she decided on a course of action, her parents' answering machine came on. She looked at her watch, checking the time. It was still early in Virginia. She left a quick message, then dialed the second number. The phone was picked up on the second ring.

"Madi."

"Hey, girl, where are you? I tried to call you yesterday. Are you still in New York? I talked to Hope and Faith and they said that you canceled lunch and shopping with them. What's going on? Are you at home or are you still at work?"

"No, I'm not at home. I didn't go to work yesterday. I called in sick."

"Are you okay?" Madison asked, knowing that Kennedy rarely took time off, particularly when she was putting together an exhibit.

Kennedy smiled. "I've never been better."

"I'm sure you're exhausted. But I guess the exhibit is pretty well taken care of for you to take the day off."

"Yeah, my part is pretty much done. Yolanda has a bit more to do, but I didn't call to talk about that."

"What's up?" Madison asked.

"I tried calling Mom and Dad this morning but their machine picked up. Where are they?"

"Crescent Island, they went down for the weekend. They'll be back on Sunday."

"Oh, I needed to talk to them."

"Why, what's going on?"

"Madi, are you sitting down?"

"Oh listen, before I forget, J.T. and Juliet are back from their honeymoon. They're positively beaming. I told them we'd get together tomorrow night at Mom and Dad's house. Are you free?"

"No. Yes. No. Wait a minute. Just answer the question, are you sitting down?"

"No, I'm in the kitchen with Tony. Trey's having lunch with us," she said nonchalantly. "Why."

Kennedy heard them chime in the background, "Hi, Keni." "I need to tell you something but I need for you to be sitting down and I need you to get Tony there beside you to listen also."

"Hold on," Madison said as she moved to the sofa and slowly sat down. A muffled call to her husband brought Tony next to her. "Okay, I'm sitting. What's going on?"

"Is Tony there with you?"

"Yes, he's here. What going on?"

"Have Trey pick up the other receiver."

Madison and Tony shared the receiver while Trey sat across the room on the other phone. "Hey, Keni," Tony said as he laid his hand on Madison's stomach and rubbed the kicking babies.

"Keni," Trey began, "whatever it is, I'm not doing it. I'm laying low until Mamma Lou finds a new target."

Tony and Madison chuckled. "Okay," Madison finally said, "I'm sitting and we're all here. What's going on?"

"I'm in Las Vegas."

"What's in Vegas?" Madison, Tony and Trey said in unison.

"My husband. I got married last night." The line went silent. "Tony, Trey, are you there? Where's Madi? What's happening? What going on? Is she okay?"

Laughter burst from the other side of the phone. Trey was hysterical. Tears barreled down his face as his laughter boomed through the receiver. Barely able to speak, he finally calmed himself and answered.

"Calm down, calm down, everything's okay, Keni," Tony said.

"Where's Madison?"

"She's here. I think she's just speechless."

"Madi?" A guttural choking sound answered. "Madi, are you okay?" Giggles erupted, then squeals of joy, and finally heartfelt laughter. Kennedy relaxed back into the comfort of the sofa.

"Kennedy Evans, what in the world were you thinking? Who did you . . . ? No, you didn't? Did you? The bad boy bodyguard, right? But you said. Oh my God, you did. I can't believe it. When? No, wait, how did you decide? Oh God, I can't believe you did it!"

The conversation, such as it was, completely understood by Madison and Kennedy, had Tony and Trey looking at each other as if subtitles would be forthcoming. Eventually they shrugged and shook their heads, knowing that this was one conversation best heard second hand. Trey hung up and Tony stood and went back into the kitchen, following Trey and leaving Madison and Kennedy to speak the language they did so well.

Fifteen minutes and an abridged explanation later, Kennedy hung up smiling. She'd told her sister and then made her swear that she wouldn't tell anyone until she got back the following day.

"Good morning."

She turned to see Juwan standing at the opening between the bedroom and the living room. "Good morning," she replied. He had showered, shaved and dressed in his new jeans and shirt.

He came over and reached his hand down to her. "Feel like seeing the sights of the town?"

She grasped his hand and was pulled up into his arms. "Sure, sounds great." She kissed his cheek, then noticed a charm hanging around his neck. "What's that? I've never seen you wear that before. It's beautiful." She reached out and touched the small pendant hanging around his neck.

"It's a Tuareg cross from the nomadic Berber-speaking people in the western Sahara Desert." He removed it from around his neck and placed it in her hand. "Some of them still wear it. It's believed to be magical and have strong protective powers."

Kennedy held it up and examined the detailed and intricate workmanship. "It's beautiful," she proclaimed, then glanced at him with smiling eyes. "Magical protective powers, huh? Is that why you wear it, to protect you?"

He smiled. "Once, yes, but not anymore. My parents gave it to me a long time ago. It helped me to feel close to them. And now I want you to have it and feel close to me, no matter what happens." He took the necklace from her hands and slipped it around her neck, securing and fastening the clasp.

"What could possibly happen? You're legally married to an American citizen. You can't be deported now, right?"

He smiled at her innocence, knowing better. "Right."

"So tell me more," she began, taking his hand and moving back to the sofa. They sat and she cuddled next to him. "Your parents, they died, right?" He nodded. She shook her head. "This is so strange. We're married and it's amazing how little I really know about you."

"What do you want to know?"

"Okay, what other family do you have?"

"A younger sister in New York and two younger brothers still in college."

"Wow, I have a whole new family. I never thought about that part. Okay, tell me about my new sister," she announced happily. "What's her name?"

"Yasmine." He paused to consider giving her the full name, then decided to take the chance. He had to begin acclimating her to her new life. "Yasmine Mason Mebeko Pole."

"Is she married to one of Ambassador Mebeko's sons?"

"No, she's his adopted daughter."

"But that would mean that you're also his . . ."

" . . . Yes, I'm his adopted son."

Kennedy sat up and looked at him strangely. "What?"

"Maurice and my father were best friends through college. He's our godfather and when my parents died, he and Adarah legally adopted us. I was fifteen and Yasmine was five."

"What?" Kennedy repeated. "You didn't think that something like that was important enough to tell me before? Your name is Mebeko."

"It's your legal married name as well."

"What?" she repeated, then hurried to their marriage certificate lying on the dresser in the bedroom. She had signed her name first, then the judge gave him the paper to sign his. She never thought to examine the document after that. But she did now. She read the names listed, then looked back at him as he approached. "You are kidding me, right?"

"No. Technically it's an honorary title bestowed on Maurice. He's a monarch and as I am the eldest son, the title has, therefore, fallen to me." He slipped the paper from her hands and returned it to the dresser. "But for all practical purposes we will be Mr. and Mrs. Juwan Mason and you'll be Kennedy Evans-Mason, if you'd prefer."

Kennedy began laughing as she attempted to walk away. Juwan grasped her arm, just as he'd done in the garden that first night. "Kennedy. What's in a name? That which we call a rose/by any other name would smell as sweet," he said, quoting William Shakespeare's *Romeo and Juliet*. "Nothing has changed."

She took a deep breath. Technically he was right. Nothing had changed. They were still married and she was still in love with him. "So, Prince Juwan Mason Mebeko, what else aren't you telling me?"

He smiled and moved closer to within inches from her mouth. "In time," he promised. "In time." He kissed her the way a husband kisses his beloved wife, and with that, nothing much mattered anymore, not even her new name.

"This isn't over," she said when the kiss ended. He nodded, knowing that they would talk about this and more. "No more surprises today." He nodded. "We still need to talk about this." He nodded again. "Okay, let's go." She turned to leave, but he held her tight.

"Whoa, whoa, whoa, wait a minute. I have a better idea."

Then, just as he leaned in to kiss her again, his cell phone rang. He frowned. He must have inadvertently turned the ringer back on when he checked his messages earlier. He opened it and looked at the number. "It's an associate, I need to take this."

"Go ahead, take it," Kennedy said grabbing her purse and heading to the door. "I'll meet you downstairs at the concierge's desk." He nodded, seeing her open, then close the door behind her, and then answered the call.

"I tried calling you a dozen times yesterday. Your forty-eight hours is up. Wherever you are, you need to get back here—now," Kevin said as soon as Juwan answered.

"What's going on?"

"Colin is looking for his suspect. He's ready to bring her in, but he just found out that she's skipped town. He suspects she went to Petre."

"She didn't skip and she's not with Petre. She's with me."

"And you are where?"

"Nevada."

"Nevada?"

"As in Las Vegas, Nevada."

"What are you doing in Las Vegas?" Kevin asked, almost afraid to hear the answer.

"I'll tell you when I get back tomorrow. I received a few messages from Culpepper. He's ready to make a deal. As a matter of fact, he wants to get this over with as soon as possible, his words. I have a feeling that Petre must be pressuring him."

"Great, when and where?"

"He wants to meet tomorrow afternoon. The place isn't set. I'll let you know as soon as I get a location."

"Perfect. I assume you'll be back by then."

"Definitely."

"Good, I'll have the team on standby. We'll pick Culpepper up and have him lead us to Petre."

"Exactly."

"What do you want me to tell Colin? He's pretty gung-ho about ending this."

"Tell him to stand down. Or, better yet, chill out. I'm on top of things. I'll see you tomorrow."

"Juwan, I hope you know what you're doing."

Juwan hung up and smiled. He knew exactly what he was going to do. Looking at his watch, he saw it was 11:30 Pacific time. He set a thirty-six-hour alarm. In that time he was going to bring Petre and Culpepper in with the stolen art, close the case, accept the promotion, announce his move to D.C. and have a life with Kennedy.

Ten minutes later Juwan stood by Kennedy's side as she shrieked with joy at winning at the crap tables. They visited several other casinos, saw some sights, ate an early dinner, then went back to their hotel. Hours later they caught a flight to Washington, D.C. By seven o'clock Sunday morning they had landed and were headed back to her house in Georgetown.

Kennedy looked around the living room as if it were brand new. It seemed as though it had been ages since she was there. But it was really just a little over forty-eight hours ago.

"I have to go," Juwan said, holding her in his arms.

"I figured that."

"I'll see you this evening and then we need to seriously talk."

"I know. I'm going in to the museum this morning. If you need me, call me on my cell phone, I have a feeling I'll probably be working on the exhibit most of the time."

"It is amazing, I'm very proud of you."

"Thanks." She blushed. "Okay now go. Get out of here. You have to bring home the bacon for two now." She turned him around and pointed him in the direction of the front door. "I need to change and get to work. There are still a few things to take care of before the reception and opening next week."

Juwan left feeling good. He looked at his watch. Perfect, ten hours remained. He was right on schedule. He had just enough time to get to the office and make the final preparations for his meet with Barry.

Chapter Twenty-Two

As soon as Kennedy entered the already opened and crowded museum, she went directly to her office. She unlocked the door and looked down. Her floor was littered with messages slipped under her door. She picked them up and sorted them as she walked to her desk. She spent the next twenty minutes on her computer answering most e-mails while ignoring the rest.

As she checked her computer e-mail and phone messages, she had several nondescript ones from Barry asking her to see him at her earliest convenience and one from Maya detailing and listing the progress that had been made Friday in her absence and addressing the few lighting points they'd talked about Thursday evening.

Kennedy smiled happily. Maya's efficiency was unmatched. Of all the stupid things Petre had done in the past, recommending Maya to be her assistant was certainly his brightest moment.

She glanced at her dwindling list of things to do. Choosing the top one on the list, she dove right in, working steadily for the next two hours. It wasn't until she received a phone call from maintenance requesting her presence in the exhibit that she paused to take a break.

A half hour later, after taking care of clean-up concerns in the lab's storage area, she returned to her desk. As soon as she sat down, the phone rang again, taking her by surprise. No one knew that she was at work except . . . She smiled, thinking of Juwan. She picked up.

"Kennedy, it's security at the front desk. There are two men here to speak with you."

"Who are they?" she asked, knowing that she wasn't expecting anyone on a Sunday afternoon.

"They say it's important. You'd better come."

"Can they speak to someone else?"

"No, they need you."

"Okay, I'll be right there."

As soon as she arrived in the lobby, she noticed the stern expressions on their faces. It was obvious that they weren't art lovers. She assumed they were some form of security. As she approached, one of the men reached into his jacket pocket and pulled out his identification. "Ms. Kennedy Evans?" one of the men asked as he stepped forward to take charge. His cold, narrow eyes gave her a chill. He glared accusingly as he spoke.

"Doctor Kennedy Evans, yes," she corrected. The museum's security guard smiled, amused by the man's stunned expression at being corrected.

"I'm Special Agent Colin Sheppard with the Federal Bureau of Investigation and this is my associate." The other man smiled briefly and nodded politely. Kennedy made up her mind instantly that she liked him better than the one speaking. His abrupt dispassionate manner was an immediate turn off. "I'd like to have a few moments of your time."

"Is this about Petre Siegal and the Nubian Museum?"

"Ma'am, it would be better if we talked privately."

"Sure, of course," she said, immediately gesturing to the elevator. "Shall we go to my office?"

"Actually." He stepped in front of her quickly. "This would be better at our office."

"Fine, may I get my purse and coat?"

"Of course, I'll be happy to accompany you to your office."

"As you wish," she said, then turned and walked away. The agent followed Kennedy down to her office, then back to the security desk to meet with his waiting partner, walking in silence. They drove in silence as well, with the partner driving and Sheppard in the back seat sitting next to her.

Kennedy looked out the window. She had been expecting this. Remembering what DeWitt said, she didn't realize that the questioning would be so formal. But she went along cooperating. The last thing she needed was to draw attention to herself. "Can you tell me exactly what this is about?" she asked as they got out of the parked car and headed to the elevator entrance.

"This way," Sheppard said, ignoring her question. They took the elevator to the tenth floor, got out and walked through a series of hallways. They stopped in front of a door marked Interview Room Six. "May I take your jacket and purse?"

"No," she said plainly.

"Excuse me?" he asked as if he didn't understand the words that came out of her mouth.

"No," she repeated a second time. "That won't be necessary."

"I insist," he said, reaching to take her things. She didn't speak but instead looked at him, daring him to touch her belongings. He relented, seeing his intimidation tactics sorely lacking, nodded and took a step back. "As you like." He walked away, leaving her to the second agent, who took her through the door into a waiting area.

She was eventually escorted to a small empty room with a table, three chairs facing a mesh-screened window. Kennedy looked at her watch as soon as she arrived. It was two-thirty. She walked over to the window and looked out. The white-frosted paneled window afforded her a perfect view of nothing. She shook her head and went back to the table.

She dropped her jacket and purse down and took a seat. Looking around, she noticed that the room looked like every interrogation room she'd ever seen in every cop movie and television show. Typically bland with dull off-white walls and a simple hanging lamp over the table in the center of the room. It even had a distorted mirror, which she assumed was actually two-way glass.

She imagined that Agent Sheppard was behind the glass watching her, waiting for her to confess to the disappearance of Jimmy Hoffa. She shook her head, hoping that this was an exception and that her government did better than this when it came to interviewing and interrogating suspects.

She stood, she walked, she sat, and then had finally had enough. She looked at her watch. The wait had gone on for thirty minutes. She stood and as soon as she walked to the door, it opened and Special Agent Colin Sheppard and a female agent entered. "Sorry to keep you waiting," he apologized with an empty smile.

He had a small notebook and file and she had a notepad, pen, and tape recorder. She placed her items on the desk, then stood by the side and waited.

"Ms. Evans . . ." Colin began and motioned for her to have a seat. He leaned across the table to turn on the tape recorder.

"Doctor Evans," she said, correcting him again.

He opened the file he'd carried and ran his finger down the first page and nodded, "Yes, of course, Doctor Evans, if you'll have a seat, we can get started and get this over with as soon as possible." She sat. He cleared his throat and began. "Doctor Evans, we are well aware of you intimate relationship with Petre Siegal and his associates. We are also aware that he has tried on occasion to contact you."

"How would you know that?"

"You've been under investigation by one of our undercover special agents and he has gathered some very damaging evidence on your recent movements."

"Undercover special agent, who is he?" she questioned as the pit of her stomach dropped and she immediately erased the preposterous thought from her mind.

"Please answer the question, Doctor Evans."

"Yes, Petre has contacted me twice. Each time I suggested that he turn himself in."

"And . . ." he prompted eagerly.

"And nothing. You don't have him so I assume he didn't do as I suggested," she said calmly, fighting back her anger.

"Doctor Evans, we can play these word games all evening. I assure you I have the time. But I assume you have something better to do than to sit here and answer my questions over and over again."

"What exactly do you want, Mr. Sheppard?"

"Special Agent Sheppard," he corrected. She nodded. "Ma'am, what I want is to have the people responsible for the Nubian Museum theft punished. You can, of course, appreciate that." She nodded again. "Good, why don't we start from the top and you tell me everything you know about the theft?"

"I don't know anything about it other than what I've heard or read about in the newspapers."

"But you do know Petre Siegal."

"Yes, I also know several senators and a movie star, not to mention a dozen or so judges. That doesn't mean I'm working with them."

"But you did work with Petre Siegal."

"Yes, along with a number of other people." He paused a while and began flipping through the open file. "Is that all?" she asked.

He looked back up at her. "Hardly. What exactly was your involvement in the theft at the Nubian Museum?"

"I had no involvement."

"Do you know where Mr. Siegal is?"

"No."

"Are you protecting Mr. Siegal?"

"You've got to be kidding me."

"I assure you I am quite serious."

She looked at him sternly. "I want my attorney."

"I must warn you, Doctor Evans, protecting Mr. Siegal will be considered conspiracy after the fact. That's time in a federal prison. I know you don't want that. So answer the question, where is Mr. Siegal?"

Juwan was relaxed as he sat facing the entrance to the mall in the seat Barry had proposed for their meeting. He looked around casually, seeing his team in position. Talking to several of his associates, he made sure that everyone was in place. He looked at his watch. He was early. But he knew that Barry should be arriving at any time. Then from a microphone in his ear, he got the word from the perimeter team that Barry had possibly arrived. But they weren't exactly sure if it was him or not. Juwan frowned; the last thing he needed was to have the play fall apart at this point. Barry was unmistakable; how could anyone not be sure it was him?

But before he could finish his thought, he looked up to see Barry entering the mall and walking toward him. Dressed in all black, he looked positively ridiculous. He wore dark sunglasses, a trench coat, a wig and baseball cap and bright brand new white running sneakers. He walked quickly, carrying a crumpled grocery store shopping bag under his arm. Juwan chuckled at the absurdity of his outfit. He'd obviously seen one too many spy movies. As soon as he approached, Juwan stood. "No, sit down. We don't know each other," Barry hissed quickly and walked past Juwan.

Juwan, barely able to keep his composure, looked away and did as he was instructed. Barry pulled a newspaper from his coat pocket, sat down on the bench directly behind Juwan and pretended to read. He set the shopping bag on the seat beside him, then looked around suspiciously. Satisfied that he hadn't been followed, he leaned back and called to Juwan, "Do you have the money?"

Juwan, silently chuckling, couldn't help but ask, "Why the wig?"

"Disguise," he stated still scrutinizing the immediate area.

"And the white sneakers?"

Barry was stunned that a professional black market fence and buyer as Juwan claimed to be didn't have a clue about disguises and making a quick getaway. "To get away fast just in case something goes wrong."

"Oh, you mean in case you get caught trying to sell stolen art?"

"Shhh, keep it down," Barry said, looking around, then focusing on a young child with a red balloon and a dripping ice cream cone getting his face and hands wiped by his mother. "You never know who's watching or who's listening."

"That's true," Juwan said as he looked at an openly laughing undercover operative standing at the jewelry counter across the way, then at the woman shaking her head miserably while examining a pair of shoes in the nearby store. "Is this the first time you've done this, Barry?"

"Of course not," Barry boasted proudly. "I've handled dozens of transactions. It's just that my partner usually took care of the one-on-one meets."

"Your partner, is she here?"

Barry chuckled. "There was no female partner, I made it up," Barry smirked proudly. "I didn't have the statue because it hadn't arrived yet. My real partner is out of the picture."

"Where?"

"Who knows? Who cares?"

Juwan faked a chuckle. "Funny, I thought you and Devlon Motako were partners."

"Nah, although I did ask him for his assistance. I figured with his reputation, he must know someone who could help me sell this."

"Did he?"

"He turned me down."

"His loss is my gain. Tell me, how did you and your partner hook up to do this job?"

Barry, bragging about his brilliance as usual, went into a five-minute confession on how he and Petre worked together years ago and now had been stealing art and artifacts from unsuspecting museums. With Petre's knowledge and his brilliant planning they had been extremely successful. He went on to admit that Petre got greedy and stole the one piece that drew attention and got several of their associates arrested. But now that Petre was out of the picture, they could have the same arrangement.

Juwan listened, as did six other special agents and a surveillance camera. He asked a few more questions and Barry went on again detailing each move and the lapses in the museum security. He proudly acknowledged his usual contacts and their interest in anything else he could move.

"Sounds like we have a deal. Why don't we get down to business? Do you have the statue with you?"

"Yes." He peeked into the shopping bag.

"Good, I have the money. Let me see the statue."

"Later."

"Do you seriously think I'm going to hand over several hundred thousand dollars without seeing if what I'm purchasing is authentic?"

Barry paused. "How do I know that you won't run as soon as I show you the statue?"

"If this is the statue I think it is, then I assume you can get other pieces. Why would I jeopardize my future earnings?"

Barry though a moment, then agreed. "Fine," he finally said, then put the shopping bag on the floor beside him and slid it back to Juwan.

Juwan picked up the bag and looked inside. He lifted the piece and examined it carefully. Satisfied, he nodded. "Okay, why don't you stand up to leave and pick up the briefcase on the bench beside me?"

"You must be kidding. Do you think I'm crazy? I need to count the money."

"Okay. Fine. One question, how exactly do you propose to count a hundred thousand dollars in tens and twenties while sitting on a bench on a Sunday afternoon in the middle of a crowded shopping mall without bringing attention to yourself?"

Barry went silent. "Okay, we'll do it your way. But as soon as I get to my car, I'm counting the money. And don't follow me."

"I have no intention of following you, Barry. Are you armed?"

"No, I mean, yes. I have a gun in my pocket and one in the car—a shotgun, loaded."

"Good for you." Juwan picked up the briefcase at his feet and laid it on the bench beside him. "It was good doing business with you, Mr. Culpepper."

Barry stood, walked around to where Juwan sat and picked up the briefcase lying beside him. He smiled openly and hurried to the exit. The man at the jewelry counter followed, along with the woman in the shoe store. Juwan sat watching as they left. A few moments later an older man came and sat beside Juwan. Juwan handed him the shopping bag. The man took the statue out and looked at it. He nodded his approval.

"That's it. It's done, pick him up," Juwan said into the microphone in his jacket lapel. Two additional agents immediately walked outside following the other two as Juwan and the man sitting on the bench with him stood and followed. They walked to the door and a black minivan drove up and stopped. Juwan and the older man got in and left the arrest of Barry to his associates.

As the black van drove away, he saw Barry surrounded by agents. He was looking particularly disturbed. "Did we get what we needed?" Juwan asked the man sitting at the recording panel in back of the van with him.

He started chuckling. "Yeah, we got it all. I've never heard or seen a more cooperative thief. He just wouldn't shut up. We have him on burglary, conspiracy, possession, and about fifteen other federal counts."

"Good work."

"We really didn't do anything." He laughed openly.

"All the same, thanks."

The van drove back to the main FBI building. Juwan looked at his watch. According to his self-imposed timetable, he was right on time. He'd go back to the office, fill out some paperwork, give Kennedy a call at the museum to see if she was done for the day, then pick her up and have a nice long talk.

As soon as he got to his office, Kevin appeared at the door. "You need to go to the interview room."

"Don't worry about it, the team can handle him." He chuckled and shook his head. "I'm sure Barry's spilling his guts even now. They don't need me." He gathered several files from his desk including a few photos and handed them to Kevin. "It's all here." He handed everything to Kevin and attempted to leave.

Kevin stopped him. "No, you need to listen to this."

"I would," Juwan said, smiling joyfully. "But tonight I have other plans."

"No, Juwan, you don't understand. First of all, no one knew he was going to do it. As a matter of fact, he went to the museum personally. Apparently in his eagerness to get the promotion, he took matters into his own hands."

"What are you talking about?"

"Colin, he brought her in this afternoon. I tried to call you, but your phone was shut off." Juwan stared at him blankly. He always shut his phone off when he was making an undercover arrest. The distraction could possibly mean someone's life.

"Colin went to the museum and brought who in?" Juwan asked.

"Kennedy Evans. She's downstairs in the interview rooms."

A solid wall of cement blocks crashed in on him. His ears began ringing, but Kevin's last words were foreign. Instinctively his fists balled and his jaw muscle tightened. He wasn't hearing what he just heard. The look he gave Kevin was enough to have him take a step back.

"What?"

"Colin brought Kennedy in for questioning."

"What?" Juwan's eyes narrowed. "Where is he?" Kevin told him. A second later he was out the door. Kevin was on his heels. The last thing he wanted was for Juwan to lose his promotion for committing murder.

Colin had spent twenty minutes warning Kennedy to speak for her own good. He instructed her that her attorney would be useless at this point and that it was to her benefit to talk first. A deal would be readily forthcoming if she would tell everything she knew, including the whereabouts, of Petre and any other associates.

Frustrated at her lack of cooperation and by her dead silence, he turned off the recorder and rushed out, followed by the female agent, leaving her alone again.

Ten minutes later a second man hurriedly entered and sat down across from her. His smile was pleasant and his manner far less regimented than that of agent Sheppard. "Dr. Evans, I'm afraid there's been a slight error."

She looked at him with interest. "Are you supposed to be the good cop?"

"Excuse me?" Kevin said.

"Good cop, bad cop. Are you supposed to be the good cop?"

"No, ma'am."

"Good, in that case I want to speak either to my attorney or with the undercover special agent in charge of this."

Kevin looked to the door, knowing that Juwan was right behind him, having stopped in the hall to have a few words with Colin to discuss recent developments. The words, of course, were loud enough to raise the dead. "You might prefer to speak with me for the time being, ma'am," Kevin said anxiously.

"Then you might prefer to speak with my attorney." They looked at each other sternly. She continued, "Or I can speak to whoever's in charge, you make the call."

The door opened behind her, Kevin looked up, and she turned around. The man in charge walked in, a badge and name tag hanging from his belt loop. Kennedy's eye blurred as she blinked several times. His walk was familiar as were his eyes. Deep and penetrating they stared. He was stunned and speechless. She chuckled, smiled then shook her head. Smirking, she finally spoke. "Nice touch, I see you're wearing the same clothes from this morning." Kevin discreetly excused himself and left the room.

"I've been out of the office all day. I didn't get a chance to . . ."

"I want a straight answer." She cut him off before he finished speaking. "Can you do that?" He nodded. "Was it all a lie?"

"Kennedy, I love you. That's all you have to remember."

"Don't." She held her hand up as he approached the table. "What exactly do you want from me?"

"You have intel."

"What?"

"Information."

"I know what intel is," she snapped. "What could I possibly know that would be of interest to you or your people—whoever they are? Who exactly do you work for?"

"The government"

"Whose government?"

"Our government. The United States government. I'm an FBI special agent. I'm with the Criminal Investigation Division. Specifically, I work with the violent crimes and major offenders section, major theft and transportation crimes unit."

She looked at him blankly, completely unbelieving.

"I hunt and recover stolen art and put away those responsible."

"That's why you know so much about art?"

"Yes."

She nodded. "You were never a bodyguard. So why the pretense?" He fell silent as the solution dawned on her. "It was me, wasn't it? You were after me all along. Everything that happened between us was all part of this game of yours."

"No." Unflinching, she looked at him. "We were given misinformation . . ."

"So I was the target."

"No, it wasn't like that, not after . . ."

"And making love to me, that was part of it, too?"

"Kennedy . . ."

"Then, of course, marrying me, I'm sure that was the coup de grace."

"Kennedy, I can't lose you . . ."

"You already did."

"I love you."

"And that's why you lied to me, then married me?"

"Yes. A husband can't be forced to testify against his wife. I was protecting you."

"Right, that's why you believed that I stole a hundred-thousand-dollar statue and what, hid it in my bedroom? I assume you searched my house."

"I told you we were misinformed. Everything we had, all of Petre's papers and documents pointed to you. If we hadn't gotten the anonymous tip that something was about to happen at the museum when we did, you would have been the prime suspect, not him. He set you up to take the fall alone."

"Don't. I don't want to hear it."

"It's the truth. Petre used you from the beginning. It was the anonymous call that saved you." He paused and looked at her oddly. "It was you. You called. You gave us the tip, didn't you?"

"Okay, fine, you have me. I called. I knew something was going to happen so I called, I did my duty and look where it got me—under arrest."

"You're not under arrest."

"Really, that's not the impression I got from your friend."

"Colin didn't realize that I was handling this."

"Oh, he seemed quite informed to me. He mentioned that he would see to it that the show is canceled and my career is over."

"He was trying to intimidate you, force you into talking. Nothing has changed. Your career is fine and the show will go on as scheduled, except Barry won't be attending."

She looked at him sternly. "Why, what happened to Barry?"

"I took him into custody this afternoon. He was Petre's partner. Together they stole quite a few pieces from the Nubian Museum as well as other institutions."

Kennedy shook her head, not at all surprised by the news. "Great, you've got your man. What do you still want from me? What information can I possibly have now that you need so badly?"

"Barry was picked up, now it's about Petre."

"What about him?"

"We need to find him and you're our best lead. He'll contact you and when he does, we need you to let us know."

She stood, grabbed her jacket and purse from the table. "Am I free to leave?"

"Kennedy," he said, quickly walking over to her. "We need to talk."

"We just did. I answered you questions."

"We need to talk about us."

"What about us? Everything was a lie. You were undercover to get you mark. I believe that's how your friend put it. Now am I free to leave or do I need to call my attorney?"

"Yes."

She headed to the door, opened it then paused. "If he calls me, which I doubt he will, I'll let you know. In the meantime expect annulment papers in the morning." She slammed the door and left.

Juwan sat in the room alone for the next half hour. He needed to make this right, but he didn't have a clue where to begin. He stood and walked over to the window. His thoughts raced in all directions. He was a pro at assimilating information and developing an action plan, but this time he had no ideas. The only thing he had was regret.

"Is this a good time?" Kevin asked as he poked his head in.

Juwan turned, seeing Kevin in the doorway. He motioned him inside. "Sure, come in. What's up?"

"Just to let you know that Barry is still talking. As a matter of fact, he's been talking for almost three hours now. I don't think we could shut him up even if we wanted to. Names, places, he has a detailed list of all of his contacts, buyers, sellers—we have it all. It was a good bust."

Juwan nodded, knowing that he had done a good job.

"Also, Colin's heading back to London tonight. He said that with Barry's cooperation and testimony, he'll be able to gather the rest of Petre's associates." Juwan nodded again. "And if it makes you feel any better, he openly admits that he was wrong."

"It doesn't. I'm just glad it's finally over."

"He's also giving you full credit for the bust. The promotion is yours, man. You can pick your city, London, New York or Washington. Congratulations."

"Thanks."

"So, how did you leave it with her?"

"She's going to let us know if or when Petre calls."

"That's not what I meant, how did you leave it between the two of you?"

Juwan turned back around to face the window. The shadow of regret still covered his face. He shook his head. Kevin nodded his head and left him alone. A few minutes later his watch alarm sounded. It was six o'clock, exactly twenty-eight hours later.

Chapter Twenty-Three

Early Sunday evening Kennedy walked into her parents' home. She had made her sister promise not to tell them about the marriage since she wanted it to come from her. So now it was up to her to not only break the news about her Las Vegas marriage but also to break the news about the annulment.

She walked through the house solemnly. Her heels echoed through the quiet emptiness of the large home. The kitchen was the gathering place for the Evans family and she could hear voices. She was the first one to arrive and preparations were in full swing. Both her mother and father were in the kitchen, her father, Jace, standing at the stove slowly stirring a large pot and her mother, Taylor, standing at the counter chopping peppers, onions and celery. They were laughing and discussing the evening's menu. They both looked up as she entered.

"Kennedy, you're early," Taylor said as she began to cut chunky pieces of lobster, shrimp and sea scallops.

"Good, you can take over for me," Jace said eagerly as he began untying his apron. "Your mother has me standing here stirring garlic and butter for her seafood gumbo when a perfectly good game is on the television."

"Oh, no, you don't," Taylor said. "Keep adding flour. I need that roux ready in about five minutes."

"Mom, Dad, we need to talk," Kennedy said.

"Sure, honey, grab an apron. I need you to take care of the French bread for me. It's already risen twice. I need you to brush it with butter and get it ready for the oven," Taylor said as she pointed to three loaves of bread on a tray covered by a damp towel.

Kennedy walked over to the marble chilling counter. Large dishes of lump crab, andouille sausage and chicken breast were already cut and ready along with dishes of okra and cut corn on the cob and tomatoes. "It's important," she added.

"Sure," Taylor said and she looked at Jace, who had just finished washing his hands. She moved the pot off the burner and turned the heat off, then sat down on a stool. Taylor washed her hands and sat down next to her husband. Kennedy followed and sat down, too.

"It sounds serious," Jace said as he poured three glasses of white wine and set them on the counter in front of his wife and his youngest daughter.

"It is."

"Does this have something to do with the man you were seeing in Africa, what was his name, Petre?"

"His name is Petre and, yes, it does have to do with him—indirectly." Jace and Taylor exchanged glances and waited impatiently as Kennedy took a deep breath and began. She started with meeting Petre, his arrest, meeting Juwan and their subsequent marriage in Las Vegas, and finally, her afternoon at FBI headquarters.

They were speechless by the time she finished.

"Did you call our attorney?"

"No, they realized that it was Barry they were after."

"How could they possibly confuse you with Barry?"

Kennedy shrugged. "Apparently they knew someone at the museum was involved, and since Petre and I were friends, more than friends, they naturally assumed that it was me."

"There's nothing natural about that assumption," Jace said hotly. "What happens now?"

"They, Juwan, the FBI asked me to let them know if or when Petre calls me again."

"Has he called you before?" Taylor asked.

"Yes, twice."

"He needs money," Jace said rather than asked.

"No, actually he wanted me to get a package that was being delivered to the museum, but I think Barry got to it first."

"So that's everything that happened," Kennedy said, relieved that she finally got it off her chest.

"Not quite." Kennedy looked at her mother questioningly. "Tell us about Juwan."

"There's nothing to tell, not anymore."

"You married him, Kennedy, there must be something to tell," Jace said.

"I married him because I thought he was being deported."

"No," Taylor said quickly. "You go to the federal building and get answers. You call in favors. You consult an attorney. But you don't elope to Las Vegas. You married him for a reason."

"I loved him."

"And you still do," Taylor presumed correctly.

"Yes."

"Even after everything that's happened?" Jace asked. She nodded.

"How does he feel about you?" Taylor asked.

"He says that he loves me."

"He has a funny way of showing it, by having you hauled into the FBI building and interrogated all afternoon."

"I wasn't him personally, Dad. He wasn't even there and, apparently, when he found out, he was furious. I heard loud yelling in the hall that might have been him."

"Okay, I know why you married him. Why did he marry you?" Jace asked.

"Good question," Taylor said as she placed her hand on her husband's arm.

"A husband can't be forced to testify against his wife. And since most of the information they were gathering still pointed to me, Juwan said that he was protecting me. Since he was the key witness, he couldn't be forced to tell what he knew."

"I see. So he does love you." Kennedy nodded reluctantly, still feeling the pain of his charade. "What now?"

"Nothing."

"I mean with the marriage."

"I don't know. We can't go back, there's too much."

"Then you go forward," Taylor said gently. "Granted it wasn't the romance of the century, but neither was mine and your father's." She looked over to Jace, who smiled and nodded, agreeing. "Nor would I have wanted you to go through this, but he does seem to love you."

Jace continued, "So much so that he was willing to sacrifice his job and his freedom."

"What do you mean?" Kennedy asked.

"I'm sure if push came to shove and this wound up in federal court and he refused to testify, he would have been found in contempt of court and imprisoned."

"What?" She looked at her mother for confirmation; she nodded her agreement.

"An annulment is always possible. In the eyes of the courts the marriage would be void and would have never taken place," Jace said.

"That's *if* you want to end it," Taylor offered. "You're angry now and you have every right to be. But later on, after you've calmed down, you might see things differently."

"I already spoke with our attorney. He's filing the paperwork and will have annulment papers delivered to Juwan at the embassy first thing in the morning."

"Are you sure this is what you want to do?"

Before she could respond, her cell phone rang. She answered.

"Kennedy, it's me," Petre said quickly, his accent thick and pronounced.

She recognized the voice instantly. Her heart lurched. "What do you want?" she asked as she walked into the dining room, leaving her parents still in the kitchen.

"We need to meet, tonight, now."

"I can't, I'm busy."

"It's important, Kennedy. It's my life."

"You tried to set me up," she hissed.

"No, it wasn't me, it was Barry. Please, you have to believe me. I loved you, I still do. I'd never set you up. How could I?"

"What do you want?"

"Meet me tonight, in an hour."

"I told you before, I'm busy right now."

"Okay, when?"

"Give me your number, I'll call you back," she said.

"No, it's too dangerous. I'll call you back in two hours. I'll tell you where we can meet then." He hung up.

Kennedy closed her cell phone and walked back into the kitchen. Taylor looked up as soon as she entered. "Everything all right?" she asked.

Kennedy nodded. "Looks like Juwan was right. That was Petre. He wants to meet with me."

Still distracted, Juwan heard the second louder knock on the door as he placed his toiletries in the small bag. He barely registered what he was doing. Having driven to the embassy, he began packing his things. He resolved to return to London as soon as possible. The earliest flight he could get was the following morning.

He walked over and opened the door, expecting to see Maurice or possibly Hawk or even Hoyt. But he never expected to see Yasmine. She instantly dove into his chest, wrapped her arms around him and held on tight. He kissed the top of her forehead. "When did you get here?"

"Friday night," she said, playfully punching him in his chest. "But, of course, you wouldn't know that. You weren't here to meet me, you were probably somewhere out gallivanting."

"Friday night," Juwan said, half chuckling, barely remembering just two days earlier. In the span of forty-eight hours his life had whirled through a gamut of dramas. "It's good to see you," he said, feeling truly delighted to have her here. "Are you staying here at the embassy?"

"No, Kevin and I are staying at his parents' house in D.C. I just stopped by to say hello and, hopefully, talk you into going to the children's hospital with me."

"I'd love to, but I'm leaving tomorrow morning for London."

"London. What? You just got here. I just got here. We haven't had any time to visit. Why are you going back to London? Your house is sold and all of your things have already been shipped here."

"There you are," Maurice said as he appeared at the open doorway, then came into the room. Both Juwan and Yasmine looked up. "I've cleared my schedule. We have this evening and tomorrow to visit."

"Juwan's leaving tomorrow morning," Yasmine said.

"That's ridiculous, you just got back. What is so urgent that you have to rush off again?"

"I've decided to accept the promotion to assistant director."

"That's wonderful," Yasmine said as she hugged him again.

"Congratulations," Maurice said, shaking his hand. "But I thought that position called for you to relocate here to the D.C. office. Why are you going back to London?"

"It does, but I've decided to take the same promotion offered in the London office."

"And what about Kennedy?" Maurice asked. "Have you completed your interest with her?"

"Kennedy," Yasmine said. "Who's Kennedy?"

Juwan paused, then decided that it was time to tell them everything. "Kennedy is my wife."

"Your what?" Maurice and Yasmine said in unison.

"We got married Friday in Las Vegas."

Yasmine's mouth gaped open as she slowly sat down on the side of the bed while Maurice reached out and hugged Juwan joyfully. "I'm proud of you, son, and I know that your parents would have been overjoyed. Kennedy Evans is a remarkable woman and you have married into a very influential family. I'm delighted that you decided to keep her in your life. She is truly a gem."

As the news settled, Yasmine leaped up happily. "Oh, Juwan, this is wonderful news, congratulations. I'm so happy for you. I can't believe it. I have a sister." She grabbed Juwan and hugged him hard. "I can't wait to meet her. Where is she?"

"There are complications."

Maurice frowned. "I was afraid of that. Might they have something to do with your job and the fact that you're undercover—investigating her?"

"Yes," Juwan said.

"And she found out," Maurice added.

"Yes," Juwan repeated.

"You've got to be kidding me. If you were undercover investigating her, then she's a suspect for a major crime. So if you know she's guilty, why would you marry her? What were you thinking?"

"I needed to protect her. I'm in love with her."

"Juwan," Yasmine moaned ruefully. "How can you protect her by marrying her? You can't have a life together. She has to pay for her crimes."

"She's innocent, isn't she?" Maurice asked, interrupting. Juwan nodded. "And being innocent," he continued, "she didn't take your deception and lies very well, did she?"

"No, she didn't."

Maurice nodded and turned away.

"She's innocent and you accused her of stealing," Yasmine said, shaking her head. "Now she's pissed. I would be, too."

"Our intel pointed to her. Everything we had pointed to her. She knew the main suspect. She'd been in contact with him. And she was always in the wrong place at the wrong time."

"But in your heart you knew she was innocent."

"Yes."

"Well, did you get the right person?" Yasmine asked.

"Yes, we picked him up earlier. It's over."

"So what happens now? You just pack your things. Go back to London and forget about everything. Forget about your *wife*?" she asked.

"She doesn't want to hear from me."

"When have you ever taken the easy way out? Go, fight for her, make her understand. If she married you, she did it because she loves you, too," Maurice said.

"She married me because she thought I was being deported. She was trying to save me."

"Oh, this just keeps getting better and better," Yasmine continued. "You marry her to save her and she marries you to save you. Did either one of you consider that you actually loved each other?"

"We do, but there's too much between us now. I messed up. She won't have me back. How could she?"

"You'll never know if you don't try. She loves you. Go to her." Maurice's words were just what he needed. A sudden burst of encouragement strengthened his resolve. He wanted Kennedy back and he was willing to do anything to get her back. As he headed out the front door of the embassy, his cell phone rang. He looked at the number. Kennedy was calling him. He answered. "Kennedy."

"I just got a call from Petre. He wants to meet."

"When and where?"

"I don't know, I told him that I was busy for the next hour or so, so he's gonna call me back in about two hours."

"Where are you?" Juwan asked.

"At my parents' home in McLean. But I'm sure you already know that."

"Can you meet me at your house in half an hour?"

"Why?"

"We need to talk about bringing Petre in."

She paused a moment, then agreed. "Fine, I'll see you there."

The decision to call Juwan had been instinctual. As soon as she hung up from Petre, he was the first person she thought of. Not because he was an FBI special agent or because it was his case, but because he was the man she loved. She made her apologies to her parents, then drove home. Juwan was waiting outside for her when she arrived. She noticed that he was carrying a large briefcase. She opened the front door and he followed her inside. As soon as he closed the door behind them, she turned and began.

"What do you need from me?"

"Your cell phone."

She reached into her purse, pulled it out and gave it to him. "Anything else?"

"No," he said as he opened the case and began connecting small gadgets to the phone. When he finished, he placed the phone on the coffee table and began connecting another set of gadgets to the house phone. She watched silently as he worked. When he finished, he closed the briefcase and turned to her.

"What exactly do you want me to say to him?" Juwan proceeded to brief her on what to ask and what to say to get as much information as possible from him. "Is that it?"

"Kennedy, we need to talk."

"It's late, Juwan, I've talked all afternoon. I'm tired."

"There are things you need to know."

She looked at him steadily. "I presume I have a file."

"A what?" he asked, confused by the abrupt conversation.

"A file, you know, all the little details of my life, everything there is to know about me." He nodded. "Did you read it?" He nodded. "Earlier, before, you were surprised that I could cook, I presume that's not in the file." He shook his head no. "And the panic attacks, are they in the file?" He nodded. "And the fact that I can't get pregnant, is that there, too?"

"No," he said, finally speaking. "If it were, I would have pulled it out by now."

She looked relieved. "I want to see it."

"The file?" he asked. She nodded. "I can't do that. It's not protocol."

"Was making love to me protocol?" she asked.

"No." *Touché.* Memories of their passionate lovemaking flashed before him like a far-off dream. No, it definitely wasn't protocol. "I'll see what I can do," he promised. She nodded. "Anything else you need to ask me?"

"So the Juwan Mason I met and knew was basically created for me, right?"

"What do you mean?"

"Everything you did, everything you said, that was all just part of the cover, right? You read my file and invented a man that I would immediately fall for. You were made for me."

"No, Kennedy, very few people get to know the real me, inside. You got to me, inside, in here." He pointed to his heart. "I didn't have to pretend. Yes, it was technically undercover, but it was my life—it is my real life. I love art because of my mother. I traveled when I was younger because of my father. I cook because I live alone and have to. I dance because I like to."

"Who are you?"

"You know the answer to that."

"No, I don't," she snapped instantly.

"I didn't create some alter ego named Juwan Mason for

you. I am Juwan. I'm the same man you asked to marry you two days ago. The same man you fell in love with. The same man you're fighting not to love now."

"No, you're not. You're nothing like that man. That man was honest and kind and loved talking to sick children. That man would never have hurt me like you did."

"Kennedy, if there was any other way . . ."

"That's just it, Juwan. There was. You could have just been honest with me from the beginning."

"How could I? According to all the evidence we obtained from Petre's files and records, you were involved up to your neck."

"So why not just bring me in from the beginning?"

"They wanted to. I was supposed to. But I couldn't."

"Why not?"

"Because I fell in love with you."

"You didn't even know me."

He stepped in closer and reached out to stroke the side of her face. "I loved you before we even met. The first time I opened your file, you on the motorcycle on the parkway, yeah, and even at the entrance where we first met."

"You planned that?"

"No, we actually met by accident. I didn't plan on seeing and meeting you until the embassy party Friday night."

"Oh my God, I almost slept with you that night. You must have thought that I was the biggest . . ." She couldn't say the word.

"I thought you were just as you are now." He reached out to her. "Incredible."

She leaned back. "Don't."

"Kennedy, nothing has changed about my feelings for you. I love you. Yes, I lied. It was part of my job. That's what I did. Ask me anything, I'll tell you."

"Did? You quit?"

"No, two months ago, before Petre and the robbery, I was

promoted. I needed time to clear things up before I accepted the new position."

"I don't want to hear any more of this." She turned away.

"I lived in London for six years. Before that, Italy and Spain for a year. Cairo for two years. Before that, Germany for two years. Before that, Washington and Quantico for three years. Before that, Boston. That's where I was born and primarily raised. My mother was an art historian and taught at Boston University. When I was twelve years old, my father was appointed to a position here in Washington. They were killed three years later. I joined the FBI right after college. I've been with them for fourteen years." She kept her back to him.

"Yes, I lied about a lot of things but never about my feelings for you. Kennedy, I know you're angry with me right now. I understand and I'm sorry for what I did. I can't change the past. If you feel more comfortable having someone else here, I'll understand." He picked up his jacket.

"Stay," she said quietly, knowing that she loved him—even after all the lies, she loved him.

Her phone rang. She looked at her watch. It had been two hours and fifteen minutes. She looked at Juwan, and he nodded encouragingly. "Answer it," he instructed, then stood by her side.

She picked up the cell phone from the coffee table and flipped it open, careful not to dislodge the attached recording devices. She held the phone out from her ear so that both of them could hear the conversation. "Hello?"

"Kennedy, it's me."

"You need to stop calling me, Petre. Just turn yourself in."

He ignored her suggestion as usual. "I need your help. I can't find Barry; you're the only other person I can contact."

"I told you I'm not getting whatever you want from the museum. You know how I feel about what you've done."

"Don't believe everything you hear."

"Petre, you stole from a museum. How can you deny that?"

"Yes, I did it. But that doesn't matter now. I have nothing to show for it. No money. No art. Nothing."

"You don't get it, do you? It wasn't yours from the beginning. You stole it. You had no right to it."

"So I wind up with nothing, is that fair?"

Kennedy half chuckled. She realized that she wasn't getting through to him. "So, what do you want from me?"

"I need money, lots of it. I need to disappear for a while. A couple hundred thousand should get me started. I need it now, tonight."

"Where am I supposed to get that kind of money tonight?"

"You're rich, your family's rich. You can get the money."

"And I'm just supposed to have that kind of money lying around waiting for you."

"How long will it take to get it?"

"I don't know, a couple of days, maybe."

"I need it tonight, I have to get out of town."

"Well, I suggest that you just turn yourself in then."

"All right, tomorrow, can you get it by then?"

Kennedy looked at Juwan. He nodded. "I'll see what I can do. Where and when?" she asked.

"Meet me at the museum right before closing."

"Fine."

"Kennedy, remember, whatever happens, know that I still love you and would never intentionally harm you." She hung up without responding.

"That was good," Juwan said as he detached the recording apparatus from the earphone plug of her phone. She nodded. "Well, that's it until tomorrow," she said as he repacked his briefcase. He picked up his jacket and walked to the front door; she headed to the stairs. "Goodnight," he said. She nodded and went upstairs to her bedroom alone.

Chapter Twenty-Four

Having canceled his flight to London when he returned to the embassy late that evening, Juwan spent a restless night tossing and turning as anxious thoughts of Kennedy and her safety troubled him. He knew that Petre wasn't considered particularly dangerous. He was more talk, bluster and charm than action. But precautions needed to be taken just in case.

Juwan got up early that morning before dawn and made several phone calls, arranging around the clock perimeter surveillance and undercover observation inside the museum. He wanted everything to be as secure as possible knowing that the tighter the net, the better chance they would have of capturing their objective.

Since Kennedy's meet with Petre wasn't until that evening, Juwan felt confident that he would have the immediate area as secure as possible. But even with all the added security, there was still something about Petre's tone that Juwan didn't trust. If it was possible that he suspected Kennedy of betraying him, then there was no telling what he might consider.

Juwan listened to the recording he'd made of their conversation the night before. He'd already heard it a dozen times, listening for background sounds and other hints to Petre's whereabouts. Familiar with the minimal background sounds, he now listened closely to the voice particularly Petre's unusual appeal for trust. It seemed odd and forced.

Trained to spot a liar, Juwan immediately recognized the strain in his voice and the awkward pitch in his tone. Although he vowed his love, his tone, nervous and fearful, revealed desperation, and a desperate man was capable of doing anything. It was a well-known fact that Kennedy had money, but money might not be the only thing he'd want—a wealthy hostage was also a consideration.

As Juwan left the embassy, he was informed that a registered package had been delivered for him. He picked it up at the reception desk, tossed it on the seat beside him, then headed for the office.

He spent the remainder of the morning filling out reports, deciphering Barry's files, reading testimony, and accepting accolades from his superiors. It was a job well done. He had recovered the stolen piece and the perpetrator had been detained. The only thing left to attend to was bringing in the main suspect, and he was certain that he would have that taken care of before the day was over.

Shortly before noon he made a phone call to an unexpected couple, and a half hour later he was escorted into the formal living room of the Evans family home. Taylor stood as Jace and Juwan entered. She watched him attentively, observing him as he approached.

Attractive and astute, he was just as she imagined, tall dark, and handsome. He had an inner strength and power that came through as confidence and self-assurance, but his cool, detached manner gave her pause. As soon as he entered, his eyes focused on a single target, Taylor, and she took full advantage of the situation. Their eyes, though guarded, were focused, until she nodded, giving him permission to relax. He didn't; instead he seemed even more reserved. Taylor smiled inwardly. Apparently he wasn't going to be a pushover.

Jace made the introductions, then offered Juwan a seat. He sat down and came right to the point.

Uncomfortable yet nonstop Juwan talked about himself, his career, his past, and his love for their daughter. They listened intently while asking pertinent questions, which he answered honestly and openly.

"Do you intend to remain married to our daughter?" Jace asked.

"Yes, sir, I love Kennedy. I always will. It's my intention to be married to her the rest of my life if she'll still have me."

"How legal was this Las Vegas wedding?" Taylor asked.

"It's completely legal. We stood before a friend of my family. He's a federal judge."

"And you married to keep from having to testify against her?" Jace questioned.

"I married your daughter because I love her and because it was a way to keep her safe in the event I couldn't make the case against her associate. I hope in the future we can renew our vows in a more appropriate setting."

Taylor nodded. That was exactly what she wanted to hear. "Juwan, you realize, of course, that my husband and I have absolutely no influence on Kennedy's decision to stay married to you. She has to make up her own mind."

"I understand."

"So why exactly did you come here today? This couldn't have been easy for you," Jace said.

Juwan smiled, agreeing. "No, sir, it wasn't. But I needed to meet you face-to-face, to explain to you what happened, and to assure you that I love your daughter. I didn't mean to hurt her, although I realize I did, badly. I know the type of woman she is and I know she will forgive me in time. I also know that she loves me."

"Tell us about the rest of your family, Juwan," Taylor asked. Juwan began with his mother and father and went on to tell of his relationship to Ambassador Maurice Mebeko.

He spent the next hour telling Kennedy's parents about himself. The more he talked, the more comfortable and relaxed they became and the more assured they felt that he was the right man for Kennedy.

As gossip will, the story of Barry's arrest spun wildly out of control. Kennedy had heard a reasonable facsimile of the true events early that morning. Then by the afternoon the story had changed into a shoot-out and a thirty-mile police chase around the outer loop of the Beltway. The board of directors convened a special meeting and the public relations department was at the top of its game in spinning the bad publicity. They had turned Barry's arrest into an organized sting dedicated to stopping museum theft.

By the time the story reached the international news, it appeared that the museum had set up the sting to draw out corrupt employees. In the process the museum had stirred interest in the collection, which promised to add tremendous traffic to the opening of the Nubian exhibit.

Kennedy stayed in her office all morning and left only when absolutely necessary. By early afternoon she had finalized the scheduling of the exhibit's additional programs. A series of lectures and film events to accompany the exhibit had been planned and she completed the breakdown of family programming. As she left her office to go over to the exhibit, her phone rang. Her heart jumped and she looked at her watch. It was still early but she was still nervous.

"Dr. Evans, you have a visitor."

"Who is it?" she asked, fearing that Petre had arrived early.

"Mrs. Pole."

"If she's a newsperson, have her speak to someone in public relations. No one else is making statements."

"She's not with the media. She said that it's personal."

"Fine, I'll be right up."

Flustered, Kennedy went directly to the main entrance. The museum was packed. The news of Barry's arrest had brought out the curious as well as the nutcases. It was her understanding that Barry had even received several marriage proposals plus book and film offers. As soon as Kennedy walked into the open foyer, she looked around expecting to see a woman dressed in a white wedding gown. Instead she saw a few dozen schoolchildren waiting in the lobby and a number of patrons preparing to tour the museum.

Kennedy looked at the security guard. He motioned to the small timid woman standing at the window looking out. Dressed in a stylish business suit and designer heels, she looked like a prim and proper librarian. Kennedy walked over cautiously. "Excuse me, you wanted to see me. I'm Dr. Evans."

The woman turned. Her eyes sparkled and her smile, genuine and serene, expressed surprise and delight. "I'm delighted to meet you. My name is Yasmine Pole. Juwan Mason is my brother."

"Of course," Kennedy said, remembering the name instantly. "It's a pleasure to meet you." Kennedy held out her hand to shake, but Yasmine reached out and hugged her instead.

"I have so been looking forward to meeting you, ever since I heard the news yesterday. I realized that this is your place of business and I know that I should have called or even waited for Juwan to introduce us, but I was too eager; I just couldn't wait."

"It's no problem. Is your brother with you?" Kennedy asked, glancing around the now emptying area.

"No, he's not. As a matter of fact, he has no idea that I've come here today. I just wanted to stop by and introduce myself. My aunt and uncle have told me so many wonderful things about you that I feel I know you already."

"Your aunt and uncle?" Kennedy asked.

"Adarah and Maurice Mebeko." Kennedy still looked confused. "I assume Juwan told you about our parents."

Kennedy nodded. "Well, we've always called Adarah and Maurice aunt and uncle, and even though they're our parents technically, the habit has stuck."

"Yes, of course. How are they?"

"Both are well. Adarah will be arriving later this evening."

"Really? That's wonderful. I'm looking forward to seeing her again. She's a wonderful woman."

"Yes, she is," Yasmine said as she looked around the open reception area. Most of the children had gone and only a few patrons still mingled around the atrium. "You know, as many times as I've been to this city, I don't believe I've ever actually walked through this museum. Do you mind if we . . ." She motioned to walk around.

"Not at all. Why don't we start on the lower level and work our way up?" Yasmine readily agreed. They took the elevator down, then worked their way up. Together the two walked through the galleries with Kennedy pointing out the many different displays in the museum's collection.

As they walked, they talked generally about art and the art world. Yasmine wasn't as knowledgeable about art as her brother, but she had an open mind and plenty of interest. She asked questions and gave her opinions freely.

By the time they'd gotten to the top gallery level, they decided to stop at the cafeteria. Kennedy suggested a cup of tea and Yasmine agreed. As they sat down at the table with their cups, Yasmine looked over and smiled at Kennedy. "He said you were beautiful. He was right."

"Thank you," Kennedy said before sipping her tea. "I guess you know that our relationship is somewhat strained at the moment."

"Yes, he told me and if I were you, I would have punched him out and been done with it."

Kennedy smiled and half chuckled at her remark. "Believe me, I wanted to," she confessed. Yasmine nodded, agreeing completely.

Small in stature, she seemed delicate and frail, but her vivacious and spirited personality belied first impressions. She was anything but a pushover. As they talked and got to know each other, Kennedy found herself liking Yasmine and enjoying their conversation tremendously.

"Yasmine, may I ask you a question?"

"Sure, of course."

"About Juwan, he can be . . ." Kennedy began.

"Distant, detached, bewildering," Yasmine said, drawing a smile and nod from Kennedy. "I know exactly what you mean, but he wasn't always like that. After our parents were killed, he literally grew up overnight."

"He mentioned that your parents died. I didn't realize they'd been killed."

Yasmine nodded. "It happened when I was five and Juwan was fifteen. I don't remember much, just bits and pieces and vague flashes every now and then. But, apparently, one night when Juwan was sleeping at a neighbor's house, he smelled smoke. He says that he doesn't know how he knew, but he apparently knew that it was our house. He ran home.

"The house had been ransacked and was in flames. Juwan broke through the front window and ran inside. He saw that our parents had been shot and killed and I was badly wounded. Juwan got me out of the house, but in the process I was also slightly burned. He blamed himself for the longest time."

"But he saved your life," Kennedy said. "How could he possibly blame himself?"

"But he did. He felt that if he hadn't gone out that night, he might have been able to protect us all, to save us."

"But he was only fifteen."

"I know that and you know that and I'm sure that a small part of him knows that, too. But he's carried the guilt for a long time. After a while he became like stone, unfeeling and unemotional. He seemed to think that if he didn't care about anyone or love anyone, then he'd never be hurt like that again."

"That's why he became an FBI agent, to protect people."

Yasmine nodded. "Yes, I think so. And that's why he's in stolen art. I think he's still looking for the people who killed our parents."

"So they were never caught."

"No. He knows that on some level that the art is long gone to a private collector who probably has no idea of its painful history. That's why he was so affected by the Nubian Museum robbery. It's what our mother collected and specialized in. She taught art history at Boston University."

Kennedy was heartbroken after the story. It all made perfect sense. She now knew why Juwan was so intense and dedicated to his job.

"Anyway, after the fire I went to the burn unit at Children's Hospital not far from here. He visited me every day for over two months. He's a godsend and he's saved my life in more ways than you can imagine." Yasmine smiled and looked away.

Kennedy remembered the night she and Juwan went to the amusement park and their stop at the hospital. Juwan was right at home and his feeling for the young child with the operation the following day was heartfelt and genuine. No wonder he was so compassionate and understanding. He had consoled his sister through the same trauma.

"I bet that I sound like some big brother cheerleader, but he really is wonderful. And I can see why he fell in love with you." She reached over and took Kennedy's hand. "Thank you for everything you've done for him. He seems so different and I know that's your doing."

"I didn't do anything," Kennedy said.

"But you have, you've opened his eyes to the possibility of love, something that I thought I'd never see." They looked at each other without speaking. Moments later Yasmine looked at her watch. "Anyway, it's getting late and I've taken up enough of your time. I forgot you're still at work."

"It was wonderful talking with you. I really enjoyed our conversation." They stood and hugged.

"I noticed that you're wearing a Tuareg cross." Yasmine pointed to Kennedy's neck. Kennedy reached up and touched the small pendant that had hung around her neck since Juwan had given it to her. She'd forgotten that she even had it on. "Juwan gave it to me."

"I'm glad. You know, it's supposed to have magical healing powers. I've never seen Juwan without it. I'm glad he gave it to you. Well, it was wonderful meeting you, Kennedy. And even though I did come with an ulterior motive of somehow reconciling you two, I just hope that I helped you understand him a bit more."

"You did, thank you."

Kennedy walked Yasmine back to the main lobby. They said their good-byes again and Kennedy went back to her office. She sat at her desk and reflected on her conversation with Yasmine. Her heart went out to the man who took the weight of the world on his shoulders and had yet to let go. "Maybe," she muttered aloud, "maybe."

Moments later her phone rang and within minutes work consumed her. It wasn't until Yolanda stopped by that she realized the time.

"I just went through the exhibit," she said as she poked her head into the office. "We did a good job," she said proudly.

"No, we did a great job," Kennedy said.

"Are you staying late?" Yolanda asked.

"Just for a little bit. See you tomorrow."

Yolanda waved and left Kennedy waiting. An hour later she was still waiting. She realized that Petre hadn't showed and wasn't going to call. It was a good thing because she hadn't seen Juwan or any FBI agents all day; so much for them protecting her. She grabbed her jacket and headed to the employees' exit. As soon as she got to her car, Petre walked up to her. "Did you get the money?"

Before she could turn and open her mouth, sirens sounded and a massive police presence descended on the area. Car doors flung open and they were surrounded instantly, with Juwan leading the way. Petre, too stunned to speak, was placed in handcuffs and put into the backseat of one of the unmarked cars. He was whisked away instantly without a single word.

Kennedy, astonished by the level of proficiency, looked at Juwan, amazed by his skill. He spoke with several officers, thanking them for their presence, and congratulated his team for another job well done. By the time he turned his attention to her, she was shaking. He reached out and held her in his arms. She was protected, she was valued, and she was loved. A slow tear fell down her cheek. This was what she'd been waiting for all her life.

"Juwan," one of the FBI agents called to him. "We'll meet you downtown for the debriefing." He nodded as Kennedy stepped back.

"You have to go in?"

"Yes, paperwork. Extraditions can be complicated."

She smiled, proud of his ability. "Of course."

"I'll probably have to escort him back personally."

"So you got your man again." He nodded. "Then everything is done, over, finished. So what happens now?"

"A new beginning," he said. It was the only thing he could think to say. After sitting in his car for hours waiting for Petre to make his move, he'd gone through dozens of scenarios of how the moment would play out. But each time he came up lacking. There was no way he could impose his will on Kennedy. His heart and his emotions were too tied to her. He couldn't let her go, that he knew for sure.

A new beginning. His words hit her like a ton of bricks. Her heart ached and reached out to him. Whether she wanted it to be or not, she knew that this was the last time she was going to see him.

He reached out and took her hands and held them, drawing her into an embrace. He closed his eyes, remembering everything about this moment, the smell of her perfume, the taste of her skin, the sound of her breathing. If this was the end, he needed memories to last a lifetime.

She leaned back slightly and looked up at him. "There's so much . . ." she began, shaking her head.

"I understand." He looked down into her soft eyes, seeing the bare honesty of her hurt and the confusion of her love for him. "I do love you," he mouthed.

She leaned up and kissed him tenderly, her heart forgiving everything but her mind still in turmoil. The love she felt for him was unending and she couldn't bear giving him up again.

"You look tired," he said as she closed her eyes and lowered her head to lean on his chest. He stroked her back lovingly.

"I am, I guess the superspy gig isn't my cup of tea after all."

"Nor mine, not anymore."

She looked up at him. "You're taking the new position?"

"Yes."

"Congratulations."

"Thank you."

"I know you have to go. Thank you for everything," she said sincerely.

"Thank you," he mouthed, then turned, got into his car, and drove off. Kennedy watched as he drove away. A sad emptiness filled her. It was over.

Chapter Twenty-Five

"Wow, that's incredible," Madison sighed, holding her hand to her heart after hearing Kennedy tell her the whole story. "So, he wasn't just a pretty face after all." She shook her head, amazed by the deception. "An undercover FBI agent and he was after you all along. I can't believe it. That's just too incredible."

"Yeah," Kennedy said. "Tell me about it."

"So what happened next?"

"Nothing."

"What do you mean, nothing? Something must have happened. Did he stop by later that night or did he call you or did you call him, something?"

"Madi, this isn't a soap opera or a romance novel, it's my life. Nothing happened. I haven't spoken to him."

"I know, sweetie, and I'm sorry it didn't work out like you planned. But it's also so romantic."

"What?"

"Keni, the man sacrificed his career and could have possibly gone to jail for you, for love. Even you can't not be impressed by that."

"He lied to me."

"Yes, he did, and it was wrong, I totally agree with you.

I'm sure what he did and how he did it wasn't exactly by the book. But the end result was that he realized that you were innocent and while going after the real bad guys, he tried to save you, and did."

"You make it sound like some grand noble gesture."

"You know you wouldn't be so upset if you didn't love him."

Kennedy opened her mouth to object but closed it again when Madison gave her that don't-even-try-denying-it look. "I never said that I didn't love him, Madi."

"So, how do you feel about him now, after everything that's happened?"

Kennedy took a deep breath and sighed wearily. "You can't just shut love off like a light switch. I wish I could, then it wouldn't be so hard to stop thinking about him. Then I could just start all over again and I wouldn't have to feel so bad and it wouldn't have to hurt so much." The sadness in her eyes and the pain in her heart poured out as her voice stressed and cracked.

"Oh, sweetie, I know, love sucks," Madison said as she opened her arms to her sister and they held each other in a warm sisterly embrace. "And it's also the most wonderful, fantastic thing in the world. And when it's right and you're not together, it hurts like hell."

"I still love him," she whispered.

"I know you do, so what are you gonna do about it?" Madison asked.

"There's nothing I can do," Kennedy shrugged.

"What do you mean nothing you can do?" Madison asked. "What happened to my brave daredevil younger sister who jumped off the roof of the porch just because Trey dared you to do it? And what about the time you jumped into the ice-cold freezing pond out back in the middle of winter just to see how far you could jump?"

"I was eight and ten years old and incredibly stupid."

"You were incredibly brave," Madison insisted.

"I broke my leg from jumping off the roof and nearly caught pneumonia from the pond. Not to mention I was on punishment until I was thirteen."

"Okay, what about the time you raced J.T. to the top of the giant oak tree out back and won? You had to be about a hundred feet in the air. That was incredible."

"The fire department had to come and get me down. I believe I was on punishment until I was fifteen for that one."

"Okay, what about the time you rode every roller-coaster ride in the amusement park, five times in one day?"

"I was sick and dizzy for a week. I didn't need punishment; I suffered enough." They laughed, remembering the fun times and silliness of growing up and the outrageous things she did in the name of adventure and excitement.

"Okay, okay, I give up. But the point is—you tried and didn't just give up. Yes, there were consequences, but nothing you couldn't live with. So why aren't you trying now? Why aren't you going after what you want?" She smiled broadly. "Just think of the consequences now by having Juwan in your life, living happily ever after with your very own Prince Charming, literally."

"I hate it when you're right."

"I know you do," Madison said happily and rubbed her belly.

"Are you okay?" Kennedy asked.

"Yeah, just cramps," she frowned, then smiled. "I have a feeling that one or both of these two is gonna take after their aunt Keni."

"Good," Kennedy teased.

"No way." The conversation lapsed for a few minutes as they continued walking. "So tell me, have you heard anything at all from him after that night?"

"He left a message at the office at two o'clock in the

morning. He said that he was on his way back to Africa with Petre, then back to London. But that was three days ago."

"And you think that he went back to stay?"

"I don't know, maybe."

"You always wanted a major adventure. All your life you searched for something exciting to happen to you. Now you have it in Juwan. Forgive him, keep him, go get him."

"It's too late. I don't think he's coming back. He told me that he'd been promoted and there was a position waiting for him in London."

"What about the annulment, do you still want it?"

"A transcontinental marriage would be out of the question."

"Yeah, you're right. Maybe he can come back to the States. You said that there was another position available here too."

"But even if he comes back, so much has happened, I wouldn't even know what to say to him."

Madison smiled. "Oh that's easy. Just say, I love you."

Kennedy looked at her sister and nodded, then looked out over the grounds of their parents' estate in McLean. Autumn had arrived, the leaves had begun falling and a chill was in the air. "I love this time of year," she said.

"Me too." They paused to reflect on the moment. "So," Madison began, "are you ready for tomorrow evening?"

"As ready as I'll ever be."

"Everything's all set?" Madison asked. Kennedy nodded. "I'm so excited. I can't wait to see it. What did you come up with as the centerpiece of the show?"

"We didn't. I can always add something later on."

They continued to walk back to the house. They spotted their brother on the back deck, waving his arms in full animation. Trey and Tony were standing with him nodding their heads. "Oh boy, is J.T. still upset?" Madison asked.

"When is J.T. not upset? You know how protective he is."

"You know he's even threatened to break you husband's neck when he meets him," Madison said.

"I wouldn't try it if I were him," Kennedy warned. "But if I remember correctly he wasn't particularly happy with Tony either, was he?"

"No, he wasn't. Let's face it, J.T. is going to be a big brother no matter what. There's just no changing him."

They watched as Juliet came outside and walked over to J.T. She linked her arm in his and he immediately stopped. She reached down and took his hand, smiled and began walking, and he followed.

"I really like her," Kennedy said with a chuckle.

"Hear, hear," Madison replied, chuckling, too.

"Come on, I'll race you back inside," Kennedy said.

"Okay but give me a head start."

"Deal, how much of a head start do you need?"

"Oh, about three weeks ought to do it." They laughed, linked arms and walked back together.

An hour later, Kennedy headed home. She was glad she drove her motorcycle. The wind whipped around her, making her feel free and happy. Although dark clouds threatened on the horizon, she didn't care. She had made up her mind. Madi was right; she had given up what she had always wanted and it was time to do something about it.

Juwan spent two days and two nights traveling. He had gone directly to Africa and delivered Petre to the Nubian authorities with the understanding that his freedom was not for sale at any cost. Then, back in London, he had attended enough meetings, appointments and debriefings to last a lifetime.

After his instrumental role in tracking down and capturing Petre and Barry and recovering the stolen statue, he had been offered and had accepted the promotion. He was officially free to return to Washington and accept the position in the main office.

He arrived in Washington later than he expected, but instead of going to the embassy, he went to Kennedy's house. He rang the doorbell and waited; she didn't answer. She wasn't home. Just as he turned to leave he heard the hum of a motorcycle engine coming down the street. Knowing exactly who it was, he had to smile.

He had thought about her every moment for the last three days. But it wasn't until he finally opened the envelope he'd received at the embassy that he felt the pain of her hurt. Trapped on a flight from London to the United States, he began reviewing the files he still had in his possession. He found the manila envelope in with his paperwork, then remembered having received it the day before he left. Assuming that it was just more museum employee profiles, he opened the envelope and pulled out the papers.

The word *annulment* hit him instantly. He read the legal document, then went still. With his mind on one thing and nothing to do but wait, he read the annulment papers a hundred times more.

Given his personality, he never made a move without first analyzing every available option. Having never felt the urge to act on impulse, he still had no idea why he had come here. It was the first impulsive act he'd taken in a lifetime of carefully planned moves.

A typical *good guy*, he always played by the rules, followed orders without question and abided by the laws governing the land—whichever land he happened to be in at the time. He had a code of ethics and honor instilled in him that was unshakable. Recklessness had never been part of his nature, not until he met Kennedy. She was his temptation, and being with her was addictive. She had awakened the restless spirit inside him and now it refused to be appeased.

He saw the single headlight as it came down the dark street. He watched as she drove up her driveway beside his car and parked. She was sexy beyond his wildest dreams; his body yearned for her. She kicked the stand and allowed the motorcycle to rest on itself. Then she sat back still on the bike, removed her helmet and looked at him.

"Hello, Kennedy."

"Hello, Juwan."

He held up a folder. "I brought something for you."

Assuming that it was the signed annulment papers, she got off the motorcycle and walked to him. "Thank you," she said. He nodded and began to walk past her. She turned. "Juwan," she called out. "Did you want to come in?"

"Probably not a good idea." She nodded as he got into his car and drove away.

Kennedy opened the envelope as soon as she went into the house. It was a copy of her FBI file. She smiled as she read. Juwan had given her her life back.

Chapter Twenty-Six

"Kevin Pole, please," Kennedy said after the security guard at the front desk asked who she wanted to see. He nodded, offered her a visitor name tag and a seat, then picked up the phone and dialed a number.

She sat down. Her heart beat like a thundering drum. She felt her breath quicken as her mind soared and adrenaline pumped. Her palms moistened, her nerves tingled and her stomach tensed. But this was no panic attack. This was the ultimate adventure, the thrill of a lifetime. She smiled. Madison was right. If she could climb to the top of a hundred-foot oak tree and jump off a porch roof and spend a day twirling in circles on a roller coaster, and put together the most uniquely exquisite exhibit of its time, featuring Nubian art spanning centuries, then she could do anything. And she intended to.

Everyday opportunities are lost by those unfortunate ones not willing to even take a chance. She had never in her life been that way and to start now would be cowardice. Brave, bold and fearless, she had surfed, skied, and jumped from planes. But that was comparatively easy. In a few minutes she intended to get the whereabouts of the man she loved, and no matter where he was, she was going to go to him.

Two minutes later Kevin greeted her in the lobby of the

Washington, D.C., FBI Headquarters. "Doctor Evans?" he said as she stood to shake his hand. He invited her upstairs to his office where she took a seat across from his desk. "I have to say, I'm a little surprised to see you here, particularly since the exhibit will be opening this evening."

"I'm on my way to work, but I needed to come here first."

"What can I do for you?"

"First of all thank you for being so kind to me the other day. I appreciate your understanding."

"Again, Doctor Evans, we're very sorry about bringing you in like that. It wasn't supposed to happen—obviously."

"Thank you. Also I wondered if you knew how I can get in touch with Juwan Mason. He's not at the embassy, and the cell phone number I have for him has been disconnected."

Kevin nodded. "It was more than likely a temporary number. There are hundreds of them. Undercover operatives change them or discard them after an assignment is complete."

"I see." The disappointment on her face was obvious.

"I'll be happy to direct you to his new office."

"His new office, here, in this building?" she asked.

"Yes."

He gave her directions. She thanked him, then stood to leave, but turned as he stood to walk her to the door. "One more thing, your last name is Pole." He nodded. "Are you related to Yasmine Pole by any chance?"

"Yes, she's my wife."

Kennedy smiled. "So I guess that would make you and me brother- and sister-in-law."

"Yes, it does. Welcome to the family, Doctor Evans."

"Thanks, call me Keni."

Moments later Kennedy found her way to an open empty reception area and an open office door. There were boxes neatly placed on the floor and desk, bookcases and file cabinets lining the back wall. Juwan was standing at his large window looking out at the breathtaking view of downtown D.C.

She waited a moment before disturbing him and took her time just watching him. He was dressed in a white shirt and a perfectly fitted business suit. She smiled. He still looked like a bad boy to her.

"So this is where you work now," she said as she walked in and closed the door behind her.

He turned, his eyes wide with surprise as he saw her standing across the room. His mouth opened but he didn't speak. She walked around to the bookcase and started reading the titles of the books on the shelf. She ran her finger across the spines, then turned back around to him and smiled.

"Kennedy," he finally said.

"Hi, Juwan."

"You're here," he said, more to himself than to her.

"Yes, I'm here." She stood across the width of the room from him.

"Why, I mean . . ." he corrected.

"I'm looking for a bodyguard," she interrupted. "Do you happen to know where I can find one?" She began walking toward him slowly. As she passed his desk, she looked down and noticed an envelope addressed to him with *legal documents* stamped on the outside. She recognized the envelope. It was the same one that had been sent to her for annulment confirmation purposes. She picked it up and pulled the papers out.

"No, I can't say as I do." He moved from the window and began walking toward her. "Why do you need a bodyguard?"

"Because someone has something that used to belong to me," she said, getting closer to him.

"Well, maybe I can help," he said as he continued walking to her. "What was this something that used to belong to you that someone else now has?"

She looked into his eyes as she grew nearer. "My heart."

He smiled. "That's funny, there must be an epidemic, because I seem to have lost the same thing."

"That's a shame. What do you think we should do about it?"

"I've had a few thoughts."

"Anything you'd like to talk to me about?"

"Everything I'd like to talk to you about."

She stood right in front of him. In a single motion she ripped the annulment papers in half and tossed them back on the desk. "The past is the past. Hi, my name is Dr. Kennedy Evans. I work at the National Museum of African Art." She reached out her hand to shake.

He nodded. "The past is the past. Hi, my name is Juwan Mason Mebeko. I'm Assistant Director for Criminal Investigations for the FBI." They shook hands.

She smiled and reached up to the Tuareg cross still hanging around her neck. "I guess this really is magical."

"I'll never stop loving you."

"Good, 'cause I love you, too."

Their words had done their job and there was nothing left to say, so she leaped up and reached around his neck and kissed him—starting a new beginning.

The knock on the door surprised them apart. "Come in," Juwan called out.

An older woman with a stern face and a no-nonsense demeanor entered. "Good morning, Mr. Mason. Is there anything you need before this morning's briefing?"

"No, thank you, Margaret," he said. "This is my wife, Dr. Kennedy Evans."

They each walked to the center of the office. Kennedy held out her hand to shake. "It's nice to meet you, Margaret, and that's Dr. Kennedy Evans-Mason."

"Likewise," she nodded. "Is there anything I can get you, Dr. Evans-Mason?"

"No, thank you, Margaret, I'll be leaving soon."

She nodded again, then turned her attention back to Juwan. "Sir, you have a briefing in ten minutes, shall I call and delay?"

"No, give me five minutes, I'll be right there." She nodded and quietly stepped back and closed the door behind her.

"I like her," Kennedy said as she picked up her coat and purse. "I'd better go. I still have a lot to do at the museum before this evening."

"I was just looking over there."

"Over where, at what?" she asked.

He reached out, took her waist, and guided her to stand at the window in front of him. "The museum, see?" He pointed across the open space. "It's right over there." She nodded. He leaned down to her neck and dipped his face to her profile. "I need to ask you a question."

She turned. "Sure, what is it?"

He walked over to his suit jacket hanging on the coat rack and came back. He immediately dropped to his knee and opened a beautiful black velvet ring box. Kennedy's mouth dropped open. "Kennedy, will you do me the honor of becoming my wife, again?"

She stared down at the huge sparkling diamond surrounded by a dozen more sparkling diamonds. "It's beautiful. I love it. I love you." She reached down and cupped his face gently. "Yes, Juwan, I'd love to marry you, again."

He stood and they kissed and in their hearts the moment lasted a lifetime.

Epilogue

The opening of the "Nubian Art, Its Past and Its Future Together as One" exhibit was a huge success. Unfortunately, Kennedy would have to hear about it from others.

Everything was in place.

All of her family and friends were there: Trey, Jace, and Taylor, Mamma Lou and Colonel Wheeler, J.T. and Juliet, Raymond and Hope, Dennis and Faith, Maurice and Adarah, Randolph, Yasmine and Kevin, even Hoyt came, surprising everyone with Laine Harrington tucked securely on his arm.

It was a night of celebrations.

Kennedy's diamond engagement ring paled only by the sparkle in her eyes. She introduced her husband to the rest of her family with special concern when it came to J.T. Trey lightened the moment as usual with a quip and theory about women and diamonds, which caused everyone to groan loudly and walk away.

The chairman of the museum's board of directors stepped to the podium and offered a few words. He gave special thanks and consideration to the many foundations such as Evans Corporation for their more than generous donations to the worthy endeavor. He also congratulated and applauded all the dedicated staff involved in assembling the exhibit with special accolades going to Dr. Kennedy Evans-Mason and Dr. Yolanda Chambers.

Kennedy stood and waved, as did Yolanda, who had finally brought her mystery man to the reception. No one was particularly surprised to see Devlon Motako seated at her side. The two woman walked to the platform with the other members of the board. Together they grasped the cord attached to the mural cover and pulled.

Gasps of delight were instant as the first sight of the exhibit garnered a rousing round of applause. As the board members turned to lead the way through the exhibit, Kennedy waited for her family and friends to accompany her.

She shook hands and kissed cheeks as others passed by. As Juwan came to her side she looked at her watch and frowned. "What's wrong?" he asked, seeing her troubled expression.

"I wonder what's taking Madison so long to get here."

"I'm sure she'll be here in a minute. In the meantime." He wrapped his arms around her waist and held her tight to whisper into her ear, "I am so proud of you." She reached up and kissed him tenderly.

Both J.T. and Trey cleared their throats. As soon as the other members of her family and friends reached to the entrance of the exhibit, cell phones began to vibrate en masse. Kennedy took her phone from her purse. She answered. "It's time?" she questioned, then shouted, "Oh, it's time!"

Tony had called everyone at once, thanks to a new computer gadget J.T. had worked out for him. He and Madison were at the hospital. She was in labor.

As the exhibit opened behind her, Kennedy walked in the other direction, followed by the Evans and Gates families and friends.

With the ambassador's security escort matched only by the President's, everyone arrived at the hospital en masse in just moments, sending the emergency room hospital staff into an uproar. Limos pulled up outside one right after the other and discharged the occupants dressed in glamorous evening gowns and stylish tuxedos.

Directed to the maternity waiting room, they only waited a few moments before Tony, dressed in surgical scrubs covering a tuxedo, came dashing out between swinging doors with a smile on his face as wide as Texas. "They're here," he exclaimed as only a new father can. He quickly caught everyone up on Madison's condition—joyfully exhausted—and the perfect ten-fingered and ten-toed babies.

"So," Jace finally asked the question everyone had forgotten to ask, "two boys, two girls, what did we have?"

"One each," he said proudly. "Here they come," he said, pointing to the two nurses as they brought the swaddled babies into the nursery and laid them in the clear cribs.

Ohs and *ahs* echoed as everyone stood and pressed against the nursery window. The nurses wheeled the two tightly wrapped bundles of joy to the front glass, one pink and one blue.

"Did you ever imagine?" Jace whispered to Taylor softly and he placed his arm around her shoulder.

"They're beautiful," Taylor said.

"Congratulations, Pop," Trey said as he slapped Tony on the back playfully and handed him several boxes of pink and blue bubblegum cigars.

J.T. and Juliet looked lovingly into each others' eyes and smiled hopefully. Raymond wrapped his arm around Hope, as did Dennis and Faith.

Juwan held Kennedy lovingly around the waist and pulled her back close against his body. "Difficult, but not impossible," he whispered into her ear. She nodded. And held on to her Tuareg cross.

Colonel Wheeler held Louise's hand and squeezed gently.

"Well, Mamma Lou," Trey said, "you'd better get started matching up these two little ones since you missed out on matching Kennedy and Juwan. They romanced, they married and they beat you to the punch." He chuckled.

"Actually," Kennedy said, suddenly remembering, "Mamma Lou told me at the embassy reception that she wanted to introduce me to an FBI special agent who loved art."

Juwan nodded. "She told me the same thing about a museum curator who was absolutely beautiful."

"Proximity," she said, winking, starting Colonel Wheeler into a fit of unending laughter. Jace and Taylor joined in. "But I do have a few ideas." She glanced down at the two babies again.

"Hold on a minute," Tony said, stepping up to the fatherly challenge. "At least give them a chance to learn to walk and run." The two babies began to cry and Trey cracked up laughing until Mamma Lou turned to him.

"Well then, Trey, I'll just have to work on you, won't I?" He stopped laughing immediately. "I have a friend who has a granddaughter . . ."

Dear Reader,

I hope you enjoyed the winding struggles of Kennedy Evans and Juwan Mason as they journeyed to find a lasting love in *The Fine Art of Love*. Both are troubled and searching. Finding each other was a dream come true, and their commitment to love and hope for the future will carry them to their special happily ever after.

My next release will be part of the BET 2006 Valentine's Day anthology and is entitled "A Taste of Romance." Afterwards, Roberto Santos returns, and this time he means business.

Please feel free to write and let me know what you think. I always enjoy hearing from readers. Please send your comments to conorfleet@aol.com or Celeste O. Norfleet, P.O. Box 7346, Woodbridge, VA 22195-7346. Don't forget to check out my Web site at http://www.celesteonorfleet.com and my blog at Celebritycafe.blogspot.com.

Best Wishes,
Celeste O. Norfleet

The Fine Art of
Love Contest

The Tuareg (TWAH-rehg), fiercely independent
descendents of the nomadic Berbers, are said to
have lived in Northern Africa for over 2,000 years.
The Tuareg Cross, still worn to this day, is
engraved with geometrically designed protective
symbolism often translated to mean
One protected by God, the center of the universe.

Enter to win your own Tuareg Cross like the one
given to Kennedy by Juwan. Send a postcard, e-mail
or letter with your favorite part of *The Fine Art of Love*,
along with your mailing address and/or e-mail contact
information to:

Celeste O. Norfleet
The Fine Art of Love Contest
P.O. Box 7346
Woodbridge, VA 22195-7346
or
conorfleet@aol.com

The winner will be randomly selected from all entries
received by January 31, 2006.

Good luck, and remember to enter as often as you like.

BOOK YOUR PLACE ON OUR WEBSITE AND MAKE THE ARABESQUE ROMANCE CONNECTION!

We've created a customized website just for our very special Arabesque readers, where you can get the inside scoop on everything that's going on with Arabesque romance novels.

When you come online, you'll have the exciting opportunity to:

- View covers of upcoming books

- Learn about our future publishing schedule (listed by publication month and author)

- Find out when your favorite authors will be visiting a city near you

- Search for and order backlist books

- Check out author bios and background information

- Send e-mail to your favorite authors

- Join us in weekly chats with authors, readers and other guests

- Get writing guidelines

- AND MUCH MORE!

Visit our website at
http://www.arabesquebooks.com